Linda Barnes is the award winning author of four previous Carlotta Carlyle mysteries: *A Trouble of Fools*, *The Snake Tattoo*, *Coyote* and *Steel Guitar*. She lives in Massachusetts, with her husband and son, and is working on a sixth Carlotta book.

Snapshot

A Carlotta Carlyle Mystery

Linda Barnes

CORONET BOOKS
Hodder and Stoughton

Para mi hermana, Carol

The following friends and family members contributed their time, expertise, and valued opinions during various stages of development and writing: Dr. Steven Appelblatt, Richard Barnes, Brian DeFiore, James Morrow, Gladys Roldan, Alexandra Paul-Simon, R.N., and Dr. Amy Sims. I thank them. I also wish to recognize the valiant efforts of the T-shirt committee, Cynthia Mark-Hummel, John Hummel, and Beth King.

Gina Maccoby continues to do Carlotta proud—and Carlotta joyfully welcomes Carole Baron to her team.

I dreamed that one had died in a strange place
    Near no accustomed hand;
And they had nailed the boards above her face,
    The peasants of that land,
  Wondering to lay her in that solitude,
    And raised above her mound
A cross they had made out of two bits of wood,
    And planted cypress round;
And left her to the indifferent stars above
    Until I carved these words:
She was more beautiful than thy first love,
    But now lies under boards.

                    —"A Dream of Death"
                    William Butler Yeats—1891

What goes out of your eyes also gradually leaves your heart.

—Persian saying

1

Every April my mother used to host her own version of the traditional Passover seder. A mishmash of Hebrew, Yiddish, English, and Russian, it involved all Mom's old union pals—Jews, Christians, Muslims, and pagans—who'd give rapid-fire thanks for the release of the ancient Hebrews from Egyptian bondage, and then launch into pre-chicken-soup tirades against General Motors, J. Edgar Hoover, and the FBI. I grew up thinking they were part of the religion.

I liked the Passover songs best. One of my favorites, "Dayenu," a lively, repetitive reminder that "It would have been enough" had God brought us out of Egypt but not given us the Torah, and "It would have been enough" had God given us the Torah but not given us the land of Israel, must have had about twenty-seven verses. Sung after the ritual consumption of four glasses of wine, sometimes it had forty-three.

Dayenu, I found myself thinking when the whole mess was over. It would have been enough to get the snapshots in the mail.

The first snapshot came on March 20, camouflaged by a sheaf of "urgent" political messages, market circulars, coupon giveaways, and appeals from various charities about to go belly-up unless I forked over twenty-five bucks. My cat and I have an arrangement that allows me to throw most of my mail directly into the wastebasket. It is he, T.C., Thomas C. Carlyle, aka Tom Cat, who subscribes to *Mother Jones* and *The New York Times Book Review*. It is he who fearlessly lists his full name in the phone directory, warding off the heavy-breathers that mere initials invite. When I scoop the mail off

1

the foyer floor, I sort it into two piles, one for me, one for the cat. His stack is always twice as high as mine, but I hold my jealousy in check.

T.C. gets nothing but junk. I used to read it; I know.

Not that the mail with my name on it is such hot stuff. Most of it might as well be addressed to Occupant.

But on March 20 the mail included one hand-addressed envelope, which I suspiciously examined for the telltale return address of a famous person. Some marketing gurus out there genuinely believe I'll rip open a flap just to see what my old buddy Ed McMahon wants to tell me.

My tongue made an abrupt clicking noise, an involuntary response to the lack of a return address on the blue envelope—a shockingly misplaced statement of faith in the U.S. Postal Service as far as I was concerned.

Red Emma, my inherited parakeet, thinking I'd addressed her, began a stream of "pretty birds" and similar pap.

"Stick your head in a water dish," I suggested. I've been trying to rid myself of that bird ever since my aunt Bea died. Or at least teach it to swear.

The envelope was party-invitation size, a bit larger than three by five. Not dime-store stuff either; it had the feel of stationery from a fancy box instead of a banded pack. I allowed myself a brief moment of speculation before slitting the top fold. I don't know a lot of people who issue formal party invitations.

I might as well not have bothered to dredge up the few sociable names. Inside was no invitation, no letter, no card, just a color snapshot of a baby, an anonymous wrinkled raisin of a face swathed in a multicolored pastel thing the name of which I'd forgotten. My aunt used to knit them for the expected grandchildren of her mahjongg ladies. They—the outfits, not the ladies—looked like little bags with zippers down the front and tiny hoods. I flipped the photo over, expecting some kind of birth announcement.

Just KODAK QUALITY PAPER repeated on a series of slanted lines from the upper-left-hand corner to the lower right.

A guessing game: Name that baby. On my desk I keep a magnifying glass, pencils, pens, scissors, and rubber bands in a coffee can. I polished the lens with spit and Kleenex. Under closer scrutiny, the baby's face looked like a wrinkled prune. Turning my attention to the envelope—specifically, to the postmark: Winchester, Massachusetts—I flipped through a mental Rolodex.

I don't know a soul in Winchester.

I slipped the photo under a corner of the blotter and proceeded with the bills. I study the phone statement like a hawk ever since Roz, my third-floor tenant, housecleaner, and sometime assistant, had a late-night vision and dialed a chatty Tibetan monk at my expense.

Exactly one week later, the second photo arrived. The envelope was the same sky-blue. No return address. Postmark: Winchester.

I'm no baby expert, nor do I wish to become one, but I pegged this tot for about a year old. Fair hair, light complexion, with wind-whipped crimson circles of excitement on her cheeks. I say "her" because the baby was wearing a frilly pink dress and tiny black patent Mary Janes so glossy they'd probably never touched the ground. The occasion could have been a first birthday party, although no cake was in evidence.

Nothing, as a matter of fact, was in evidence, just green grass and a couple of leafy elms.

I located last week's photo and got out my trusty magnifying lens. Could have been the same baby, a year older. Could have been another kid altogether.

I was in no mood for games and thought about tossing the snaps in the trash along with T.C.'s Sharper Image catalog and his invitation to use a $6,000 line of credit with Citibank MasterCard.

But I didn't.

The third came on April 3, one week later, right on schedule. I almost expected it. The little girl was wearing bibbed pink overalls and a matching pink-and-white-striped shirt. Same girl as in the second photo; I could see that now. She'd changed, maybe aged

3

another year, but the eyes were the same shape, the mouth had the identical bow.

Same amount of information, too. Zero. I thought about missing kid cases, wondered whether I'd seen the girl on the back of a milk carton.

It was the briefest of thoughts. I shoved the three photos underneath the blotter. I guess I don't feel right about tossing photographs. I keep them around, the way I save leftovers in the refrigerator.

The fourth photo arrived on the tenth of April. My Winchester correspondent had the U.S. mail figured better than I did. When I drop something in the blue box, sometimes it gets delivered the next day. Then I mail a letter from the same place and it takes a full week to make it to the same destination.

Number five, when it appeared, was definitely a birthday photo. A cone-shaped hat was tilted to one side of the girl's head, secured by an elastic band under her chin. Was I going to get a new picture of this child every Friday for the rest of my life?

Kid was a heartbreaker, no doubt about it. It wasn't any one of the features; it wasn't the features at all. The eyes were too close together, the nose small and unformed. It was the grin, a light-up-the-eyes squint that could have melted polar ice caps. Maybe somebody was sending them to cheer me up at the end of each week.

Probably not.

They stayed on my mind, like a measure of half-forgotten music, a melody tantalizingly out of reach. Almost a week later, on Thursday, I spread the photos across my desk and went over the lot with the magnifying lens, speculating about relatives. My mother had no family, except for Aunt Bea, and she was dead. Aunt Bea had never married. I'd lost touch with my father's kin even before his death. He'd never had much use for them. Was some long-lost cousin trying to slowly acquaint me with his or her offspring? Was this the opening salvo of a charity touch?

I do have a little sister, not a blood relation, but a sister from the Big Sisters Organization. Because of a sticky situation with her mom, I haven't seen Paolina for over four months. Could the Big Sisters be trying to soften me up to accept a replacement child?

Forget it.

I put away the magnifying glass with a sigh, sarcastically congratulating myself on some truly momentous discoveries: The child's face had thinned out as she'd turned from baby to toddler to little girl. Her hair had grown. The anonymous photographer had managed well-composed, centered shots with no chairs or lamps growing out of the kid's head.

Brilliant detective work. With the photos laid out like a hand of solitaire, I could watch little raisin-face begin her transformation into a curly-haired, blue-eyed, blond American princess.

Paolina, my little sister, is Colombian, with chocolate eyes and shiny dark hair. Her face is too round for perfection, and will probably stay that way even after her cheeks lose their baby-fat chubbiness.

So who wants perfection?

I gathered the snapshots together like a pack of cards and aimed them at the wastebasket's gaping mouth. At the last minute, I held the shot. Not that I figured they'd lead anywhere, but I found myself more intrigued than irritated by their presence.

After that night, I no longer thought about tossing them. I don't trust anything to the trash.

Not since the attack of the garbage thief.

2

Yes. The garbage thief.

I know it's hard to credit. If I hadn't been leaning out the window, I wouldn't have seen it. If I hadn't seen it—if, say, Roz had reported it to me the next morning—I wouldn't have believed it. And if I'd been wearing any clothes, I'd have stopped it.

"If" is one of my least favorite words.

As it happened, I was bare-ass naked, seated cross-legged on a doubled-up futon that serves as a couch, my elbows propped on the windowsill, my face turned to a flickering sliver of moon. All the lights in my second-floor bedroom were off and my modesty, such as it is, was further protected by some twenty inches of wall separating the low futon and the sill.

A night-chilled breeze brushed my hair. If I closed the window, the screech of badly joined wood would break the silence and send a shiver up my neck. Instead of the deep sky, the barely budding elm tree, the moon, I'd catch a reflection of my sleepy face in the glass. Wide-set hazel eyes that I call green. Pointy chin. A nose broken often enough to acquire either "character" or a bump and a tilt, depending on the relative merits of flattery and honesty.

I left the window open. If I stared hard, I could see the full circle of the moon, the dark part defined by the silver crescent.

I'm an insomniac, a card-carrying member of the club. Since enrollment is secret, I'm the president of my own chapter and I make up the rules. Number one: "Don't lie there. If you can't sleep, get up and do something else."

I recited the other commandments in my head.

7

"Get plenty of exercise." Well, I sure do. I play killer volleyball three mornings a week. I swim laps at the YWCA pool.

"Eat right." Definitely a failing. I'm a junk-food addict, and the thought of a nice warm glass of milk before bedtime makes me want to puke.

"Always go to sleep at the same time." Sure. I'm a full-time private investigator, but when I can't pay my bills, I drive a cab nights. There is no soothing regularity to my schedule.

"Don't nap." Who has time to nap?

"Cut out the caffeine." Pepsi is a way of life to me.

I did quit smoking. I give myself extra credit for that.

Not for the first time, I considered sleeping pills, the scattering of Dalmanes and Halcions I'd inherited along with Aunt Bea's house. I rejected them, as usual. Live with an addict and you grow wary of medication. Marry and divorce one, you practically convert to Christian Science.

"Exercise." I went back to the second commandment because I thought I'd read somewhere that you shouldn't try any strenuous activity within four hours of going to sleep. I glanced at my bed, shadowy in the moonlight, at the sheet-draped form of Sam Gianelli. Maybe he was my problem. Making love isn't supposed to count as late-night exercise. It relaxes you, right? Makes you sleepy.

Hah. It makes me feel loose, slippery, and warm. But not sleepy.

I considered tossing a pillow at Sam's head. Why should he sleep? Specifically, why should he sleep at my place when he could go back to his Charles River Park apartment? I padded over and kneeled down to reach for my guitar case. I'd ease it out quietly, go downstairs, and practice some finger picking.

The guitar was beyond my reach, centered under the queen-size mattress. Dear God in heaven, Roz must have vacuumed under the bed.

I crawled back to the futon and watched the moon disappear behind a sea of brightening clouds.

The car didn't have its headlights on.

I heard it before I saw it, the closest streetlamp being twenty-five yards away. The motor sputtered to a stop near my driveway. The carburetor needed work.

A car door opened, but the dome light didn't flash. The next sound puzzled me until I realized it was the creak of the trunk. Maybe the driver needed a jack to change a flat tire.

In pitch blackness?

By this time the car had my full attention.

I craned my neck, realized the limitations of my nakedness, and wondered where my clothes were. I felt like yelling "What the hell are you doing down there?" I kept quiet, realizing that the fast-moving moon would soon tell the tale.

It reappeared in a V-shaped break of cloud cover.

A heavyset guy was lifting one of my garbage cans into the gaping trunk of his car. I blinked and shook my head. When I opened my eyes, he was still there.

In my Cambridge neighborhood, barreling is an old and time-honored tradition. The rules are clear. Residents put out big items —old chairs and rickety tables and clunky washing machines—the last Thursday of the month.

It was the third Thursday of April. No one would expect to mine gold in a third Thursday trash collection. And who would rummage for the odd unreturned five-cent-deposit soda can in the middle of the night?

"Stop!" I hollered as loudly as I could. I didn't want the sucker to get away with the trash can. I have only two of them, big wheeled ones that cost $39.95 a piece at the local hardware store. He turned his face and I ducked instinctively. I didn't want to turn the lights on till I found a robe.

I scrabbled around on the floor until I touched cloth. Sam's shirt—hardly long enough, but something to shroud me while I searched more diligently.

I snapped on the light. "Sam!"

"Huh?" He didn't even roll over.

I grabbed my red chenille bathrobe, the one that clashes with my hair, out of the closet. How'd it get in the closet? Roz must have really gone on a cleaning binge.

"Wha'?" I heard Sam mutter as I ran barefoot down the steps.

I have three good locks on my front door. You can't even get *out* of my house without a key for the deadbolt. My purse, with keys inside, was probably on the kitchen counter. Might as well have been on the moon. I ran to the living room and snatched the extra key from the top drawer of my desk. Then I raced back and let myself out in time to see the car two-wheel the corner and disappear.

With both my trash cans.

I stood at the edge of the driveway, in the same spot the cans had occupied a moment before, cursing under my breath, staring at empty darkness but seeing the speeding car, the screeching turn, the mud-smeared license plate. Four. Eight. The last two digits: a four and an eight. Definitely.

My gut reaction: Why me? I'm no rocket scientist. I have nothing to hide. And then I thought, goddammit, yes I do! I have plenty to hide. I don't want anyone to know how much mocha almond ice cream I eat in a week, much less a single detail of my correspondence. I particularly don't want the names of my clients spread around. They hire me for confidential reasons, and, within the law, I do my damnedest to preserve their anonymity.

I did a quick inventory of what I'd been tossing besides the cat's junk mail. Had I received any checks lately? What cases was I still trying to collect on?

A missing husband whose wife should have thrown a farewell party for the bum instead of paying good money to find him living with her stepdaughter. A runaway son-in-law. A habitual bail jumper every private eye in New England has taken a run at . . .

I tried to catalog the trash, but my mind blanked at the scope of the task. And maybe the garbage thief wasn't even after me. Maybe some garbologist was doing a study of Roz's reject artwork. To me, it always looks like Roz frames and attempts to sell every botched endeavor, but what do I know about postpunk art?

Hell. I didn't care if the target was Roz or me. I didn't care if some grad student was doing a thesis on banana-peel disposal in the 02138 zip code. Whoever it was, the garbologist was going to have to research somebody else's garbage.

I wiped my bare feet on the damp grass. Four-eight, four-eight, four-eight, I repeated. With my eyes closed, I teased my memory for details. Color: blue, maybe gray. Rectangular taillights.

I'd have to put a hook near the front door, hang the deadbolt key on it. Should have done it long ago, in case of fire. Of course, with the key hanging there, any burglar who came through a window would be able to open the door and steal the big items—the couch, the bed, the goddamn refrigerator, if he wanted it—as well as the usual small stuff.

I thought about thieves. I thought about garbage. I thought about thieves who steal garbage.

Now, empty trash cans have their uses. Landscapers use them to haul dead leaves and branches. The hawkers who sell soda outside Fenway Park use them to store ice.

But this moron hadn't tried to dump the trash on my front lawn. He'd sped off with Hefty bags full of juice cartons, catfood cans, and old newspapers smeared with parakeet droppings.

If he'd wanted the cans, why steal the garbage? If he'd wanted my garbage, why steal the cans?

3

What with the garbage thief and insomnia, I didn't stir until eleven o'clock the next morning. Sam had long since returned to Charles River Park, complaining that he hardly ever felt rested after a night at my place.

As I groggily crossed the hall, listening to a throbbing hum in my head and hoping the shower would ease it, the day's mail hit the foyer floor with a thud.

Friday. Terrific. Time for another snapshot of little Miss Winchester. Well, she could wait till I'd washed up, eaten breakfast, lunch, or both, depending on the contents of the fridge. She could wait till I'd started my pursuit of the garbage snatcher.

How many light blue, or possible gray, late-model Firebirds had a four and an eight for their final two license-plate numbers? Was I sure it was a Massachusetts plate?

The thought almost drove me back under the covers. Instead I stood in the shower for ten minutes with the temperature at lobster-boil. Then I put in a full two minutes under ice water because somebody told me that cold water is better for rinsing conditioner out of your hair.

Dressed in jeans, sneakers, and a turquoise cotton sweater, I headed downstairs. I pass through the foyer on my way to the kitchen. No harm in stopping to take a peek, I decided. Give me an opportunity to bend over and shake out my wet hair, which I comb as infrequently as possible because it's too thick and too curly and it hurts. I could view the day's photo while chugging orange juice. No time wasted.

I sorted through the pile twice to make sure, but there was no blue envelope. I felt curiously deprived, as if I'd come to the end of a novel borrowed from the library and found the final chapter razored out.

The throb of my headache met its match in the smack of a hammer against a nearby nail.

"You like this here?" The voice came from an unlikely height. Perched on a chair, my tenant, Roz, had gained about a foot in stature. She's short and I'm six-one. Our eyes were now on a level.

I said, "I thought you were going to check with me before you hung any more paintings on my walls." To contrast with her fright-white hair, which she dyes more often than I shampoo, Roz was wearing skin-tight black pants and a redder-than-red T-shirt emblazoned with NINE OUT OF TEN MEN WHO'VE TRIED CAMELS PREFER WOMEN. I read it twice to make sure I'd gotten it right. I don't know where Roz finds her enormous wardrobe of bizarre T-shirts. Maybe secret admirers send them. She has a body, particularly in the T-shirt slogan area, that earns much admiration.

She plucked a nail from between her teeth. "I thought you meant just with offensive stuff."

"This is not offensive?"

"What? You're with the National Endowment for the Arts?"

"Just because it has vegetables in it doesn't make it a still life," I said. "What the hell is that man doing with that carrot?"

"You don't like it?"

"Roz, this is not only my home, it's my office. Clients come here. People who might otherwise consider hiring me."

"Hang it someplace else, huh?"

I nodded my heartfelt agreement.

"Should I yank the other nail out, or try a different painting?"

"Depends on the painting."

"I've got more vegetables. Acrylics really groove with vegetables."

Whenever Roz needs subject matter, her first target is my refrigerator.

The telephone interrupted a promising aesthetic argument.

"Should I answer it?" she asked.

I nodded. "Stall while I get orange juice."

I grabbed the carton from the fridge and raced back in time to hear Roz, in the nasal twang she deems secretarial, report that I was currently taking a foreign call on another line.

"It's okay," I said. "Geneva hung up."

She glared at me. "Ms. Carlyle will be right with you."

"Speaking," I said crisply.

"Hi. Maybe you remember me. I'm the psychiatrist in the brown triple-decker two doors down."

"Sure," I said, "um—"

"Keith Donovan."

Maybe he'd had his trash stolen too. Maybe he wanted me to trace it for him. "What can I do for you?"

"You've been receiving photos in the mail."

"Baby pictures. Kid pictures. Yes."

I could hear him breathing. I wondered what he was waiting for. He exhaled again, inhaled. "I have a patient who's been sending them. I'm sorry. I'd mentioned your name—as someone who wouldn't be, um, a threatening presence, if she decided to investigate a certain matter . . ."

"And?"

"She's having trouble making a decision, and she thought she'd —I don't know—prepare you in some way, in case she decided to seek your counsel."

"Is she in your office now?"

"Yes," he said. "She knows I'm speaking to you."

"Does she want to see me, make an appointment or something?"

"Can you hang on a minute?"

"Sure."

I could hear indistinct muffled voices. I couldn't make out individual words. I tried to remember what he looked like, this Keith Donovan. I remembered the name from some Homeowners Association meeting. Was he the pudgy guy who always complained about the neighborhood dogs? The area I live in, within spitting distance of Harvard Square, is thick with psychiatrists.

"Ms. Carlyle?"

"Yes."

"She—my patient—wonders if you might see her now? I would come along."

"I don't usually have a consulting shrink present."

"Is it out of the question?"

I reviewed my caseload. Tracking down the garbage thief was not going to earn me a fee.

"Come on by," I said.

4

He seemed too young. Perhaps I'd misunderstood. Maybe he was a therapist of some sort or other, but hardly the kind entitled to call himself "doctor." With a haircut fresh off a Marine base and an eager grin, he looked like a big goofy kid. His tweed jacket and muted paisley tie had probably been chosen to make him appear older, and he must have inherited the half-moon reading glasses tucked into his breast pocket. He sure hadn't aged enough to need them.

She was a willow-thin blonde with nervous hands. It took her ten minutes just to remove her raincoat, fingernails clacking against the buttons. She wasn't paying attention to the task; her eyes were darting all over the place, noting the water stains on the ceiling, eyeing the furniture as if she were pricing it for an auction gallery.

I was glad I'd made Roz take the painting down.

I did some appraising of my own. The beige suit, piped in a darker shade, maybe six hundred bucks, and I constantly under-value due to years of Filene's Basement shopping. Double it to include the shoes, bag, and leather gloves. The raincoat had a plaid lining and a Burberry label. Her slim gold watch and massive soli-taire diamond told me she could probably afford both a private eye and a therapist.

The skirt of the fancy suit gapped at the waist and bagged at the hip, as if she'd recently lost weight. Deep purplish-gray shadows tinted the skin under her eyes. A woman who spent megabucks on a precision wedge haircut ought to concentrate more on her makeup, I thought.

Keith Donovan made a ceremony of hanging her raincoat on the coat-tree while she fumbled with her gloves. Clasping her handbag tightly against her chest, she managed the single step down to my living room with an elbow assist from the therapist.

Normally I invite clients to sit in the chair across from my rolltop desk, but I hadn't readied a second chair so I motioned them farther into the room. The woman chose my aunt Bea's favorite rocker, with its needlepoint cushion and faint welcoming creak. Donovan waited for me to take the couch before selecting an easy chair.

The woman absorbed the surroundings with a practiced glance, and I wondered what deceptive conclusions she'd drawn from the antiques and Orientals. The room is exactly as my aunt left it when she died, except for the addition of my desk.

Her eyes fastened on the silver-framed photo centered on the mantelpiece. She mumbled and looked at me expectantly.

"What?"

"Is she your daughter?" she asked in a low urgent tone.

"My little sister."

"Do you have children?"

"No."

"Ms. Carlyle," Keith Donovan said, "I'd like you to meet Mrs. Woodrow, Emily Woodrow."

She twisted her hands, rubbed them along the length of her thighs, clasped them in her lap. Said nothing.

"Would you like a cup of coffee?" I asked.

No response.

"You've been sending me pictures of your daughter?" I made it a question only by inflection.

"She looks like me, doesn't she?" the woman said. On the surface her pale face seemed as passive and calm as an old portrait in an art museum, but I felt uneasy scrutinizing her. She had an odd voice, faint and hoarse.

"She's beautiful," I said. "Your daughter."

The woman lowered her head suddenly. Her hair, falling in wings from a center part, covered her face, so I couldn't tell if tears came with the wrenching sobs. I had a fix on her hoarseness now. Crying jags roughened vocal cords more quickly than Jack Daniel's and cigarettes.

Donovan seemed to be studying his knuckles. I wondered if he was billing my time as one of the woman's treatment sessions.

She did the hand routine again, her fingers rubbing her thighs as if she were searching for something to grasp or tear. Her long fingernails were unpolished and neglected.

"Is there something I can do for you?" I asked.

Color flooded her cheeks. Her chest rose and fell so quickly I thought she might hyperventilate and pass out. I hoped Donovan, young as he was, had some medical experience.

"Doctor," she muttered to him. "I don't know where to—"

"Would you like me to provide some background information?" he asked gently.

"Yes," she said, seizing the words like a lifeline. "But first, I want—I'd like to give her this."

It was a pale blue rectangle. I was going to get my Friday photo after all.

The envelope seemed identical to the ones underneath my blotter, but the enclosed photograph was a formal study, on thicker stock. The child . . . well, the girl wore a hat, but the floppy-brimmed straw was no cover for the fact that she'd lost her bouncy curls. I could practically see bones through her papery skin. She was gamely attempting her angelic smile, but it couldn't make the jump to her sunken eyes.

I swallowed and was glad I hadn't eaten breakfast.

Centered at the bottom, beneath a black border, elaborate calligraphy spelled out: Rebecca Elizabeth Woodrow. 9/12/85–1/6/92. The newborn in the hand-knitted bunting—funny how the word for the damn thing came back to me—the two-year-old in the pink striped shirt and bib overalls, hadn't made it to her seventh birthday.

I glanced up. Emily Woodrow stared at my little sister's photo with an intensity bordering on hunger. I was glad I held her daughter's picture in my hand. It gave me something to look at, besides her face.

"I'm sorry," I said. "She was beautiful."

The woman tried to smile. A mistake. Her lips quivered.

"Mrs. Woodrow has been seeing me since her daughter's death," Keith Donovan volunteered, his voice low and soothing.

"Three months ago," she whispered, as if she were reminding herself. Her hands were working again. The nail on the index finger of her left hand was broken, jagged. "Have you ever had a serious illness?" she asked abruptly.

"No," I said.

"Then you don't know what it's like when a doctor looks at you in that special kindly way, and then he rips your heart out."

I tried to guess how old she was. Forties by the hands. Thirties by the face.

"Do you want to tell me about it?" I shot Donovan a sidelong glance, but if he'd caught me doing my imitation of a therapist, he didn't react.

She lowered her eyes and addressed the carpet in a voice as flat and melancholy as a foghorn. "There's no place to start. No beginning. Becca seemed to get a lot of colds, maybe three times as many as the year before. And the fevers. Scary high fevers, where she'd just go limp, with her face flushed and her hair soaked."

As she spoke, Emily Woodrow lifted a hand to her own hair, as if she were unconsciously feeling for dampness. She left her hand there, forgotten, suspended, and went on.

"One day I kept her home from school, even though she wasn't running a fever. Her father says—said—I babied her. But the listlessness; it wasn't like her. I called our doctor. He said bring her in —no appointment, just bring her in—and I was scared." She swallowed audibly. "For the first time. I was always scared after that. He gave her a quick exam—eyes, ears, throat, heartbeat—and said she seemed okay. She went back to school, but I could tell she wasn't right. She cried a lot, cried for no reason, and she'd never been a complainer. And then she got a bruise on the inside of her leg, big as an apple, but she couldn't remember bumping into anything, and it didn't go away, so I took her back to the doctor—I remember that day. There was such a wind howling; I held her hand. I thought she might blow away. She'd gotten so thin; she'd stopped eating. I bought her whatever she wanted. Pistachio ice cream . . ."

"Go on," said Donovan.

She shrugged and glanced down at her expensive shoes. "Something was wrong with her blood. Platelets. He sent us to a specialist. And another one. They diagnosed Becca with ALL."

"Which is?" I asked.

"Acute lymphoblastic leukemia. It's ninety-five percent curable. That's the cure rate. Ninety-five percent. They kept telling us that, over and over. When she lost her hair, when she couldn't eat, not even applesauce like a baby, when she'd throw up every five minutes, too weak to turn her head, so I was afraid she'd choke on her own vomit, they always came back to that. Ninety-five percent."

I didn't like the way this was going.

"Mrs. Woodrow," I said as gently as I could, my voice barely above a whisper, "I'm sorry. Believe me, I am sorry for your loss and your pain. But five percent die. If the cure rate is ninety-five percent, then five percent die."

Emily Woodrow accorded my observation the same polite interest she might have given if I'd commented on the weather. "At first it didn't matter. Nothing did. My daughter . . . my only child . . . There had to be a funeral and people came and people went and brought food and took food away. Casseroles and covered chafing dishes. Bread. Pots that steamed but never smelled. Nothing smelled, except the flowers. I didn't want any flowers. I hate lilies. The first day, they're beautiful, especially the star lilies, and by the second day, they reek. I remember I couldn't go to her bedroom. I stood in the hall by her door, but I couldn't go inside. I remember that. Her chair is at the kitchen table. I won't let Harold take it away. I want to move, but Harold, my husband—"

Dammit, I ought to keep a box of Kleenex on my desk. She fumbled for tissues in her handbag.

"I was taking pills, medicine. Pills and water, pills and water. Waking and sleeping, waking and sleeping again. I never ate. There's an oak outside my window. I watched its branches rustle. Empty branches. An empty tree. Dead, but living. Why should it be dead, but living? I thought I heard God talking to me. Just the once. He said—or she said—it was a whispery kind of voice: 'If you don't believe in me, it's because you haven't suffered enough.' And I felt almost triumphant, as if I must have found some sort of religion— because I had suffered enough. Not like Becca, but enough."

I glanced at the therapist, tried to send him the silent urgent message that this was his country, not mine.

"The funny thing is," she went on, "I made phone calls and commitments. Friends would ring and say, 'Where were you? Why didn't you meet us for lunch?' And I wouldn't know what they were talking about. I had these perfectly sane conversations, talking about books and gardening, and I made plans, and I don't remember any of it. It was like floating in a fog bank. I never could see or hear anything clearly.

"I spent a lot of time thinking. Brooding. About what I'd done wrong. About why I was being punished. About how I hadn't listened to her when she first said she wasn't feeling well, about how I hadn't taken her to the doctor soon enough, and then about how I must have taken her to the wrong doctor. Keith says I was angry, terribly angry, but I turned my anger inward . . ."

Keith. Not Dr. Donovan. I glanced at his pleasantly earnest, unlined face, and wondered who would choose a shrink so apparently unscarred by life.

Mrs. Woodrow seemed to have run out of steam. Even her hands lay idle in her lap.

"I'm sorry," I said, again as gently as I could, forming the words with the care a child takes in trying to blow a large soap bubble, "but I don't know what you want me to do."

"I'm getting to it," she snapped, her voice brittle, her eyes staring deeply into mine. "I can't just tell you cold."

I was sorry I'd interrupted. I'd seen the photos: the baby, the toddler, the child, the beautiful girl. I'd watched her grow.

"I have a picture in my mind," the woman said. "And I can't make it go away."

She sat for a time, a statue frozen in her chair. Lines appeared and disappeared in her narrow face. Sometimes they seemed deeply etched; sometimes a superficial shading of the light. At the right side of her jaw, a tiny muscle twitched.

"You have to remember how hard it was for me," she said finally. "I was taking pills, medicine. Did I say that?"

"Yes."

"It's about the last day, her last day."

"Did she die at home?" She flinched when I said the word.

"At the hospital," she said, staring directly into my eyes, holding them with her gaze. "It was her regular chemotherapy session. The doctors had been, well, noncommittal. But encouraging, very encouraging. She was handling everything well . . ."

"Yes?"

Her eyes were blue, an icy bottomless lake. "I have this picture in my head. The last day. It went wrong so fast. I was sitting near her, in a beige chair, on the right side of the bed, so close I could stroke her forehead. We were in the regular room, the one with the blue wallpaper. Blue wallpaper, with a white lattice pattern and flowers, yellow-and-gold flowers. Zinnias. I used to stare at the wallpaper when I couldn't stand watching the pain in Becca's face. Only for a moment; otherwise, I felt like I was deserting her. But there were times when I'd stare till there were only yellow and blue blotches. It was quiet. The regular nurse was present. She hadn't had any trouble inserting the IV. Everything was ordinary—if horrible things, if your child's pain, can ever be ordinary. And then there was a man in white, a man I hadn't seen before, but he must have been a doctor. Bursting in like that. Yelling. And he pushed me out of the room, shoved me. And through a tiny window, I saw the mask over her face, over Becca's face. He jammed it over her mouth, her nose. The noise she made, I hear it in my sleep—".

"It's okay, Emily," Keith Donovan said quietly. "It's okay. It's okay."

Her silence was more unnerving than her sobs. She sat motionless, staring inward, seeing her child's last moments with the intensity of a fever dream.

"Where was your daughter treated?" I asked.

"JHHI."

The Jonas Hand/Helping Institute, created when the small Jonas Hand Hospital and the even smaller James Helping Institute merged in the late seventies, is housed in a dilapidated building in an area that swings between urban renewal and urban decay, teetering back and forth on the pendulum of local politics, never quite making it into the respectable zone. For years, there've been rumors of JHHI closing, or moving, but they've always proved false. JHHI endures, the major reason the neighborhood never quite succumbs to gang violence, racism, or sheer neglect. Said to be one of the nation's top medical centers, it draws patients from as far away as Cairo and Santiago.

The locals bless the hospital for the police presence it commands. Most of them call the place Helping Hand, and believe it was named for some anonymous Good Samaritan. It's no fly-by-night miracle-cure center, no south-of-the-border laetrile clinic.

Mrs. Woodrow rubbed her temples. "We took her there because of Muir, of course. Because of his reputation."

I didn't respond to the name. She looked at me as if I'd missed a cue.

"Dr. Jerome D. Muir," Emily Woodrow insisted. The name did have a certain familiarity, like a name I might have read once in a newspaper.

"Wouldn't Children's Hospital have been the place to go?" I

inquired. "Better known?" I'd certainly heard more about Children's than I'd read about Muir.

"No. No," Mrs. Woodrow said earnestly. "We checked very carefully. My husband does know doctors. He talked to them. We were afraid of a teaching hospital, of some enormous place where you never know who's actually doing what. I mean, I realize medical students need to learn, and I know they need to learn on living people with real illnesses, but I thought, no, not on my daughter. So we chose JHHI. Because of Dr. Muir."

Donovan said, "He's the best man in the area, maybe in the country." The woman seemed comforted by his assurance.

I asked, "Was Muir your daughter's primary physician?"

"Yes."

"Do you think an error was made in your daughter's medical care?" I asked Mrs. Woodrow.

"I don't know."

"Sounds to me like you want a malpractice attorney."

"I don't," she said vehemently. "I can't and I don't. My husband is an attorney who works closely with doctors, setting up corporations, partnerships, that kind of thing. I can't risk his livelihood by starting up a lawsuit based on shadows. I don't know anything for sure. Maybe I dreamed it. Maybe the drugs I took afterward . . . maybe they altered my perceptions. . . ."

"You must have asked your daughter's doctor what happened."

"He explained. He explains, but it doesn't make sense. He uses words I don't understand, words with twenty syllables, and the next time I ask, after I've looked things up, he uses a different word and says I must have misunderstood him. And lately, he's always out— on rounds or whatever. And the nurses, they don't even bother to hide it anymore. They just whisper to each other. 'It's her again, the crazy woman.' "

A lawyer once told me that more doctors get sued because of rude receptionists than rotten care.

"You lost your daughter," I said. "That's enough to make anyone crazy for a while."

I wondered what Keith Donovan thought about the nontechnical term, *crazy.*

"Becca looked like me, but she wasn't like me," the woman said fiercely. Her jagged nail snagged a beige stocking. She tore it loose, ripping a hole. Didn't notice. "She was matter-of-fact. She accepted what was. Whatever they did to her, whatever those doctors and nurses did to her, she simply assumed they were doing their best. Even when she was so weak she could hardly talk, she never blamed me. She never blamed anyone. She cried when she couldn't go to her friend Jessie's birthday party, but she didn't cry because she had leukemia. She just wanted them to make her well again. So her hair would grow back, and she could jump rope on the playground. And they said they would, and they didn't."

Children died. Parents lived. It broke your heart. Before I could open my mouth to tell her I couldn't help her, she sped on.

"I want you to tell me, assure me, that nothing, absolutely nothing unusual or odd or wrong went on. I owe that much to Becca. To Becca and myself. I need to hear someone say it, before I can go on."

"You want me to talk to her doctor?"

She licked her lips, spoke rapidly, softly. "I need to know that everything that could have been done was done, and done right. That no one could have done more. I don't want to sue anybody. I don't need money. I have money."

"I'm not a whiz at medical terminology," I said.

"I could help with that," Donovan volunteered.

I turned on him. "Do you think this is necessary? Or wise?"

"You mean, do I think it will help Mrs. Woodrow?"

"Yes," I snapped, surprised to find myself angry. I didn't need any psychiatrist to tell me what I meant.

He paused, considering his words. "I think it may help to close off this area, wall up the past. So she can move forward."

"Move forward," Emily Woodrow repeated, shaking her head slowly. She kept moving her head back and forth as if she'd forgotten how to stop.

I sucked in a deep breath, tried to find another way to say what I needed to say. Couldn't. This is what came out: "Mrs. Woodrow, I'm sorry, but I have to say this. Your daughter is dead. What Dr. Donovan means when he says 'move forward,' what he means is that no matter what I discover, no matter what I learn, your daughter will still be dead."

Her eyes closed and she flinched as if I'd hit her. I glanced at Donovan. He inclined his head slightly as if I'd said the right thing, but it didn't make me feel any better.

She wanted to write out a check immediately. I persuaded her to take a day to look over my standard contract, suggest any changes. I assured her that she could mail me the check.

I don't usually go out of my way to avoid prompt payment. Usually I demand it, but there was something about this case—probably the woman's visible pain—that made me want to stall. And what was the hurry? I asked myself. It wasn't like the events had occurred yesterday.

She teetered on her heels when she stood to leave. Since she had her doctor along, I didn't feel required to see her out.

When she reappeared in the doorway, clad in her Burberry, her index finger to her lips, I was surprised. Surefooted now, she glided across the room till she was well within whispering range.

"He thinks I'm looking for my glove," she murmured. "Tell me quickly: Do you own any stocks? Do you speculate?"

"No." I thought she was probably mad but I answered. It was something in her eyes. An intensity, a brilliance.

"Do you work for yourself?"

"Yes."

"For anyone else?"

"I drive a cab."

"What company?"

"Green and White."

"I can check on them. Do you own a gun?"

"Yes."

"Can you use it?"

27

"Yes."

"Have you?"

"Have I what?"

"Used it. Killed with it."

"Yes."

"Would you do it again?"

"If I had to."

"What does Cee Co mean to you?"

"Seiko? The watch people?"

She handed me a slim envelope. "This is for you. Keep it. And stay here for me. On hold. Don't take any other client. You'll get something in the mail or by messenger. Keep it safe. Keep it for me."

"Wait. Wait just a minute. Hire a safety deposit box."

"No. It has to be this way. Please. You have to." For a moment, her fierce gaze faltered.

"What is Cee Co?" I asked.

She ignored the question.

"Are you in danger?" I asked, louder this time.

"I don't think so."

"Why ask about guns? Do you need protection? Are you afraid?"

"Afraid? Afraid of what? There's nothing to be afraid of now. When you've lost everything, there's nothing left."

She swiveled her head, as if she'd heard a noise, footsteps. All was quiet.

"No," she murmured softly, turning to stare at me again. "No, I take that back. You're right: I am afraid. I'm afraid I'll forget her someday." Her voice was a choked whisper, and the words came faster and faster. "Forget the feel of her hair. Forget the moment I named her. Forget the creases under her eyes when she smiled—"

"Did you find it?" Donovan hovered at the door. Instinctively I slid the slim envelope under my blotter, out of sight.

Emily Woodrow, her gait unsteady, yanked a glove from beneath the rocking chair. I hadn't seen her plant it.

"Here it is," she said automatically, the mask almost back in place. "Sorry to have troubled you."

"I'll be in touch," I said.

She shot me a warning glance. "This is something I won't discuss on the telephone. I cannot discuss it over the phone."

"Still—"

"If you'll do as I've asked," she said mildly, her fierce eyes hooded, "everything will be fine."

Sure, I thought.

"Ms. Carlyle," she said, turning back as she reached the doorway.

"Yes."

"Your little sister—"

"Yes?"

Her voice faltered. She bit her lip and took a deep breath before she could go on. "She's very beautiful."

5

This time I closed and bolted the door behind them. I peered through the peephole as Donovan guided Emily Woodrow down the three steps. Then I hurried back to the living room.

The white envelope, while of lesser quality than the stiff blue ones, was not cheap. I slit it with a letter opener and eased out the contents. Two items: a folded sheet of paper and a powder-blue check. The paper was a photocopy of a death certificate. Rebecca Elizabeth Woodrow's. The date of death was the same as the one on the photograph.

Emily Woodrow's daughter had died. That much of her initial story was true.

The check was big enough to earn an involuntary whistle. And all I had to do to earn it was wait.

I tapped my fingers on my desk. My blunt-cut nails made no noise. Waiting is not what I do best. Nor is it my natural inclination.

I peered into the envelope, dissatisfied with its contents. My eye caught a flash of silver at the bottom. I yanked the sides of the envelope apart and shook until something fell onto my blotter.

I got a stinging paper cut for my effort, and a shiny bit of foil-like paper, about one inch square. When I held it to the light, it seemed to change color. One edge was slightly bent, another looked as if it had been snipped with a nail scissors, separated from a larger item.

What that item might be, I couldn't guess.

My stomach rumbled, so I made breakfast, swallowing the rest of the carton of orange juice, then frying up four slices of bacon and two eggs in a cast-iron skillet.

Ah, the joy of bacon! I'd never tasted its crisp fattiness till I was eighteen: No pig products allowed in my mother's kosher home. As an adult I've found that eating such defiantly *treyf* fare gives me the warm glow of disobedience, as good a fuel as any for trying to pump information out of often-reluctant sources.

I deserted the dishes in the sink, where Roz might or might not notice them, and returned to the living room. Emily Woodrow's check, drawn on a BayBank in Marlborough, had her name and address printed neatly on the upper-left-hand corner. Her own name, not her husband's. I dialed a 1–800 number, asked to speak to Patsy, and sipped my first Pepsi of the day while stuck on hold. Somebody played saccharine-stringed Beatles Muzak in my ear.

Patsy Ronetti's Bronx blare woke me up.

I met her when I was a cop. She's a prize. Took a job right out of high school, a trainee with Equifax, one of those high-profile information-gathering corporations. Spent four years as an insurance investigator, and now she knows it all: data-base access, public-document searches, credit reporting. I send her a bottle of Johnnie Walker Black Label every Christmas. Most of the investigators in town probably do the same. She could run a liquor store on the side, but mostly she reports credit.

I ran Emily Woodrow past her, gave her Harold's name as well, assuming he had the same last name as his wife and child, read her the Winchester address on the check. Then we talked money and time. Her rates are not cheap, but she's fast. I could hear her punching keys on her terminal as we bartered.

I wanted both a credit report and an employment search, and was arguing in favor of a two-for-one deal.

"You hooked yourself a live one," she said.

"Yeah."

"I'm backed up here to Tuesday, Carlotta. Half the country's checking on the other half. I'm not gonna do any rush job on this, understand? But here's a teaser for you. He's a lawyer—"

"I already knew that."

"You also know he pulls down six large? Maybe you can afford the car."

"Huh?"

"You're buying a car, right? Or leasing?"

"Not that I know of," I said while imaginary warning bells pealed in my ears.

"Wait a minute. Carlyle, right?" She spelled it out.

"Yeah."

"I got a call, must be three days ago. Car dealer, I coulda sworn."

"Got the paper on it?"

"Geez, I dunno. I think it was a phone deal."

"Patsy, can you pull my file and see who exactly was doing the asking? Because I'm not buying any car."

"Hang on."

Muzak drowned out the furious clatter of keystrokes.

I gulped Pepsi and brooded. I don't mind using electronic data banks. It's just I hate the thought that somebody else can use one to find out about me.

Her voice was smug. "Stoneham Lincoln-Mercury. What did I tell ya? Memory like a trap."

"Hang on." My phone doesn't feature Muzak on hold. She had to listen to the sound of my lower-left-hand drawer opening and closing. I found the Yellow Pages tucked behind a sheaf of files. I balanced it on my lap, riffled the pages.

"There's no such place," I said.

"Gee, he sounded nice, too," she offered.

"A man."

"Yeah."

"You must have had a phone number or something, so you could tell the guy I was a bum risk."

"Gotta go," Patsy said. "Later."

I was getting used to her abrupt disconnections. Her bosses at E–Z Electronic, a far-smaller outfit than Equifax, didn't know about her free-lance career. Nor would they have approved.

I waited five minutes, but she didn't call back. No telling when she would.

Somebody steals my garbage. Somebody checks my credit. And I hadn't even applied to work for the FBI.

I drummed my fingers on my desk for five more minutes, then I picked up the receiver and dialed Mooney.

When I was a cop, I worked for Mooney, and most of the time he made it seem as though I worked with him, not for him. Green as I was, just out of U.–Mass. and the police academy, I didn't fully appreciate the camaraderie. I thought it was the way all cops worked.

He's a lieutenant now—homicide—and I don't think he'll rise any higher because he's too good at what he does. Too busy closing cases to play politics.

I mentally composed a recorded message because he's out of his office a lot. When he answered on the second ring, I was caught flat-footed.

When Mooney starts sounding good to me, I worry. Not that he doesn't have a nice voice; he does. Not that he's bad-looking. Tall, well-muscled, round-faced—I jokingly tell him he's too white-bread for my taste. He—disapproving of Sam Gianelli—tells me I'm attracted to outlaws, not cops. When Mooney starts sounding good, it makes me wonder how things are really going with Sam and me.

"Moon, hello."

"Hi, there."

"How're you doing?"

"Fine, Carlotta."

"Busy?"

"Usual."

"Somebody's in your office."

"How'd you guess?"

"Intuition." I could have said, "And you haven't asked me out yet," which he usually does right after "hello," but I didn't want to start anything.

"It's a lady," he said. "Somebody who's getting to be a very close friend."

I wasn't sure if he was telling the truth, but I felt a sharp stab of something that felt uncomfortably like jealousy. "You gonna arrest her?"

"Haven't decided yet. What can I do for you?"

"Run a plate?"

Mooney and I keep an ongoing balance sheet in our heads. Anytime I can help him out, I do my best. Private cops need official pals to break bureaucratic logjams.

I said, "I'm looking for a late-model Firebird, light blue, maybe gray."

"Just give me the plate."

"Yeah, look, I'm sorry to bother you at the office. The last two numbers are four, eight."

There was a moment's silence. "Nah," he said, "you gotta have more than that."

"I don't."

"Give the client the money back."

"I would if I could."

"Spent it?"

"It's a personal thing, Mooney. Try it with the Registry, okay?"

"Those clerks hate me already."

"They respect you, Mooney."

"Carlotta, don't even try to butter me up."

"Why not?"

"Might work."

I smiled. "One more thing."

"Where have I heard that before?"

"What does Cee Co mean to you?"

"Huh?"

"Just free-associate, Mooney."

"This a test?"

"Moon, try."

"Short for Coca-Cola?"

I hung up. While I waited for Patsy to call back, I made a list. Seiko. Seeko. See Ko. Ceeko. C. Ko. Somebody Ko. I tried the White Pages and learned that Ko is quite a popular name in the Chinese community. The entries numbered twenty-six and ran from Chi-Fen Ko to Zyuan Ko, with a pedestrian Thomas Ko thrown into the mix.

Patsy didn't call back.

After staring interminably at both the shiny side and the dull side, I carefully placed the foil square back into Emily Woodrow's envelope. Under my magnifying lens, it seemed dotted with a faint crescent-shaped pattern. It didn't look like anything I'd ever seen before.

I sighed. Maybe Roz would have a different take on it. She usually does.

When the doorbell rang, I was relieved.

Waiting is hard.

6

Keith Donovan, hands buried deep in his trouser pockets, was rocking back and forth on my front stoop. Alone. He'd exchanged his jacket and tie for a blue crewneck sweater.

"May I come in?" he asked with a quick on-and-off grin.

"Okay."

He headed to the living room, aiming for the easy chair again. I followed. Last time, he'd kept his feet on the floor, his hands in his lap. This time he leaned back and crossed his legs, relaxed. If he'd been a prospective client, I'd have quoted him top dollar. I go by the shoes.

Give him a break, I scolded myself. He might have a pile of grubby sneakers in the closet. And it's not his fault he looks too young to practice anything more complicated than tying the laces.

His wheat-colored hair would look great when it grew out. He was about my height. Decent build—narrow shoulders, but even narrower hips. He sat high in his chair, evidence of a long torso. Most of my length is in my legs.

"I wanted to thank you for listening to Mrs. Woodrow," he said. "It's quite a painful story."

"Thanks for rustling me up a client. You want a commission?"

The corners of his eyes crinkled, making him look a shade older. "No, really, you were fine. You helped her. Just having somebody listen the way you listen helps."

"Anytime," I said, wondering why we couldn't have exchanged such pleasantries over the phone.

"Look," he said, "this isn't something I usually do. I hope you don't feel like I'm passing the buck."

I recalled the gratifying size of Emily Woodrow's check, and her desire for secrecy, even from her therapist.

"Any bucks I can collect, I'll take," I said lightly.

"No. Really, this step, um, my visit was fairly unorthodox. Psychiatrists aren't exactly known for their activism."

There. He'd said it again. Psychiatrist. How old was he?

"Even in the People's Republic of Cambridge?" I asked.

"You do get a more radical branch of therapy here," he admitted, "but nonetheless, I feel somewhat uneasy about involving you in what will probably turn out to be a waste of your time and Mrs. Woodrow's money."

He seemed to speak in two different voices. One, his shrink voice, used words like *nonetheless* and *somewhat*. The other voice, the easy one, went with the smile. When he used his shrink voice, his forehead wrinkled. I wondered if he practiced in front of a mirror.

"I'm a grown-up," I responded. "I could have said no. Therefore, it's no longer your responsibility, Doctor."

"Keith," he said in the easy voice.

"Keith," I repeated. He had nice brown eyes, a firm but expressive way of moving his hands.

"Mrs. Woodrow's version of reality," he continued in full therapist cry, "may not be entirely responsible."

"Oh?" I said, raising an eyebrow. "What are you trying to tell me, exactly? That she didn't see some guy enter her daughter's hospital room? That she imagined the business with the mask?"

He straightened up and planted his feet on the ground. "You see, when something goes so horribly wrong in a person's life, that person may automatically seek for a reason, a fault, a devil if the individual is of a religious bent, as a way of obtaining some comfort against the horrible randomness of death and disease."

He sounded like he was quoting a textbook, but his gaze was direct and sincere. Too direct and sincere.

"You think she's lying about that last day? Dramatizing?" I admit I was enjoying his academically roundabout way of talking, his frank open gaze. I got the feeling he'd taken a med school course in how to hedge everything he said. If I listened to him long enough, maybe I'd learn.

He lowered his voice conspiratorially. "Hospitals can be enormously confusing places. People come and go; it's all hurry up and rush. And Emily Woodrow clocked a lot of hours at JHHI. She may think she's telling us exactly what she saw, but she may have the time factor off."

"It happened on another day?"

"Possibly."

"I'd think the day her daughter died would be pretty well fixed in her mind."

"She's gone over that day, uh, Carlotta. Over and over it. Rewriting it. Sanitizing it. Making it bearable."

"Fictionalizing it?"

"It's possible that Emily's version is very close to the truth. Whoever was administering the chemo probably saw the child's vital signs failing and called a code."

"A code?"

"Every hospital has a code system. So visitors aren't unduly alarmed by loudspeakers booming 'heart failure in room nineteen.' "

"What would have happened if somebody called a code?"

"All hell would break loose. The place would be flooded with strangers. Someone—a doctor on duty—would grab an emergency cart and rush into Rebecca's room, try to revive her."

"Emily didn't say anything about a crowd or a cart."

"Exactly." He paused, leaned back, and crossed his legs. He seemed to be enjoying himself. "And she didn't tell you that one of her major childhood memories concerns a tonsillectomy that occurred when she was approximately four years old. She doesn't remember much about it. Mainly the mask coming down and covering her face. The smell. The fear."

I didn't like his solved-it-all expression. "You think she's confusing the two episodes in her mind," I said slowly.

His smugness evaporated, and he was all earnest understanding again. "I know the doctor who treated her daughter," he said, "and believe me, if anything irregular went on in that room, Jerome Muir would have been on it like a hawk. He has an international reputation, an impeccable one. He's extremely personable and respectable, and he won't be very pleased to talk to you about this."

"Better me than an attorney," I said. "I don't take depositions."

He sighed deeply, uncrossed and crossed his legs again.

I said, "So what do you do with Mrs. Woodrow? Talk about her childhood, huh? Age four and on?"

"Mainly she talks."

"And you listen."

He took the reading glasses out of his pocket and tapped them thoughtfully on one knee. I wondered if they taught that maneuver at shrink school. "I don't think it would be helpful for this to go on too long," he said slowly. "The therapeutic goal is to get Mrs. Woodrow to pick up the thread of her life. A prolonged investigation would hardly help."

"Quick and dirty?" I inquired.

"Quick, anyway."

I smiled. "Well, I'm sure you didn't mean to come over here and insult me, but you're getting close. If you brought Mrs. Woodrow by for a dose of warm fuzzies, you made a mistake. I'm not a shrink and, frankly, your therapeutic goal does not interest me. If Mrs. Woodrow's imagination is running wild, I'll find that out and close up shop. But she's my client now and you're not. Understand?"

"You're very touchy."

"Am I?"

"I didn't mean to impugn your professionalism."

"Yeah, I'm sure you didn't."

"Do I detect a lack of respect for therapy?"

"Possibly," I admitted.

I went to a therapist once. The cop brass sent me, after I shot and killed a man, right before I left the force. Standard procedure: you off somebody, you see the departmental psychiatrist. I'd hated the departmental psych on sight. A pudgy, balding egomaniac, he'd reminded me of a buzzard circling wounded prey, urging me to tell him all about it, scrounge up every last detail. Please, Detective, when did you first touch the trigger? Please, Carlotta, when was the exact moment you felt you had to fire? Please, tell me, what did you feel when you pressed that trigger? Excitement? Relief? A sense of release? Anything sexual? Oh, please, anything at all sexual? Tell me, and it will be our little secret.

It's not that I didn't react to killing another human. It's not that I don't cry. But I resent being forced.

And I kept wondering what they'd have done to the goddamn felon if it had gone down the other way. Would the same shrink be asking my killer the same questions? And when did you first feel you absolutely had to pull the trigger and shoot the cop?

"A great many people mistrust therapy," Keith Donovan said mildly, "but others are helped by it."

"We all have our ways of dealing with shit," I said.

"Yeah? What do you do when you're angry?"

"Yell. Play volleyball. Smack the ball around."

"Hmmmm," he said.

"And what's that supposed to mean?"

"Just hmmmm. And what do you do when you're down? Depressed?"

I hesitated on that one. "Play guitar."

"What were you going to say? Before you settled for guitar."

Our eyes met and I almost smiled. He grinned, and I thought oh-oh. Whenever I start arguing with a guy for no reason, it's a sure sign the old chemistry's kicking in.

"What kind of guitar?" he asked.

"Blues," I said. "Old-time blues. Mainly Delta, a little city stuff."

He said, "I play drums. Used to, anyway. Rock. Punk."

I have no-fail chemistry. A guy turns me on, he's the wrong one for me.

"Since you're here," I said, bringing the conversation back to a professional level, "maybe you can answer a few questions for me."

"Such as?"

"How does Mrs. Woodrow pay her bills?"

"By check. She's reimbursed by her insurance company."

Nice, I thought. I ought to have that arrangement. Investigation insurance. "And you've been seeing her for three months now? Weekly?"

"I saw her more often right after Becca died."

"Who made the connection? Why you?"

"Why not?"

"You seem, uh, young."

"So do you."

"Are you with Harvard Health or Bay State Medical or anything like that?"

He shrugged. "Another patient may have mentioned me to her."

I temporarily accepted the evasion. "Okay. She mentioned drug blackouts."

"Disorientation," he corrected.

"Right. What's she on?"

"Um. I don't know that I should—"

"I can ask her. You don't have to tell me if it violates any professional standards."

"What's going on here?" he said, his eyes narrowing.

"An investigation."

"You take your work seriously."

"Don't you?"

"I only meant to say that Mrs. Woodrow's suspicions are not uncommon among those who've experienced an unexpected loss."

"You can bring anybody else who wants an unexpected loss investigated over to visit, if you'd like," I said.

"Look, I just felt I should warn you there's a good chance you might be dealing with delusional behavior here. I certainly haven't ruled that out. I think it's highly likely."

"What do you mean by delusional?" I asked. Oh, this was fun. I could sit and ask "what do you mean by that?" questions all day.

"Mrs. Woodrow is certainly suspicious and hostile. Something terrible did happen. Her daughter did die. But I have no way of knowing whether Mrs. Woodrow was already suspicious and hostile before this event set her off. I came in on this case as a fireman. I wasn't seeing her before the crisis. I just want you to understand that."

"You toss around words like *suspicious* and *hostile*. How about *paranoid*?" I asked. I once knew a private eye who did regular business with a psychiatrist. Whenever the shrink requested it, the PI would pass his electronic debugging equipment over the dental fillings of extremely paranoid patients. The shrink swore it reassured them tremendously.

Donovan blew out a breath. "*Paranoid* has definite clinical overtones," he said slowly.

"Would you use it to describe Emily Woodrow?"

"Not as a one-word label, no."

"You sound like you regret introducing me to your client," I said into silence.

"My patient," he corrected me. "I only want to reinforce that the patient is seeking closure."

"Or possibly truth."

"Her daughter died of leukemia. That's truth."

"When I was a cop, I got into the habit of treating every death as a suspicious death. Otherwise I found myself tromping all over the evidence before I'd decided to check it out."

"I didn't know you'd been, um, with the police."

"A cop. Would that have kept you away?"

He tried the smile again. "I'd have to think about it. But, no, I don't think so. I find it extremely interesting."

"What?"

He shrugged. "A woman. In your line of work. I hope I don't offend you by mentioning that."

I shrugged in return. "Anything else you'd like to tell me about Mrs. Woodrow?"

"Just this: If you speak to Dr. Muir, I'd prefer you didn't use my name."

"Aha," I said, arching one eyebrow.

"Is that your first clue?"

"Could be helpful. What can you tell me about this Jerome Muir? Aside from his international reputation?"

He thought about the question for a while, opening his mouth to speak, then reconsidering, shifting in his chair, frowning.

"Well?" I prompted.

"I never knew him in his prime."

I wondered what years Donovan considered "prime" ones. Teens? Twenties?

He crossed his arms over his chest and went on. "Muir's a genius. It's that simple and that complicated. The amount he's accomplished, the amount he accomplishes . . . I don't know if he never sleeps, or what. He's the guiding spirit behind Helping Hand, the CEO, the Chief of Staff, and he still manages to see the occasional patient."

"Does he pick and choose patients?"

"If some oil sheikh's kid got leukemia, yeah, Muir would probably see him. But he keeps his hand in, takes a few regular cases. He's part of a practice."

"What practice?"

"The Muir Group."

"And modest, too," I said.

"He is. I mean, if he'd wanted it, they'd probably have named the whole damn hospital after him. He put the deal together that saved the place. You ever hear of MedCare, Inc.? They buy up hospitals—in poor areas, a lot of the time. It's a for-profit chain, mainly in the South, and they can stay there for all I care. If it weren't for Muir, MedCare would have eaten the old Hand place. The merger with the Helping Institute kept it alive and vital, and that combo would never have come together without Jerome Muir.

44

He held MedCare at bay almost single-handedly, and did some smooth financial dealing to arrange funding for the merger. Brought people together, bankers, politicians, doctors, neighborhood activists. As far as the Muir Group goes, the other docs probably begged him to let them use his name."

"So he's a genius," I said.

"He's . . . I don't know how to put it . . . engaging. He has a great manner. He's a force. He gets behind something and it moves, it happens."

"Is he a good doctor?"

"There are doctors who go through the motions, and then there are healers. Genuine committed healers. Muir's a healer." He stuck out his chin defiantly, as if daring me to say something bad about his idol. Defiance sat on him awkwardly, made him look vulnerable.

"Do I sense a bit of hero worship here?" I asked.

"Chalk it up to my youth," he said dryly.

"If you happen to be on staff at Helping Hand, you could tell me things about the place. If you want to cooperate."

"I'm all for cooperation," he said, "provided it's a two-way street."

"Well, I'm taking the case," I said. "Isn't that what you want?"

"If Mrs. Woodrow wants it. If she decides to go ahead."

"Have you met her husband? Harold?"

"No. I've certainly heard about him. But nothing I'd want to share. Anything else?"

"Yeah. Now that you mention it," I said. "I would like to ask another question."

"Shoot."

"How old are you?"

I caught a momentary flash of annoyance in his eyes before the grin reasserted itself. "Thirty," he said. "Why?"

"Honest?"

"Twenty-nine."

"That's kind of young to—"

"I graduated high school at sixteen and then I took an accelerated six-year med school program."

"What was the rush?"

"I don't know. And you?"

"Me?"

"How old are you?"

"Older than you."

"Want to tell me the story of your life?"

"No. But if I wanted to look at your notes on Mrs. Woodrow, what would you say?"

"My clinical notes?"

"Yeah."

"I'd say that after you check out Emily's story, maybe even talk with Dr. Muir, we should have a drink."

It seemed like an interesting possibility.

"Maybe," I said.

"I'll let you get back to work," he said.

"Good-bye."

As soon as I heard the door latch, I dialed JHHI and confirmed my hunch. Dr. Keith Donovan was indeed a member of the staff.

And, I thought, tapping a pencil against the phone, I'd bet good hard cash that someone at the hospital, possibly even the great Muir himself, had referred Emily Woodrow.

7

After Donovan departed, I righteously typed, filed, and tied up loose ends, intermittently dialing Patsy until I was informed by a cheerful voice that she'd left for the day. I hoped she hadn't been fired.

Friday afternoon is no time to begin an investigation. Of course, since all I'd been instructed to do was wait, I could honestly say I was fulfilling my end of the deal. My eyes kept veering toward the photo on the mantel as I considered the looming weekend. For the past four years my Saturday mornings have belonged to Paolina. And dammit, there's absolutely no reason they shouldn't still belong to Paolina.

Except her mother.

Marta Fuentes is someone I'd never go out of my way to be-friend, but since she is the mother of my little sister, we have—in the past—been tolerant of each other's behavior. In certain ways I admire her. She had the sense to figure out that her lone girl child might have the need for another female in her life, somebody who wasn't burdened—as Mama was and is—with rheumatoid arthritis, the tendency to take up with rotten men, and three younger kids, all boys. Someone who'd act as a role model, sure, but more important, someone who'd listen to Paolina, care about her.

When I first met my little sister, she was barely seven years old —older than Rebecca Woodrow would ever be—with a hand-shaped bruise splayed across her face where Mom's latest flame had left his imprint. One thing I can never figure about Marta is that she doesn't seem to mind playing punching bag for the current man in her life. On the other hand, she unfailingly protects her kids. The guy who'd smacked Paolina was history before the bruise purpled.

I ran my fingers over the telephone, thought about calling Marta and asking for another chance.

It's too easy to hang up a phone. Too simple to leave it off the hook. So I tidied my desk by shoving all unfinished business into the top drawer, got into my car, and banged the door, imagining that I was slamming it on Marta's stubborn head.

I've tried everything. I've apologized. I've begged. I've attempted bribery.

Time to try again.

Marta lives in a Cambridge project that's not the worst housing in town. Close, but not in the same league as the city-owned high rises. Her development runs to a series of look-alike four-families with scraggly patches of lawn and a concrete playground flanked by a pair of broken, netless basketball hoops.

It's always a struggle to find a nearby parking place, but I persisted and jammed the Toyota into three quarters of a space that other drivers shunned.

The front door to Paolina's building was wedged open by half a cement block. I wondered whether someone was moving in or out, or if the security system had been trashed again. Maybe the door was ajar as shorthand to the neighborhood gangs: nothing left worth stealing.

I buzzed Marta's apartment and hiked up the stairs. Possibly some tenant cursed with a sensitive nose had opened the door to air the stairwell, which smelled like it did double duty as a urinal.

I wondered what Emily Woodrow's Winchester house looked like, if her daughter had been happy in its imagined splendor.

The door to Marta's flat was closed. I knocked once, then again, pressed my ear to the wood, listening for the blare of the TV, usually a constant. Nothing. I knocked louder. I thought I could hear someone fumbling with the lock.

Little Alvaro is only three. I was surprised he could turn the door handle. He looked up at me from under dark curls, gave a shy smile, and ran inside. I said "Hi!" to no one in particular, entered, and closed the door behind me.

Marta's no great housekeeper, but I'd never seen the place so filthy. Dishes were heaped on the table, smelly and coated with food. Bedding lay in piles on the floor, as if the whole family were camping out. Two boys stretched out on their stomachs in front of the TV, which was on, but silent. They stared at the moving images as if they were more real than I was.

"Is your mother home?"

The oldest nodded toward the single bedroom.

"*¿Quién es?*" The voice was definitely Marta's. "Paolina?"

I leaned in the bedroom doorway.

"I tell them no to open the door," she said. "I tell the boys. Do they listen? No."

"Marta, are you okay?"

"It looks maybe like I'm okay?"

"What's wrong?"

"*Nada.* Only my stomach. I can't keep the food down. *Me duele.* It hurts." Her last words came out through clenched teeth.

"You taking your medicine?"

"What there is. *No puedo caminar.* I no walk to the store like this."

"You can have it delivered."

"Don' you tell me what I do. What you doin' here is what I ask."

"Marta, is the phone working?"

"*No. No esta trabajando.*"

"Why?"

"*No es su problema.*" None of your business. That was clear enough.

"Money?"

She turned her face to the wall.

Her middle boy, asleep on another bed, hadn't stirred during the entire discussion. I placed a cautious hand on his forehead. It seemed cool enough, but I wondered if a four-year-old should be asleep at dinnertime.

I wondered if the kids still ate dinner.

But mostly I wondered where Paolina was. Marta always slept on the fold-out couch in the living room. Why was she resting on Paolina's bed?

I checked the brick-and-board makeshift shelves that lined the room. Paolina's clothes were there, neatly folded, along with her meager collection of books.

Marta kept her face stubbornly to the wall. I went back into the living room.

"Hi."

I couldn't remember the name of Alvaro's oldest brother. It made me feel bad. "How are you?"

"Hungry. You cook?"

I picked up the phone. Dead.

"Can you lock the door and then open it when I knock?" I asked. There's a pay phone on the corner.

"I'm not supposed to."

"I might bring something to eat."

"I'll open it."

The pay phone worked, an unexpected blessing. I hit 411 because there was no phone book, and got the number of the nearest Pizza Delite. I ordered two large—one with cheese, one with the works—hung up, and fumed.

I couldn't remember the name of the social worker assigned to Marta's case. Probably she couldn't remember Marta's name either. Most likely, she was the last person Marta would want me to call, a rule-bound bureaucrat who'd take one look at the place and start talking about moving the boys to a more "child-centered environment."

Roz picked up on the third ring.

"What time are you going out tonight?" Friday nights, I don't bother asking if she's going out. Hell or high water, hair-dye emergency or acrylic inspiration, Roz makes the weekend scene.

"Ten, eleven maybe."

The hours she keeps, you'd think she partied in New Orleans instead of Boston. "Want to earn a few extra?"

"Sure."

"Stop at a store and buy cleaning stuff. Basics. Meet me at Paolina's."

"You didn't say cleaning."

"You didn't ask."

"I'll have to change clothes."

"You can do it. See you soon." I vocally underlined the last word.

The oldest boy was disappointed that I didn't bring goodies, but I assured him help was on the way. Then I sighed deeply, and plunged in.

I hate routine cleaning with a passion, but this was so far from ordinary that there was a certain satisfaction involved, reminiscent of an archeological dig. I could make discoveries, like the true color of a dish, or the actual pattern on the linoleum. I should have asked Roz to bring a friend. Several.

"How long has your mom been sick?" I asked the boys.

"I dunno. Long time."

"You eat lunch today?"

The little one held out an empty cracker box.

I was afraid to open the refrigerator.

I folded bed linens, wondered where the closest Laundromat was located. Where was Roz?

Where was Paolina?

Marta wasn't speaking and the boys just stared at each other solemnly when I inquired. So I scrubbed the countertop near the sink with a pitiful remnant of sponge, and awaited fresh supplies.

When the bell rang, I thought it might be her. It wasn't. I tipped the nervous pizza-delivery boy well. Neither cabbies nor delivery folk adore the prospect of a project destination.

The kids, the freshly awakened four-year-old included, fell on the pizza like starving animals. I found a can of chicken soup without a dent in it, scrubbed a battered pot. No trays, so I balanced the bowl on a plate when I carried it into the bedroom.

"You still here?"

"Can you sit up?"

"Why you do this for me?"

"Because I want to see Paolina again."

She grunted while I shifted the pillows. It hurt her to move, to sit. I made the mistake of waiting for her to grasp the spoon. When she didn't, I glanced down and saw what the arthritis had done to her hands.

I held the spoon while she sipped.

She hesitated, her jaw clenched, then said, "Is okay with me. You and Paolina, I mean."

"Does she want to see me? She never answered my letters."

"I talk to a new social worker. She don' think is right, you an Anglo. She thinks is maybe better I find Paolina a Spanish sister."

"Does Paolina feel like that?"

"She don' answer you because I throw the letters away. Now you get me a glass of water, no?"

I bit back an angry response. "So who's this new social worker? What's her name?"

"Cynthia, the old one, she quit. She say she make more money clerking a grocery store. Why go to college for that? I tell her marry some man. Is better."

Ah, Marta's magic cure-all for women. Marry some man. Is better. She, still wedded to a guy who took off while she was pregnant, was living proof.

I sighed.

"You bring the water?"

"What you need is a doctor."

She seized my wrist and held on with surprising strength. "No doctor," she said. "No social worker. Nobody. Or you never get back with my Paolina."

She turned her face to the wall again and I walked out.

Roz had arrived and was staring at the apartment in horror and amazement. I hadn't heard her knock, but one of the boys must have let her in. I wondered what creation she'd been modeling before she changed. Could she own something more bizarre, less appropriate, than the fringed thigh-high outfit she now wore?

Roz is a karate expert. Dress like that, certain skills come in handy.

The pièce de resistance was her hair.

"Roz?"

"Yeah?"

"You shaved your head." Sometimes I'm compelled to break my vow never to comment on Roz's appearance.

"Less than half. You like it?"

It was more like a quarter of her head, to be honest. A strip extending from just above her right ear to about an inch below where the part might be on anyone so hopelessly conventional as to part her hair on the right. The bald strip had scalloped edging, sculpted and precise as topiary.

She must have reached total hair-dye saturation, I thought, experimented with every available shade. And now, imagine the possibilities—new horizons in hair art.

She'd remembered to bring rubber gloves. They lent a science-fiction touch to the ensemble.

"Whoa. Gross," she marveled, wrinkling her nose. "Is this a crime scene or what?"

The kids had eaten more pizza than I would have believed possible. The middle boy wiped a tomato-stained hand across his mouth and calmly inquired about dessert. Without a pause, Roz whipped a box of Girl Scout cookies from her canvas tote. God knows what else is in there.

"You want milk?" I asked the boys.

"Coke," they demanded. "Root beer."

Maybe Roz had something yummy in her purse. I fetched Marta's water, first washing the glass. The counter on the far side of the sink was so littered with pill bottles it looked like a pharmacy. I read the labels: Naprosyn, Medrol, Nalfon. All empty. Zorprin, full.

Feldene, empty. A warning label said to take this medicine only with or following food.

The warning label was in English.

I opened a window and inhaled a noseful of early spring before going back into the stale bedroom.

"Did you stop taking your pills because you ran out?" I asked while she sipped.

"I have more."

"Are you taking them?"

"Cuándo el dolor es muy fuerte." Only when the pain is real bad. "They make my stomach hurt."

"You have to take them with food."

"A veces no puedo comer." Sometimes I cannot eat. "Then I can no take the pills?"

"You need to eat," I said.

"The boys, they eat?"

"They ate. What about Paolina?"

"You only care for her. The boys are good boys. They help me."

"Where is she? Please."

"Is Friday? She has maybe a date."

"C'mon, Marta. She's a kid."

"You want to ask where is this kid, no? Maybe after you hear, you no want her for your sister."

"Don't worry about that."

"The little girl, the kid, has got herself a man. Twenty-five, maybe thirty years he's a day. I see him walkin' with her. I see them in his car. Lots a times. She says no. She says I'm crazy. Her own mother."

"Paolina? With a guy?"

"You don' believe me, maybe?"

"In his twenties? Has to be a teacher or something."

"Oh, you a stupid lady. Guy like that don't teach no school."

"Guy like what? You know his name?"

"She don' bring no man like that to her house. I throw her out, I see her with a man like that."

I wanted to ask what kind of men she'd expect Paolina to fall for, with such a sterling example of how not to pick 'em for a mother.

Instead I made her another bowl of soup.

"When will Paolina be home?"

"Soon, I think."

Roz beat it to the Laundromat with two giant bags of reeking clothes, leaving me the moldy bathroom to scour.

"Soon," Marta constantly assured me.

When the last light had faded from the sky, I wanted to call the cops. That's when Marta told me not to worry, she'd suddenly remembered: Paolina was staying the night with her aunt Lilia. And no, I couldn't phone the aunt to make sure all was well. Lilia left her receiver off the hook after nine o'clock. Too many wrong numbers. Too many salesmen. Too many perverts.

I drove by the aunt's place. All seemed quiet and dark.

Back home, I played my National steel guitar late into the morning hours, fooling around with an old tune, trying out different bass runs and slides till my calloused fingertips ached.

> Baby, please don't go.
> Baby, please don't go.
> Baby, please don't go down to New Orleans,
> You know I love you so.

I played all the standard verses, borrowed a few from other songs, even made up a couple of my own. I settled on a down-and-dirty bass and a bottleneck slide.

And I worried.

8

By Saturday morning I'd decided to see for myself. Which might be difficult. Marta's hardly my greatest fan, but her sister Lilia—Paolina's only aunt—really despises me. She'd take great delight in spitting in my eye.

The way she sees it, I cost her a job, almost single-handedly shutting down her place of employment. Of course, if she'd taken my advice and applied for immigration amnesty, she could have gotten other work easily. But her distrust of the government is almost as strong as her dislike of me.

Instead, she relies on badly forged papers, and she's been fired twice in the past year.

Paolina's life was endangered during the same case that cost Lilia her job. That's the root cause of our estrangement. It wasn't all my fault. A lot of the blame rests with Marta, which is probably why she's so keen to shift the entire burden to me.

I'm not the one who lied to Paolina about her father.

Anyway, I knew that Lilia would foam at the mouth if my car so much as appeared on her street in daylight, so I decided to use a cab, which makes as good a surveillance vehicle as anything outside a power company van.

Gloria, massive dispatcher and half owner of the Green & White Cab Company, was sitting in her wheelchair behind her battered metal desk, phone to ear, listening, talking, and eating at the same time, a trick perfected only by Gloria and certain politicians on the campaign trail.

I never understand why Green & White's Allston garage hasn't been shut down by some sort of health or public safety bureau.

Payoffs probably, arranged by none other than my lover, Sam Gianelli, the coproprietor of the company.

Maybe that's his main contribution to the business: veep in
charge of bribery.

Or maybe he supplies Gloria with junk food.

I glanced at the top of her desk in shock. On a typical visit, I
expect to find, within arm's reach, a sampling of America's best, say
a box of Bugles, a six-pack of Hershey Bars, a one-pound bag of
M&M's, an openmouthed jar of marshmallow fluff, and a can of
Planter's peanuts.

There was nothing but a single sack of Orville Redenbacher
microwave popcorn, empty and forlorn.

"Dieting?" I asked, my voice layered with disbelief.

"My dumb-ass brothers," she said angrily, hanging up the
phone and momentarily ignoring the flashing lights on her console.
"My brothers are saying I got to diet, watch what I eat and all. I
come in here and they cleaned me out. Nothin' but rabbit food,
carrots, and shit."

Gloria's got the three largest brothers imaginable, but you
wouldn't call any of them fat. You wouldn't call any of them anything. Former sports stars all, they now earn bucks as bar bouncers,
or in less savory trades.

You might call Gloria fat, but not in their hearing.

"You want food?" I asked, hoping she'd say no because who in
her right mind wants to oppose the world's biggest brother act?

"Hell, long as they make pizza to go, I ain't gonna starve. And I
got stashes they ain't found yet. They let me have this popcorn stuff,
but where's the butter?"

"I need a cab," I said. "You got something barely functional?"

"Let me guess. You want a cut-rate lease."

"Ask me, all your junkers ought to be cut-rate."

"You just gonna charm it right outa me."

"Give me a deal and I'll bring you a package of Hostess Cream-
filled Cupcakes."

"Make it four packages." She patted one plump dark cheek and let a laugh rumble up from deep inside her. "Chocolate's good for my complexion."

"You drive a hard bargain."

"And you get to drive an old Ford. Keys on the pegboard. How long you gonna keep it out?"

"You'll know when I get back."

"Six packages. And some Twinkies."

She was still outlining her grocery list when I slammed the door.

Lilia lives in Cambridgeport, a slightly slummy part of the University City, on the top floor of a triple-decker. The place is no showpiece with its peeling gray paint, but it's better than her sister's project. Lilia's fifteen years older than Marta and she's got problems of her own, like chronic unemployment. But if Marta had asked, she'd take in Paolina. No doubt about it. For her, family is family.

Only rarely did I wish I had one.

Oh, maybe somebody else's family, some idealized make-believe family. But I certainly felt no longing for the barely masked hostility of my parents' marriage, no nostalgia for my own brief attempt.

It was convenient for sex, my marriage, but life isn't lived in bed.

Thoughts of sex led to images of Sam Gianelli, which segued into fantasies of Keith Donovan. I have strict rules about not getting involved with clients. But then he wasn't technically a client. And I break my own rules all the time.

Sam and I have had an on-again-off-again affair steaming for more years than most marriages last. It will never lead to wedded bliss. I'm not in the market and, by his father's standards, I'm off limits, being both divorced and non-Catholic. Was I using Sam for relatively safe sex in this scary AIDS-ridden time? Hell, was he using me? Yeah. Both. But it wasn't the safety that attracted me; I hadn't met a lot of guys who turned me on the way Sam did.

Donovan was a distinct possibility. Too young, of course, but that had its good side. He probably wasn't looking for a long-term commitment. Yet.

I'm monogamous in my fashion. One at a time. No marrieds. Was I ready for a total breakup with Sam?

Cradle snatching. That's what a fling with Dr. Donovan would amount to. The mirror image of what this older guy was trying with Paolina. If I believed Marta . . .

I settled back in my car and stared at nothing. On surveillance I can semidoze, almost go into a trance. I don't think of it as patience, just the ability to turn off and turn on when necessary. It used to be one of my best cop traits. What a boring job that was. On the good days.

One Pepsi, two tiny boxes of raisins, and a banana later, I saw them approaching out of the corner of my eye. I didn't move. I'd expected Paolina to be leaving the house, not returning to it. I'd expected her to be with Lilia. Or alone.

He was in his twenties. At least. Marta had been right.

He wasn't holding Paolina's hand, but they were walking close together, and she was smiling up at him in a way that transformed her from a child to a strange and precocious young woman. I realized I was biting down on my bottom lip.

I'd only wanted to see her. To make sure she was safe. To speak to her if she was alone, pass some secret signal if she was with Lilia. Now I felt like a voyeur. The man said something and she rewarded him with a dazzling smile.

He was big, beer-bellied big—a look I associate with bars and motorcycle gangs. Studded belt, leather jacket, frayed jeans slung low on his hips. If I'd been a vice cop, I'd have hauled him in on probable cause.

What the hell did Paolina find attractive in a man almost old enough to be her father?

Bingo. I'd just answered my own question.

I sat like a statue, my mind racing. Should I jump out and confront him? Ask him what the hell he was doing with a girl young enough to define jailbait? How would Paolina react?

She was dressed for spring in spite of the chill, wearing tight pink leggings. A long purple shirttail hung out from under her multizippered red jacket. A red beret plastered her bangs to her forehead. She wore earrings. Earrings! When the hell had she started doing that?

He didn't walk her up to Lilia's doorstep. Instead, they loitered on the sidewalk. He shook a cigarette out of a pack, mockingly offered her one, then lit up. They talked three cigarettes' worth. I couldn't see her face.

I cracked the window of the cab, but I was parked too far away to hear anything but mumbling. His voice dominated, deep and husky. He pulled something from the back pocket of his jeans, maybe an envelope, or a card. Paolina shook her head no, but her resistance gradually weakened, and after ten minutes, the item passed from his possession into hers.

I heard a bang, and jumped. Paolina glanced up sharply, but not at me. On the third floor of the gray building, a window had opened. I could hear Lilia's angry voice.

I'd be angry too, my niece littering the sidewalk with trash like that guy.

Paolina blew a defiant kiss at him and raced up the walk. He flipped an upraised middle finger at Lilia, turned and started back down the sidewalk.

I sat till he passed me, till he turned the corner. Then I gunned the engine, banged a U-turn, and followed. If he stayed on foot I might have to abandon my wheels and do the same, especially if he made for any of the Central Square subway entrances. Shadowing a guy solo in the subway is no fun.

Where had she met the creep? Not at school; it was ten years out of his league. Hanging around the projects, more likely. An unemployed loser. Or illegally employed.

He walked two quick blocks in the direction of Central Square while I considered the possibilities. There's no place to leave a cab on Mass. Ave. where it won't get towed or stolen. I could park it now and walk, or trust to providence to find a space. Last time I did that, I wound up retrieving my car from the city lot, paying eighty-five dollars in tow fees, and practically getting eaten by a German shepherd guard dog. I tried to figure how close to Central Square I could safely approach before taking the last available parking space.

They ought to mark them the way they do gas stations: last space before the Mojave Desert.

He was still walking at Pilgrim Street, brisk stride, cigarette in hand. I'd obviously passed the last parking space. The loading zones, even the fireplugs were occupied territory.

He strolled across Mass. Ave., dodging traffic, hung a left, and started toward Prospect Street and the MBTA station. Took a surprise right into the alleyway next to the liquor store that used to be a Greek restaurant. I put on a burst of speed, two-wheeled the next corner. I thought I'd pick him up easily on Bishop Richard Allen Drive.

No sign of him. Two black ladies in full Easter finery strolled toward the church across the street. A tiny Oriental girl balanced a boom-box on her shoulder.

A steel-blue Firebird came barreling out of the parking lot.

The last two numbers on the plate were four-eight.

Paolina's friend was driving. I swung in behind him.

9

He signaled right on Main Street, left on Mass. Ave., tooling along easily in the smelly wake of a bus. I started to radio Gloria with a quick message to call the cops. Then I hesitated. What did I have on this guy? Probable garbage theft? Offering a cigarette to a minor? The cops wouldn't exactly put out an all-points.

He swerved past the bus in front of MIT, sped up, and headed over the Harvard Bridge into Boston, hitting a major pothole so hard I was amazed he didn't lose his engine, much less a hubcap.

Left on Commonwealth. Didn't the jerk ever check his rear-view mirror?

Right on Gloucester. He'd been inching along so slowly that he caught me when he squealed a left on Boylston, catching the very tail of a yellow. If I'd had my own car, I'd have chanced it, but Gloria hates to have the least little dent on one of her fenders.

When I drive for her, I carry a secret repair kit consisting of one bottle each of green and white nail lacquer. Punk fashion has helped me camouflage a couple of nasty scratches.

I watched the Firebird do a tricky little scoot into the Pru Center garage. This guy believed in paying for parking. I don't.

I tapped the steering wheel impatiently. The light took forever to change. Instead of following him into the garage, I decided to ditch the cab in front of the Lenox Hotel. The head bellman knows me, and I was making up a likely story when I saw a junky Renault vacate a space in front of the drugstore. I crossed three lanes of traffic without a qualm. There was time on the meter.

On foot, I sped back across the street and down the ramp into the shadowy garage.

Once past the punch-a-ticket machine, motorists could turn in any one of three directions to seek parking. No humans to pinpoint the trail of the steel-blue Firebird.

I walked the lanes, crisscrossing the green level.

The car was the only way to trace him. I couldn't cover all the pedestrian exits. He could have chosen from two banks of elevators, eight separate staircases. Lost himself in a department store. Entered the Prudential Center Tower, wound his way through the plywood boardwalk of the under-construction shopping mall clear to the Sheraton. Strolled through the glass bridge to Copley Place and descended the escalator into Back Bay Station.

The car was not on the green lower level. Which left the blue.

As I made the upper circuit, I unconsciously started counting the number of Japanese and German imports. As a native Detroiter I have a hard time believing things have come to such a pass. But then, as the driver of a Toyota, I have met the enemy and she is I.

The long and the short of it is I lost him. I couldn't find the damned car. Had he spotted me? Driven straight to an exit with some phony wrong-turn story?

I located a pay phone. Tried Mooney. He was not in the office. Good for him, I thought. Somebody should be enjoying Saturday. I tried his home number and he picked up as if he were waiting for someone to call.

"Good," he said as soon as he heard my voice, not giving me a chance to speak. "Look, I can't get zip from the last two digits of a plate. It's the way the computers are rigged. You've got the first two digits, my guy says, he could give you a print-out—thousands of names, but a print-out anyway. But they're not geared for the last two digits, or the last digit or anything. I'm gonna raise hell. I mean, we get a lot of partials, and if they can find the first two numbers, why the hell shouldn't they be able to find the last two, especially with a make of car—"

"Mooney," I said. "Listen."

"Everybody gets off blaming the Registry. So do I, so I don't mind about you asking, and I'll be glad to—"

"Five-three-six, Mooney," I said. "Five-three-six—zero-four-eight. A Mass. plate. Still a late-model Firebird."

"You got all the numbers?"

"That's what I've been trying to say."

"This guy's hanging around? Hassling you or what?"

"Not exactly," I said hesitantly.

"Wanna give Papa the whole story?"

"You're not old enough."

"Papa loves dirty stories," he said.

"Gonna run the plate?"

"I'll run it," he said after pausing long enough for me to wonder whether he would.

I hung up. I'd put a quarter in the slot for a dime call, because a quarter was all I had. I wondered about change, but decided not to risk sticking my finger in the coin return. Kids put used chewing gum in them. Worse.

Since I'd found such a great parking place, I decided to take advantage of it. At the Pru Star Market, I stocked up for Gloria. I bought junk, but I tried to sneak in a little nutrition on the side—oranges, a couple apples. I asked the check-out clerk to bag it separately, the unembarrassing stuff in one plastic sack, Twinkies and cupcakes in the other. I'd tote in the wholesome bag first, disappointing Gloria, but decoying any brother who might be hanging around in between bone-cracking sessions for a local loan shark.

Gloria and I dined together, with me sticking to a minimal portion of Kraft Macaroni and Cheese, while she downed the rest, along with multiple Tootsie Rolls, Mars Bars, and a large box of chocolate-covered graham crackers. I spent the whole meal scared her brothers would show up.

At least I knew Paolina was okay, alive.

Sunday was a bust. No progress on the plate. No messages from Emily Woodrow. No mail at all.

10

By Monday morning I'd had it with waiting.

As soon as I got back from the Cambridge Y, still sweaty from volleyball, I tackled New England Telephone, rising higher and higher in the supervisory ranks till I reached someone who took my threat of dire legal repercussions seriously enough to promise to reconnect Marta's phone. Flushed with victory, I dialed Patsy Ronetti.

"Sorry," she murmured in what, for her, were dulcet tones. I held the receiver an inch away from my ear instead of the customary five. "I got hung up on a trace."

"You got what I need?" I asked, pencil poised.

"Yeah."

"Shoot."

"Harold Winthrop Woodrow. Age: forty-eight," she began. She rattled through his social security number and date of birth. "Harvard University. Rutgers Law. *Law Review.*" She gave me a list of firms where he'd been employed, and I envisioned how much easier life would be once I joined the computer set. Electronic mail was the only way to go, I thought while scribbling at breakneck pace. Otherwise I'd have to learn shorthand. Spelling.

"Currently a partner at Irwin, Woodrow, and Place," she continued, naming an influential local firm at which I had absolutely no contacts. I know lots of lawyers; I mainly work for them. But IWP boasts such a blue-blooded clientele that they rarely do business with investigators. Or if they do, they keep it quiet.

"So he's that Woodrow," I said.

"Fancy taxes are his speciality."

"Her?"

"Inherited major money."

"From his name, sounds like he did, too." Nobody in my family has a middle name like Winthrop.

"Nope. He made it the old-fashioned way. Married it. She's a Ruhly. The department-store Ruhlys."

"She pay the bills?"

"No need. Hers sits in investment accounts. Okay? You know where to send the check, right?"

"Wait. What about her?"

"I told you. Rich."

"Employment history. She work?"

"No."

"Never?"

"I didn't check on her. Just him."

"Kind of a sexist assumption," I said.

"Classist. Why should she work?"

"Classist, sexist, whatever, if I'm paying for an employment check, I want both of them."

"Okay."

"Hey, anything turn up on that guy who was asking questions about me?"

"Sorry," she murmured softly. Then she hung up. Dammit, I was going to have to cultivate somebody who did less apologizing and more conventional farewells.

I chewed my fingernails till the mailman brought my usual pile of bills and political pleas. Maybe Emily Woodrow, unwilling to break the weekly rhythm, would time her mysterious, vital, and probably cuckoo information to arrive this Friday, or next Friday, or the Friday after that.

The hell with waiting. I'd deposited her check. At least I could meet the players.

I reviewed my notes. Jerome Muir, Becca's doctor, the man with the impeccable international rep, the "genius," according to Keith Donovan, seemed the logical place to start.

After some deliberation, I selected a card from my ever-growing phony business-card file, took a few duplicates as well. Upstairs I tried to dress to match my new identity. I might, someday, if this investigation ever blossomed, wish to meet Dr. Muir as myself. An initial foray called for disguise.

I pity male detectives, I really do. Some may laugh and ask where a six-foot-one redhead's gonna hide, but I have my response down pat: A *female* six-foot-one redhead is as easy to hide as a trip to your local wig shop.

I could do it with hair dye, like Roz—or Roz before she discovered the clippers—but the truth of it is, I like my own particular shade of flame, and I take umbrage when anyone suggests I may have helped nature's hand. So I do wigs. They're not especially comfy, and the cheapies, the kind they foist off on undercover cops, are a guaranteed headache. So I stick to two decent ones, a long straight brunette and a curly blond.

I gazed at the business card's neat type. Sandra Everett. Sandy. Definitely curly blond. Cute is not easy to achieve at six-one, so I decided on earnest. Older than me, maybe thirty-five to forty. Well groomed. Wealthy. Unaccustomed to the word *no*.

I own a single good navy business suit, purchased at a Filene's Basement sale. Paired with a prim white silk blouse, it would see me through. A hat would be good. In one of the many rooms I could rent to Harvard students if I bothered, I keep the few things of Aunt Bea's that I didn't send to charity. I plucked the frivolous silk flowers off a straw boater, pinned it to my wig so it would sit at a properly unbecoming angle.

Pearls would have been nice if I'd owned any.

I found a pair of Italian leather flats that pinched my toes, another Filene's Basement deal. I wear sneakers most of the time, but they wouldn't do for Sandra.

Disguised, I spent some time with the current Yellow Pages. Muir wasn't listed under Physicians, but he was part of a special feature, the GUIDE TO PHYSICIANS AND SURGEONS, ARRANGED BY PRACTICE. Under Oncology at the Jonas Hand/Helping Institute. Tiny letters beneath his name spelled out: Chief of Staff, Pediatric Oncology-Hematology. I cut to the big print: Longwood Avenue. I cross-checked the reference under Hospitals, but the ad for JHHI gave no specifics, not even physicians' names. Just a single all-purpose phone number.

While I ran my finger down the lists of names and places, I tried to imagine how Sandy Everett would sit in her clothes, how she'd move. Since she'd opted for flats rather than heels, I decided she'd try to try to make herself seem shorter. Ducking my head forward and hunching my shoulders, I felt a surge of righteous determination.

I made sure my message machine was operational, grabbed my purse with a more ladylike motion than usual, and left the house.

When I drive a cab, I keep strictly away from the Longwood Medical area, preferring a tricky left turn and a crescent-shaped detour onto the Riverway to avoid the whole of Hospital Row, which boasts—in addition to Helping Hand—Children's Hospital, Beth Israel Hospital, Brigham and Women's, the Deaconess, the Dana-Farber Cancer Institute, and probably a few new health-care havens that have opened since the last time I checked. The traffic is appalling. People late for doctors' appointments, hurrying to give birth, or racing to see loved ones *in extremis* tend to be less than mindful of their turn signals. Add the fact that every intersection in the one-mile stretch has its very own traffic light, and the result is a caliber of gridlock unique even in Boston.

An old yellow Saab decided to turn left in front of me. From the right-hand lane. No signal.

I usually cab nights because I don't have the patience for day-time driving. I'd rather risk midnight muggers than hang out behind a five-mile-an-hour stream of honking commuters. While traffic crawled, I slid Bonnie Raitt's *Collection* into the tape deck, a much-practiced maneuver I can perform blindfolded on an S curve.

Another reason I avoid the Longwood Medical area is that once you hit your destination, there's no place to park. The few metered slots are regulated in scant twenty-minute allotments. There is nothing you can do in a hospital in twenty minutes, right? So the meters are perpetually red-flagged and traffic tickets adorn every windshield. But that doesn't create any more parking spaces, and the garages are incredibly expensive.

Whoa, I said to myself. Incredibly expensive is Emily Woodrow's middle name. And since this visit was on her, I could afford a garage.

I crossed Brookline Avenue after two lights worth of left-turners. Kept up a stop-and-go pace in front of Children's Hospital.

Unlike the rest of the medical outfits, JHHI lies south of Huntington Avenue. I began looking seriously for a garage. The chance of car theft increased dramatically on the wrong side of the streetcar tracks.

JHHI had its own meager parking facility. I yanked the car into the barely marked drive. The ramp spiraled steeply, a two-way job too narrow for more than a mile-an-hour creep. The structure beyond the ramp featured cramped spaces, mostly occupied. Few cars seemed to have parked entirely between the yellow lines. For two bucks a half hour, it was no bargain. I squeezed between a badly parked Mercedes and a battered Plymouth. Signs and arrows directed me to an arched passageway that led to the lobby.

I wondered if the passageway, newer than the garage, had been built to shield the hospital from its surroundings, ushering patients from parking lot to front door without making them confront the boarded-up tenements across the street, the littered playground to one side, the seemingly abandoned factory on the other.

I glanced quickly around. No one in sight, so I gave my wig a quick downward tug with both hands, settled the straw hat on top, and eased through the automatic doors wondering how Marie Antoinette had ever kept her hairdo afloat.

The high-ceilinged lobby was pleasant enough. Both the elegant chandeliers and the ultra-utilitarian reception desk seemed out of place in opposing ways. To the left, a low fountain spilled into a shallow pool. Pennies and silver coins glittered in the shallows. Of course: A body of water in a hospital would soon become a wishing well.

Make my child healthy. Keep me whole.

A dark-skinned woman pulled a contraption halfway between a wagon and a wheelchair around and around the fountain. In its depths, a reclining child, pale as the pillows behind her head, lay tethered to a machine that gurgled and spat. A second machine, attached to her arm, flashed green blips across a screen.

A nurse pushed an IV stand across the wagon's path. It squeaked as it rolled by.

A young mother, impossibly burdened with diaper bags and car seats, tried to bundle her two small children against the chill. A third child, older, possibly four, splashed in the fountain, drenching the sleeves of his navy-blue jacket and giggling. She yelled at him, then glanced furtively around the lobby and bit her lip.

The lobby was hot. Sandra Everett was sure going to sweat in her suit jacket. Perspire. Sandra would perspire.

I sweat.

I approached the information desk.

"Where would I find Dr. Muir?"

The aging attendant looked up at me with instant respect. On her desk was a chart, printed on graph paper. She ran a fingertip down one column, then another. "It's a clinic day. With the construction, let's see, he'll be on Eastman Two. Take the last elevator on the right, or you could just climb these stairs if you want to."

"Thank you."

"You have an appointment with Dr. Muir?"

"Yes."

"He's a wonderful man," she said, looking off in the direction of my right shoulder. "I hope everything works out for the best."

I followed her gaze and found myself staring at a row of portraits, stiff men in formal dress, lined up like ancestors in a family gallery. JONAS HAND read the bronze plaque under one. James Helping, a plump smiling presence, hung next to him. Jerome Muir had already earned a place of honor on the wall.

He was extraordinarily handsome. I would have taken more time to study his likeness, but the receptionist kept her eyes fastened on me, making me feel guilty, as if I were late for a genuine appointment.

I climbed the stairs quickly. Surrounded by all the wheelchairs and wagons, I was grateful I could.

Directly ahead, an area was boarded off, under construction. Hammers pounded and a buzz saw worked. A temporary plaque on a column announced EASTMAN TWO. A signboard listed names and displayed arrows, sending patients to a waiting room on the right or one on the left. I scanned the list and veered right.

Jerome D. Muir, Dr. Renee Talbot, Dr. Simon Piersall, and Dr. Edward Hough worked to the right. Presumably the Muir Group.

The waiting room was nothing much. Blues and grays. Tweedy aged carpet. Landscape prints on pale walls. Magazines overran a square coffee table and sat haphazardly on a couple of the upright blue chairs. Seating for thirty. The place smelled of disinfectant. Or maybe I was just imagining it, confronted by all that white behind the reception counter.

The main room had an adjoining alcove, a children's wing, featuring low furniture in primary colors, stacks of kiddie books, and cabinets full of Raggedy Anns and toy racing cars.

Behind the counter, backed by a wall of tabbed files, two women peered at computer terminals, single-mindedly entering data. The dark-haired, middle-aged one wore glasses that had left red moon-shaped weals on either side of her nose. The other was a knockout: slim, young, and black, with strikingly tilted eyebrows. Neither acknowledged my approach, so I waited. Sometimes if they just notice you standing there, they feel guilty. Not often. But I've conducted a survey, and if you interrupt, they're almost always in foul humor.

The middle-aged woman glanced up first. "Can I help you?" she asked with no hint of apology.

I drew in a deep breath and started the gag.

First I handed over my card and smiled as if I were doing her a favor.

"The *Suffolk News*?" she said.

"Oh, don't let that alarm you," I said easily. "I'm not here in my capacity as a reporter."

"I don't understand."

"Well, of course you don't," I said generously. "I told the advisory board that we should have called first, but they wouldn't hear of it. And since I was going to be in the neighborhood—"

"Miss Everett, I don't—"

"Mrs. Everett, dear. Now if Dr. Muir can't see me right away, I'll absolutely understand. I'm quite willing to wait, but the board insisted that I deliver the invitation personally."

"Invitation," she repeated.

"Yes. Invitation. I'm the current vice-president of the local Silver Crescent chapter. We're a charitable organization, and each year we honor an individual who's made a major contribution to our community. Dr. Muir is an overwhelmingly popular selection, and the consensus of the nominating committee was that I approach him in person."

"He's extremely busy." It was a line she was so used to dishing out, she probably didn't even hear herself say it.

"It's just eleven fifteen, and I've brought lots of busy-work," I said. "I can catch up on the minutes of the last meeting, work on the phrasing of the press announcement. I only need a few moments of his time, and I know he'll be pleased. The Silver Crescent isn't in the Shriners' league, dear, but we do what we can."

The middle-aged woman exchanged a quick glance with her young co-worker. Which one had called Emily Woodrow crazy? I wondered.

The black receptionist shrugged and bent over her typing. She might as well have announced that she was the less senior of the two. The older one would have to flip the coin and make the call. I pressed a little harder.

"Look," I said, with a smile glued to my face, determination shining through, "I know it might have been preferable, from your angle, to arrange matters formally with the public relations department. But there'll be plenty of time for that. Right now, the ladies of the Silver Crescent are waiting for my report, waiting to hear how Dr. Jerome Muir reacts when he learns that he's been named our very special speaker of the year. I'm willing to wait. It's a waiting room, isn't it? And sooner or later, I'm certain he'll find time to see me." I put more warmth in my smile and added, "I'm really in no hurry, Barbara."

I sure would hate to wear a name tag to work, especially one that gave only my first name.

"Dr. Muir is extremely busy," she repeated, wavering.

"He must be a wonderful man to work for."

She inserted her tongue between her teeth. She'd made a mistake and she knew it. She should have implied that he was out, on hospital rounds.

I quickly retreated to a chair and busily shuffled through my handbag. If that didn't get me into the presence I didn't know what would. I'd used the key words: charity, contribution, Shriners, honor. No receptionist would want to be tagged as the obstacle who'd blocked a hefty donation.

I'd taken a chance using the reporter's card rather than an ordinary calling card, but I wanted an excuse to question. This way, any apparent lack of tact could be attributed to journalistic habit.

I surveyed the waiting room's inhabitants—a young woman staring into space, a couple holding hands, a tiny black teenager wearing a turban—trying to make eye contact, develop likely sources of gossip. No one took any notice of Sandra Everett.

Two wan children, one about five, the other eight, sat listlessly nearby, ignoring the toys.

"It could be some time," the receptionist warned.

"I can wait," I said. And I did.

11

The staring woman jerked back to reality when a nurse called her name. Leading the eight-year-old, she hurried past the reception counter and down a curtained hallway. The young couple never exchanged a word, but they never stopped holding hands either. The five-year-old made airplane noises and drummed his feet.

I entertained myself by trying to remember my mother's favorite Yiddish maxims concerning doctors. She had quite a few, all passed down to her by my grandmother, an awe-inspiring woman by all accounts, union firebrand and scab nemesis extraordinaire.

The only one I could remember was: *"Far der tsayt ken afile a dokter a mentshn nit avek'hargenen."* Or, "If your time hasn't come yet, even a doctor can't kill you."

I'd folded and stuffed a sheet of typing paper into an envelope before leaving my house. Under the watchful gaze of the receptionist, I carefully inscribed a few sentences. Too bad Roz hadn't been home. She could have fixed me up with something fancy, even parchmentlike. This phony testimonial business cried out for her artistic touch.

A man wearing a white smock over khaki overalls passed by with a brisk step. His keys jingled as he opened a metal lockbox next to a column. He withdrew wrapped test tubes, stashed them in a pouch, and disappeared with a nod in the direction of the desk.

I finished writing, reinserted paper into envelope, shifted my weight, and smiled, self-importantly and pointedly, at Barbara, the receptionist. She returned my stare blankly and I wondered if she'd bothered to inform Muir of my arrival.

The exotic black woman fetched noontime sandwiches for herself and her colleague. She didn't ask if I was hungry.

By one o'clock I was starving, but I didn't want to give up my seat, my silent battle of wills with the receptionist.

One o'clock ticked slowly into two o'clock. I removed my straw hat; the wig was making my scalp sweat. Waiting-room magazines revealed that seafood was potentially hazardous, while beef would definitely kill you—provided the ozone layer held out for another twenty years. Sexual harassment was moving out of the office and into the courtroom, and three out of four movies featured slice-and-dice killers.

I started getting the waiting-room willies. Anytime I'm stuck in a room smelling of antiseptic, I flash back to my father's death. It wasn't like I saw him every day; he and my mom had long since separated. But viewing him so shrunken, so different from his larger-than-life cop self, so diminished by tubes and drains and cotton hospital johnnies . . . The memory still makes me want to snatch cigarettes out of the mouths of teenagers.

The couple disappeared down the hallway shortly after the mom with eight-year-old departed. I waited. More patients were called. More arrived to occupy their vacant chairs.

I kept an eye on my receptionist. Carlotta Carlyle was steaming under the collar, but that was unimportant. How would Sandra Everett handle the situation?

Sandra, I decided, had two kids, was recently divorced. Determined to make a career in journalism, her old college major, she was genuinely puzzled that there weren't more opportunities out there for ladies who'd taken ten years off to raise the kids. The kind of woman who prefaced her sentences with "Well, I'm not a feminist, but—" Maybe a touch of the South in her background. A woman taught to value niceness over just about anything else.

A woman who might use her volunteer work to gather quotes from the wives of community leaders, but who'd never *ever* print anything scandalous.

I fingered my synthetic blond curls. Time for a reminder, I thought. A gentle reminder.

I waited until the black woman was handling the desk alone.

"Has Dr. Muir given you any idea when I might have a few minutes?" I asked.

"I'm sorry," she said. "I just don't know."

"Could you give him a buzz and find out?"

"Not if I want to keep my job."

"Like that?"

"Like that." She gave me a rueful grin that changed as she looked over my shoulder. She bent immediately to her work and I assumed my dragon lady had returned. Instead I heard a man's voice.

"Savannah," he said to the black woman, "you guarding the desk all by yourself? Think you can manage that?"

SAVANNAH was printed plain as day on her badge. But it was evident from his tone that he knew her.

"Barbara will be right back," she said with a faint edge to her voice.

"You ought to do fine," he said coolly. "Ring Jerome and tell him I'll be in his office."

"He's, uh, tied up, Dr. Renzel," Savannah said.

"Where's Barbara?"

"Oh, Dr. Renzel. I didn't see you come in!" The middle-aged receptionist rushed up, smiling and ineffectually patting her hairdo.

"Hey," the doctor said, his deep voice warming with her arrival, "you look great. I see they've got you breaking in another one. You ought to earn extra as chief trainer."

Barbara's plain round face turned blotchy with pleasure. She chuckled while Savannah stretched her lips in a meaningless parody of a smile.

"I'll be waiting in his honor's office. You let him know, okay, Barbara?"

"Well, he is with a patient." She smiled indulgently, negating any reproof.

"What else is new? I've got five minutes." With a broad wink, the man sailed through. Fortyish, medium height, a narrow bony face with knife-blade cheekbones. Thick glasses. He didn't quite live up to his pleasing baritone.

Barbara immediately pressed a button on her phone console.

"While Dr. Muir's on the line," I urged, "please remind him that I'm waiting."

She mentioned only Dr. Renzel, not Sandra Everett, before hanging up.

I glanced at the black woman. She lifted her lovely eyebrows in a weary gesture of resignation. Savannah what? I wondered. A dissatisfied employee can be an information gold mine.

My scalp itched under my wig. "Where's the ladies' room?" I inquired.

Barbara began a complicated string of instructions that would have taken me downstairs through the lobby and halfway to the Himalayas.

"There must be one for the patients," I murmured softly when her phone rang, commanding her attention. "I'll only be a minute."

She didn't see me dodge down the narrow opening into which Renzel and the patients had disappeared. The corridor opened into a chamber decorated with gilt-framed diplomas. The name *Muir* appeared on no less than four. I studied his degrees, reading the parts that weren't in Latin. Harvard. Johns Hopkins. Yale. University of Michigan. Not exactly offshore diploma mills.

I figured Sandra Everett had a fifteen-minute head start before the reception witch came hunting, and the searching-for-a-bathroom ploy is as tried and true as any, so I moseyed down the door-lined hallway.

It irked me that this Dr. Renzel had crashed the secretarial barricades so easily. Maybe I should have posed as a doctor. Sure. Easy. I'd just need to cram for eight years to carry off the impersonation.

There was an open doorway five feet down the corridor. I stepped quickly inside and shut the door behind me.

It was a small examining room, a cot against one wall, a wooden step stool leading up to it. The walls were painted, not papered. No trace of the blue-and-white lattice design Emily Woodrow had described. A scale dominated one corner. A blood-pressure cuff was secured to the wall over the cot. No trace of an oxygen mask.

I wondered where the chemotherapy rooms were located, whether they were equipped, like operating rooms, with wall outlets for oxygen and air. Were oxygen masks wall-mounted as well? I twisted the doorknob slowly, peered out into the empty corridor, and began a search for floral wallpaper. Hospitals rarely paper individual rooms; possibly all the chemo rooms were similarly decorated.

The examining-room doors featured small ledges on which to balance patients' file folders. Rooms without ledges seemed to be offices. None bore so much as a stenciled name or number.

I passed a metal canister labeled MEDICAL WASTE in bright red letters. It had a domed top, a WARNING! label on each of its four sides. A nearby philodendron plant needed watering. A flushing sound came from behind a wooden door marked W.C.

A woman passed and nodded. A child cried and a male voice murmured soothingly.

I heard voices issuing from a room with no door ledge. One was the mellow baritone of Dr. Renzel. I assumed the lower, gruffer voice belonged to Jerome Muir.

Sandra Everett discovered that her panty hose were slipping. She bent to straighten them. I took advantage of her strategic location to eavesdrop.

At first it sounded like Renzel was reciting letters. I shifted closer and got sentences. "One Florida place has been taken over three times in six months. Started with Humana and then went to SurgiCare and then CritiCare. Drove the billing department nuts."

I heard footsteps and swiveled to find the dragon lady in hot pursuit.

"Mrs. Everett," she said firmly, "the restrooms in this area are reserved for patients only. You'll have to go back to the lobby."

Right outside Muir's door seemed as good a place as any to dig in my heels. I made sure my voice was loud enough to penetrate wood.

"Really," I said. "Have you any idea how the ladies of the Silver Crescent might react if I can't make our presentation to Dr. Muir personally? Today? How can we print up the invitations? How can we set the level of contributions? I understand that he's a busy man, but good news is not to be ignored. He is certainly not the only medical man worthy of this honor—"

I could have continued, but I didn't have to. The door swung open on well-oiled hinges.

12

Dr. Renzel appeared, staring at me quizzically. "I was just leaving, Barbara," he said. "Hope I haven't made a hash of your schedule."

"What seems to be the problem?" I heard a gruff voice demand from within.

I sidestepped both Barbara and Renzel, stuck my foot in the door.

"A minute of your time, Dr. Muir," I said.

The gruffness was age, I realized. Much older than his lobby portrait, he sat in a high-backed leather throne behind a slab of mahogany and inclined his head a fraction of an inch in my direction. I felt almost as if I'd been granted a blessing. His crisp white shirt and red speckled bow tie were hardly clerical garb, but I was vividly reminded of an old priest my father, a much-lapsed Catholic, had revered. Jerome Muir's hair had turned beautifully white, without a trace of yellow; his moustache and bushy sideburns were elegant.

"The lady from that charity," Barbara murmured in a low voice, as if she thought I might be hard of hearing. "I'm still checking on her. The newspaper . . ."

The number on my *Suffolk News* business card is hooked into the Green & White Cab Company's fancy phone system, courtesy of Sam Gianelli. It's not just an unlisted number; it's unpublished and pretty close to untraceable. Sam's picked up a few tricks from his mobster dad over the years. The efficient Barbara would have reached an answering machine: "All lines are currently busy. Please hold."

"Checking!" I echoed indignantly. "Surely, Dr. Muir, you've

heard of the Silver Crescent. We're currently seeking affiliation with the Eastern Star."

"Barbara, perhaps I'd better handle this directly." Muir's broad face was slightly florid and crisscrossed with a fine web of lines. His piercing blue eyes rarely blinked. He focused his full attention on me, and it seemed like a gift seldom bestowed, something the speaker needed to earn.

Renzel's casual, "Can I stay?" made it sound as if there were going to be a movie screening, with popcorn and Coke.

I said, "The membership gave me very specific instructions. They wanted me to do it just so."

Renzel said good-naturedly, "Don't let me stop you."

Barbara turned on her sensible heel and departed without a word.

"You've upset her," Renzel said. I wasn't sure if he was talking to me or Muir. Talking about me or Barbara.

"Oh, Jerome, I almost forgot," Renzel went on. "Have you decided on the Portugal conference?"

While the two doctors debated the merits of meeting with colleagues in Lisbon, I inspected the office. Matching bookcases lined two walls. A marble-topped table held an ornate Chinese vase. A collection of creamy, spiraled shells filled two shelves of the right-hand bookcase. A full-rigged frigate in a bottle sailed another. Two oil paintings looked like the real thing, but who knows, what with Polaroid reproductions? Muir had covered the wall behind his desk with framed photographs. Student groups from college days, gowned graduation photos, Muir standing beside a man in flowing Arabian robes, Muir smiling while he clapped a well-known congressman on the back.

A power wall.

In most of the photos he wore a polka-dot bow tie. As he apparently did in real life.

"I'll consider it," Muir said firmly. "Decision by Wednesday. Now, young lady, please sit down." Muir nodded me into a plush blue chair. "I do hope Barbara hasn't made your life difficult. She's extremely protective of my time."

I sat.

"I'm sorry if we seem to have behaved rudely," he continued, "but we were under the impression that you were a reporter. We have strict procedures—"

He'd shifted to the royal *we*, but it didn't seem ludicrous. Didn't even seem inappropriate.

"I'm not here on a story." I withdrew the envelope from my handbag, unfolded my precious sheet of paper. "May I read?"

"Please." Muir carefully stifled a yawn so that only the edges of his nostrils fluttered. I wished I'd spent more time gazing at the painting in the lobby. He must have been incredibly handsome.

My speech was brief, but I spluttered a little and made several mistakes, to make it seem as if I hadn't just written it in the waiting room, as if I were nervous at being in the presence of JHHI's Chief of Staff and CEO.

To my surprise, I was nervous. If I'd known Muir was going to be like this, I thought, I'd have taken more time composing my speech.

"Whereas the ladies of the North Shore Chapter of the Silver Crescent," I intoned, "select each year a person of good character and great achievement, and whereas Dr. Jerome Muir has been duly nominated and considered for this honor, we, the undersigned, hereby name him Silver Crescent Man of the Year with all the honors and benefits traditionally accorded thereunto."

And Mumbo Jumbo, Alakazam, I silently added.

"Charitable donations, bequests, and volunteerism," Muir said after a long pause, "are the lifeblood of the community hospital. On behalf of this institution, and myself, I thank you." Another benediction conferred.

"The presentation copy got delayed at the printers," I offered apologetically. "But we were afraid to wait any longer. The membership has asked me to formally congratulate you on your impressive contributions to the medical well-being of New England, and to request that you honor them by appearing as this year's Silver Crescent Lecturer at our November twenty-fifth banquet. We feel that Thanksgiving is the true start of the giving season, and if you'd like us to direct our fund-raising toward a specific hospital project, we could certainly accommodate any request."

Renzel said, "This is great, Jerome. God knows we've got projects to fund."

The phone buzzed. Muir picked up on the first bleep. His hands hadn't aged as well as the rest of him; they were gnarled, the knuckles scarred and red. "Yes, Barbara, I know. I know. I'm on my way."

"Do you accept?" I asked eagerly. "Can you do it?"

"I'm extremely honored," he said solemnly. "And I'd be delighted. I'll need to check my calendar, make sure I'm available. Hank, do we have any conferences near Thanksgiving?"

"Not that I remember," Renzel said. "Unless that Hoffman-La Roche thing—no. That's December in Hawaii."

Muir smiled warmly. "Mrs. Everett, please extend my gratitude to your membership, and do leave your phone number with Barbara. I'll have her get back to you within the week."

"That would be wonderful. Thank you so much." I took a deep breath and plunged on. "We were worried you'd be all booked up, and after Emily Woodrow recommended you in such glowing terms —well, we did hope you'd accept."

Muir grew very still. "Emily Woodrow?"

"Her daughter was treated for leukemia here."

He examined my face searchingly. "Are you certain it was Mrs. Woodrow who recommended me?"

"Yes, I am."

He smoothed back his carefully combed white hair. "How extraordinarily generous of her. I thought she might have harbored some . . . hard feelings. You know her daughter didn't respond to . . . her daughter died." He seemed genuinely distressed, possibly more upset than a doctor who'd seen death so often ought to be.

"Oh, I'm sorry," I said. "I could be mistaken. But I thought—no, I'm sure it was Emily."

"It doesn't matter," Muir said, almost his regal self again.

"No," I said hesitantly, "I guess it doesn't. Only—well, I suppose I ought to ask. The ladies might think me rude, but please, don't be offended. I feel I have to follow through on this. There isn't any reason why you *wouldn't* wish to be our speaker, is there?"

"I'm not sure I know what you mean."

"You're not expecting any difficulties, uh, nothing of a legal nature, concerning Emily's daughter's death?"

The sparkling eyes froze and I got a glimpse of steel. "Certainly not. Not to my knowledge."

"I'm sorry. It's just I know that Emily's husband's a lawyer, and lawyers do tend to sue anytime things don't work out."

He made a dismissive noise and straightened his perfect tie. "Some people believe there always has to be a happy ending. Perhaps it's the television they watch. I don't know."

"The death of a child is hard to accept," I said.

"Indeed," Muir responded. "For all of us."

The phone buzzed again, two short bleats.

"I really must go now, Mrs. Everett."

"Thank you so much for your time, and for all the good work you do." I stood and offered my hand. He crossed to take it. His handclasp was firm and dry. He was wearing a spicy after-shave that successfully blocked the hospital smell. With his door shut, we could have been in any fancy corporate office.

Dr. Renzel interrupted our farewells. "I could show you a couple of current construction projects, if you're interested," he said.

I turned to him and he flashed a quick smile. I studied his face. Ordinary, except for the prominent cheekbones. Not quite enough chin. His voice was another story. Smooth as a well-bowed cello. Put him to work in telephone sales, he'd have a hell of a future.

"Mrs. Everett, this is Dr. Renzel." Muir made the belated introduction hurriedly, then added, "Mrs. Everett's from a local newspaper," as if Renzel hadn't been hanging on our every word. I wondered if Muir stressed my newspaper affiliation to remind Renzel to discuss only printable matters.

"A newsweekly, really. But I'm here only as a representative of the Silver Crescent," I reminded them.

Renzel smiled enthusiastically. "Well, maybe I can talk you into doing a puff piece for us. Something that will get a few philanthropists to stop sitting on their wallets."

"That's an idea," I said.

"Have you seen any of the newer areas of the hospital?" he asked me.

"No." I patted my phony curls. Maybe blondes do have more fun. And maybe I could talk him into a guided tour of the chemotherapy treatment rooms.

Muir left the room before we did, his back imperially erect. We followed him like sheep, like courtiers.

13

"First of all," Renzel said, leading me briskly into the waiting room, taking a sharp right, then a left toward the elevators, "do you have all our literature? We do a quarterly magazine that details our progress. Scholarly articles. Chitchat. Who's new on the staff."

I fumbled a notebook out of my purse: Sandy Everett, resourceful reporter, always prepared for a story. I doubted I could get him to tell me the *right* story, but maybe I could finesse him into tossing me a lead.

"This is very kind of you," I said, "but first things first. Like who exactly are you?"

He lowered his lashes and gave me a little-boy-lost look. His thick-lensed glasses microscoped his brown eyes.

"Probably most of the people around here know who you are and what you do," I said. "But I've got to start with the basics: who, what, when, where, why."

"Just because people at JHHI may know who I am," Renzel said contritely, "is no reason to come off as a self-important windbag. I'm sorry. I get carried away. My enthusiasm for the hospital takes off."

The legendary Muir, I thought, might rate as a self-important windbag, but so far Renzel, with his great voice and his willing tour-guide offer, certainly hadn't.

"I'm Chief of Pharmacy," Renzel declared. After a brief pause, he added, "Everybody calls me Hank."

"Not Doctor?"

"Oh, that, too. I am a doctor. A Ph.D. doctor. A scientist, not a clinician."

He pressed the elevator call button. "I'm going to show you the new floor," he said, the way a doting father might say "I'm going to show you the new baby."

"And how long have you worked here?" I asked.

"Four years or so. It surprises me I've stayed this long. I'm an academic at heart."

"Chief of Pharmacy certainly sounds impressive," I said. "If Muir can't give the Silver Crescent lecture, maybe you can pinch-hit for him." I was trying to figure how far I could push my reporter ruse. Why had Renzel volunteered so cheerfully to show me around? Was he lonely? Underworked?

"Well, it may sound impressive," he said ruefully, "but it would be a lot more impressive if I held a key chair at a medical school as well. You know what it costs to endow a university chair these days? Two biggies. That's two million dollars."

I whistled. "More than the Silver Crescent could raise."

"And, admit it, your ladies would be disappointed if they had to put up with a relative nobody like me. Around here, Jerome Muir's pretty much the show. Rightfully. He deserves it. I'm more the professorial type. I'm used to people calling me Professor, not Doctor. What are you used to?"

"Huh?"

"I mean, do people call you Mrs. Everett or what?"

I almost confessed to Carlotta. He had a way about him, an engaging bedside manner. "Sandy," I said.

He reached over and formally shook my hand. "Pleased to meet you, Sandy." He was slow to end the handshake. Close up, his bony face seemed interesting rather than homely.

"You seem fond of Dr. Muir," I said. "Do you see him as kind of a role model, a father figure?"

"Why do you ask?" His mouth curved into a smile.

"Oh," I said, "I don't know. I guess it's because I've been seeing a therapist lately. Stuff like that rubs off."

"You've had some troubles?"

"It's nothing," I lied cheerfully. "My divorce."

"That's not nothing, Sandy," he responded earnestly.

The elevator slowly opened its doors. We got in and he brushed his hand against mine. Muir had been wearing after-shave. Renzel's scent was definitely cologne, pungent and sweet.

"So tell me," he said. "Are you dating yet?"

"Not really," I said.

"Well, you ought to be." He edged a little closer.

I took a step back and felt the wall behind me. "Soon, maybe," I said.

The doors closed.

"Um, you mentioned a new floor," I said. "You're expanding up? Why is that? I noticed a lot of vacant buildings nearby."

"The changing ethnic character of the area is a fund-raising problem," he said. "We're confining ourselves to renovation at the moment. We freed up the sixth floor by streamlining our records. Computerizing. Contracting out some of the billing and accounts. Medical technology changes so rapidly, it's all we can do to keep pace. Real expansion would cost more money than we've got. Unless Silver Crescent runs a close second to the Shriners."

"We don't. Sorry." I was starting to feel guilty.

"Well, we have great hopes: a major bequest in the wind."

"Can you tell me more about that?"

"No."

"Well, can I get a little more background?"

"Like what?" he asked.

"Dr. Muir," I said quickly. "How old is he?"

"I thought you were going to ask about me. My job. But everybody's interested in Muir." He sighed deeply and shot me a grin. "Did you ask him how old he was?"

"No."

"Why?"

"I didn't have the nerve. It would have seemed so rude."

"He has that effect, doesn't he? You don't want to discuss anything unpleasant in front of him. And age, well, there's no reason to think he won't go on forever."

The elevator opened its doors. Renzel took my arm and ushered me into an unfinished lobbylike area.

"You're not answering my question," I said.

"You're right." He seemed in no hurry to rush into guided-tour mode. He looked comfortable enough, just standing and talking. Didn't seem to mind that I had a couple inches' height advantage on him. Some guys hate that.

I tried another tack. "His memory, how good is it?"

"He probably has to write down a few more things now than he did when he was twenty, if that's what you mean. But don't worry, he'll do a bang-up lecture for your group."

"It's not that."

"What?"

"I'm surprised he remembered Emily Woodrow's name right off."

"The woman whose daughter died?"

"I think it's sort of touching, him remembering, as busy as he must be."

"It doesn't surprise me," Hank Renzel said resolutely. "I'm sure he loses sleep over every child who doesn't make it."

"Oh, come on," I said. "I'm not writing this down."

"You can write it or not. It won't change. Jerome Muir's a gentleman, an old-fashioned word for an old-fashioned man. I know. I travel with him. Time-zone changes, lost luggage, fouled-up hotel reservations, he sits politely and waits, as if he were a small-town schoolteacher instead of one of the most powerful voices in American medicine."

"That might make a good story," I said. "Sort of a companion piece to the Silver Crescent award. Play up his humble side."

Renzel went on. "We do a lot of traveling together. On business. Mainly abroad, but in the states, too. Do you like to travel? Weekends? Up north? I have a little place in Vermont, just a cabin really, but it's on a hill and the view is astonishing."

"Maybe I can work it into the story," I said pensively, ignoring the dating-bar chat, "about his remembering that little girl, Rebecca Woodrow."

"Did you know her?" Renzel asked.

"No, but the family's socially prominent," I said.

"The kind of name that sells newspapers?" he asked pointedly. "Funny. Jerome remembers the mom's name and you remember the girl's."

Time to abandon newspaper talk, I thought. Even if it meant a brief return to the dating bar. "So tell me about your job," I said.

"Mainly managerial," he responded. "Not enough funds to do the kind of research and development I'm trained to do."

"Which is?"

"It's all biotech, now. Genetic engineering. Never enough space, never enough money. These days, you really need university backing. Here, let me show you around the floor."

He touched my arm again and led me through a corridor, past tarpaulin-covered sawhorses and partially glassed-in chambers. I couldn't see a construction crew, but hammering and hollering told me they weren't far off. The creamy wallboard hadn't been painted yet.

"We're doing amazing things, amazing," the Chief of Pharmacy said. "You can't tell by this, but the whole floor—you can see the blueprints, if you'd like—will be absolutely devoted to patients undergoing bone-marrow transplants. An entire sterile floor, because the immune system becomes so compromised in these patients that the chance of opportunistic infection skyrockets."

I heard more about bone-marrow transplants than I wanted to know. The man was a motor-mouth nonstop Helping Hand booster. They should have hired him as a professional fund-raiser.

"Will the chemotherapy rooms be located up here?" I asked, hoping to stem the tide of information.

"No," he said. "Why?"

"Doesn't chemotherapy lower your resistance to other diseases?"

"To some extent, but conventional sterile methods are generally considered adequate."

I sighed. "I guess I was still thinking about Rebecca Woodrow. How she died."

"We have hundreds of patients who get well. Why not do a story on one of them?"

"Dog bites man, you know, that's the story. This one little girl who didn't make it, in spite of the odds."

"I don't like it," he said, staring down at glossy linoleum, cut and stained to imitate parquet. "I'd skip that one, if I were reading your paper."

"It's human interest," I said with a shrug. "You wouldn't want to help me out on it, would you?"

"How?"

"Well—just off the top of my head—I could start with a peek at the room where she died. Maybe do sort of a mood piece."

He shrugged. "I wouldn't know where it was."

"Probably a lousy idea anyway. My editor's more of an upbeat guy. Loves sports."

"Do you know about our bike race?" Renzel asked eagerly.

"Huh?"

"Bike race. With research costs out of control, and with the government cutting back and insurance rates taking off, we have to rely on charity more and more. We have wonderful organizers here. Every year, there's a cross-country bike race, a balloon race, a carnival, a Las Vegas night. You name it."

"Um," I said. "That's really interesting."

"If your editor's into sports, the bike race is a natural."

"Maybe," I said.

"You don't sound enthusiastic."

"If it's biking, he'll assign one of his buddies to write it. I'll come up with the story idea, and somebody else will get the by-line and the paycheck."

"Too bad."

"Yeah," I agreed wholeheartedly, as we passed another wing of unfinished rooms. "But, you know, I may have another idea."

"What?"

"Well, tell me what you think of this," I said, reaching back to Donovan's story about Emily Woodrow's early memory. "When I was really little, I had my tonsils out."

"They hardly do that anymore," he said. "I'm surprised they took yours out. It couldn't have been fashionable when you were a kid. You're way too young."

He was right. I hadn't adjusted for the age difference between Emily and me. "Mine were infected," I said hastily. "But the main thing I remember is a doctor putting something over my mouth, like a mask, and I guess I passed out after that."

"Anesthesia."

"I mean, there must be a lot of people with the same memory. Maybe I could sell my editor on an update, what they do in a modern place like this. I bet you don't just knock kids out like that anymore, right?"

"Anesthesia's not my area."

"Is there somebody I could talk to? Somebody you'd recommend? I don't mean today. I'd go through regular channels, do it right, get in touch with PR."

"You'd want to make an appointment to see Dr. Hazelton. Or even Dr. Peña."

I scribbled their names in my notebook. "Why do you say 'even' Dr. Peña?"

"Well, he's a new resident. He's here so many hours, he probably sleeps here. He wouldn't thank me for volunteering him for more work."

"I'll try for Hazelton."

"I'd do that. I'm not sure Peña is as up-to-date in his methods."

"I thought you said he was new."

"My understanding is he didn't exactly graduate at the top of his class."

"A place like this, I'd think you could pick and choose."

"We used to," he said, lips pursed disapprovingly. "Tell me, do you do this, uh, reporter work, full-time?"

"No," I said, deciding to turn him off the personal stuff once and for all. "The kids take up most of my time. The twins, especially."

"You must be busy," he said, edging back from the precipice. I pretended not to notice his discomfiture, but I was almost certain he'd been on the verge of asking me out.

He glanced abruptly at his watch. "I'm sorry. I have to get back to my office." It was a definite kiss-off. Little doubt about it; he'd played escort because he needed a date for Saturday night.

I smiled politely. "Well, thank you. And I'll be sure to tell the ladies about the new construction at the next meeting."

"Can I see you out?"

"I think I ought to stop by Dr. Muir's receptionist first. Make sure he's not going to be out of town November twenty-fifth."

"You remember the floor?"

"Two."

"I'm on four. If you decide you want to do a story on the pharmacy. Or if you need an escort for that Silver Crescent bash."

Well, if twins and a two-inch height difference didn't discourage the man, what would?

"I'll keep it in mind," I promised with a genuine smile. Maybe if he wore contact lenses . . .

Looks change, but great voices are great voices.

14

I thought I was in luck. The black woman, Savannah, was in sole possession of the counter. She recognized me and smiled.

"Still here?" she inquired.

"Would you know where I could find a guy named Peña? Anesthesiologist?"

Barbara, the dragon lady, came up behind me and cleared her throat to let me know she was in charge.

"Hi," I managed pleasantly. "An anesthesiologist named Peña, would you know where I might find him?"

"Dr. Peña?" It was more a correction than a question.

"Doctor," I agreed, perhaps with less than the proper reverence.

"I wouldn't know," she said disapprovingly.

The young black woman piped up with, "I saw Pablo about ten minutes ago in the lounge on the fourth floor. Drinking coffee. Big dark-skinned guy, kind of vague-looking."

"Thanks," I said, regretting the dragon lady's untimely return. "Appreciate it." I left without asking the black woman her last name. I figured she was in enough trouble, first-naming a doctor.

Pablo. Pablo Peña. On the whole, I thought his parents should have considered a different choice. On the other hand, they could have christened him Pedro, which would have been worse.

People like me, cursed with alliterative names, think about stuff like that in elevators. Sandra Everett had no such problem. I decided Everett was probably her married name. She was the kind who'd keep it for the kids' sake. I'd never taken my ex-husband's name, even though it would have moved me out of the alliterative ranks.

I roamed the fourth floor in search of something resembling a lounge. I couldn't wander far; JHHI was housed in a tall building, but not a large one. I strolled past another roped-off construction area with a sign that read: PLEASE EXCUSE OUR APPEARANCE. A RENO-VATED JHHI TO SERVE YOU BETTER! The pharmacy seemed to take up more than a quarter of the floor space. I wondered at its location. More convenient on the ground level, I'd have thought. But then, old buildings rarely seem designed with human needs in mind. The pharmacy looked busy and efficient. One line of customers stood at a counter to hand in prescriptions and another waited by a register to pay. A stream of white- or green-clad individuals bypassed the civilian queues and went about their business behind the counters, in a warren of rows and shelves and refrigeration units.

Hank Renzel was nowhere in sight, but then I wouldn't expect the Chief of Pharmacy to hold down some front-desk clerical posi-tion or count out pills.

As long as I kept up a purposeful stride no one challenged my right to pass. I kept walking, not wishing to endanger my status by asking for directions.

I did a perimeter search, then picked a bisecting hallway.

Four small tables and a collection of vending machines behind a partially closed curtain made up the lounge. It was deserted ex-cept for a man who matched Savannah's description. His hospital greens were wrinkled and stained, and a surgical mask drooped below his chin. He rested his elbows on a table, his head in his hands.

"Dr. Peña?" He wasn't that dark. More the color of heavily creamed coffee.

He didn't lift his head. "What?"

"Dr. Muir said I'd find you here." Since I was planning to lie anyway, I thought I might as well start by dropping a name that would carry weight.

"Muir? What's he want?" Peña muttered in hardly the awed tone I'd come to expect. He had no trace of an accent.

"He said you wouldn't mind speaking with me. I won't take much of your time."

He finally glanced up at me and Sandy awarded him her very best smile. He reached to straighten a nonexistent tie. Pure reflex action.

"Time, I've got. Sit down." He stared at his watch. "I'm on for another six."

"Six hours?"

"Thirty down, six to go."

"You want a cup of coffee?"

"Nah. I forget whether I'm tired or not after the first twenty-four. It's better that way."

Sandy giggled. I let her. Me, I never giggle.

"What did Muir send you for? See if my health insurance is paid up?"

"He said you'd give me a good quote. I can see why. You're funny."

"He said that?"

"Not exactly."

"I'm surprised he knew I was on duty."

"I got the impression he took a personal interest in the staff."

"Look, he's great. I'm tired. Way past tired. It's just—"

"Just?"

"I mean, I heard so much about him. Before. I guess nobody could live up to press like that. Greatest doc in the world, you know, and all he does is worry about the building fund. What do you want to talk to me about?"

I handed over another of Sandy's phony business cards. I don't know why, but cards seem to inspire confidence. "I'm writing a story about a little girl who died here."

"You're from a newspaper? And they let you in?"

"I'm a personal friend of Dr. Muir's," I said. I sound much more convincing when I lie than when I tell the truth.

"Oops," he said.

"Oh, I'd never repeat what you just said to Jerome. I mean, no one would trust me if I gossiped, would they?"

"Well, what do you wanna know? A lot of kids die." His voice was flat and uninterested. His words about kids dying—well, he could have been talking about plants wilting or rain falling.

"The girl's name was Rebecca Woodrow. I'm doing a feature story about her last day."

"She spent it here? Too bad. She should have gone to the beach."

"It was January."

"She should have stayed home, then."

"You remember her?"

"You want coffee?"

"If you have a cup, I'll have one."

He patted all his pockets and looked bewildered and vague, and I wound up buying the two plastic foam containers of brown liquid.

A uniform, even just hospital greens, makes it hard to get a fix on somebody. His watch was good, but not flashy. Probably something he needed for work, an accurate watch with a sweep second hand. He wore paper hospital slippers, so I couldn't use his shoes to figure his financial worth or fashion flair. He was a big guy, even sitting down. Maybe six-two or six-three. Twenty pounds overweight. He had a habit of licking his lips.

"You remember Rebecca Woodrow?" I asked when I'd sipped enough coffee to regret buying it.

"It's a big place."

"How big?"

"Two hundred and twelve beds."

"That's not huge."

"I put 'em to sleep and wake 'em up."

"This one didn't wake up."

"I don't remember names."

"A six-year-old girl. In for chemotherapy."

"You're talking to the wrong person. I don't supervise chemo. Nurses handle that." His eyes were almost closed, his speech faintly slurred, as if he couldn't make the effort to be more precise.

"Have you slept lately?"

"Twenty minutes here, half an hour there. I'm fine, really."

"You don't look fine."

"Muir send you to check up on me?"

"No."

"I got less than a year to go and then I'm out in practice."

"You're not a real doctor yet?"

"Of course I'm real. I'm just not paid like I'm real yet, okay?"

"I thought this wasn't a teaching hospital."

"It's private, but even private places take in a few residents. They need to. Time I'm putting in, I'm probably earning a buck an hour. System's built on slave labor."

I drank bad coffee and let him talk.

"Guys collecting the fees and the guys putting in the hours, they're two different sets of people," he complained.

"Paying your dues," I suggested.

"Yeah, and when I'm out of here, you think I'll be able to cash in the chips? Hell, it'll be National Health by then. These old guys, they did a number. Milked the system so bad, the rest of us are gonna pay. If I'd done an MBA, a lousy MBA, I'd be rolling by now. Kids five years younger than me got houses and two BMWs, and I'm working my butt off."

"You're a specialist. Aren't specialists well paid?"

"Oh, yeah, and now the government's coming in to tell me what to do, how to treat a patient, how long a patient can stay in the goddamn hospital, and setting my fee wherever some clerk outa high school thinks it ought to be. It's the damn DRGs."

"DRGs. Is that, like, drugs?"

"DRGs. Diagnostic-related groupings. Fitting a patient into a diagnosis, and getting paid based on which grouping you plug them into, like all people only have one thing wrong with them at a time."

He still hadn't made much eye contact, but his voice wasn't a

monotone any longer. "Bunch of legislative lawyers," he went on.
"They hate doctors. Screwing the whole system and it's just gonna
get worse. Bureaucrats'll take the money, and the patients'll end up
worse off than ever. It's not doctors, it's technology. It's tests. It's
machines. Own the machines and the technology, you've got it
made. Me, if I don't invest, I'm gonna be a wageslave working for
some bureaucrat doesn't even respect what I do."

"That bad?" I murmured sympathetically.

"And it's not like there's no money. You see the construction,
like we've got to have a new wing and a new garage and a new lab
and a helipad on the roof, the whole nine yards. You writing this
down? I thought you were a journalist."

"I'm doing a small story, focusing on this little girl, Rebecca
Woodrow. Her mother's name is Emily. Acute lymphoblastic leukemia, that's what she had. I understand it can be cured."

"Yeah. Chances are damned good."

"Rebecca died during chemotherapy treatment."

"You know what I always say?"

"What?"

"Sleazebags never die. You get some guy in a hospital, some
scumball wanted by cops in thirty states, it's a given: he'll make it.
Sweet little kid, apple of her mama's eye, she dies during some
routine thing. Never fails."

"This girl was the apple of Mom's eye, all right. Only child.
Wealthy folks. Pretty girl."

"None of that counts."

"Would any nurse here be qualified to administer chemotherapy?"

"No, no. Specially trained nurses. Nurse-practitioners."

"Part of my story involves interviewing the last people to see
this girl alive. My editor loves that kind of stuff. Human drama."

"Glad I don't have your job," Peña muttered.

"So I need to interview the nurse who handled the chemo. On
a little girl who died suddenly. In January."

"January," he repeated.

"Yeah."

"Beginning of January?"

"Yeah."

"I suppose it was Tina," he said as if he were speaking to himself.

"Tina?" I echoed very quietly, not wanting to wake him in case he was talking in his sleep.

"Tina Sukhia. Lovely woman." He added regretfully, "She doesn't work here anymore."

"The dead girl's mother says a doctor rushed into the room at the end and placed a mask over the girl's face." Emily hadn't mentioned whether or not the stranger was *wearing* a surgical mask, like the limp green rectangle dangling around Peña's neck. Surely she would have noted that, a masked man carrying a mask. "Would that doctor have been an anesthesiologist?"

"Might have been. Logical thing to do," Peña said. "First rule: Establish an airway. Somebody's not breathing for herself, you do it for her, with a bag and a mask."

"Do you remember—?"

"Look, lady—I forget your name—"

"Sandy. Sandra."

"Sandra. You think I'm gonna remember what we talked about in ten minutes, you're wrong. I'm zonked, see? I need to sleep. Some of the guys, they can take this, and I'm pretty good at taking it too. But the thing you're talking about happened months ago. I can't remember if I ate breakfast."

"Aren't you worried you're going to make a mistake?"

"No. No, once I'm working, I'm fine. Adrenaline comes to the old rescue. I know my job. You know how people say 'I could do that in my sleep'? Well, I can. I can do my job in my sleep. I just forget other things."

"Like Rebecca Woodrow."

"I don't check on the chemo. That's not what I do."

"The mother says the man with the mask pushed her, shoved her out of the way."

"That I'd remember. It definitely wasn't me. I don't push mothers around."

An overhead speaker came to life, announcing "Code Thirty. Code Thirty." Peña's beeper emitted sharp little bleats. Then it said, quite clearly, "Code Thirty, room four-oh-two. Code Thirty. Four-oh-two."

"I gotta go," Peña said unnecessarily. He was already moving.

I followed, wishing my flats had rubber soles. It was hard to stay silent, but the anesthesiologist was traveling so fast he never glanced behind him.

We shoved through two sets of swinging doors, took two quick turns down featureless corridors. He pushed open a wooden door and entered full tilt.

A glance into the narrow window next to the door, five inches wide, ceiling height, stopped me cold.

The room was crammed, jammed, as crowded as a stateroom in an old Marx Brothers film. Any resemblance to comedy ended there.

I couldn't see the occupant of the bed, only an extended arm here, a leg there. It must have been a child. The limbs were small.

A thing that looked like a tool chest on wheels, studded with drawers, half of them flung open, blocked part of my view. Plastic tubing curled from one drawer. Clear plastic bags of liquid filled another, bottles and jars a third. The top of the cart was dominated by a machine with complex dials and buttons and a computerlike screen. Paddles grew out of the top. I noticed a metal cylinder strapped to the side of the cart.

A man in a white coat held a bag and a mask near the head of the bed. A hose led from the bag to a wall-mounted spigot.

A woman wearing white slacks repeatedly slapped the back of a small hand, tried to insert an IV needle. On the other side of the bed, a second woman strapped a blood-pressure cuff to a limp arm. A man in greens, not Peña, had a hand where the child's midsection must have been. He was speaking, but I couldn't distinguish the words.

There must have been twelve people in the room, not counting the patient. Whatever Emily Woodrow had seen when her daughter died, it couldn't have been this. Not unless she'd passed out after the first stranger arrived.

I was the sole idle onlooker. Everyone in the room moved with intent, carried out a given task, performed the required steps in some secret ballet.

Peña seemed to take charge. There was nothing sleepy about him as he barked orders, moving more quickly than his bulk should have allowed. A woman handed him a syringe.

Someone was sticking patches, like small round Band-Aids, to areas of the patient's bare skin. Peña spoke and a woman scrambled to grab the paddles off the cart.

The resident anesthesiologist glanced up suddenly, and his eyes met mine. His mouth moved. A sharp-featured woman began a march to the door.

I turned quickly and ran. My wig felt too tight. It wasn't until after I'd pressed the down button, after the elevator door had closed behind me, that I recalled the room's wallpaper: blue, with white latticework and gold flowers.

If all the chemotherapy rooms were outfitted the same, then each had a single wall-mounted spigot. Oxygen, most likely. No way to make a mistake with only one source.

If oxygen was readily available in the rooms, I wondered what was kept in the metal cylinder strapped to the cart.

15

In a first-floor bathroom, I breathed deeply, washed my hands, and fluffed my fake hair until two nurses finished arguing and agreed that Isabel had one hell of a nerve dating Danny. I kept glancing at myself in the mirror. I have photo IDs—laminated official-looking badges—for both my blond and my brunette identities. Neither looks much like me, nor did the woman in the mirror.

When the nurses finally left, I hid in a stall and, with overwhelming relief, peeled off the wig, feeling my hair spring back to life. I ran my fingers over my scalp, ruffling my curls and scratching all the pesky itches, then wrapped the blond wig in crumpled tissue paper and stuffed it into my purse.

As a redhead, I returned to the mirror and unfastened the top two buttons on my blouse. Could I make it through one more interview? I placed a hand firmly over my racing heart and wondered if the child on the fourth floor was breathing yet. I exhaled enough air to fog the mirror.

One more interview. I kept my suit jacket on, just in case. My freshly released hair was wild, but a few pins and the straw hat held it down. Sandy's lipstick clashed with my natural coloring, so I dipped a rough paper towel in warm water and scrubbed my lips till they paled.

The water felt so good that I dampened another towel in icy water and pressed it to my cheeks. My heartbeat slowed.

In about a week, with Roz's help, I'd fake a Silver Crescent letterhead and cancel the whole shebang. Maybe my imaginary chapter would go bankrupt, their treasurer accused of embezzlement. Simply shocking.

Tina. Tina Sukhia. I should have asked Peña to spell it. A shaky lead, but my only one, given that my client showed a marked disinclination to talk. No hospital would give up information on an ex-employee. I'd probably have to transfer more of Emily Woodrow's advance to Patsy Ronetti in order to get the necessary address. But first, outside the bathroom, I ducked dutifully into a nearby phone alcove. Never neglect the obvious, Mooney used to preach. And damned if he wasn't right.

Tina Sukhia listed her number in the phone book. The address was on Buswell Street. The nurse-practitioner who might have administered chemotherapy to Rebecca Woodrow had given up a job conveniently close to home.

I fed a coin into the slot. Three rings and a quick pickup. "Hi." The voice was wrong. Male.

"May I speak to Tina, please?"

"Who's this?"

"Is Tina there?"

"She oughtta be home any minute."

I shifted to a more official tone. "That's perfect. I'm calling from JHHI, about Tina's exit interview. We're a little concerned."

"Yeah? Why's that?"

"As you may know, we're required to withhold her last week's salary until we complete the exit-interview process."

"Oh."

"Hang on a minute, please," I said, because real people expect bureaucrats to put them on hold. I counted to twenty-five, slowly, then spoke again. "I'm sorry. Where were we? Oh, yes, listen, this could work out very well. We have someone right in your neighborhood. She could be in and out in five minutes."

"Would she bring the check?"

"Well, no. But I'll be able to drop it in the mail as soon as our rep phones in and tells me the exit interview's complete."

"Okay," the man said. "Good enough. Bye, now."

I emerged from JHHI blinking like I'd spent the day in a darkened movie house, dazzled, disoriented, amazed by the light in the sky and the fresh air. Since I'd already hit the maximum daily rate at the garage—an astounding sum—I temporarily abandoned my car and headed up Longwood, counting crocuses. Even on heavily trafficked Brookline Avenue, a few blossoms challenged the concrete. On the less-traveled cross streets, bright patches of yellow and blue turned city lawns into gardens.

I took deep gulping breaths, gagging on exhaust fumes for my trouble. The hell with formality in the late-afternoon heat, I decided, plucking off the straw hat and shaking my hair loose. I wished I'd stripped off my panty hose in the JHHI ladies' room. I was tired of disguises.

Buswell Street is in Boston University country. B.U. tried to buy most of the area outright a few years ago and might have succeeded if not for a vigilant neighborhood association that saw few benefits in losing more of the city's rarest commodity—taxable property—to an insatiable juggernaut.

B.U. continues to chew away at Kenmore Square, threatening its seedy bars and pizza joints with gentrification, but a few blocks down Beacon Street no new dorms rise high. Just weathered brick four-stories, basking in faded glory.

According to two strips of linotype pasted over the doorbell of 551 Buswell, Tina Sukhia shared apartment 4D with Tony Foley. In Boston, where the O'Reillys tend to stick to the O'Days, and the Cabots to the Forbeses, Sukhia seemed an odd matchup with Foley.

I rang the bell. A metallic squawk issued from the speaker. "Tina? That you? You forget your keys?"

I hollered my real name and no further information since I don't like yelling my business in strange vestibules. A buzzer sounded and I pushed open the heavy oak door.

The vestibule was small, paneled in dark wood. The stairs beckoned. If people are slapping down hard-earned bucks for Stairmaster machines, it must be good exercise, right? My resolve was strengthened by a quick glance at the elevator, a cell with no evidence of a state inspection certificate.

It seemed like a long climb for only four levels. The steps

twisted and spiraled, three steep short flights per floor. I heard a door unlatch, and a deep voice, familiar from the phone, demanded, "Tina, that you?"

I'd beaten her home. I kept climbing. My appearance wiped the welcoming smile off Tony Foley's face. He rearranged it and came up with a grin that managed to be both tentative and flirtatious at the same time.

"Who're you?"

"Carlotta Carlyle. That's what I said at the door," I answered cheerfully, pleased to leave Sandy Everett behind.

"Speaker doesn't work worth shit."

"I'm here to talk to Tina."

"Coulda saved yourself a climb. She ain't in yet." He was lanky and blond, with an accent out of the rural South. As he spoke, he ran a hand through greasy hair that spilled over his forehead. Twenty-five to thirty. With a shampoo and a lot of dental work, he'd be close to handsome.

"But you're expecting her," I said. "Soon."

"You that exit-interview lady?"

"Right."

He stared at me blankly for a minute, then broke into a know-it-all grin. "You're scared she's gonna sue you, right? She tol' me. Anytime she leaves a place, they get all worried 'counta she's a minority, and did she file a complaint with MCAD or some such." He seemed pleased by the prospect, as if a lawsuit would be the punchline of a joke.

MCAD is the Massachusetts Committee Against Discrimination.

"It's nothing like that," I assured him.

He sucked on his ill-spaced teeth and aimed a pointing index finger at me, cocking his thumb for a trigger. "Well, is it, like, if she was laid off, she gets severance?" He seemed like he was earnestly trying to fit together pieces of a jigsaw puzzle.

I was trying to figure something out too, namely this guy who talked like a hayseed, looked like a sheet-carrying Klansman, and lived with a woman who was definitely not an Irish townie.

I blew out a sigh. I'm glad when people surprise me. Sometimes you think you've got it all mapped out, and then whammo.

He hadn't invited me in and he was blocking the door to the apartment. I said, "You think I could have a glass of water?"

"Elevator busted again?"

"Didn't look too reliable."

He snorted. "Come on in." He shifted a good five inches and I brushed past him.

The door opened onto a wall with a row of wooden pegs, heavy with winter jackets and bright-colored filmy scarves. From the hallway, I could see into four tiny rooms: kitchen, living room, bedroom, and bath. The place was bigger than the elevator, but not much. From the bedroom came a pungent smell of incense, smoky and floral, with a hint of something underneath.

Tony nodded me toward the kitchen.

Along one wall, a dinky two-burner range nestled next to a toy refrigerator and a half-size sink. The rest of the room was crowded with a card table, two chairs, and a stack of boxes emblazoned with the logo of a local stereo outlet.

The man rummaged in a high cupboard, found a glass, rinsed and filled it with tepid water.

"Thanks," I said.

My nose and my memory got together: marijuana. How quaint.

"So, she's got money comin' from JHHI?" the man demanded while I drank.

"Are you Tina's husband?"

"You mean, like, you shouldn't discuss stuff with somebody ain't family?"

"Something like that," I replied coolly. Near the sink, peacock feathers fanned out of a purple vase. Someone in the apartment had a taste for exotic colors, and I didn't think it was the man in the white T-shirt and khakis.

"We're engaged. I'm Tony." He offered the name as if anyone

who'd ever encountered Tina, even on paper, would automatically recognize it. "Nothin' wrong in tellin' me."

His brief nervous smile made me wonder if Tina knew about the engagement. "New equipment?" I asked, nodding at the boxes, pretending I hadn't heard his request for information.

His face lit up. A shame about those teeth. "Reason I was hopin' you were Tina. Wanted to show her. It's like her weddin' present to me. She just told me go pick it out, put it on her card."

"Nice," I said, because his enthusiasm demanded some response, and because stereo components are one of the few things I spend money on.

"Terrific," he corrected me. "'Bout time something good happened 'round here."

"Did something good happen?"

"Tina's job."

I removed a notebook from my bag, found a pen, and prepared to take notes like a diligent bureaucrat. "A new job? I'm glad to hear she found work so soon," I said.

"She hadn't had something, she wouldn't have left JHHI— Hey, I'm not gettin' her in any trouble, sayin' that, am I?"

"I'm not here to make trouble. It's just one of those follow-up studies. The institute likes to keep track. We want to make sure we're offering comparable benefits, competitive salaries—"

"Hah!" Tony had quite a line in snorts. "You guys must have your heads stuck in the sand. Competitive!"

"Tina's doing better now?"

"Better! Man, that don't even touch it!"

I waited for him to tell me more, but he didn't, so I pretended to consult a form. "Did she feel her schedule at JHHI was too demanding?"

"I sure did. Hell, I hardly ever saw her. One shift after another. We didn't even eat together, or if we did, we barely had time for takeout."

I made squiggles with my pen. "Would you say she was suffering from professional burnout?"

"She was tired, I know that. New job, she practically sets her own hours. We eat out."

"And what's the nature of her new employment?"

"Well, it's not frontline nursing care. There's no money in that. Some kind of experimental training or research."

I kept my pen poised. "Would you know her new job title?"

"I dunno." He broke into another of his sudden nervous smiles. "Say, you want to see this stuff I just bought? I got to show it off to somebody."

With minimal encouragement, he started opening cartons, eagerly setting equipment on the kitchen table. He'd apparently unsealed the boxes earlier, removing the bubble-wrap and plastic peanuts and bagging them for the trash. What I was watching was more like a ceremonial unveiling with running commentary.

"Look at this CD player! I didn't get the changer, the kind takes six CDs at once. Too much money. Coulda got a changer for the same money, but not this kinda quality."

He had a good two thousand bucks' worth of sound equipment laid out on the table by the time he'd finished. Top-grade stuff: Bose, Nakamichi, Denon. While he was patting it and singing its praises, I leaned out the kitchen door and took a quick inventory of the living room: Pier 1 wicker, potted plants, red-and-orange-patterned cushions. More money invested in the stereo than in anything else in the apartment.

Nurses earned decent salaries. Maybe she drove a good car, had a hefty savings account, helped out her family.

I stretched small talk to the limits, but no Tina. We moved into the living room, sat in two cushioned chairs on either side of a bow window. He offered me a beer.

"You think she might be working late?" I asked, consulting my watch. "I could try her at her new place."

"She didn't say she'd be late, but you know nurses." He leaned forward and lowered his voice. "She comes home and finds me with a pretty gal, you just bet she'll be pissed."

I was glad I'd turned down the beer. There was a framed photo of a young woman on the windowsill. The frill of white lace balanced on her head made her skin seem ebony. She had a heart-shaped face, knowing eyes.

I let Tony see me studying the photo.

"She's beautiful," I said.

"Yeah," he agreed happily. "Sure you won't have a beer?"

"No, thanks."

"You got incredible hair, you know. Super color. Want to take your jacket off, or anythin'?"

"No, thanks. Maybe I ought to try her at work. I wouldn't have, like, any language difficulties, would I?"

He grinned, displaying those awful teeth. "With Tina? 'Cause of her name and the way she looks? Hell, her folks speak English better 'n me, and they're the foreigners. Tina's never even been to Pakistan. I mean, she likes to wear the clothes, the whad-ja-call-it, but she's a hot-dog all-American."

"No problem trying her at work, then?"

"Can't it wait?"

"No," I said.

His eyes narrowed. "Don't get huffy. Hey, you're not one of those Q.A. people, are you? Quality whatever? About taking good care of the patients? 'Cause you know, Tina is one damn fine nurse."

I made a noncommittal noise and lowered my voice confidentially. "Well, you know, we did receive a letter about her," I said, wrinkling my forehead in a concerned frown.

"Don't sound like no card from a grateful patient," he said.

I studied his face. "It was from a Mrs. Woodrow. Did Tina ever mention her, or Rebecca Woodrow, a six-year-old girl? She was Tina's patient—oh, three months ago. She died."

"Look, Tina worked with dyin' kids all the time, and we didn't discuss it over dinner a whole lot. Too depressin', you know? I'm glad she's out of it."

"You think she's happier at her new job?"

His face clouded briefly, then he flashed the nervous smile. "I dunno. I hope so."

"Before I can clear her exit interview, I have to speak to her about this letter," I said. "Thanks for the water. The new place close by?"

He shrugged.

"You know, you never said where she worked. My boss would kill me if I forgot to get that."

"Place called Cee Co."

I kept my voice level, uninterested. "How do you spell that?"

"I dunno."

"Well, just the address then," I said.

"I never been there. I mean, everybody knows where JHHI is, and I went to plenty of parties there with Tina, but she just started this other place. We ever meet at one of them parties, you 'n' me? At JHHI?"

"I don't think so," I said. "I'd have remembered. Is Cee Co. the whole name?"

"Short for somethin' else, I guess. You know, I never get any of that shit straight. DG is Data General and DEC is Digital and that's short for Digital Equipment Corporation—"

"You in computers?"

"No."

"What is it you do?"

"I get by," he said with a quick grin.

"Is Cee Co. with a *C* or an *S*? Do you know?"

"*C*, I think. Some long name."

"And they do medical research?"

"I guess."

I stood up and returned my notebook to my purse. I was fed up with all this Cee Co. hanky-panky. Dammit, I'd call Emily Woodrow tonight, in spite of her instructions, demand a few answers.

In the meantime, I gave Tony Foley my real card, the one with Carlyle Detective Agency on it. "Ask her to call me as soon as she comes in," I said brusquely. "Thanks for your time."

"Tina's never this late. You want to have dinner or somethin'?" he said speculatively, arching an eyebrow.

"Save it," I said.

"Hey, what's this?"

He was finally reading the card. "Detective agency?" he spluttered. "What kind of crap is that?"

I didn't join him for dinner.

16

I hoofed it back to the Longwood garage and paid the ransom for the car. Considering the price, they should have washed and waxed it.

Cee Co. was a business. C-something Company. Emily Woodrow had mentioned it in an urgent whisper, Tina Sukhia worked there, and I'd never heard of it.

Traffic crawled over the B.U. Bridge and inched sluggishly along Memorial Drive. I cut down River Street and started using twisting cabbie shortcuts, turning every two blocks. I'd rather drive miles out of the way than sit still. I punched on a tape and sang along with Chris Smither's "It Ain't Easy," silently agreeing with the lyrics, and trying to avoid thoughts of food. A quick stop for a burger and fries was tempting even after last night's junk-food orgy with Gloria.

I usually don't eat much when I dine with Gloria. Watching her sock away Tootsie Rolls humbles my appetite.

No time for food now. I turned down Flagg Street, made my way to Mount Auburn. The business pages of the *Globe* might identify Cee Co. Maybe Cee Co. was a stock-market abbreviation. I'd hit the tables, the New York Stock Exchange, the American, NASDAQ, the local Boston exchange.

Cars snarled Broadway near Cambridge Rindge and Latin, the high school Paolina would attend one day. I sighed and hit the brake. A stalled car, an accident, maybe. It wasn't the usual place for a rush-hour jam.

Would Paolina, discouraged by her mother's remarks, overwhelmed by home responsibilities, drop out before high school?

117

What could her friend want with my trash? My mind balked at the word *boyfriend*. *Friend* was bad enough. What does an eleven-year-old need with a twenty-year-old friend?

I ought to keep food in my car. Trail mix. Beef jerky. Behind me, a man in a blue Chevy had the nerve to honk. I love it when the seventh driver in line decides to honk. I didn't bother giving him the finger. Every other driver on the street beat me to it anyway.

The problem: a stuck traffic light at Cambridge Street. Once past it, I flew, making it home in three minutes only to find a man pacing my front stoop. For a minute I thought it was Mooney with a name to match the garbage thief's license plate, but the shape was all wrong. I didn't know this guy. Maybe he was waiting for Roz.

I revised that opinion on the way up the walk. He was too old for Roz. Too ugly. Roz has a penchant for the male body beautiful—not Schwarzenegger types, but solidly built hunks. This one looked forlorn, unkempt, and a little bit angry.

"Miss Carlyle?" he said accusingly.

I didn't fit the key into the lock, just kept the ring in my pocket, where, almost unconsciously, I'd closed a fist around it. I learned that as a cop: If you need to hit somebody, keys make a great substitute for brass knuckles. "Yeah?"

"I wonder if I might have a word?"

"You got one."

"I'd like to speak with you."

"Who would I be talking to? About what?"

"My name is Harold Woodrow."

I unclenched my fist and worked the key. He followed me into the living room like a docile puppy, sat stiffly in the straight-backed chair next to my desk.

It was his nose, I decided, that made his face unpleasant. Thin, sharp, and long, it made him appear arrogant even before he opened his mouth.

"What can I do for you?" I asked, giving myself points for sounding far more polite than I felt. I was hungry and I desperately wanted to kick off my flats and run cold water on my abused toes.

"You can explain this." He removed a folder from his inside jacket pocket. His speech and manner did nothing to warm the arrogance. His shoes were soft leather with an expensive sheen.

The folder was his wife's check register. He tapped it with a manicured fingernail.

"My wife paid you a thousand dollars. The memo says 're-tainer.'"

I pretended to study the entry while trying to read the adjacent lines. She didn't write many checks.

"Why has my wife hired you?"

"Mr. Woodrow, I understand you're an attorney, and you do a considerable amount of financial consulting and advising—to doctors."

"Yes."

"How would you react if I asked you about one of your clients?"

"You haven't asked. I have." He had a light complexion, a thin-lipped mouth made smaller by the prominent nose.

"Ask your wife," I suggested.

His mouth tightened. "My wife told me you were a psychic, and that the amount in question covered several séances and a detailed tarot reading."

Thanks a lot, Emily.

I said, "Everybody's got to earn a living."

"I mentioned Emily's bizarre conduct in consulting you to a fellow attorney who deals in criminal matters. He knew your name. Remembered it. Said you were an investigator."

"What's your friend's name?"

"That's not what I'm here to talk about."

"Talk about what you're here to talk about," I said dryly.

"I want to know what you're doing for my wife."

"Talk some more," I suggested.

"I expect some answers."

I stared at my desk top, glanced around the room, and sighed. I hadn't fed the parakeet in days, and the cat was probably poised to claw me as soon as I stepped into the kitchen.

"Fifteen eighty-eight," I recited. "That's the year of the Spanish Armada. I don't know why I remember that one, but it's up there with 1620 and 1492 as far as answers go."

"You don't take this seriously."

"Ah."

"Young woman," he said, "you are going to take this seriously before I'm finished."

"Oh," I said, "and why is that?"

"If my wife hired you to spy on me, you'll be very sorry. You people are licensed by the state." He hesitated before the word *people,* made it sound like *vermin.*

"My wife is under the care of a psychiatrist," he continued. "She is not a well woman and I won't have her taken advantage of by some rumor-mongering private eye."

He'd lost a child not four months ago, but I found myself having empathy trouble.

"My wife, much as I, uh, love her, is not a completely truthful woman at the best of times. And now, well—you have to understand where she's coming from."

I wasn't about to tell him anything, but if he wanted to confide in me that was a different story. I eased my heels out of my shoes, waggled my toes.

"It's not often you come across a spoiled child of forty," he said, snapping out his words, "but that's my Emily. Up until—up until our disaster—I don't think she ever wanted anything she couldn't have. You've seen her type before, haven't you? Rich, pretty, homecoming queen. And now she's behaving as if she were the only person in the universe to lose a child, the only one to suffer. She acts as if . . . as if she's completely forgotten that Rebecca was my daughter as well.

"Emily's the one who's frozen me out, not the other way around. I'm not an unfeeling man. She may have made it sound like I'm uncaring, but it's not as if she's played the perfect little spouse."

His voice shook, but he pretended to cough and firmed it up. He put a hand to his cheek, rubbed it as if he were checking to see whether or not he'd shaved recently. "Good God," he murmured softly, his voice gaining volume as his chagrin turned to anger, "this is what she's driven me to, babbling in front of a—I beg your pardon, young woman. I shouldn't have come here at all."

"You're probably right about that," I agreed.

"Dammit." He squeezed syllables out from between clenched teeth. "One more chance, all right? What exactly did my wife pay you for? What service do you offer for a thousand dollars?"

I reached over and picked up the telephone.

"What are you doing?"

"Calling your wife," I said, jamming my heels back into my shoes. I was actually punching Roz's upstairs number because it's nice to have a karate expert around when you're going to throw somebody out of your house.

"Stop."

"It's ringing."

"I don't want her to—"

"Don't you think it's time to go?"

He gave me the kind of look actors use to signify that they'll get even someday, and crossed to the hall. I opened the door for him, locked all three locks as soon as he'd departed. Then I leaned against the wall.

Why had I thought of actors? Something about the performance hadn't rung true. Words or emotions? Which?

My wife, much as I, uh, love her . . . Had his hesitation spoken of more than Yankee embarrassment at a declaration of affection? Did he love his wife? He'd seemed convinced that I'd been hired to spy on him. Query: When does a wife hire a private eye to follow her husband? Response: When she believes he's having an affair. Less so nowadays, what with divorce-law reform. Still, evidence of infidelity can be a potent weapon in child-custody cases.

Here, there was no longer a child to consider.

I freed my aching toes and padded around the house barefoot, digging through the daily rubble until I found the *Globe* neatly folded on the hall table. Nearby, Roz had hung a glistening portrait of two large onions draped by a bunch of limp parsley.

No good. Monday's paper didn't carry the stock quotes since the exchanges were closed on Sundays. Slovenly housekeeping, however, has its bonuses. I located the Saturday paper under a chair, took it to my desk, and ran a finger down the tiny print of the Stock Exchange listings. CCO, maybe. I found a C COR on NAS-DAQ, but that was corporation, not company. My eyes started to hurt. I gave up the tables and read the entire section, front to back, and all the miscellany in between. A columnist advised me to *Keep My Stock Records Up to Date.* I learned that health-care funds slumped in the first quarter.

Nothing about Cee Co.

T.C. yowled while I yanked the flip-top ring and presented him with a tin of Fancy Feast. I put a big pot of water on to boil for spaghetti. I use sauce straight from the jar, with a dollop of red wine to give the illusion of homemade. It's not great, but it's quick. Eating takes enough time out of life. Who has hours for cooking?

I practiced some tricky guitar riffs from Rory Block's new *Ain't I a Woman* tape, listening for the telephone, the doorbell.

I didn't hear from Tina Sukhia.

I didn't get a package from Emily Woodrow.

My fingers stopped picking in the middle of a song while I considered Tony's assertion that his fiancée was a fine nurse. Had he sounded overly defensive? He'd asked if I was from the Q.A. Department—Quality Something. Quality Analysis? Quality Assurance?

And what about the timing? When exactly had Tina left JHHI?

A death and a departure. No reason for them to be related.

My fingers chose an old Robert Johnson tune:

I got a kindhearted woman, do anything in this world for me,
I got a kindhearted woman, do anything in this world for me,
But these evil-hearted women, man, they will not let me be.

17

I spent the next morning juggling phone books, checking out variants of Cee Co., riling secretaries with useless calls, and finding no trace of the company that employed Tina Sukhia, who, for her part, neither answered her phone nor responded to the messages I left on her answering machine.

When the doorbell rang just after two o'clock, I ran a hand through hair uncombed since volleyball practice and smoothed my ratty gray sweatshirt over black jeans that were ripped at both knees and faded from too many go-rounds in the washer.

I peered out the peephole and saw Mooney, his weight evenly balanced in classic traffic-cop stance. I figured he'd come about the license plate so I started unchaining chains and unbolting bolts. No quick dives into the powder room necessary; Mooney's used to my come-as-you-are appearance.

He wore a beige cotton sweater, chinos, and sneakers. Loose comfy stuff he could run in if he had to. It was nice of him to come by with the plate rundown. He could have called. I grinned when I opened the door. He didn't smile back. "Can I come in?" he said somberly. No sparkle in his eyes. No handshake, no mock-brotherly squeeze.

"Something happen to Paolina?"

"No. I must look pretty grim."

I sighed. "You do. You want a beer?"

"Orange juice?"

"Okay." That meant he was working. Not working, Mooney drinks beer. He followed me into the kitchen and scraped a chair across the linoleum as he pulled it away from the table.

"This guy Paolina's seeing is a known child molester, right?"

"What guy? Sit down," Mooney said. "It's not about Paolina."

I sat.

Mooney drank juice.

"You gonna break it to me gently?"

"You went to visit Tina Sukhia yesterday."

I quickly cast my mind back to the street outside her apartment. Had I strolled into somebody's surveillance? I remembered the stale marijuana smell in the tiny apartment, but I didn't think cops cared about marijuana anymore, not with crack around. Not with heroin, crystal, speed, PCP, and an Uzi in every other high-school locker.

Mooney said, "Her boyfriend gave us your card."

"Why?"

"I guess because of the coincidence—you showing up, her dying."

Dying.

"No," I heard myself say.

"That must mean no, it's not a coincidence—because I just saw the body, and yes, she sure is dead."

"Hell," I said, and then "damn," over and over. It sounded like my voice was coming from far away, working on its own, without the cooperation of my lips or larynx.

"So I need to know why you wanted to talk to her. And you're gonna tell me because it's part of an official police investigation."

"Homicide?" I asked, stalling, knowing Mooney wouldn't be here if it wasn't.

"A definite possibility."

"But not a certainty?"

"Listen when I talk. I said possibility."

"How likely?"

"Likely enough that you ought to answer me instead of playing games."

"Shit."

"So do we talk here?"

SNAPSHOT

"Or what? You gonna haul me down to the station house, use a rubber hose?"

"I'm not in the mood, Carlotta."

"Sorry. Me, I'm in a great mood."

"I coulda sent somebody else. I come all the way over here and you're gonna give me crap?"

"I work for a living, Moon. Same as you. My clients deserve a little discretion."

"Any client who sent you to see Sukhia better not leave the jurisdiction."

"Why don't you tell me how Tina Sukhia—a lady I never met in my life—died? I haven't read the papers yet."

"That's not how this song goes."

"You want to keep the details from me because you think I killed her and then left my business card with the boyfriend—who told me yesterday, by the way, that he was the fiancé."

"Boyfriend, fiancé. They were shacked up, is what."

"You use phrases I haven't heard in ten years. Shacked up."

"You use phrases I don't hear much either," he said. "Except from hookers." Mooney was brought up a strict Catholic. Women did not swear, not even a discreet *hell* or *damn*. They didn't become cops, either.

"The boyfriend-fiancé a suspect?" I asked.

"Seeing as it happened in a hospital, and we can't place him there, no more than anybody else."

"JHHI?"

"Good old Helping Hand," he said.

"She worked there."

"You working for them?"

"Them?"

"The hospital?"

It's not that I mind telling lies, it's that I know it's not smart to lie to Mooney. Withold information, maybe. But he's got an incredibly good mental lie detector.

"And why would the hospital hire me?" I asked.

"Nice try," he said.

"Come on, Mooney."

"It looks very much like the lady overdosed on barbiturates."

"People OD on downers all the time. What's against it being an accident?"

"No evidence she was a user at all."

"When did she die?"

"Body found about six forty-five this morning. That's all I've got till the M.E. talks."

"That's probably all you'll ever get then," I said sympathetically. M.E.'s are pretty useless when it comes to precise time of death. Oh, they can shove thermometers into orifices and plug numbers into equations, but there are too many variables. The more they learn, the less they know.

"It's not even cast in concrete on the six forty-five. Doctors," Mooney said, raising his eyebrows. "Deaths in hospitals—no matter what the circumstances—cops are considered the last resort. Doctors think there's no such thing as a situation they can't handle."

"Doctor find her?"

"Nurse. Anne Reese, R.N. Didn't know the victim. Didn't care. Mainly irritated because she was at the end of her shift and wanted to go home."

"Nice."

"Like I didn't want to go home, too. But a death's a death. You don't just walk off and leave it."

"At hospitals they do."

Mooney made a face.

"You didn't like the nurse," I said.

"Bingo. And she didn't like me."

"And you're so charming, Moon. Tell me, the boyfriend see Tina last night?"

"Nope. So he got good and stewed, far as I can tell. Eyes bloodshot, but you can't tell if it's from crying or booze."

"If Tina was a user, that could be why the hospital let her go," I said.

126

"I already thought of that," Mooney said.

"There could be money in this someplace. Fiancé had new stereo equipment up the wazoo."

"So?"

I waited for him to mention Tina's new job as a source of the windfall. He didn't.

"The hospital been leaking drugs?" I asked.

"The question crossed my mind," Mooney admitted.

"Anybody answered it yet?"

"I haven't asked yet. I've got appointments with some docs: Chief of Staff. Chief of Medicine. Chief of Pharmacy. Chief trouble-shooter. Probably Chief of PR."

"But you decided to pick on me first? I'm not gonna give you headaches like some medical bigshot?"

"Carlotta, you know that's not—"

"Mooney, it looks to me like you've got an accidental death, and I don't think my client ought to be hassled about an accidental OD. I don't think I ought to be hassled, either." While my mouth was saying *accidental,* I have to admit I was thinking *suicide.* Maybe Tina had quit JHHI. But there was also the possibility that the woman had been dismissed. Maybe she'd done something wrong, screwed up so badly that Rebecca Woodrow had died as a result. What do you do for a comeback if your negligence causes the death of a child?

Maybe return to the scene of the crime and atone for it.

"What do you mean, hassled?" Mooney's voice interrupted my thoughts. "This is hassling?"

"Yeah."

"Hah." He smacked his glass down so hard I thought it would break. "If you want that plate number, owner, you give up your client."

"Unfair," I said.

"So?"

Dammit. Mrs. Woodrow had insisted that a stranger, a doctor, a man in a white coat had been present when her daughter died.

Keith Donovan had asserted that Emily was hallucinating the incident. Harold Woodrow had intimated that his wife was a liar. Pablo Peña, JHHI's resident anesthesiologist, had denied shoving anyone out of a hospital room. And now I couldn't ask Tina Sukhia which one, if any, had been telling the truth.

With a sinking sensation in the pit of my stomach, I wondered exactly where Emily Woodrow had been when Tina died. I hadn't yet received the day's mail, but I found myself hoping it wouldn't contain a confession.

"Mooney, let me get back to you."

"Carlotta, the more time goes by, the less chance I've got."

"Don't quote the stats at me. There's no pressure here, Moon. It's not like you found a city councillor with a knife in his back. The press is gonna see a minority nurse dead in some drug scam. Inside page, Metro, under the fold."

"Tomorrow," Mooney said.

"What about the license plate?"

"Tomorrow."

"Moon, please."

"What is this crap? I can wait, but you can't? If this plate has to do with Sukhia, the whole deal's off."

"Mooney, it's Paolina. The plate belongs to a guy who's hustling Paolina."

He gave me a hard look, but then he sighed and yanked his notebook out of his pocket. "This loser's twenty-eight years old," he said.

"That's why I want to stop him fast."

He made a face. "Plate's registered to Paco Lewis Sanchez. One five eight Peterborough, Boston."

"What else?"

"Height: five-ten. Weight: one ninety-five."

"What else?"

"That's all I got."

"You could run him through NCIC," I suggested. "Keep the crime computer ticking."

"It'll cost," Mooney said.

"Repayment in kind," I replied.

"Like first thing tomorrow, everything you know about Tina Sukhia?"

"She's dead," I said. "And the only way I even know that is from you."

"You can trust me on it," he said.

"Trust has to go both ways," I replied.

"Like love?" he asked after a pause. Mooney's been trying to turn my attentions away from Sam for as long as I can remember. He might have succeeded, too, if we'd never worked in the same chain of command.

"Like lust," I said. "I don't know a lot about love."

"Yeah?"

"And what I do know about love," I said, "I don't trust."

18

She'd told me not to phone.

I punched her number as soon as Mooney's footsteps cleared the porch.

I've never yet tossed a client to the cops, but there's always a first time. I figured I'd use Tina's death to throw a scare into Emily Woodrow, speed up the process, get her to level with me. About her promised packet of information. About Cee Co. About why she needed a person with firearms expertise to take charge of her mysterious paperwork. Or else.

As the phone rang, I doodled on my blotter and tried to envision Emily, in her elegant beige suit, plunging a loaded hypodermic into Tina Sukhia's arm. Or, more likely, forcing her to swallow a quantity of pills.

Had Emily ever been a nurse?

If Patsy Ronetti had done her job, I'd already know. Why the hell hadn't she gotten back to me?

"Hello?" The voice was harried, anxious. I'd reached Harold, the husband, which seemed odd in the middle of the day. When I gave my name and asked to speak to his wife, he erupted, but not in the way I'd expected.

"She's not here," he shouted. "She's not with her mother. Her friends don't know where she is!"

"Calm down."

"She didn't come home last night. Her asshole therapist, the jerk, doesn't know where the hell she is."

"She didn't tell you where she was going?"

"Shopping, for Chrisake, something like that. What do I know? How do I know?"

"Have you, uh, called anyone?"

"The police, you mean?"

"Yeah."

"Why on earth would I call the police? Bitch walks out on me. On *me!* What did you tell her about me?"

"Huh?"

"It's not like she's been a comfort lately, you know? A help-mate. If she ever spoke to me in a civil tone anymore . . . It's not like . . . Well, things might be different with us, that's all. Ever hear the one about how there are two sides to every story?"

"I'm not sure what story you're trying to tell me," I said.

His voice grew tight with suspicion. "Is she with you?"

"Yeah," I said sarcastically, "that's why I called to speak to her."

He hung up. I bit my tongue and winced.

Roz came speeding by and homed in on the refrigerator. She wore black from her leggings to her bustier. On the side that wasn't shaved, her white hair was developing greenish streaks. It looked like she was aging in a fashion usually reserved for plants.

I said, "Busy?"

"No more cleaning," she pleaded. "C'mon. My hands stink. Something in Marta's refrigerator went right through the rubber gloves."

"Soak them in turpentine," I suggested.

Instead she displayed them five inches from my nose, full of odd rings and chartreuse nail polish. "Smell." Her toenails were the same chartreuse.

"No, thanks." I described the guy who'd escorted Paolina to her aunt's house. Then I scribbled Paco Sanchez's address on a scrap of paper. "See where this guy lives, what he does, who he sees. Drives a blue Firebird." I wrote down the plate number as well.

"Maybe I can borrow Lemon's van."

"Good idea. See if you can borrow it without borrowing him."

"Two's better." Lemon is her karate instructor and sometime lover. They share a penchant for slogans: hers on T-shirts; his plastered on the bumpers of his van—everything from friendly whales spouting SAVE THE HUMANS to travelers' warnings such as NEW YORK CITY—WHERE THE WEAK ARE KILLED AND EATEN.

"Two's better for what?" I asked.

"Surveillance."

"One's cheaper," I responded. The Woodrow riches weren't going to pay for this investigation.

"If it doesn't cost, you got any objection to him coming along for the ride?" she asked.

"Just don't miss the Sanchez guy 'cause you're busy screwing in the back of the van, okay?"

"Would I do a thing like that?"

"Oh, Roz," I said. "Yes. You have and you would. But why rake up the past?"

19

When I dialed the Foley-Sukhia number, I got the recording again. Tina must have made the tape, and it was disconcerting to hear the cheerful voice of a dead woman over the line. While I listened, I recalled her photograph, white cap perched on glossy hair, smiling unlined face. I left no message.

After a glance at my watch, I quickly changed from torn jeans to black slacks. The grubby sweatshirt hit the laundry basket. I yanked a pea-green cowl-neck over my head, a sweater I've had since my Detroit high-school days, made of some indestructible acrylic fiber that never balls and never rips. I'm sure the clothing industry outlawed it years ago.

I combed my hair with my fingers as I dashed down the stairs.

My house has a stoop. Keith Donovan's house, two doors down, has a porch big enough to call a veranda. I rang the bell and paced, hoping I'd timed it right. Five minutes before the hour to five minutes after the hour, a psychiatrist ought to answer his bell.

He came to the door wearing a gray oxford-cloth shirt and charcoal slacks, his unknotted tie draped around his neck.

"Hey," he said. "Caught me off guard. This patient's always late."

"Spare a minute?" I asked.

"Have you seen Emily? Spoken with her?"

"My questions exactly."

"She's not at your house?"

"She's not at yours?" I returned.

He pulled at one end of his tie and glanced hastily up and down the street. "Why don't you come in?"

His floor plan wasn't much different from mine. Foyer with staircase. Single step down to the living room. Dining room straight through the foyer. There the resemblance ended. If he did his own decorating, he was wasted as a therapist. A job at *House and Garden* beckoned. The foyer had been set up as a waiting room with a hunter-green loveseat and two inviting chairs. The wallpaper picked up the green of the loveseat. The area rug was a plushy Oriental.

He peered into a gilt-framed mirror, executed a flawless Windsor knot. If my foyer looked like his, I could raise my rates.

He'd taken the entire living room for his office, not just a corner of it like I had. It made me wonder about him. Where did he do his entertaining? Where did his friends hang out? Was he the workaholic the room suggested?

His inlaid mahogany desk probably cost more than every stick of furniture in my house. He couldn't have been a practicing, high-earning shrink for long. Cambridge is full of trust-fund babies. I wondered if he was one of them. Maybe he had an exceptionally wealthy practice. Or an extremely rich wife.

If he had a wife, there was no evidence of her existence. No ring on the man's hand. No framed photo on the desk.

I avoided sitting on the nearby couch. Made me feel too much like a patient. I settled for a tall chair with its back to the window. From the expression on Donovan's face, I'd copped his favorite seat.

"I haven't much time," he said.

"Did you and Emily Woodrow ever talk about the nurse-practitioner who was with Rebecca when she died?" I asked, skipping to the meat and potatoes.

"Emily's husband called me, all worked up—"

"I've spoken with him. Any reason he'd expect to find Emily at your house?"

"What do you mean?"

Looking at his guarded face, I could tell he knew exactly what I meant. Lately, you open any newspaper, there's a story about some therapist who's getting sued for seducing a patient.

"I mean what I said," I responded. "Mrs. Woodrow calls you Keith. You call her Emily. I thought you might be close."

"You thought I might be sleeping with her? As part of her treatment?" He sounded amused rather than outraged.

"Not really," I admitted.

"But you needed to ask."

"Unlikelier events have occurred," I said.

"She's not my type," he offered.

"So what about the nurse?" I asked.

"You don't want to ask me what my type is?"

"Not at the moment. The nurse."

"Emily talked about her," he conceded. "Can I call her Emily without you drawing any cheap conclusions?"

"Did Emily talk about her by name?"

His raised eyebrows implied he'd be humoring me by answering such a ridiculous question. I hate that.

"Did Emily use her name?" I insisted.

"If you want to know the name, I'd have to check my notes—"

"Tina ring a bell?"

"Tina. Yes."

Dammit, I thought. "A last name?" I asked.

"Is it important?"

"Start looking at those notes. Did Emily ever seem to blame Tina for Rebecca's death?"

He made no move toward his desk or wherever he kept his files. "In the past three months, Emily has gone so far as to blame Congress for her daughter's death," he said with a twist of his mouth.

"Have any congressmen been found dead today?"

"What's that supposed to mean?"

"The body of a nurse named Tina Sukhia was found at JHHI this morning."

"Sukhia." He recognized the name, all right.

"And now Emily's missing," I said. "And that might be a coincidence."

"It would have to be a coincidence. What else could it be?"

"I can think of a startling number of possibilities."

"Such as?"

"Tina Sukhia came into some money recently. *After* she lost her job." I left out the new job. I didn't intend to discuss Cee Co. with Emily's therapist. If she'd felt comfortable talking to him about it, she wouldn't have invented a ruse to see me alone.

"Maybe she quit *because* she came into money," he said.

"See. You can play the game, too," I said.

"Your turn."

"Emily has money. She could have used it to buy information."

"Such as?" Donovan asked.

"The identity of the man who was in the room when Rebecca died."

"The man Emily *says* was in the room," he retorted.

I got the feeling he was less than happy with the present situation, that he'd much prefer to lean back in his own chair, above the fray, and ponder somebody else's problems. "Another thing you can buy with money is silence," I suggested.

"So? Go on."

Could Cee Co. be some abbreviated form of the Ruhly department-store chain, the source of Emily's wealth? Maybe the Ruhly empire consisted of a group of "Clothing Co-ops" or "Cecilia's Corners." Maybe Tina's new "job" was to blackmail Emily Woodrow.

"Is it possible that Emily could have monkeyed with a piece of machinery, done something that inadvertently caused her daughter's death?" I asked. *And that Tina might have seen her do it,* I thought.

Donovan removed his reading glasses from his pocket, tapped them against his thigh. "Emily feels a basic responsibility for the child's death," he admitted. "Of course, that's not unusual."

"Do you think she could have deliberately killed her own daughter?"

"You have a high opinion of people, don't you?"

"I earned it," I said. "Do you know if the child's life was insured?"

"It would never have occurred to me to ask."

"I suppose the girl could have been wealthy in her own right," I said. "A trust fund. Money from a grandparent that would revert to a parent on the child's death."

"Whenever Emily mentioned money, which wasn't often, she spoke of it as a given, as a matter of fact."

"Was she jealous of her daughter?" I asked.

He paused long enough to swallow, and when he finally spoke, he avoided a direct response. "Women rarely kill," he said softly. "And when they do, they almost always kill abusive husbands or boyfriends."

I was a woman who'd killed twice, once as a cop, once after. My ex was alive and well, far as I knew.

I said, "Emily never discussed what happened in that room that day? Before Rebecca died?"

"I think she's told me every word she exchanged with her daughter, just remembering it, validating it, sharing it. She's talked about the possibility of a medical mistake, never murder."

"Did she ever talk about suicide?"

"About killing herself?"

"Yeah," I snapped. "She's missing. People who go missing sometimes turn up dead. That's what I mean."

"Let me put it this way: Most people who haven't lived sitcom lives, at one time or another think about killing themselves."

"I'm not asking you about most people. Did Emily talk to you about wanting to do it?"

"Have you ever thought about doing it?" The question came out wrong, full of sexual overtones. The silence in the room grew. He polished his glasses, restated himself carefully. "I mean, killing yourself?"

When my mother died. The thought came so quickly I was afraid I'd spoken it out loud.

"Don't analyze me," I said instead, my voice tight with anger. "Or patronize me."

"Okay," he said. "I'm telling you this in confidence. Understood?"

"I'm not a lawyer. It's not a privileged communication. But I'm not a blabbermouth either."

He leaned forward, extending his fingers and steepling his hands. He regarded me for a long moment, as if he were gauging exactly how far I could be trusted. "Okay then. When I first saw Emily, she wasn't sleeping. She said she never slept, or she slept for two hours and then roamed around the rest of the night. I prescribed Dalmane, a very common drug. Minimal side effects. She said it didn't work. I tried another. Serax, I think, was next, more an anti-anxiety medication, with drowsiness as a side effect. Didn't work."

"Is that unusual?"

"Yes. I tried Xanax, a tranquilizer, then something else. She still seemed resistant. And then it hit me. I realized she wasn't taking them."

"Huh?"

"She'd get a two-week supply or a month's supply, and stash it. I figured she was saving up, hoarding a lethal dose of sleep against the day she couldn't take the pain anymore."

"What did you do?"

"I cut her off cold. I spoke to her. She said she threw the pills away."

"Said."

"She seemed to be making progress."

"What kind of progress?"

"Her retaliatory thoughts seemed to become more other-directed than internalized."

"Did she specifically threaten to kill this nurse?"

"Whose side are you on here?"

"Do you have any idea where Emily might be?"

"I've told my answering service to put through her calls night or day. That's really all I can do."

"Psychiatrists not being interventionists," I said dryly.

"What would you suggest?"

"Go through your notes, and try to get in touch with every person she ever mentioned." I could see the protest in his eyes, so I added, "Or go through the notes and give me the list of people."

He nodded grudgingly.

I went on. "With Emily Woodrow unavailable I need a way to get her daughter's medical records. As Mrs. Woodrow's shrink, why don't you apply for the files?"

"I suppose I could do that."

"Too interventionist?" I asked.

"No," he said defiantly. "Why do you need them?"

"I want to know who was in that room at the end."

"I'll try," he said.

"And let me run some names by you, people who've come up in my preliminary check."

"I can give you till the doorbell rings."

"I spoke to Dr. Muir."

"You did?" His voice dropped as if I'd had an audience with the pope.

"Everybody tiptoed in his presence. Treated him like a national treasure. Except for one guy, an anesthesiologist named Pablo Peña. You know him?"

"Never heard of him."

"A resident. Three-quarters asleep."

"That explains it. He was probably too exhausted to salute when he heard Muir's name. You work a hundred and ten hours a week, you get tired."

"Tired enough to get confused? To panic and give the wrong drug?"

"Anesthesiologists don't give chemo."

"Think about it this way. Maybe he's on duty, thirty-fifth hour of a thirty-six-hour stretch, and something goes wrong with Rebecca. Tina Sukhia calls for help—what do they say?—calls a code, and this guy, asleep on his feet, rushes in with a mask, but instead of attaching it to the oxygen outlet, he grabs some cylinder on the emergency cart—"

"Stuff's color-coded. A cylinder on a crash cart would be either oxygen or air—"

"What if he intended to kill her?" I said. "Anesthesiologists have access to killer drugs."

"You're thinking like a cop. Why would he want to kill her?"

"Off the top of my head? Because he gets off on the power, the life-and-death stuff of putting people to sleep and waking them up —or not waking them up. Or maybe Rebecca saw something she wasn't supposed to see. Heard something she wasn't supposed to hear. Maybe the guy's a child abuser, and he'd tried his act on her."

"Carlotta—can I call you that?"

"Yes."

"Have you ever seen a code called?"

"Yeah. I have. Very recently."

"There would have been a minimum of ten people in Becca's room, within seconds. You think Peña would have killed her with all those witnesses?"

"In a mob scene, with everyone focused on a specific task, he might have seized an opportunity."

"If there was anything odd about Becca's death, Muir would have demanded an investigation."

"I'm not so sure about that," I said.

Donovan pressed his lips together and tried to hide his indignation. "You've met the man exactly once."

"Believe me, I was awed. But I got the feeling that he was a man who cared about his reputation. And his reputation is tied up with JHHI's rep, right? Bound together with steel bands."

"Yes," Donovan admitted.

"Who wants to send a kid to a hospital where there might or might not be a killer loose? If I ran that place, I might be tempted to play my cards very close to my chest."

Donovan raised his eyebrows, gave me a look.

"It's happened before," I said, egged on by his skepticism. "Hospitals can be a killer's favorite place. Where else can you wear a mask and not get thrown in jail? Where else can you find such a helpless population? There was a nurse's aide who split his time between Ohio and Kentucky, killed dozens before anyone even considered him as a suspect. Richard Angelo was a nurse who killed four on Long Island."

"And you're ready to add Peña to the list? Just because he's sleepy?"

"I spoke with a guy named Renzel," I said. "Chief of Pharmacy. He didn't seem to think much of Peña."

"That figures."

"Why?"

"I'm talking too much."

"Go right ahead. It's all confidential," I reminded him.

"Renzel's very close to Dr. Muir."

"Is that why Renzel dislikes Peña? Are they rivals for Muir's favor? Is one of them going to take over when Muir retires?"

"Nothing like that. Truly, I don't understand the Muir-Renzel relationship. They're friends. They travel together. Maybe Renzel's a laugh-a-minute conventioneer. I feel like you're asking me to do five-second psychiatry."

"That's because I am."

"I have an impression—I wouldn't call it more than a feeling— that Hank Renzel resents nonwhite physicians. Among men of a certain age-group, it's not unusual."

"Alan Bakke," I said.

"Who?"

"Wasn't that his name? The white guy out in California who sued because he didn't get into med school. Said they dumped him in favor of a less-qualified black."

"For some borderline white applicants, affirmative action was the end of the dream."

"For Renzel?"

Donovan shrugged. "He's a Ph.D. Not an M.D. And his father was a well-known surgeon. Almost as big a name as Muir. Medical careers tend to run in families."

So, I thought, Renzel's comment about Peña—that he might not be as "up-to-date" in his methods as the WASPy-sounding Hazelton—could stem from pure prejudice.

Donovan stared pointedly at his watch. His next patient was tardy.

I decided to try a quick change. "Harold Woodrow. Does Emily know he's having an affair?"

He grinned and refused to bite. "Do you know? Or are you guessing?"

"Let's just say I wondered."

"Here's a question for you. Do you ever feel you do more harm than good, digging around like this?"

"I didn't set this in motion," I said.

"Are you sure about that? Did you see this Tina woman before she died?"

I only wished I had.

"Can I ask you something else?" he said. "If you've run out of questions for me."

"Till the doorbell rings."

"You dating someone?"

It must be something in the air. Now Donovan.

"Yeah," I said flatly. "I'm seeing someone."

"*The* someone?"

"The someone who?"

"The man you're going to marry."

Good sex can blind you to a lot of character flaws, but even with great sex, Sam was not marriage material. Which was fine with me.

"And then would I get to live happily ever after?" I inquired sweetly.

"Where do you think this conversation's headed?" he asked.

"Nowhere."

"I was planning to ask you out."

"Because we have so much in common?"

"Because you interest me."

"Clinically? As a subject for further analysis?"

"I haven't met many women who seem as comfortable with violence as you do."

"I'm not proud of it," I said.

"No?"

"Let's sit this one out," I suggested.

"Until Mrs. Woodrow turns up."

"We'll see," I said.

"Just let it simmer?"

"We'll see."

The doorbell rang.

I said, "Did you ever prescribe Halcion for Mrs. Woodrow?"

"In moderation, under the administration and supervision of a doctor, there is nothing wrong with that drug."

"And it makes one hell of a criminal defense," I said.

"I have a patient." He stood and walked quickly across the room, his face rigidly under control. "Good-bye."

20

Tony Foley still didn't answer his phone. When Tina Sukhia's recorded voice cut in, I banged down the receiver.

I dialed the phone again, hung up again. Maybe Tony was home, stubbornly resisting the telephone's lure. Considering the statistics on boyfriends killing girlfriends, the police had probably grilled him past exhaustion. The reporters would be next in line, pursuing him for poignant quotes. Given similar circumstances, I wouldn't answer my phone for a week.

I sat at my desk and twisted a strand of hair, a childhood habit I've never outgrown. Most of my hair is silky, but the occasional kinky filament teases my fingertips. The game is to isolate a lone curly stalk and pluck it out.

I'll probably be bald before I'm thirty-five.

I needed to ask Tony Foley some more questions. And stats aside, I didn't see him as a valid murder suspect. Call me sentimental, but I figured he'd have waited until Tina paid off the VISA bill for the stereo.

I debated phoning the Woodrows. Had Emily reappeared?

I reached into the drawer for the photographs she'd sent me, dealt them face up on the desk: baby, toddler, little girl. All I'd ever seen of Tina Sukhia was a single photograph, a smiling image.

Police photographers would have taken shots of her body, pictures that might hint at the circumstances of her death. But I wouldn't see them, not unless I told Mooney everything, including my client's name.

Roz was momentarily handling the garbage-thief search. I hoped Lilia was looking after Paolina.

I yanked, and six inches of curly copper wire came loose, a lone hair trapped between my thumb and finger. I wrapped it around the photos of Becca Woodrow and thrust them into the drawer.

I took back roads to Buswell Street, avoiding Memorial Drive.

Tony Foley wasn't answering his doorbell any more than he was picking up the phone. I settled into a metal folding chair at a Laundromat half a block away and tuned in to the spin cycle. Read the *Globe*, focusing on the tiny paragraph concerning the discovery of a body at JHHI. Former employee. Identification delayed pending notification of kin. No cause of death implied. What would coverage be like tomorrow?

The Laundromat was slightly too warm and smelled of bleach and Downy fabric softener. I took off my jacket, sat down again. Fidgeting escalated to pacing. If Foley didn't come home soon, I was going to start folding laundry.

He'd been out running; no mistaking the regalia. I stifled the thought that he ought to be wearing a black suit instead of royal blue shorts over gray sweats. Physical activity has always proved a healer for me.

I did a little sprinting myself and was by his side as he turned up the front walk. He glanced at my legs. When his eyes traveled up to my face, he abruptly U-turned and started running again.

"Hey!" I said. He didn't stop.

"Tony," I yelled. "Come on."

No reaction. He ran well, long easy strides down Park Drive. He already had thirty yards on me.

I took off after him.

I don't run long distances for exercise or pleasure. I prefer volleyball, with other people and competition, and swimming, with buoyant water and no shin splints. But I'd waited a long time to talk to Tony Foley and I wasn't about to lose him.

He wasn't racing, just pounding along at a good rhythm, a distance man's run, the kind of pace that he could probably maintain for an hour and that would kill me in half.

He turned a corner at St. Mary's and headed toward the university. Afraid he'd hide in some alley or vestibule, I speeded up another notch. When I caught sight of him again, I'd gained a few yards and he was looking back worriedly. I hoped he'd already done a hard day's workout, a marathon at least. Get tired, you bastard, I thought, my sneakers smacking concrete.

He seemed to be heading toward the river, which made sense since the banks of the Charles are the major running path for those who don't enjoy traffic roulette. Racing across Commonwealth Avenue, I almost got smashed by a red Buick. I heard the screech of brakes, kept my head down, and ran.

I thought he'd take the footbridge to the Esplanade, but he kept going, hung a right, sped over the crest of the B.U. Bridge, cut another right, and headed toward MIT.

The going got easier along the river, turf and muddy ruts replacing the pavement, springier but more uneven. Now I had to look down to keep my footing. When I did glance up, I seemed to be getting closer. But I was starting to breathe hard, and my right side was aching.

I don't know if I'd have caught him if he hadn't stumbled. Stupid ideas were crowding my brain. I saw another runner nearby and thought about yelling at him to tackle Tony, considered a traditional cry of "Stop, thief!" But it would be just my luck to get an avenger on the trail, some bozo who'd shoot first.

I could see myself trying to explain it to Mooney.

He went down near the spot where the geese hang out, across from the Hyatt Hotel ziggurat. I put on a burst of speed. He looked back, lowered his head, and struggled to his knees. I was close enough to see the sweat on his forehead and hear the rasp of his breath.

"What the hell?" I stopped next to him, hands on my aching thighs, panting so hard the words could barely surface.

"Leave me alone." He forced the words out between gasps, and I felt vindictively glad he wasn't daisy fresh after practically maiming me.

"You hurt?" I asked, hoping for a positive response.

I got a stream of expletives.

"Why the hell did you run?"

"I don't have to talk to you."

"You twist the ankle, sprain it, or what?"

He put weight on it, winced. "It's gonna blow up, I don't get ice on it."

"I don't usually carry ice," I said. "Maybe if you wait long enough, the river'll freeze."

He tried to stand, but his foot wouldn't take the weight. He hopped a couple of futile yards before collapsing again.

"You gonna help me here?" he asked angrily.

"Oh, sure," I said sarcastically. "What's in it for me?"

"Yesterday, I didn't figure you for a detective. Today, you're actin' like some fuckin' supercop."

"The fuckin' supercop would like to ask you a couple questions," I shot back.

"I didn't know you were a runner."

"I'm not a runner."

"Your wind's good."

"Thank you very much."

"Think you could help me over to the hotel?"

"Answer the questions?"

"Hell, once I get ice on the ankle and a drink in my hand, I'll tell you my fuckin' life story."

"Deal," I said.

It was plain luck we didn't get run over crossing Memorial Drive.

21

Our sweaty appearance was not greeted by hotel staffers with any great consternation. In fact, we were pretty well ignored. The place was jammed, the seafood restaurant off the lobby filled to bursting, humming with conversation and background music. Velvet theater-lobby ropes and a black-and-white sign declared it off limits to the dining public this evening, taken over by the American College of Gynecologists and Obstetricians.

"Whole shit box fulla doctors," Tony Foley complained. "You see one volunteerin' any aid, you let me know, and I'll go have a heart attack."

I said, "Maybe they can't tell you're pregnant."

"Hell, OBs are regular doctors, too."

A harried maître d' finally noticed us. I asked for a bucket of ice and got the feeling Tony wasn't the first injured runner the head-waiter had encountered.

"Can we get a drink?" My surly companion's request sounded more like a demand.

"Certainly, sir. I'll send a waitress over. Why don't you, uh, take a seat in the lounge?"

I smiled at the maître d' and he ruefully returned the grin. The "lounge" was a couple of chairs plunked near the check-in desk for weary travelers.

Tony limped toward the restaurant proper, glaring. "You want to take a guess how many of these sharks are eatin' on their own dime?"

"You really ought to sit down."

"Every time some Joe takes a friggin' aspirin, it goes into a doc's pocket."

I took an elbow and steered him. He lurched into a yellow armchair, sank into the cushion with a groan.

"Think he'll bring the damn ice today?" he muttered, already bent over untying the laces on his worn left Nike. "Shoulda told him I tripped on the hotel grounds, over some goddamn tree root. Shoulda told him I'm some kinda lawyer. Get him hoppin'."

A waitress approached warily.

"Double scotch," Tony demanded. "And bring it before you go back and serve those fat butts their wine, okay?"

"Beer. Whatever's on tap." I thought I might learn more from Tony if I drank with him. Separate myself from the cops anyway.

The waitress was young and easily flustered. She edged around Tony's chair. "It's real busy," she murmured softly.

Tony glowered. She turned and practically ran.

The maître d' brought not only ice but an ice pack improvised from a folded hotel towel. Foley stopped cursing long enough to mumble a hostile thanks.

The waitress served our drinks in a rush of squeaky shoes and dropped napkins. Foley glared at her and gulped his scotch.

"Ice and a drink," I reminded him. "Life-story time."

"Pretty tame stuff," he said.

"Up till now."

"What's that mean?"

"Now you get to be the number-one suspect."

"Hell."

"Meaning?"

"The cops are full of it." He took a deep breath, then another pull on his drink. "Nobody killed Tina. Nobody ever would."

"Then what happened?"

"She made some kinda mistake is all."

"You saying she used drugs?"

"Not like that."

"She pop pills when you were around?"

SNAPSHOT

"You recordin' this or what?"

"You watch too much TV."

"Hell," he said, "what I figure, Tina—look, I love her. I do, but this is how I see it. I mean, she's a good-time gal. She'll try practically anythin' once. Hell, so will I."

"You think she got the dose wrong?" I asked skeptically. "A nurse?"

"How do I know? How the hell do I know? What I know is I never got to thank her for the stereo. I never bought her a goddamn gift worth more than twenty bucks. We'd go to flea markets, and I'd buy her cheap earrings. That's all I ever bought her. Cheap earrings."

He stopped talking abruptly and applied his mouth to the glass. Sitting so near, he seemed as silent and remote as Tina's photograph.

I took a sip of beer and decided I ought to be more particular about ordering by brand name. "Do you know what Tina was doing at JHHI last night?"

"Try another one. Cops asked me that all day."

"Taking a class, filling in for a sick friend?"

"Look, I been through this."

"You find yourself a dinner companion last night?"

"Ordered in pizza. Hope to hell the delivery boy remembers."

"If he took the stairs, he'll remember." It was warm in the hotel after the race along the river. My sweater was starting to stick to my back. "Think Tina went to JHHI to steal drugs?"

"I don't have to answer—"

"How about if I dump you over by the geese and you can crawl back?"

He summoned a ragged smile. "I want another drink."

I flagged the waitress. If cops could ply suspects with liquor, they'd make more arrests.

"I never guessed you for a private eye," he said as soon as the timid waitress departed. He grimaced as he spoke, either from the

153

pain in his foot or the pain of the admission. The number of people who don't guess my profession is one of my major assets in the field.

"You gave my card to the cops," I said. Why had he run away from me? Because he thought I'd be angry about the stupid business card? Did he think I'd shoot him for telling the cops I was looking for Tina?

Did he think I'd killed Tina?

"Yeah, I sure did," he said. "Why'd you give it to me anyway?"

"I was impatient," I admitted. "I wanted some answers fast. Wanted to know if I was wasting my time checking out some rich woman's fantasy."

"This rich woman hired you to ask Tina questions?"

Not exactly, I thought.

Tony lowered his voice. "If you tell the cops I was hittin' on you, I'll flat-out say you're lyin'."

They must have questioned him long and hard about his fidelity. I said, "The subject won't come up."

"Anybody says I didn't love Tina is crazy. I wouldn't do anythin' to hurt her ever. Hell, I didn't even know where she was last night."

"She stay out all night often?"

"She worked nights, some."

"You had an exclusive thing?"

"Mostly. Look, I'm not saying I been a saint, but Tina, I figure she's the faithful type."

"Sure about that?"

"Sure as anybody is."

"Did you call the police when she didn't come home?"

"I fell asleep. They called me."

A businessman replete with yellow power tie and alligator briefcase gave us a haughty glance, as if to say "Why are these homeless people cluttering up my lobby?"

"Are you taking the day off today?" I asked Tony.

"I'm not workin' right now. Cops loved that. I got fired three friggin' weeks ago. Crummy economy, you know."

"Where did you work?"

"Bicycle shop over on Cambridge Street. Little repair, little sales. Little was about it, that's why they laid me off."

"You looking for a job?"

"You offerin' one? Sorry. I been thinkin' things over, if I oughta go back to school or what." He jerked his head over his shoulder. "I'm not like those fellas. I'm not an ambitious kind of guy, tell the truth. Tina had enough ambition for the both of us." He tried out another smile, but his bottom lip shook. "You know, I had ideas of myself as a daddy, a full-time daddy."

"Tina liked to work?"

"Yeah. She sure did. She was the planner, the one figuring on striking it rich. And no, she wasn't pregnant. It wasn't anything but dreamin', and now it's nothin' at all."

He frowned and took a gulp of his fresh drink. "You ever eat here?"

I glanced at the fern-bar decor. "Nope."

"Looks like a buffet setup. Think they'd miss a few clams?"

"You want 'em, you got 'em," I said.

If the cops could ply suspects with seafood, they'd make more arrests.

I liberated a lavish plateful. A waiter glared at me. I glared back. No one tried to stop me.

"Want one?" Tony asked.

"All for you," I said. "Did you see Tina last night?"

"No," he intoned, like he'd given the same response a hundred times.

"Well, did you talk to her last night?"

He peered at me from under pale lashes, his mouth full of food.

"She telephone you?" I asked.

"Yeah."

"You tell the cops this?"

"Sure, I did."

"If you didn't, you'd better."

"Well, I did."

155

"Where'd she call from?"

"I dunno."

"Did you tell her about me?"

"I guess. I read her your card."

"Did you ask her about it?"

"Sure."

"And?"

"She said she didn't know what the hell you could want."

I sighed. "How's the ankle?"

"Another drink?"

"Not on my tab. Look, I need some stuff about this Cee Co. place."

"Like what?"

"How did Tina hear about it?"

"I dunno."

"Did she go for an interview?"

"I dunno."

"Did anybody at the hospital tell her about the job?"

He just looked at me blankly.

"Did she want to leave JHHI? Was she unhappy there?"

"She was . . . depressed about somethin'."

"Something that happened at JHHI? Look, last night, you thought I might be from some quality board, a committee that checks on patient care. Right?"

He peered at his empty glass, looked around for the waitress.

"What happened?" I asked softly. "What got Tina upset?"

"Why should I tell you? She's dead. She was a damn fine nurse. They're tryin' to say she was messed up with drugs, one more dark-skinned girl dead from drugs, no big deal, right? But it's not like that."

"Then don't let them write her off," I said.

"Nothin' I can do, is there?"

I shrugged my shoulders. "Maybe not," I said, taking a sip of warm beer, keeping silent, watching him decide.

He started slowly, in a low, flat voice. "A while back, beginning

of the year, just before she left JHHI, she came in from work a
mess, went right into the bedroom, wouldn't hardly talk to me."

"Yeah?"

"I cooked dinner. She wasn't hungry. I tried talkin', she wasn't
listenin'. Wound up watchin' TV reruns most of the night. *The Tonight Show,* but she didn't laugh once. Didn't even hear the jokes."

I kept quiet. He held his empty glass in one hand. The index
finger of his other hand traced a circle on the arm of his chair, the
same circle over and over.

"She took a shower before bed. I always know it's really bad if
she takes a shower at night instead of in the morning. Like she
wants to wash somethin' offa her. So when she comes out I ask her
flat-out did she lose a kid? Seven years she's a nurse, it still rips her
up to lose a kid. And she gets this look on her face and she says, 'You
know, I had bad days before, but this is some kinda personal best.' I
remember she said that, 'personal best,' 'cause she's a runner, too,
like me. And she tells me she lost three. Three in one day, one right
after another. All real sick, yeah, but she don't understand it, and
she's worried as hell thinkin' maybe, maybe, she did somethin'
wrong. Thinkin' about how it'll look and all. Three."

Three.

"Can you pin the date down on that?"

"Huh? How?"

"What did you watch on TV? Anything besides *The Tonight
Show?*"

"I don't remember."

"Was it the first week in January?"

"Could be."

Becca Woodrow had died January sixth.

"Did she get fired?"

"No."

"Was there an investigation?"

"I dunno."

"She didn't talk about it?"

"No. And I didn't ask. I didn't want to get her upset again. I was just damn glad when she left that place is all."

"Left for Cee Co."

"She only mentioned the name Cee Co. once. And then she kinda laughed."

"She only mentioned it once?"

"That's what I said."

"You didn't ask her about it?"

"What's to ask? 'You have a nice day, honey?' Yeah, I'd ask her stuff like that. 'Say, what's the real full name of that company you work for?' Naw, that didn't come up."

I swallowed my exasperation along with a mouthful of tepid beer. "How about this? How soon after her bad day at work did she leave JHHI?"

"Maybe a month later."

"Think hard, Tony. Do you ever remember Tina mentioning a woman named Emily Woodrow?"

"No. Sorry. I don't."

"Isn't there anything you can remember about Cee Co.?"

"Honest, no. I didn't pay it hardly any mind, and she didn't seem to work much, to tell you the truth. Put in a few hours is all. Nothing like the hours she worked at JHHI."

"A few hours?"

"Some days she didn't go in at all. Then, the last few weeks she spent a lot of time away. But some of that was at the library."

"What library?"

"I dunno." He seemed momentarily abashed by the scope of his ignorance, but then brightened up and offered, "She was readin' about Pakistan. Know-your-roots stuff, I guess."

"Pakistan? Was she planning a trip?"

"Nope. Just readin' about it is all."

I took a sip of beer and wished I'd had a chance to meet Tina Sukhia.

Not many women are killers, Keith Donovan had said. And he was right. But a nurse in a Texas hospital had killed sixteen children with a lethal drug a few years ago. Made national headlines, that one. She said she'd done it to show administrators how much the hospital needed a pediatric intensive-care unit. The lady was in jail and would stay there till she died.

I wished I'd remembered that little tidbit when I was sparring with the shrink.

I called a Green & White cab for Tony Foley before I left.

22

The light slipped from the sky as I walked back over the bridge into Boston. The air had cooled and a breeze whipped the dark river. A lycra-clad bicyclist swerved to avoid a pedestrian. A dented Volkswagen blared its impatience at the traffic light.

Chase a bereaved man away from his home, buy him drinks, and desert him, friendless, in a bar. I congratulated myself on a job well done. Time was, I'd have stayed with him, munching stale peanuts, nodding and listening. But the plain and simple fact was that I didn't want to hear the precious details of his pain.

I shook my head and plodded on. I've felt empty before, depleted of compassion. I quit being a cop when I felt that way all the time.

Worries slowed me like pebbles in my shoes. Paolina. Marta. Emily Woodrow. Becca and Tina were dead and couldn't profit from my anxiety anymore.

Hell, if I were Tony Foley, would I go home to that solitary apartment, to Tina's peacock feathers and filmy scarves, to the bed they'd shared? I'd moved back to my aunt's house after I'd split with Cal, and he wasn't even dead, although he might as well have died, for all the good he did me, zonked out on cocaine.

I passed a phone—not a booth, just a public phone stuck on a metal stem. The 411 operator took her time before parting with the Woodrows' number. Harold picked up on the first buzz, like he'd been hovering over the instrument, willing it to ring.

No, Emily was not home. No, she had not been home.

"Don't you think you should call the police?" I asked. "She's been missing for more than twenty-four hours—"

"What do you mean, 'missing'? It's her choice. You think that's what she's waiting for? Me to call somebody, let the general public know my wife's turned into a lunatic?"

"Look at it this way. If something's happened to her, if she's in a hospital somewhere, it won't look good if you haven't lifted a finger to find her."

"I've informed my attorney. Desertion is grounds for—"

"This is a no-fault divorce state, Mr. Woodrow, as you know. Look, I hate to bring this up on the phone, but I'm concerned about your wife's welfare—"

"And I'm not, I suppose?"

"Are there pill bottles in your medicine cabinet? Did you notice a lot of prescription bottles?"

He gave an exasperated snort. "What are you getting at?"

"I think you ought to hire me to look for your wife."

"Hire you? Hah. Use the thousand she already paid you, the money you bilked her out of already. Don't come to me for more."

"It's not money I need, it's authorization! I can't tell you what your wife hired me to do, but I can tell you she didn't hire me to find her!"

"I'm hanging up."

"Wait. I'm sorry I raised my voice. I won't do it again. You said her mother hadn't seen her—"

"Her mother's in a nursing home. She can't speak. The attendants haven't seen my wife in days."

"Is there anyone else? A sister or brother?"

"I phoned her half sister in Rhode Island."

"Can you give me that number?"

"You think Emily's there, but she doesn't want to speak to me?"

"It's possible."

"She's not close to her half sister. No love lost there. Greta would have begged me to come fetch her."

"What about her friends from before you got married?"

"Before we married? Well, I wouldn't know about them, would I?"

"This is no good. On the phone like this. I need to see you. It'll take me, what? Half an hour, forty minutes—"

"Not tonight."

"Fifteen minutes of your time. No more."

"Absolutely not. Not tonight."

"Tomorrow, then. Ten o'clock."

"You won't be late?"

"No."

"Nine thirty would be more convenient."

"Nine thirty, then."

"Good-bye." The receiver cracked into the cradle and a rusty dial tone hummed in my ear.

How inconvenient, I thought, to have a missing wife.

Tomorrow. Wait till tomorrow. What the hell would I tell Mooney tomorrow? That my client was missing? That she might or might not have killed Tina Sukhia? That she might have killed herself as well?

I turned blindly and walked uphill toward the bridge. A teenager in a B.U. sweatshirt jogged past, breathing hard. She started to smile at me, stopped with her lips barely stretched, and looked quickly away.

Poor Emily Woodrow. Mother in a nursing home. Husband cold as ice. Daughter dead. I stared at the high iron railing surrounding the bridge. High enough to discourage midnight jumpers? Or did the polluted Charles River beneath, the thought of an unclean death in murky water, do that? For a moment I thought I could see Emily in the gloom, still and small in her neat suit, stockings torn, poised on the brink. Just out of my reach.

My mother used to throw up her hands and cry, *"Eyner vil lebn un ken nit, der tsveyter ken lebn un vil nit."* "One person wants to live and can't, another can live and won't." Her all-purpose comment on the basic injustice and futility of it all.

If Tina had been killed by someone other than Emily, my client could have been murdered as well.

Where in hell were those documents Emily had promised to send? Did Harold know about them? Had she confided in her husband? Would he confide in me?

I walked.

I could have gone back to comfort Tony Foley.

"What is it you do when you're down?" Keith Donovan had asked.

I could have gone home to play guitar and eat frozen pizza.

I called Sam Gianelli.

23

"Hey," I murmured gently, running a light finger over Sam's ear, "wake up."

He smiled and sighed. His eyes stayed shut.

Me, I'm a second-round lover. Unless I have a steady bedmate, a regular night-and-morning man, I find the guy too eager to come, too easily satisfied, too quick to drift off to sleep. I'm slow to rouse and slow to finish. Sam knows that. He forgets.

But when I wake in the middle of the night and reach for him, Sam isn't surprised. That's the coziness of old lovers, who know just where to lick and touch and probe.

"C'mon," I said, a little louder.

Sometimes I miss the craziness of new lovers, who haven't got a clue, but are more than willing to search. My subconscious flashed an image of Keith Donovan knotting his tie. Substituted one in which he unbuckled his belt.

"Mmmmm," Sam said. "That's nice."

"How to put the romance back into your affair," I said.

"You could wear lace," he murmured.

I peeled off my menswear tank-top undershirt. "Black lace?" I asked. "Kinky?"

"Kinky," he agreed solemnly.

I've never been into dress-up sex. Music's my aphrodisiac, and since Sam tolerates my old blues albums, maybe I ought to give itchy lace another chance. I've got a black underwire bra I haven't worn since high school. The push-up kind, bought when I thought every girl needed Miss December breasts. Had I thrown it out?

"Pay attention," Sam said.

I did. The sheet and blanket entangled us, but they finally surrendered and tumbled to the floor. We managed to stay on the mattress, me on top, wriggling and slowly, slowly sliding, while Sam, his big hands free and busy, did his own underwiring and encircling.

When the phone rang, I was winded, pleased that it had waited till I'd climaxed.

"Relax," I said to Sam, lifting my hair off my sweaty neck with one hand. "It's probably just a ransom demand for my garbage."

I tilted the receiver off the hook before it could shrill a fifth ring. The woman on the other end of the line cursed me in Spanish. I was tempted to hang up, but I knew the voice too well.

"Marta," I said firmly. *"¡Por favor, repita!"*

That had no effect at all.

"¡Mas despacio!" I demanded.

The flow of sound slowed and started to make sense.

"How long ago? Did she take any money?" I spoke in Spanish. I know better than to try English on Paolina's mother when she's in a state.

"¿Cuanto? Gracias. Now tell me exactly what she said. Word for word. Spanish, English, whatever! If I don't understand, I'll ask." I shut my eyes and ground my teeth to keep from screaming.

Sam leaned over and flicked on the light.

" *'¿Jamás?' ¿Cómo se dice en inglés?* Never? Same as *'¿nunca'?* Stronger, when you use them both? What else? Okay. Okay. *Cuanto antes."* I hung up while she was still shrieking at me about how it was all my fault and she would sue me, kill me, if anything happened to her daughter.

"Bad?" Sam asked, already sitting up and starting to pull on his pants with the speed of a man who felt guilty about missing the earlier episode with the trash cans.

"Paolina. She ran away." I started punching buttons as soon as I heard a dial tone.

"Cops?"

"Not yet."

"Green and White Cab," Gloria sang on the first ring. She didn't try to interrupt while I sketched the outline. "Poor lamb," she muttered. "Poor darlin'." Then "You hang on two seconds, hear?"

It was more than two seconds, more than two minutes. I spent the time foraging for clothing on the floor, handing an occasional article to Sam, balancing the receiver between my shoulder and chin while donning the rest.

"You called it right, babe." Gloria's voice was so soothing I wondered why I didn't dial her whenever I got an insomnia attack. "Johnny Knight picked her up on Portland Street, dropped her in front of the Delta terminal fifteen minutes ago. Sweet child knew enough to flag a Green and White. No perverts workin' here. 'Course she probably hoped she'd get you."

"I doubt it," I said. "It's not like I'd have driven her to the airport. They don't start flying out of Logan till it's light, do they?"

"I already checked that on another line. No departures till six eighteen. Not from Delta anyway."

"She'll want Delta."

"Should I call airport security?"

"No. I'm on my way."

"Let me know if I can help."

"You already have. Thanks."

Sam was ready when I was.

"How'd you know she'd take a cab?" he asked.

"She took money from Marta's purse, and she's not dumb enough to hitch. Come on."

I slammed the car door, twisted the key in the ignition, and floored the accelerator.

"Want me to drive?" Sam asked quietly.

"No," I snapped. "I should have known."

"Known what? You haven't seen her for months."

"I haven't spoken to her for months. I saw her Sunday, spied on her. Oh, goddamn—" I remembered the envelope the beer-bellied man had passed her, the quick argument that had preceded the exchange, the aura of conspiracy. Money?

"Still—"

"She had a fight with Marta. Usual stuff, but worse. The brothers kept teasing her, she didn't have any privacy. And Marta says, 'You're no better than the rest of us, girl. Don't complain to me.' And it goes on. And gets into the business about her dad, and Paolina says Marta's right, she's not like the rest of them. And then she says, '¡Nunca, jamás, volvere a verte!' "

"What's that?"

"She pulls out a bag, already packed, from under her bed. And she says to her mother, 'I'll never, *ever* see you again.' "

"Kids say that."

"And Marta says, 'Wherever you go, they'll send you back.' "

"So?"

"Paolina uses the Spanish word *extradición*. Sounds pretty much the same in English, and you don't use it if your final destination is in the U.S."

"You figure she's going to try to track down her real father? That bum in Colombia?"

There was a long silence in the car and then Sam added, "We'll find her." He tried not to wince as I screeched a corner onto Memorial Drive.

It was sheer negligence on the part of the police that I didn't get a ticket. I flew the route at twenty miles over the speed limit while Sam hung on grimly to the chicken stick and didn't say a word, bless him. I had less than an eighth of a tank in the car. Plenty to make the airport unless the Callahan Tunnel was jammed, an unlikely event in the predawn blackness.

I shot a yellow at Leverett Circle, yanking the wheel hard to the left to bypass a truck already stopped in my lane.

"Why Delta?" Sam asked.

"They do the Miami run," I said. "Miami's halfway to Bogotá."

"She have enough money for that?"

Why would Paco Sanchez give her money? Why would a twenty-eight-year-old hang out with an eleven-year-old? I used to be a cop. I know there are men who steal children—especially young girls—men who spin them tales of instant movie stardom—or reunions with long-lost fathers.

"I'm afraid she might. She took sixty bucks from Marta. She's got her baby-sitting money. And there's this guy who might have loaned her some." I didn't tell Sam any details about Sanchez; it made him seem less real.

"And she's that hot to meet her old man?" Sam murmured.

"Wouldn't you be?" I asked. "If you'd never seen him? If you'd never even known about him till you found out by mistake?"

"I'd be delighted if I found out my father was a mistake." Sam's voice had an edge to it. It's a sore subject. He's the son of a Boston mob underboss, the kind of guy who chews a cigar on the evening news and mumbles "No comment" out of the corner of his mouth.

I fishtailed into the short-term lot at Delta. You want your wheels stolen, park them at Logan International. The professional car thief has the brains to boost from the long-term lot, but the junkies don't care.

I made sure all the doors were locked. My Toyota was going to have to take its chances.

I didn't want to alert airport security. Once you start your basic attack dog in motion, it's hard to call him off, and the last thing I wanted was a bunch of bored gun-happy guards tagging at my heels.

She'd have to buy a ticket at the counter, or, better, talk somebody into buying one for her. She'd want to stay out of sight until she could blend with a crowd. Maybe find a nice sympathetic family she could temporarily join. Paolina's a pretty good liar. If she went up to some lady with a story about how her mom had to drop her at the door with money and rush Aunt Cecelia to the hospital to have the new baby, and now the people at the counter won't pay attention to her because she's just a kid . . . well, you'd probably do her a favor, and take her cash, and put her ticket on your credit card, too.

If there was a cheap under-twelve fare to Miami, she'd definitely join a family. I tried to think myself in her shoes, but eleven years old is a lifetime away from thirty-odd. I don't remember eleven, except that everything—a quiz, a boy, a pimple—was life-and-death important.

The terminal was hushed and fairly empty. Cleaners bused the ashtrays where desperate smokers had stoked up before venturing into the smokeless skies. A skinny young man stared into space as he moved his linoleum polisher in widening arcs. I asked him if he'd seen a little girl hanging around and it took me a while to realize that he was plugged into a Walkman and hadn't heard a word I'd said.

"Nope," he muttered when disengaged. "Ain't seen nothing."

Good witness. Typical.

We tried the restaurant, the snack bar, the bookstore, the two magazine stands, the souvenir shop. There was a special waiting area with cheerful slides and ride-'em airplanes for Disney-World-bound children. Empty. Sam's leather soles smacked the linoleum. My sneakers were silent, except for the occasional hurried squeak. I remembered the elevator and thought she might have taken refuge there. She likes elevators.

The doors slid open on no one.

"Maybe we should wait by the ticket counter," Sam said, grasping my hand.

"You wait, okay?"

"Where will you be?"

"Just make sure she doesn't buy a ticket."

"What am I gonna do? Grab her and carry her out to the car? What if she screams?"

"Do what you have to do, Sam."

"If I get shot by airport security, one of Dad's goons will want to know why. Bear that in mind."

I leaned into a quick kiss, took off in the direction of the rest-room sign.

There are six restrooms in the Delta terminal complex. I pride myself on knowing the location of every ladies' room in Boston—which ones have Tampax machines, which have rats and roaches, which are clean enough to use. The knowledge came in handy as a cop, especially on surveillance, and it comes in handy as a cab driver.

Two flight attendants chatted in number one. A cleaning crew was swabbing the floor in number two. Number three was empty. I opened all the stall doors, ducked into the special baby-changing alcove.

By number four I had to pee. That's what propinquity will do for you.

Number five was it. A hint of Paolina's cologne entwined with the smell of disinfectant. She doesn't wear it often, just on special occasions, and then she always splashes on too much. I waited while a woman patiently helped her daughter sit on the toilet, then washed the girl's hands in the sink and showed her how to start up one of those dumb air blowers that takes so long to use that your flight has left by the time your hands are dry.

The daughter stuck her face in front of the vent and let the hot breeze ruffle her hair. The machine had entertainment value I'd never appreciated.

After the woman and her daughter departed, I stood absolutely still for two minutes. Then I tiptoed to the one closed stall and peered underneath.

She was wearing the red shoes I'd sent for her birthday, flats with big shiny bows. I could never have had a biological sister with such tiny feet. At the sight of them I swallowed hard.

I cleared my throat. The feet tried to scoot out of sight.

I wanted to yell. I wanted to scare her the way she'd scared me. I wanted her to know that there were people in the world who'd take unimaginable advantage of her innocence.

I filled my lungs, but the scalding words wouldn't come because I was so damned relieved to see those little feet. I could hear her breathing, quick and shallow.

"Paolina," I said.

The right foot reappeared, then the left. She started to sob quietly.

"Open the door, baby."

"Go away."

"I can't."

"Let me go. Please."

I didn't make a fuss about opening the door. If I had to, I could crawl under it.

Months ago, Paolina stumbled on a family secret: she doesn't share the same absentee father as her three younger brothers. She's presumably the daughter of a wealthy man, an offshoot of one of Colombia's richest families. Her mother, a servant in the big house, never married Paolina's father, although she says he promised her marriage. The old story. Complicated by the fact that the man ran off, not with another woman, but to the jungle, to lead a revolutionary guerrilla group. Which is where—the popular press declares—he first became involved with drugs. Money for *La Revolución, La Violencia.*

You've seen grainy news photos of Paolina's dad. Carlos Roldan Gonzales. A member of the Medellín cartel.

"Did you tell Paco Sanchez about your father? Did Sanchez promise he'd help you find your dad?"

Silence.

"Paolina—"

"I need to find him. I have to find my dad now."

"Open the door, baby."

"I can't. I can't. I can't get up. I can't leave here."

"Honey, calm down."

More silence, broken by huge gulping sobs. I thought about crawling under the door.

When it came, her voice seemed very small. "I'm sick, Carlotta. There's something really wrong with me, inside me. I think I'm dying."

"What are you talking about, baby?"

"I can't get up. It's happening again. It happened before, but then it stopped, and I thought if I went to church and prayed, and if I helped at home, maybe I wouldn't die."

"What do you mean?"

"It's happening again."

"What's happening?"

"I'm bleeding. I'm bleeding. Down there."

Eleven years old. Oh, my God. Eleven years old, with a mother who hadn't told her what to expect.

"Oh, honey," I said, "please open the door."

I'd gotten my period at eleven, too. A Wednesday, I remember, dance class in gym. How I'd hated, *hated* dance class. Flat-footed foxtrots with boys half my size. And then a sudden dampness spreading between my legs, and pointing fingers, and smothered giggles.

I'd been ashamed to ask the gym teacher for permission to go to the bathroom. I'd fled, convinced that death by embarrassment was truly possible. And then the horrific stain. The fear.

There was no hiding anything from my mom. The slightest shading in my afternoon greeting would tell her whether I'd passed the test or failed, met a new friend, lost an old one.

She'd been brusque and congratulatory. Squeezed me in a tight embrace, and taken me out for a grown-up lunch at the corner deli.

"If I stand," Paolina said, her voice quavering, "I'll get blood on my clothes. I have blood on my pants. I can't go out. Everything's spoiled. Everything's ruined. I'll never see my father."

"Sweetheart, just lean forward and open the door. There's nothing wrong with you, nothing at all." I made my voice as calm, as soothing, as gentle as I could, trying to force my words through the gray steel door, will her hand to flip the lock.

"I'm bleeding," she wailed.

"I know you're scared," I said. "But you're okay. I'm coming in. Don't be afraid." I sat on the floor, eased myself down on my elbows, stuck my head, my chin, under the door, and inched my way backward under the stall.

She was sitting on the toilet, her stained panties and tan pants rolled into a ball and hidden behind it.

I knelt by her side in the cramped space, put my arms around her shoulders. "Listen to me. Listen, honey. There's nothing wrong with you, Paolina. Every healthy woman bleeds like that. Till she gets too old. It just means she's healthy, she's ready. Her body's getting ready. When you bleed, it's because your body's saying that everything's in working order. Your body's ready to have a child."

She looked up at me, momentarily startled out of her tears. "A baby? I don't want any baby."

"Of course not. Not now. Your body's ahead of the rest of you, that's all. But someday, if you want to, honey, when you want to, you can have a kid. It's a choice you can make because your body's telling you it's in gear, it's working just fine."

She looked up at me with red swollen eyes, the panic and the pain still at the surface.

"I'm so sorry it scared you," I said, hugging her closer. "I'm so sorry I wasn't there to tell you."

"I'm not dying?" she said. "I don't have cancer or leprosy?"

Leprosy. Jesus.

"You're not dying. You're just older. You're a girl turning into a woman. You menstruate, that's what it's called. You bleed."

"But what do you do? How do you—?"

"Pads. You use pads." There was a Tampax machine outside the stall, but I remembered from somewhere in my past that tampons weren't recommended at first, for virgins.

Paco Sanchez. No. I wouldn't think about it. I wouldn't ask. Instead I started wadding up a stream of toilet paper, folding it over and over into a makeshift pad.

"We'll stop at a drugstore," I said. "This will do till then."

"But—are you going to make me go home?"

"Honey, you're only eleven."

"My dad's getting old. He could die. He must be fifty, my mom says."

With a life expectancy that diminished with each photo in the international press.

Paolina said, "I can't wait much longer. I need to meet him is all. To see what he looks like. If he looks like me. Can't you understand?"

I was tempted to get on a plane with her. Forget about Emily Woodrow and Tina Sukhia. Go to South America. Find the delinquent father. Get it the hell over with.

I didn't relish the thought of being arrested for kidnapping in Miami. Bad class of people in the jails down there, I hear.

"Oh, honey," I said softly. "I'm so sorry."

"You won't let me go?"

"Can't."

Tears filled her eyes and welled over. I held her until the sobs turned to sniffles. We used up more toilet paper blowing her nose and wiping her eyes.

"Well, if I'm not going to die," she announced solemnly, "maybe I could wait just a little longer. I'm really, really tired."

"Come home with me?"

"But I'm so messy." Her voice started to shake again. "I'm such a mess."

"I can fix that," I said, patting her shoulder, squeezing her hard.

We found other clothes in the battered gray carryon that she'd shoved to the side of the stall—underpants, dark slacks. She seemed to have packed half clothes, half stuffed animals, all in a jumble. I rinsed her tan slacks and bloody underwear in icy water and stuck them in a plastic bag she'd used to hold a pair of sneakers.

"You look great," I said, after she'd patted her swollen eyes with a soaking paper towel. She was taking big deep breaths, trying to accept that she wouldn't die in the airport ladies' room after all.

My little sister.

"Ready?" I asked.

"Ready."

Holding hands, we went out of the bathroom.

24

I could hear far-off shouting as soon as I opened the door, coming from the direction of the ticket counter. I thought I recognized Sam's voice.

I tugged at Paolina's arm.

"I can't run," she moaned. "I can't. My stomach hurts."

A six-foot-long black vinyl bench stretched along one wall of the corridor.

"Sit right here and don't move," I said. "I'll be back for you in five minutes. Don't move, Paolina. Promise me."

"Come soon."

I was already twenty yards down the hall, running toward the commotion.

I saw Roz first. Flanked by two much-taller men, ringed by curious onlookers, she stood out because everyone else seemed to be staring at her, either mesmerized by the green-white hair and partially shaved skull or taken with her black leather shorts and metal-studded T-shirt.

The heavyset man was the same one I'd seen walking with Paolina.

"Leave her alone." That was Sam. His voice was low, but its menace carried.

The two of them, Sam and Roz, were herding Sanchez in my direction. If they kept him backing up, he'd bump smack into me.

I swiveled and searched for uniforms—airport security or Boston police. I saw neither, just some gold-braided flight attendants. One was speaking urgently and softly into a red phone.

Security would be on its way.

I couldn't wait for Roz and Sam to push Sanchez closer. I sped toward him. "Forget about going anywhere with Paolina," I said firmly. My voice turned him around. If I'd had a gun, I would have aimed it, kept him immobile until the cops arrived. Maybe done something worse.

That's one of the reasons I don't usually carry.

"Do you own a gun?" Emily Woodrow had asked.

"Can you use it?"

"Have you used it?"

"Would you do it again?"

Use it for what, Emily? Couldn't you have told me that before you disappeared?

The defiant grin on Sanchez's face altered when he saw me. Two to one, he'd seemed almost comfortable with. Three made him sweat. "What the fuck you talking about? Get the hell out of my way."

He lowered his head and tried to charge past me, but Paolina was down that corridor and I wasn't planning to let him get a single step closer to her. I faked to the left, let him pass me on the right, did a fast reverse, and dived for his ankles. Damn, damn, damn. It stings so much less when I wear my volleyball kneepads and fling myself across a wooden gym floor. I cursed while I brought him down, and hoped it hurt him more than it did me.

He was quick, up in an instant, sprinting the other way, toward an automatic exit door, past a suddenly frozen Roz and a Sam who'd gallantly stopped to help me.

"Get him," I yelled, standing and rubbing one aching knee before scurrying back to Paolina. I could have joined in the chase, but I figured she'd be worried, all alone.

Besides, I didn't think they'd catch him. Too many places to run, too many places to hide. Roz is a good karate student; a sprinter, she's not. Sam's big, but slow, and once outside the terminal building, Sanchez's dark pants and shirt would ease him into the shadows.

So I wasn't surprised when the two of them came back, Sam

empty-handed; Roz shaking her oddly coiffed head and clutching a flat manila envelope.

Both greeted Paolina, who was practically asleep, her relief converted to exhaustion, her head lolling against my shoulder.

"You can pick that creep up again, can't you Roz?" I asked quietly.

"Sure, but he's no creep," she said.

Never trust Roz's judgment, that's one thing I've learned.

"Surprise!" she went on. "The creep's a PI, same as you."

"You're kidding," I said after a pause.

"Hey, like, I tailed him all day. The maggot works for Griffith. You know, old Carl Griffith, that slime in the Pru Center?"

I admit that Carl Griffith, an ex-cop with a colorful reputation, has never struck me as a stand-up prince on the few occasions we've met, but—"I don't understand this," I muttered.

Sam said, "Hey, how are you, Paolina? Long time. You sure have grown."

She kept on staring at the floor, but a faint, pleased smile spread over her face.

"What's in the envelope?" I asked Roz.

"Jerk dropped it."

"On purpose?"

"I don't think so. It was early on. See, I didn't know he knew I was tailing him. I thought I did a hell of a job, by the way, him being a pro, and not knowing I'd tracked him all over town. Lemon's van—"

"That jerk is nothing more than a semipro at best. I tailed him to the Pru and he never—for Chrisake," I said, "look at this."

Inside the envelope was a passport. A single navy-blue U.S. passport, for one Maria Elena Vargas, age 13. The photo was of Paolina.

There it was. Proof that Paco Sanchez had planned to help Paolina leave the country. Had he also intended to accompany her? And why?

"Honey," I said, nudging her awake. "You know anything about this?"

"No," she said.

"You had to pose for the picture."

"I remember when Paco took it. See, that's the wall over by the school, next to the playground."

"Here," I said, pointing to Maria Elena's signature, scrawled across the photograph. "Did you sign that?"

"No. Honest. What's wrong?"

"Good. Nothing. Listen." I motioned Sam to sit next to Paolina while I pulled Roz aside. "Roz, go back to Sanchez's home address. Pick him up and stick to him. Use Lemon. I'll even pay him. Follow this guy everywhere."

"But he's seen me."

"Wear glasses," I said. "Get a wig. Change into something conservative. I want to know who he sees, what he does. If he goes near a train station, a bus depot, an airport, stop him."

"Oh, yeah," she said sarcastically. "How?"

"Use your charm," I suggested. "If that fails, try a karate kick."

25

Paolina dozed in the car and so was spared the additional embarrassment of a stop at a Store 24 where the register was operated by a teenage boy who blushed at the sight of a box of maxi pads.

I placed them on the bedside table in the guest room. She didn't wake, just moaned softly when Sam carried her up the stairs. I decided to let her sleep in her clothes.

After ten minutes of telephone sparring, I managed to convince Marta that Paolina would hardly come to grief in a single night spent under my roof.

"I'm surprised Paolina didn't know," Sam said, when I explained. "Street-smart kid like her."

"Street-smart, right. Means she's heard the jokes, not the facts. She gets her period and panics, so she goes to church. Period ends; prayer works. When it starts up again, she figures she's gonna die any minute. Goddamn Marta."

"Marta's mom probably never enlightened her either," Sam offered.

"You defending her?"

"Not if it pisses you off."

I smiled grudgingly. "It doesn't." I put my arms around him and nestled my face into his neck. "Thanks for coming along."

"Will it piss you off further if I go now? I've got a major meeting tomorrow, and I could use a couple hours of sleep."

I'd have liked him to stay, but after a few hard hugs and a little body massage—just enough to get me started—he went home.

Morning came quickly, a raw gray morning more like February than April. Paolina breathed quietly, the blankets wildly scattered, as if she'd attacked them in the night. An untidy sleeper, she sprawled across three quarters of the big bed, arms outflung, as if she needed to occupy all available space.

I hesitated, hating to wake her. But I couldn't stick around. I had a nine-thirty, don't-be-late appointment with Harold Woodrow. Maybe I'd leave a note on the kitchen table, along with breakfast. She looked so happy asleep, so unconcerned and childlike.

Downstairs, the mail carrier had littered the foyer with Stop & Shop coupons and ads. No blue envelopes. Nothing from Emily Woodrow. The message counter on the answering machine stood at zero. Roz hadn't called in.

Just as well I had a date with Woodrow. I'd have to stay out most of the day to keep a step ahead of Mooney. Once he discovered the relationship between Emily and Tina . . . well, maybe I could put the threat to good use. Cooperate, I'd order Harold Woodrow, or I talk to the police.

After Woodrow, I'd try to track down Savannah, Dr. Muir's gorgeous second-string receptionist. Approached the right way, she might tell me a lot about the day three patients died.

If I were a more domestic soul, I could have left a nice platter of homemade waffles for Paolina, on one of those warming trays, along with a glass of freshly squeezed juice. As it was, with Roz responsible for stocking my shelves, there was nothing to eat.

I opened the freezer in hopes of a frozen bagel, stared at glacier formations, and wondered if Roz would ever defrost it short of an engraved invitation. I found sixteen cans of peaches at the back of a cupboard; she must have hit a sale. Also a suspiciously large number of cans of jellied cranberry logs. Maybe she was planning to use them for hair dye. Or finger paint.

I wound up eating peanut butter straight from the jar, a trick I've picked up from watching Roz too often. About all she eats is peanut butter; she uses her finger for a scoop, as part of her continuing effort to avoid washing dishes or silverware. I'm proud to say I used a spoon. A can opener is the only kitchen utensil Roz ever needs.

The phone shrilled, and I figured it must be her, reporting from surveillance. I'd have her come in and take Paolina out to breakfast at the IHOP. Lemon ought to be able to cover Paco Sanchez for a couple of hours.

The phone blared twice before I caught it.

"Hello," I said.

Nothing.

"Hello?" I thought I could hear faint breathing on the other end.

"Roz?" I said, breaking the first commandment of answering the phone to possible dial freaks: Never give them a name to use. I heard more breathy noises and a distant grunt, then banged the receiver down.

Since I already had my hand on the phone, I called Donovan. If Emily had been in touch with him, I wouldn't have to tackle Woodrow.

The psychiatrist picked up after I'd started my standard answering machine spiel. I hate that. What am I supposed to do, feel grateful that, after careful screening, somebody's decided to accept my call?

"Heard from Emily Woodrow?" I asked.

"Who is this?" He sounded angry.

"Carlotta. Your friendly investigator down the street, remember?"

"Sorry about the machine. I keep getting hang-up calls. That's why I—"

"I got one, too. Just a minute ago."

"They're out there," he said. "The weirdo patrol. And no, I haven't heard from Emily, and I'm pretty worried about it."

I'd have to threaten Harold after all. "You get Rebecca Woodrow's medical records yet?"

"No. And hello, good morning, how are you?"

"Busy."

"Me, too. That's why I haven't picked them up."

"Good."

His voice took on an edge. "Now you don't need them? I went through a lot—"

"I do need them. And more. I need the records of two other patients who died the same day as Rebecca."

"How am I supposed to—"

"You're the doctor. Use your imagination. Snow the clerks at the medical records office. Wave your M.D. in front of them."

"Who are these other people?"

"I don't have names."

"You don't have names?"

"Stop repeating me. Three patients died under Tina Sukhia's care that day."

He took his time responding, and when he did, he spoke in measured flat tones. "At a smaller hospital, like JHHI, that would be unusual."

"Find me three deaths on the same day—I assume from complications of acute lymphoblastic leukemia, certificates signed by the same doctor—"

"Dr. Muir?"

"Probably."

"I don't see where you're headed."

"Can you do it?"

A pause again. "Probably. I can fudge it. Research subjects. Family reactions. Follow-up therapy. I don't know."

"Good."

For the shadow of a second, before hanging up, I thought about asking him what I should say to Paolina when she woke. There's a temptation to listen to experts. I resisted it. Hell, he didn't even know her.

I glanced at my watch; I'd have to leave in twenty minutes. Better wake Paolina, ferry her back to her mom. Maybe I'd have time to ask her a few questions about Paco Sanchez, how he'd approached her, who'd brought up the possibility of travel—

It didn't make sense.

He worked for a detective. And it had to have something to do with me, because of the garbage.

Now, I was a cop for six years, and I've put a few pimps away for pretty long spells. There are felons and ex-felons and ex-husbands who might think they'd be better off if I'd never entered their lives.

One of them might hire a not-too-savory investigator to get the goods on me. But hurt me by stealing Paolina?

The doorbell rang. I hurried, envisioning a UPS man holding a fat, detailed file sent by Emily Woodrow.

There were cops on the doorstep.

26

"You didn't have to send the storm troopers!" I said in a voice so dangerously soft it was almost a whisper. I controlled the volume carefully; if I let myself get a single decibel louder, I'd scream.

Mooney glanced innocently up from his desk. "Hey," he said, shoving back his chair and standing abruptly, "what is this? Paolina? Honey, I'm sorry. What the hell, guys? A kid?"

The younger of the two cops smirked. "You said pick her up. She wouldn't budge without the kid."

Mooney closed his eyes and sighed deeply. "Right. I'll talk to you later. Go back to work." As soon as the door slammed, Mooney shrugged and turned to me. "Traffic patrol," he said. "I'll stick 'em both back in traffic."

"Heavy traffic," I suggested, tight-lipped and angry.

"Carlotta, look, it's for your own good. There are guys from Winchester looking for you with a warrant."

Winchester was Emily Woodrow's backyard. A muscle on the right side of my neck tightened like a fist.

"Mooney, is anybody dead?"

"Carlotta, believe me, I had no idea Paolina would be with you. Those guys. I can't believe them."

"*Is anybody dead?*" I repeated.

"No. No, honest. Paolina, come on over here and give me a hug, okay?"

"She hasn't even had breakfast, Mooney."

Paolina marched over and threw her arms around Mooney's neck. "I missed you," she said. "Those guys, they wouldn't even run the siren or flash the lights. Are they for-real cops?"

"Hey, that's my girl!"

"Mooney, I hate to interrupt, but what's going on here?"

"A minute," he said. "Paolina, Jo Triola was asking me about you the other day. When's Paolina coming by? And you know, she's got a whole boxful of doughnuts in her room. Smelled 'em when I came in."

"Mooney, just tell me quick, and let me take her out to breakfast. Okay?"

"Are you two mad?" Paolina asked anxiously.

"No, honey. But I need to talk to Carlotta alone. For a little while."

"My mom didn't call you, did she?"

"It's not about you, Paolina. Honest. Come on, let's find Jo and the doughnuts."

I waited. I fidgeted. Winchester cops with a warrant? Dammit, I ought to be in Winchester right now, chatting with Harold Woodrow. Maybe I ought to make a run for it. Hah.

Mooney's not in Donovan's league as an interior decorator. Not even a poster on the wall to take my mind off the institutional paint and the smell of police station. I glanced at his compulsively neat desk top. He'd left a single file folder dead center, labeled *Tina Sukhia*. Sealed.

I was fingering it when Mooney opened the door. He pretended not to notice. "Here," he said, holding out a napkin-wrapped bundle. "Paolina sends you a glazed doughnut, with love."

"Mooney, you can't keep ordering your hounds to pick me up. I don't work for you anymore."

"I know that. And I also know who your client is. So maybe we can have a meaningful conversation."

"I don't see where the two points follow," I said. "You think you know who my client is. So what?"

"Where were you last night?"

"You recording this?"

"Come on. I know you weren't home."

The doughnut was sticky. "Is there coffee to go with this?" I asked.

"I can get some. Hang on."

I waited.

"You break the seal on the file yet?" Mooney asked when he came back, two plastic foam cups steaming in his hands.

"You can't break it yourself?"

"I called you last night. Late. No answer."

"I was out partying," I said. "Need the gory details?"

"This is not about your social life, Carlotta. Harold Woodrow, a Winchester big shot whose name rings bells with some well-connected people, says you were busy breaking into his house."

I chose one of the coffee cups. Didn't matter which. Mooney takes cream and sugar, same as me.

So. Harold wouldn't have been too surprised when I didn't turn up at nine thirty. Harold might have arranged the whole thing so I wouldn't turn up at nine thirty. But why?

I toyed with my cup. "This Woodrow, he happen to see me?"

"He wasn't home."

I licked my sugary fingers, thought fast. "Where was he?" Out with the girl friend, I'd bet.

"Nobody thinks he trashed his own place, Carlotta."

"The cops actually went out and looked?"

"Yeah."

"So why don't they think he did it himself? Because he's a big shot?"

"Damage."

"He's probably insured." I caught a chunk of my lower lip between my teeth, worried it. Who'd break into Harold Woodrow's house? Kids out for kicks? Professional burglars? Someone who wanted whatever material Emily was supposed to send me?

"Let's talk about you instead of him," Mooney said.

I sipped coffee that was too hot to taste.

"He named you," Mooney went on when I said nothing. "Gave the cops your address and phone number. One of the guys knew me. Otherwise you'd be making the acquaintance of the Winchester lockup."

"Did I take anything, or was I just out burglarizing the homes of the well-connected?" I asked. "Does that mean mob-connected, by the way?"

"Government-connected. Important-people-connected. He's a lawyer."

"Yeah, and we all know no lawyers are mob-connected."

"Woodrow told the locals his wife hired you to keep tabs on him."

It made me angry; it really did. Here I'm prepared to spend time in jail to shield Emily Woodrow, and her husband goes and loudmouths his jackass theories to the cops.

I managed a smile.

"Did Emily Woodrow hire you?" Mooney asked.

I was sure he'd heard about the thousand bucks, maybe even seen the cancelled check. "What if she did?"

"Then you make the connection between the Woodrows and Tina Sukhia, right?"

I kept silent.

He leaned back in his chair, big feet on the desk, hands clasped behind his head. "I talk to this Woodrow on the phone, drop the name 'Sukhia,' and he hesitates, says Sukhia might have been a nurse at JHHI. Well, I know damn well she was. So I figure maybe his wife wasn't paying him much attention while their kid was in the hospital, and maybe he got together with Sukhia, who was no bad-looker. The wife guesses something's wrong, hires you, and you tell her about it."

"Good figuring," I said. "Why did I break into the house? I forget."

"Can't you just talk to me? Aren't we on the same side here?"

"What side is that?"

"Somebody killed Tina Sukhia."

"Or maybe she killed herself," I maintained, although I was less and less inclined toward that theory.

"I don't buy it."

"Intuition?" I asked.

He stuck his tongue out, gave a halfhearted raspberry. "I have to take an educated guess," he said. "Nobody's gossiping in my direction."

"What do you expect? You look like a cop," I said. "I wish you'd brought me another doughnut."

"I want to know where your client is."

"So do I."

"Come on."

"You never believe me when I tell the truth."

"Sure I do. Try it."

"Let's trade." Mooney and I have an ongoing, years-long game of *Let's Make a Deal* in progress.

"What?"

"You wouldn't have left that folder on your desk if you didn't want to tease me."

"Maybe I've got zip."

"Maybe I don't know where my client is."

We stared at each other.

"Even exchange?" I said.

"I'm not giving gifts."

I smiled at him. "Keep your precious file sealed. Just answer a few questions. Appease my curiosity. Tina stopped working at JHHI. Why?"

"Resigned."

"Not fired?"

He considered it. "She left pretty quickly. Could have turned in her resignation under pressure, I suppose. But I've read the letter on file. Nothing unusual."

"She have a new job?" I made it casual, like I'd just thought of it as a possibility.

"Told the boyfriend she did." There was something in his voice, hesitancy beyond his usual circumspection.

"Lying to him? Maybe stepping out?"

"She was earning money, getting paid a lot. And get this: no pay stubs. No checks. Cash."

Damn. I wanted an address for the elusive Cee Co. Did they even exist?

"Maybe she was more than stepping out, maybe she was hooking," I said, just to keep talking.

He scribbled a note on a scratch pad. "I'll have Triola run escort services. But a nurse hooking? I figure cash payments, plus location of death, makes it swiping drugs from the hospital."

"If that's why she was fired, for stealing, they'd tell you, wouldn't they? Once she was dead."

"Hospital pharmacies aren't corner drugstores, Carlotta. Somebody knows the right procedures, the right computer codes, they could probably steal a hell of a lot before they got caught, if they ever got caught."

"Sukhia was a nurse, not a pharmacist. Would she know?"

"Computers are computers. If one person can rig them one way, another person can rig them another way."

"You got somebody checking?"

"My turn. Is the Woodrow guy telling the truth?"

"About me breaking into his house? Forget it. Was anything stolen?"

"He doesn't think so. Is he telling the truth about why you were hired?"

I exhaled, waited.

Mooney smiled. "The romantic link to Sukhia, it's crap, right?"

"Intuition, Mooney? Instinct?"

"Better than that. Here, take a look." He grabbed a flimsy sheet of paper out of his top desk drawer, flapped it in front of my face. "You're gonna love it."

"What is it?"

"Read it. Take your time."

It was a photocopy of a typewritten note.

The salutation was heavily inked out, so heavily I didn't think even the police lab could make heads or tails of it. The meat of the message was simple:

SHE WILL LIVE WHEN YOU ALL DIE!
THERE IS NO PRICE FOR LIFE BUT DEATH.
TORTURERS. KILLERS. MURDERERS.

"You met the Woodrow woman," Mooney said evenly. "Did she write that?"

"How would I know?"

"She seem okay? She seem odd?"

"Her daughter died."

"According to the husband, she sees a shrink."

"That doesn't make her a psycho."

"Read it again. I'm glad I'm not a doc at the hospital where her kid died. Or a nurse, like Tina Sukhia."

I shrugged. "Where'd you get the note?"

"One of Muir's partners. Man named Piersall."

I hadn't seen Piersall. Could he have been the man in the white coat who pushed Emily Woodrow out of her daughter's room?

"He the only one who's received a letter?"

"Only one who's told us about it." He lowered his voice. "I need to find that woman, Carlotta. I don't like how the note says, 'you all,' like she's planning more than one death here."

I didn't like it either.

"I don't know where she is, Mooney."

"Convince me."

"Ask her stupid husband how many times I've called, trying to reach her. Ask the jerk if she's written me any more checks. He keeps tabs on her checkbook."

"What did you tell her about Tina Sukhia?"

"Nothing."

"What did she tell you about Tina Sukhia?"

"Nothing."

"I ought to let Winchester lock you up."

"You'd have to look after Paolina."

"This Woodrow woman gets in touch, you call me."

"Right."

"I didn't book you. I didn't read you your rights. I didn't embarrass you in front of Paolina—"

"I'll call you, Mooney. The minute I hear. And you?"

"Me?"

"Are you looking for Emily Woodrow? Hard? Is there an APB? I'm worried about her. Honest-to-God worried."

"If you were so worried, you should have named her yesterday."

Somebody banged loudly on the door, opened it before the echo died. "Oh, hi. Didn't know anyone was in with you. Maybe I'll—"

"Wait," Mooney said. "You get the lab report?"

"That's why I'm here."

"Those spots on her dress, they get a reading on those? Blood?"

"Rust," the man said. He was slight and thin. His moustache drooped. "Common rust."

"Rust," Mooney repeated. "Thanks. I'll catch the rest in a minute."

The man shrugged, closed the door.

"Tina Sukhia?" I asked.

"Yeah."

"Rust on her dress?"

"A few spots. In front, near the hem. That suggest anything to you?"

"What color dress?"

"Tan, beige, sorta light brown."

I thought it over. Maybe nothing more than a lousy dry cleaner. "No," I said.

"Too much to ask," he muttered.

"You have time to run that guy for me? Sanchez?"

"The Firebird guy? He's clean," Mooney said.

"Just hasn't been caught yet," I corrected him. "Mooney—"

"What?"

"Is there really a warrant out on me in Winchester? Are they going to pursue this? I need to call my lawyer, or what?"

"You got an alibi?"

"Yeah."

"Good one?"

"Yeah."

"The Gianelli guy?" Mooney stuck his chin out. He doesn't approve of Sam.

"Gianelli," I admitted.

"Well, I might be able to kill it."

"Why don't you do that?"

"As a favor," he said.

"Does that mean I'll owe you?"

"A very big one. Keep it in mind."

27

Paolina, full of doughnuts and good cheer, chatted with the desk sergeant while I dropped change into a pay phone and placed a call to Woodrow's house.

He'd involved his wife in a murder investigation. And he'd been worried about *me* being indiscreet.

Was he just stupid and angry, or worse?

Had someone actually broken into his home? Why?

I'd intended to search the house. Armed with the now-useless threat of police involvement, I'd planned to check whether Emily had left any vital information under her mattress. Had someone beaten me to it?

"Come on," I ordered the ringing phone.

Woodrow didn't answer. And if he had, he'd probably have hung up at the sound of my voice. I cradled the phone in disgust. I'd have to drive out there, maybe break in after all. If you're going to do the time, you might as well do the crime, I thought.

I got the number of Harold's law firm from Information. A snotty-voiced clerk who informed me that Mr. Woodrow didn't wish to be disturbed, reluctantly took a message.

I couldn't involve Paolina in a Winchester trip. I'd promised Marta I'd have her back in the morning, and it was almost noon.

I glanced at my little sister, grinning and joking with the sergeant, so far removed from the waif of last night. A quick-change artist.

Maybe if Emily Woodrow had been younger when her daughter died, she could have made the adjustment. Younger, she could've had another child.

I stared at Paolina. If something had happened to her, if she'd caught her plane last night, vanished entirely—

"Come on," I said to her, my voice rough. "Your mom's worried about you."

I rang Marta's buzzer as a formality. Paolina's got a key. She used it and we ascended the steps in silence. I could hear the TV from the landing, even louder than usual.

Marta staggered to the door as we entered, in a torn nightgown, her long hair uncombed. Murmuring in Spanish, she lunged to hug Paolina, missed, and landed on the floor, a tangled heap of arms and legs, making a keening noise somewhere between laughter and tears. Her unfocused eyes stared at an unseen horizon.

"Mama, Mama, what's wrong? What's wrong with her?"

I thought she was drunk, so I didn't answer. I knelt near her head, bent forward, and tried to sniff her breath. Sour, but no trace of alcohol.

"Marta!" Her eyelids fluttered. I found her pulse, which seemed strong, arhythmical.

"*Creo que esto enfermo,*" she mumbled.

"Is it your stomach?"

"*No. Sí.* I get *pastas. Estómago.* They say maybe is *úlcera.*"

"What pills?"

She waved an arm in the direction of the kitchen, then clutched her stomach. "*Por favor, llame al médico.*"

"Paolina, see if you can find a new pill bottle. It'll have the doctor's name on it. I'll get her into bed."

"She's not gonna—"

"She'll be okay," I said as reassuringly as I could.

Marta's sudden full-blown laughter was more disconcerting than weeping. Scary. She looked like a harpy, like a Victorian caricature of a madwoman, all snaky hair and crimson fingernails and white nightgown.

"See what's on the kitchen counter," I urged Paolina. "Maybe she took too much of whatever it was."

Marta babbled and giggled while I half carried her into the

other room and tucked her into bed. Her forehead was icy. She stared at me as if she didn't know me, called me Lilia. Abruptly she threw all the bedcovers on the floor.

"*Muy calor*. I'm hot," she said. "Freezing hot."

"Here." Paolina rushed in, speaking fast. "It's a doctor I never heard of."

"Call four-one-one and get his phone number," I said.

"Is she—?"

"She'll be fine. Call." I humped the sheets and blanket back on the bed, made soothing noises, and hoped the phone company had delivered on its promise.

"I called," Paolina said, five long minutes later, on the verge of hysteria. "He's on hospital rounds. He'll call back."

"Let me see the bottle."

I read it and something clicked.

Marta seemed calmer. "Sit with your mom for a minute," I said. "I'm gonna make a call."

Paolina, her cheeks pale, was far too quiet and obedient.

I grabbed the pill bottle from her unresisting hand.

Information gave me Donovan's number quickly. Maybe they heard the urgency in my voice. He did.

"What's wrong?"

"Xanax. You gave it to Emily Woodrow."

"So?"

"What is it?"

"It's a tranquilizer. A benzodiazepine."

"A friend of mine went to a new doctor who said she had an ulcer. She's got rheumatoid arthritis, too, and she takes a lot of drugs that hurt her stomach. He gave her Xanax and now she's talking crazy and she doesn't know who I am."

"Wait a minute. She said Xanax, not Zantac?"

"I'm holding the pill bottle in my hand."

"Which?"

I spelled it.

"Shit. She got the wrong one. Maybe the doc wrote illegibly. Maybe the pharmacist screwed up."

"She's hot and cold and confused as hell."

"Look, Xanax is like a big aspirin. It's mild. It's almost impossible to OD on Xanax."

"She said her stomach hurt pretty bad."

"Count the number of tablets."

"There're a lot of them."

"Count them!"

Eleven were missing.

"Get her to an ER," Donovan said.

28

I don't recommend visiting both a police station and a hospital in the same day.

Mass. General made the cop house look both efficient and humane. Of course, if I'd entered the police station under arrest, I'd probably have had a different take on the situation. In the emergency room at MGH, Marta came off as a prisoner.

Nothing against the individuals—the nurses couldn't have been nicer, even the ones stifling exhausted yawns. A young Hispanic woman with placid brown eyes took Paolina under her wing while I answered questions and filled out forms and waited, waited, waited. The doctor, once we saw one, clucked sympathetically. I found it amazing, considering the surrounding sights and sounds, that he could still summon sympathy.

Overnight hospitalization was recommended. Observation. An unusual reaction, white-coated strangers declared. Definitely atypical. No acute danger.

Words I didn't understand floated past my head. Alprazolam and Ranitidine. IV infusion and polypharmacy. Codes and colors were called over loudspeakers. Beepers bleeped, and machines that looked like they'd be at home in spaceships flashed their lights and sang electronic songs.

I dropped change into a pay phone. Lilia swallowed her indignation and agreed to fetch and temporarily care for Marta's boys. The sour-voiced receptionist at IWP insisted that Harold Woodrow was still unavailable. In a meeting. Again.

"An in-house meeting?" I inquired.

"If you don't wish to leave a message, you might try again in an hour," she said, slamming the phone down before I got a chance to reply.

It was past four o'clock. I wondered if she would deign to pick up the phone after official quitting time. I checked the street address of Irwin, Woodrow, and Place, Attorneys-at-Law, in the Boston directory. Then I hustled back to Paolina.

The Hispanic nurse nodded vigorously when I said it was time to leave. Her mother would be in the best of hands, she assured Paolina, and when her own shift ended, she'd make sure that responsibility for Marta's care passed to a Spanish-speaking night nurse.

"*Gracias,*" Paolina said.

"You're terrific," I added. "Thanks."

Paolina denied any hunger, but I stopped at a nearby Burger King anyway, ordered a bagful of assorted takeout.

"Where are we going?" she finally asked, settling back in the passenger seat and glancing out her window for the first time in ten minutes.

"Nowhere," I said disgustedly. We were crawling up Huntington Avenue behind a loaded Green Line train, at rush hour, an experience to be avoided. Traffic was snarled as Northeastern students tagged across the street like a flock of abandoned sheep.

"You okay, Paolina?" I asked.

"Yeah," she replied, her voice unsteady.

"Your mom will be fine."

"Yeah."

"You feel okay? Cramps?"

"No."

"Look," I said, "I've got a problem. I don't want to drop you at Lilia's. I don't want you to be by yourself—"

"Why can't I stay with you?" she asked quickly.

"Exactly. I want you to stay with me. But I have work to do, and it's not the kind of thing where I'd normally take you along."

"Is it dangerous?" She perked right up; I knew she would.

"Boring, more likely. Here." I groped in my purse, handed

over my case notebook. "This should be on page three or four. Read me the make and license plate number for any car registered to Harold W. Woodrow. Do you need the overhead light?"

"Not yet. He a crook?"

"Not that I know of, baby."

"I wish you wouldn't call me baby."

"I won't. I'm sorry."

"Two cars," she said, wrinkling her forehead over the scribbled notes from my conversation with Patsy Ronetti. "A BMW seven-three-five-I and a Saab nine-thousand. Rich guy?"

"Lawyer."

"We going to his house?"

"His office. The slow way."

"Why?"

"To see if he's there."

"Is he a bad guy? Is he doing something bad?"

"I have to keep secrets in my business, Paolina."

"Oh," she said, disappointed.

"But, if you want to, you can help me out."

"And stay with you?"

"Sure. As long as you do exactly what I say."

"Deal," she said.

Most Boston law firms, I wouldn't have had a chance. They're huddled around Federal Street, jammed close together with no parking, except for the major underground lots. But IWP has offices in a converted brownstone on Newbury Street—very tony, very quiet, with private parking off the back alleyway.

Once I abandoned Huntington, the crush eased. I semicircled the Pru and eased onto Boylston, turned left at Berkeley, passed Newbury, turned left again.

I drove behind the IWP offices, not too slowly. The alley was a one-way affair, wide enough to admit a garbage truck. The mouth of the tiny parking lot was visible, but not the cars.

"Okay," I said to Paolina. "You know the plates?"

She rattled off two sets of six numbers and letters.

"This lawyer might recognize me," I said. "So I'm gonna send you instead. I want you to walk back as far as the lot, stop, and look around like you're lost."

"Okay," she said.

"Be casual about it. Don't come racing back if you spot his car. Just decide you're going the wrong way and look at your watch, like you're late."

"I'll be cool," she assured me. And then she was out of the car and walking.

The Back Bay is Boston's safest neighborhood, far less crime-ridden than Paolina's project. Still, I felt funny, sending her like that. Even if it would take her mind off her mother.

I don't think I breathed until she climbed back into the front seat.

"The BMW's there," she said excitedly. "What do we do now?"

"Eat dinner," I said.

"In the car?"

"Don't worry about the upholstery. Ketchup could only be an improvement."

I parceled out wrapped bundles—sandwiches, shakes, and fries —and we ate heartily, having devoured nothing but doughnuts all day. I kept an eye on my rearview mirror and I even rigged up the side mirror so Paolina could assist. And, after a little prodding, Paolina started to tell me more about Paco Sanchez and how she'd met him in the neighborhood, and liked the way he looked at her and talked softly to her and treated her like a grown-up woman.

"Did Paco suggest the plane trip?" I asked.

"No," she said firmly, looking me straight in the eye, which could have meant she was lying. Could have meant she was telling the truth.

"He loaned you money."

"Yeah."

"Why?"

She set her jaw. "Because he likes me."

Sure, I thought.

"Was he planning to go with you? To Florida? To Colombia?"

"He always wanted to visit Colombia," she said defensively.

"You gonna finish your hamburger?"

"You want it?" she asked.

"I'd rather see you eat it."

"I'll get fat," she said.

Fat's good at eleven years old, I thought. Keeps the boys away.

The sky darkened steadily as we ate. By seven o'clock it had turned to navy velvet. If Woodrow worked past eight thirty, I decided, I'd let him go for the night.

"Hey," Paolina said. "Isn't that the car? Yeah. Look. Come on."

"Is he alone?"

"Just him. Hurry up. Aren't you gonna follow him?"

Alone, I thought. Dammit. Then he'd most likely head back to Winchester. If he *was* having an affair, I thought it likely that the object of his affection was an office mate. When long-married men stray, they rarely venture far from accustomed paths.

"Relax," I said, pulling out into moderate traffic. "I'm gonna tail him. A loose tail. Far back. Not like on TV. Just get a clear image of his taillights in your mind, and tell me if you see them turn. You'll be my extra eyes."

"He took a left."

"I'm on him."

"This is neat," Paolina said. "Like a video game."

After two more turns it was obvious that he wasn't heading home. For a moment, I thought he might be driving to JHHI, but he kept on going into the area known as Mission Hill.

"Lock your door, Paolina," I said firmly.

"Where is he? I lost him."

"He took a left. He's doing a lot of zigzags."

"Do you think he knows about us?"

"At night, all he can see is headlights. And headlights look the same," I said, taking my eyes off the target vehicle for an instant to glance at my companion.

She was leaning forward, her eyes sparkling, her lips parted.

Watching her, I experienced a moment of sheer panic: What if she became a cop?

"He took a right," she said. "He stopped!"

I wouldn't have left my Toyota on the street where he parked his BMW, streetlamp or no streetlamp. Maybe he had a fancy alarm system. Maybe he wanted his car stolen.

I drove by as he got out of his car. He bounded up the stairs of a nearby apartment building. He wasn't carrying a briefcase.

I stared at the five-story building. No lights blossomed. Either he'd entered a back apartment, or he was visiting someone whose lamps were already turned on—possibly someone who expected him.

"What now?" Paolina breathed.

I pulled into a slot three quarters of the way down the block, in a no-parking zone. Across the street, a wire fence drooped around an abandoned playing field.

"We wait," I said. "He could be dropping off something on his way home. Paperwork."

I didn't think so. IWP's clientele might own some of the surrounding tenements, but I doubted they'd live here, in a poor, ethnically diverse, racially tense enclave.

We waited almost an hour. He didn't come out. Paolina yawned with increasing frequency. "I'm going to need to go to the bathroom soon," she announced.

"Keep your door locked," I ordered her. "I'll be right back."

I walked purposefully down the block, ducked quickly into the apartment's vestibule, wrote down all the names as they appeared on a row of rusty metal mailboxes. One—Savannah Cates—caught my eye. The rest were men's names. Or initials. Or Mr. and Mrs. So-and-so.

Savannah. I flashed on exotic eyes, tilted eyebrows, an engaging smile. Mooney hadn't been so far off base after all. Harold Woodrow *had* met a woman at the hospital. Not Tina Sukhia, but Savannah Cates, Muir's young receptionist . . .

I drove my little sister home to her suitcase full of crumpled clothes, and held her hand till she fell asleep in the guest room.

I had my shirt halfway over my head, getting ready for my own bedtime, when the phone rang.

Mooney must have found Emily. I grabbed it.

Roz.

"You get my messages?" she hissed.

"Haven't had a minute."

"Dammit, I don't know how much longer I can keep him here."

"Calm down. Where are you?"

"South Station. At the oyster bar."

"Where's old Paco headed?"

"One-way, New York."

"Keep him there."

"Carlotta—"

"I have every confidence in you, Roz."

"Just get here."

"Half an hour," I said. "Bye."

29

I lied. It took me almost an hour, what with changing clothes, waking Paolina, dialing Gloria, making sure Paolina felt okay about staying home alone, assuring her that Gloria was a phone call away.

Oh, and I had to run back upstairs to get the nicely altered passport Paco had been civil enough to drop.

As I drove, I found myself peering down empty cross streets, checking the surroundings the way I used to when I was a cop on patrol. Searching the black-and-white shadows for Emily Woodrow. Wishing I knew her haunts, knew exactly where to focus. Hoping I'd find her before Mooney. Or she'd find me.

Had she killed Tina?

Had Tina killed Rebecca?

Was that what it was all about—an eye for an eye?

Or had a third party killed both Tina and Emily? Tina, for what she knew about Rebecca's death; Emily, because she'd learned the secret from Tina.

I blared an old Taj Mahal tape full volume. The music filled my head, answered no questions.

South Station has been recently renovated. An interior designer crisscrossed the floor and walls with beige-and-raspberry tiles, put in a French bakery, and sold vendor permits to hawkers with cute green carts filled with ties, fudge, and sun hats, as well as toys to bring home to the kiddies. Huge fans did their best to circulate the cigarette smoke and train fumes. You can get your shoes shined, buy a bouquet of fresh flowers and a chocolate croissant. The hurrying footsteps, whooshing doors, groaning diesel engines, and clanging bells are all that remind you that you're not in a shopping mall.

The oyster bar is tucked in a street-level corner.

I recognized a couple of veteran prostitutes right off, old friends I'd rousted years ago, no doubt rehabilitated through the wonders of our prison system and social service agencies. One was giving a brazenly outfitted hooker the unfriendly glare reserved for new talent on already-taken turf.

It took me a minute to realize that the woman of the hour, the one drawing hostile eyes, was Roz.

I guess she figured that with her clothes sense and general flair, there was no point in shooting for subtlety. But green hair, I thought, except on St. Patrick's Day, is going a little far.

Her wig made the stuff they sew on the heads of Barbie dolls look real. Nor had she taken my advice about conservative clothing —not that I'm naïve enough to think Roz possesses a knee-length shirtwaist dress. Her low-cut green taffeta number looked like a fifties prom dress gone astray.

One thing you have to say for her: She didn't look like the shaved-headed, black-clad karate warrior of the airport. No way would Sanchez link the two. Roz wore spike heels to change her height. Glasses completed the ensemble. Harlequins, with rhinestones in the corners.

She didn't look like anyone I knew. Or wanted to know.

"Don't worry, Yolanda," I murmured to the tiny platinum-haired pro. "You are totally out of her league."

"Hey. You back with the cops?"

"Relax."

"No, sugar. You check that babe. She's young and hot and she ain't let go that dude all night. Man couldn't even take a pee if he wanted one. And look at the bod on her. She's messin' up business is what."

"Good," I said. "She works for me."

"You pimpin' now? Hell."

"Yolanda! I'm private heat, and she is, too. Go peddle it someplace else."

"You gonna bring cops on me?"

"You're hopeless," I said. "Go home."

"Spot me twenty?"

"Ten," I said. "Home."

"Later, babe."

I caught Roz's eye and she sagged with relief. I could see her point. Even after Paolina had sung his praises, I couldn't ID the sterling qualities in Paco Sanchez.

Either he hadn't changed clothes since the weekend or he had many identical T-shirts and bagged-out jeans. His five-o'clock shadow had turned into scruffy three-day growth. His eyes looked bloodshot under the fluorescents.

"Hey," I said, approaching Sanchez and borrowing Yolanda's all-purpose greeting.

His face changed when he saw me. He recognized me, no doubt about it.

"Don't go anyplace till we've talked," I said.

"And why the hell not?" he blustered.

"Cause this green-haired lady, the one you been boring to death with your sorry life story, will be glad to kick you where it hurts anytime I say. Right, Roz?"

"How about now?" she said. "What took you—"

"Hang on a minute." I removed the doctored passport from my purse, held it well out of Sanchez's reach. He grabbed for it anyway. "Something you want?" I asked, tucking it out of sight.

"Hey," he said. "Maybe we can deal."

"Exactly what I had in mind," I said. "Roz, why don't you take a walk?"

"Can I stay in sight? Just in case? I'd like to kick him."

"The restroom, Roz. Lose the hair."

"That's a wig?" Paco said. He sounded disappointed.

"Let's deal," I said.

30

Roz disappeared.

"See, I want to understand something," I said to Sanchez, sipping my assistant's leftover Pepsi and thinking that for the day, I was probably well over the maximum daily caffeine intake for a small country.

"I'll bet." His moustache barely moved when he talked. It made me wonder what deformity he was hiding under its bushy growth. "Your friend have to leave?"

"I'll give you her phone number later," I promised, tongue in cheek. "Why'd you boost my garbage?"

He lit a cigarette and I inhaled fumes. "Guy I work for said to do it."

We shared a small round table, the stand-up kind meant for rushed commuters. The bar was empty except for two serious drunks in a corner, a scattering of working pros. "Carl Griffith," I said. "The investigator. He musta been ripped when you took the cans too. You know, stealing the cans makes it sort of obvious."

Paco blew a puff of smoke my way. "He doesn't tell me how to handle it. He kinda leaves stuff like that up to his ops."

I don't mind inhaling smoke. I used to do a pack a day myself, before my dad died. "You started working for him recently?" I inquired.

Sanchez opened his mouth, paused with his tongue sticking halfway out. "Nah," he said.

"Come on," I said. "This your first case?"

"Third," he said, stung.

A miracle he'd lasted this long. "And what about Paolina?"

"Griffith told me to check her out."

"He tell you to get her on a plane?"

"That was her idea," he said. "Honest. I wanted to help the kid out. That wasn't business, that was personal."

Personal, bullshit. Now *I* wanted to kick him. "Who's the client?" I asked.

"Huh?"

"Who's Griffith working for?" I repeated impatiently.

"Lotsa people."

"On the Paolina Fuentes thing."

"He'd kill me."

"He won't know."

"You don't understand."

"I don't want to understand, Paco. I want to know why you gave Paolina money."

"It was a personal loan. Nothing to do with Griffith."

"It probably comes under corrupting a minor. You know what kind of prison time child molesters get?"

"I never touched her. I liked the kid is all. Felt sorry for her."

"Who's Griffith's client?"

"He won't tell me. He won't tell you, either. Man, it's all he talks about, how nobody can push him around."

Sounded like a nice guy. The kind of guy who'd employ a creep like Sanchez. There was an ashtray on the table. Sanchez dropped his ciggie butt on the nicely tiled floor, ground it out with his heel.

"He keeps you in the dark?" I said.

"Hell, yeah, and if I get in any trouble, I'm on my own, too."

"You're in trouble."

"Well, I don't know anything." He gave an elaborate shrug.

"Let's go," I said.

"Go where?"

"Two choices, Paco. And one is the Feds. Passport forgery is Federal, right? As in Leavenworth."

He swallowed, his Adam's apple jiggling up and down. "Uh, I thought you wanted to deal."

"What time does Griffith open his office?"

"Hey, not till late. Not till after noon, at least."

"I don't want to have a lot of conversation about this, Paco. I'm kinda on a tight schedule. The way I see it, if you love Griffith like a brother, and you're gonna get all bent out of shape when I suggest visiting his office after hours, we might as well talk to that uniform over there. I'm sure he can get through to a Justice Department suit who'd love to see how you doctor a passport."

He swallowed again. "Say we do visit Griffith's place. What do I gotta do?"

"Sign in. Sign out. Work the security system. No reason the boss should know about our visit. Then you go back to work for him, you split for New York, whatever you want."

He considered the situation.

"And then you'll give me the passport?"

"I never said that, Paco."

"Come on."

"It's either the Feds or a quick peek at Griffith's files."

Before we left the train station, I found Roz sheltering behind a column and told her to get home to Paolina. Sanchez couldn't pry his eyes off the shaved section of her scalp.

When you work the middle-of-the-night shift, you don't have to worry about parking. I got a perfect slot on Boylston Street, and Sanchez and I strolled into the Prudential Center like buddies, almost arm in arm. I kept the funny passport in my handbag, its strap double-looped over my arm. I didn't trust my new buddy.

Like a lot of office-tower tenants, Griffith had unshakable faith in the building guards, uniformed do-nothings who could be counted on to make sure visitors signed in and out. His office locks wouldn't have baffled a toddler. Even worse, he'd lavished a key on Paco.

How does a guy who employs squirrelly ops like Sanchez rate a plush office in the Pru? It baffles me; it really does. The rents there are astronomical, and Griffith Investigations wasn't squeezed into any broom closet either. My socialist mom would have ranted on about inequality for weeks. Me, I just noted the thick pile carpet, the fancy Roman shades, the leather chairs, and got down to business.

Griffith was an organized bastard, maybe that was the key to his success. He kept his current cases at the front of a tall metal filing cabinet. Six of them. I should be so lucky. I studied the file tabs, spotted no familiar names.

I started with the first file, an assets search for a potentially messy divorce, read it through, looking for my name or Paolina's. Next case, another divorce, I did the same. Third case, also marital.

The fifth file was it. There was my name, heavily underlined. My address. My phone. My Social Security number. The file was headed *Vandenburg*. Some kind of code? No. Thurman W. Vandenburg. Of Miami Beach, Florida.

I glanced at my watch. It reminded me that I needed sleep. "Hey," I said to Sanchez, who was folded into one of the leather chairs, chewing the ends of his moustache. "Xerox machine in here?"

"Yeah."

"What's the warm-up time on it?"

"It's one of those little jobbies. Pretty fast."

"Turn it on and copy this. Don't 'forget' any pages either."

I didn't know a Thurman W. Vandenburg from Miami or anyplace else.

Sanchez did a good job handling the copy machine. Maybe paperwork was his forte.

"Can we get out of here?" he asked when he'd flipped off the machine and tidied up.

"My pleasure," I said.

"I dunno," he muttered, shaking his head.

"You considering calling your boss and fessin' up?" I asked.

"Nah," he said.

"Because you ought to think before you do it, long and hard. If you spill it, I'll tell him you sold me the file. And I'm a good liar. He'll believe me."

We walked out of the building after signing out with the guards. We'd used names other than our own upon entering.

"Now for one last thing, Paco," I said as we reached the sidewalk.

He said, "I'm finished doing business with you, lady."

"My garbage cans, Paco. Where are they?"

"Huh?"

"You using them?"

"I dumped 'em."

"Damn, that is too bad."

"Tough," he said.

"I expected more sympathy, Paco. I was fond of those cans. You know, you can help make up for my loss. True Value Hardware Stores. The gray wheeled cans. Two of them. By tomorrow night."

"You're kidding."

"Tomorrow night is garbage night, Paco. Would I kid about that?"

"You're crazy."

"Yeah." I sighed. "I guess I am. But if I don't get my garbage cans, the Feds get the passport, with your name, and probably your prints on it. They'll ask questions. They won't be as polite as I am."

"Shit," he said.

"Just put them by the side of the house," I said. "No need to ring the bell."

I got in my car and sped away while he was still searching for words.

I don't normally listen to the news. Usually my tape deck goes full blast, but I'd played all my tapes twenty-seven times, so I hit the radio button instead. Not a news station, a blues-and-oldies station. But even they have news breaks and I caught one. I heard talk of the thirty-seventh recent health-care proposal and slaughter in Bosnia. It sounded the same as last week's horrors, so I leaned forward to punch it off.

"A spokesperson for the pharmaceutical firm Cephagen Company has announced that a man shot dead today at the Marine

Wharf Hotel in downtown Boston has been identified as company president and CEO David Menander."

She pronounced Cephagen with a long *E* sound. Cee Co.

More, I commanded silently. More. Come on.

Three teenagers wounded in a drive-by shooting in Boston's Grove Hall area had been taken to Boston City Hospital for treatment. Police suspected gang involvement.

No! More about Cephagen with a long *E*.

The woman's voice slid into the weather forecast, fair and sunny, while rain spattered my windshield.

I drove faster, checking my rearview mirror for cop cars, and hitting fifty in the thirty-mile zones. A Store 24 had one tattered *Globe* left. I hurled my thirty-five cents across the counter top to the bored and indifferent clerk.

It was one of those inside-page late-breaking Metro stories. Splashy because the Marine Wharf is no fleabag, and soft-pedaled because tourists are easily discouraged from spending two hundred a night to endanger life and limb. Hotel PR would have been all over this one. Bad luck, the victim being a notable. That would hinder further efforts to soften the impact. My eyes skimmed the print. Possible robbery of a male Caucasian. Wallet removed. Wristwatch ignored.

I climbed back into the car. Cephagen Company. Cee Co. Cee Co. Pharmaceuticals. They had to be related. Had to be. I drove quickly through the rain. Oncoming headlights dazzled my eyes. My tires squealed on the slick pavement.

At home, all was quiet. Paolina slept.

31

I was tired enough to fall asleep in the car, but I still had one phone call to make—to Mass. General, where according to Patient Information, Marta Fuentes was in satisfactory condition and resting comfortably. "Resting comfortably" had such a nice ring to it that I hurriedly splashed water on my face, brushed my teeth, stripped, and yanked on my in-lieu-of-nightgown tank top. Then I slowed to enter Paolina's bedroom in barefoot silence, listening to her hushed, regular breathing and smoothing the rumpled sheets.

When I do fall asleep, I slumber soundly and rarely remember my dreams. I recalled this one only because the phone woke me before it ended.

"Hello?" The shrill of a phone in the middle of the night summons the elemental power of childhood terror, as well as the adult knowledge that no one calls with good news past midnight.

"Hello," I repeated loudly. The line was open. I heard something at the other end, a crashing sound, then silence.

"Who is it?" I demanded. "Is someone there?"

I muttered a curse and slammed down the receiver.

I could hear the clock tick. Ten past four in the morning. I was drenched in sweat and my pulse drummed in my ears. I gulped deep calming breaths. My throat felt scratchy. Not from an oncoming cold, from my interrupted dream.

I'd been spinning, whirling along with my bed, which floated above the floor, abruptly released from gravity. The sheet and quilt became restraints, imprisoning my arms and legs. The mask had begun its descent, covering my mouth, my nose, choking me, stealing my breath. . . .

Why had I assumed oxygen, air, *anything*, in the mask? Why not the simple absence of air? Nose and mouth covered, airways blocked . . . would Rebecca have lashed out, squirmed, and kicked? Would Tina Sukhia have recognized her distress for what it was? Suffocation.

What it might have been, I amended. I could hardly ask Tina now, and I doubted "suffocation" would appear on Becca's medical chart. I shut my eyes and tried to force myself back into the dream, to view the resolute face above the mask.

When I woke again, my alarm clock was on the floor where I must have hurled it. Sunlight flooded the curtains.

The house was still. Paolina slept, catching up for two late nights in a row. I tiptoed downstairs, brunched at my desk on crackers smeared with peanut butter.

The phone book gave only one number for JHHI. I didn't want Admissions. I didn't want Muir. I didn't particularly want Personnel. I closed my eyes and came up with the name of the floor on which I'd spent so much time waiting: Eastman Two. I dialed and repeated the words to the operator.

I was almost certain the woman who picked up was Barbara, the dragon-lady receptionist. "May I speak to Miss Cates?" I said clearly.

"Who?"

"Savannah Cates."

"Oh, Savannah. Right. She's no longer with us."

Damn. "Is she ill?" I asked.

"Who is this?"

"Her sister. I've been trying to reach her at home—"

"Can you hold, please?" Barbara said, zapping me into limbo.

She was back in a minute, sounding harried. "Look, Savannah was temping with us. Try her agency, okay?"

The line went dead. There was an S. Cates in the book. I let the phone ring twenty times before I gave it up.

Harold Woodrow and Savannah Cates. An odd couple, but if

Emily had hired me to prove infidelity, I'd have gone a long way toward earning my fee.

I gathered my uncombed hair into a messy topknot and yanked it, leaning way back in my chair and trying to figure a connection between Harold and Savannah that amounted to anything more sinister than sex. Could they have caused Emily's disappearance? Could they be implicated in Rebecca's death?

I didn't see it. Savannah wasn't the white male who'd entered Rebecca's room on her final day. And I couldn't buy Woodrow as the murderer of his own child. Arrogant, self-centered, yes. A killer, no. It was psychologically wrong.

Psychologically . . . I released my hair and hustled upstairs.

Dressed in jeans and my last clean shirt, I pushed Keith Donovan's bell, toe-tapping impatiently until he wrenched the door open with an exasperated grunt. His legs were hairy beneath a blue robe, his feet bare.

He said, "I thought it was the mailman, special delivery."

I said, "I didn't think you'd be sleeping."

"Thursdays," he said. "No patients. You heard from Emily?"

"No. You?"

"No." With that resolved, he hesitated. "Uh, how's your friend?" he asked. "The one with the pills."

"She'll be okay. Pharmacists do that often?"

"Not if they want to stay licensed. But, yeah. There are always a few cases a year, and everybody's got a horror story about some drug sounds like some other drug, and how they were just about to pop a killer dose into somebody's vein when the internal alarm bells went off. I remember—"

"Yeah?"

"See. I'm doing it."

"You get the medical records?"

"I did."

"Can I see them?"

"Right now?"

"Right now," I said. "And I'm gonna need help on the technical stuff. Also now. But I don't mind seeing a doctor in his bathrobe; my doctor's seen me in less."

He shrugged and smiled. "Come in, then. You want coffee?"

"Sure."

"Make some in the kitchen while I pour cold water on my face, okay?"

The kitchen, unlike the foyer and living room, hadn't been renovated or redecorated. I liked its uneven floorboards, battered oak cupboards, and faint smell of cinnamon. Green plants hid some of the cracks in the yellow plaster. One of those automatic-drip coffee makers, bristling with buttons and dials, looked out of place on a countertop. I was hunting for instant and a spoon when he came back, looping a belt through khaki pants.

"You got dressed," I observed. His shirt was alternating bands of tan and blue, with a placket closing. I preferred it to his oxford shirt and tie.

"Professional ethics," he responded with a grin, removing a can of coffee grounds from the freezer. He counted spoons into a filter cone, inserted it into the recesses of the clinically white machine, and pressed buttons. The gizmo gave a contented beep.

"While we're waiting for the coffee, you want to tell me your horror story?" I asked.

"The drug story? It isn't mine. A friend of mine. Anesthesiologist."

"Like Pablo Peña."

"Not him. Somebody else."

"What happened?"

"He had a patient hooked up to a continuous epidural pump. On Fentanyl. For pain. It's a narcotic, side effects are nausea and itching. Had an old lady on the pump, she's complaining about itching. Nurse calls my friend, and he says give her some Narcan. Works out the dose. All set."

"But."

"Gets paged back right away. Lady can't breathe. So my buddy goes to check it out and he finds one frightened old woman. She's more than willing to itch, just don't give her any more of that stuff. So my friend checks, and the nurse didn't give any Narcan, she gave Norcuron."

"Close," I said.

"Norcuron is used to paralyze patients during surgery. Pharmacist had no business even delivering it to a nursing floor. Sent up ten vials of the stuff, enough to kill everybody who itched and then some. See, Narcan's a liquid and Norcuron had just switched over to liquid, and there was a mix-up. There's always a new form of a drug coming out. Always something new."

"Nice story," I said. "Remind me to stay out of hospitals."

"Advice I try to follow myself," he said.

"Where are the records?" I asked.

He walked toward a small desk. "I left them down here. You know it was hard enough getting access. Copies were a bitch."

"I'm sure you did a great job."

He offered me a stack that must have been close to a foot high. "I pulled five files."

"Five?" I said sharply. "I asked for three."

"Five fit your specs."

"You're telling me *five* kids died in a small hospital on the same day and nobody rang the alarm?" I asked.

"I'm not telling you anything," he said. "I'm just handing you some extremely private files."

"This looks like fifty files, not five."

"Disease generates a lot of paper."

Each file consisted of an unburst sheaf of computer printout, with MEDICAL RECORDS, JHHI, 259 LONGWOOD AVENUE, BOSTON, MA 02117, DO NOT REMOVE, at the top of the first page.

I read the names of the dead in alphabetical order:

Avalone, Renee F.
Eaton-Fitzgerald, William P.
Milbury, Heather C.

Schulman, Justin A.
Woodrow, Rebecca E.

"Common factors," I murmured, sitting unbidden at the kitchen table. "I need common factors."

"That's how I yanked these," Donovan protested.

"All acute lymphoblastic leukemia patients, and they all died at JHHI on the same day. I know. But I need more."

After each patient's name, age was noted, then date of birth. Renee Avalone had lived the longest. She'd been eleven, almost twelve—the same age as Paolina—when she died.

I'd started with a question: Why had Rebecca Woodrow died? It was no longer that simple. Not "Why this child?" but "Why these children?" Not "What could Rebecca have heard or seen or done?" but "What could these children have heard or seen or done?"

Please, I thought. Please, let me find it in the files. Let me not have to interview Heather's mom, William's parents, Renee's loved ones.

People think the hardest part of being a cop is shooting it out with bad guys on some dark street corner. The toughest thing I ever did when I was on the force was tell a dazed woman kneeling by the side of a busy road that her four-year-old had been hit by a car.

"But he's okay," she'd insisted, even though she must have seen what I'd seen, known the truth. "He's going to be okay." She wouldn't let go of my arm. I remember she wouldn't let go of my arm.

"You all right?" Donovan asked.

I tapped a finger on the laminated table top, found it reassuringly sticky. "Yeah," I said quickly. "I'll need a list of all medical personnel in common. And treatments in common, and drugs in common. It was on my mind with my friend and the Xanax–Zantac thing, even before you told about your Narcan–Norcuron mix-up. I want to know if they all got the same drug or the same combination of drugs on the day they died."

His phone rang. "Damn," he said, making no move toward the wall-mounted instrument. "Ignore it."

"Why?"

"It's another hang-up. I've been getting them all morning."

"I got another one last night. Answer it, okay?"

He picked up the receiver.

"Hello?" He shook his head and made a face, repeated his greeting, then said, "Nothing."

"Can you hear breathing?" I asked.

"Not now. Dial tone."

"Could it be Emily?"

"Emily? I hadn't thought of it. I don't know . . ." Almost to himself, he murmured, "What do hang-up calls mean?"

"You're the shrink," I said.

"Rhetorical question," he responded dryly. "Sometimes I can't help myself."

"If I'm after a runaway," I said, "I'll put a trace on the home phone. The kid'll always call. Won't talk, but she'll call. Just to hear Mom's voice."

"Reassurance," he said.

"What else?"

"Hate calls, love calls. Annoyance calls. Anything you can imagine, people do."

"Anything that would fit with what you know about Emily?"

"I don't know enough about Emily."

"Look, I saw her for fifteen minutes," I said. "You've been her therapist more than three months. You have to know more than I do."

"Three months. Twelve weeks: a scratch on the surface with someone as reserved as Emily."

"You found her reserved? Cold?"

"Afraid. Maybe shy is a better term," he said, sitting across from me at the table. "I don't mean that she was afraid of anything specific. More frightened of life, which isn't unusual in someone who's experienced a devastating loss. She felt out of control. Lost in space. If Rebecca could get leukemia and die, she saw no reason why Harold wouldn't crack up the car on the way home from work. She expected to be struck by lightning."

"She had been."

"Exactly. It was like trying to convince someone who's been mauled by a shark that there are really very few sharks in the water."

Each file was divided into sections with subheadings: *Diagnoses and Notes, Hospitalizations, Therapies, Test Results, Internal Consultations.*

"You know," Donovan said, frowning, "I don't think Emily's fear started with Rebecca's death. I think she was timid before that."

"Why?"

Frowning, he laced his fingers together and rested them on the table. "I'm speculating now, but if she hadn't married Harold, she'd probably have stayed out of sight, hidden behind that camera of hers."

"Her camera?" I said.

"Emily Ruhly, she was. E. J. Ruhly. Ever hear of her? She took pictures—you probably saw some of them. Studies of migrant workers, Native Americans. I guess you'd have called her a photojournalist. She didn't keep up with it after she married. Harold objected to the hours and the travel, and then when she had Rebecca, she gave it up entirely."

The snapshots. So clear, so sharp, so illuminating. And yet, there was nothing in her photos of Rebecca that I'd have labeled *technique*, nothing that cried out *professional*. No tricks. Just the child, caught at the perfect moment.

"Very shy people sometimes become addicted to cameras," Donovan went on. "Or sketchbooks. It's a way to shift the eyes of the world away from themselves. To stay in the background. Oh, I know it smacks of dime psych, but the obvious is sometimes true."

My gut reaction was: Patsy Ronetti never told me, damn her! She'd never come through with the promised employment check on

Emily. My second reaction was to examine my first: If Patsy *had* told me, would I have given more credence to Emily's story? Was unfocused speculation from a mother less believable in my eyes than unfocused speculation from an ex-professional photojournalist?

"Coffee," Donovan said.

"Thanks. I need it. I mean, I'll need some before tackling these. Rebecca's file alone is what? Two-and-a-half-inches thick. It's . . . daunting."

"She was sick for months. She put in a lot of hours at JHHI." So had Emily Woodrow. E. J. Ruhly.

"All you really need to focus on is the end," Donovan said. "Right? The final day."

"Maybe."

"They all died from complications of ALL," he said.

"On Becca's death certificate, it lists ALL and then something else. Sepsis. What's that?"

"Septic shock. Bacteria in the bloodstream."

"What would cause it?"

"Sepsis? Contamination of some sort."

"Would it kill somebody quickly?"

"That would depend on all sorts of things."

"Is sepsis unusual?"

"I don't study death certificates. I'd certainly expect the hospital to check it out. Hospitals have review boards, morbidity and mortality reviews, all sorts of governing bodies."

He drank coffee and I read. It was slow, tortuous going, like reading a foreign language, jammed with multisyllabic words I had to break down into parts before they yielded information.

"Hepatic," I said. "That's liver, right?"

"Pertaining to functions of the liver. Maybe I should cook some eggs." He didn't sound enthusiastic at the prospect.

"Don't bother on my account."

"Coffee cake?"

"Sounds great."

He pulled a Sara Lee ring out of the freezer, started messing with the microwave oven while I waded through sentences laden with *extravasation* and *myelosuppression.*

"Alopecia," I said.

"Hair loss," he countered.

"Couldn't they just say that?" Several times I came close to quitting in a fit of frustration, but strong coffee and the aroma of defrosting coffee cake glued me to my chair, and I soldiered on. Occasionally I asked a question, and Donovan gravely responded.

If I gave up on the files, I'd have to face the bereaved families, rip away stitches on wounds that had scarcely crusted over.

"This," I said into silence. "What is this?" I must have spoken loudly. Donovan gave me a look.

"What? Cephamycin?" he said. "I think it's a chemotherapy drug."

"Who makes it?"

"You mean who manufactures it?"

"Where does it come from?" I said, very slowly.

"I don't know. Here. Look it up in the PDR."

He handed over a hardbound *Physician's Desk Reference* the size of the Yellow Pages, but heavier, with tinier print. I located the drug but got bogged down on "cytotoxic anthracycline antibiotic."

"What's a naphthacenequinone?" I asked, murdering the pronunciation.

He made a wry face. "Go to the beginning of the entry for the name of the lab."

Cephagen. The Cephagen Company. An Orlando address.

"Keith," I said, very quietly. "The president of this company was killed in a Boston hotel yesterday."

"Killed?" he repeated.

"How do you administer Cephamycin?"

"Give me the book."

"With pleasure."

"Here," he said after a long two minutes. "Intravenous. 'Slowly administered into the tubing of a freely running intravenous infusion of Sodium Chloride injection USP or five percent Dextrose injection USP.' "

"Huh?"

"In an IV drip," he said.

"How's Cephamycin packaged?"

"Let me check." He ran his fingers over the three-columned page, dense with print. "Two ways. As a liquid, you can get it in ten-, twenty-, or fifty-milligram vials. And it comes in a powder, too. You reconstitute that."

"If contamination—sepsis—was in an IV drip, how long would it take someone to die?" I asked.

"If the contamination were in an administered fluid—which would be extremely unlikely—the patient would get shaking chills, spike a high fever, blood pressure would drop. The patient could die within hours, sooner."

"Can I make a phone call?" I asked. "Long distance?"

"Help yourself."

My fingers hit information for area code 407, and I requested the number of the Cephagen Company.

"Cephagen. How may I direct your call?" The receptionist was female. She sounded both harried and hostile.

"Sales, please."

"We are not accepting any calls from the press." She practically spat out the last word.

"No, no, nothing like that," I said. "This is Diana Hudson. We've talked before. I'm calling from the JHHI pharmacy. Boston."

"Oh." She sounded only slightly mollified.

"Things must be really hectic there," I went on, oozing sympathy. "I hate to bother you with this. I'd call another time, but you know how it is, everybody wants things done yesterday."

"I think Mr. Knowlton is in."

"That would be great. Thanks."

He came on the line with no further secretarial interference. A gentleman pretty far down in the food chain, I guessed.

"Knowlton," he said. "How may I help you?"

I gave the Diana Hudson name again, the JHHI affiliation, the apology.

"What do you need?" he said, apparently taking me at my word.

Encouraged, I went on. "It's not an order, Mr. Knowlton. We're, uh, updating our list of approved chemotherapy drugs, with emphasis on ALL treatment. And I'm the lucky one who's supposed to make sure all the spelling's correct before we go to the printer—"

"Hah. Then the printer'll louse it up."

Good. He was buying it.

"I know, but you've got to try, don't you?" I said. "My boss is a real stickler for spelling. So could you please spell out the brand names of any drugs Cephagen would want placed on that list?"

"We just have the one."

"Go ahead."

"It's Cephamycin. I know it as well as my own name, but let me check to make sure. C–E–P–H–A–M–Y–C–I–N. One Y and one I."

"Thanks," I said.

"You're welcome. Good luck."

"Oh, one more thing. A friend of mine used to work for you. She really had great things to say about the company, and how nice it is in Orlando. The weather up here is just vile, you know?"

"Don't tell me. I used to live in New Hampshire."

"Really? Where?"

"Hollis."

"No kidding. I used to date a guy from Nashua."

"I don't miss the winter."

"I'll bet," I said. "Anyhow, my friend had to move away from Orlando, and I was thinking, you know, if her job's open, I'd really like a change of climate."

"What division was she in?"

"Gee, I can't remember."

"Well, hey, Diana—you say your name was Diana?"

"Diana Hudson. What's yours?"

"Peter. But I wouldn't know about job openings. Let me transfer you to Personnel."

"Mr. Knowlton, please. Peter. Wait a second. You transfer me to Personnel, we both know what'll happen, right? They'll just say they're not hiring, or tell me to send a résumé."

"Look, Diana," he said, softening. "I'll try to transfer you to Janet Lee. She's a friend of mine and she might be able to help."

I hung up on him. Then I quickly placed the call again, going through the same harried receptionist. "Personnel," I said this time.

"To whom may I direct your call?" She was really trying to weed out the uninformed.

"Janet Lee, please." Names are power. Any good skip tracer knows that.

When I got through to Lee, I immediately mentioned Peter Knowlton, and repeated my tale. She wasn't from New England. We had less rapport.

"We're not hiring," she said flatly. Careful, I warned myself. Don't push too hard.

"Well, this wouldn't be like new hiring, this would be just replacing somebody who left."

She relented. "What was your friend's name? At least I can check the department, to see if they've already filled the requisition."

"Tina Sukhia."

A pause, then, "That name's not familiar."

"Well, I'm sure she said Cee Co. Pharmaceutical research."

"That's what we do. Sukhia?"

It was my turn to spell. "S-U-K-H-I-A."

"Sorry," she said after a long interval. I could hear the quick clicks as she punched away at her computer terminal. "No one with that name has ever worked here."

I hung up.

"You're a good liar," Donovan said.

"And I'm comfortable with violence. An attractive combination."

"I think so," he said.

"But you haven't acted on it."

"You're the one who said to cool it. Until Emily's found. I took you at your word."

"Good. I like to be taken at my word."

"You don't look happy," he said.

"Shrinks are certainly perceptive."

"And we love to be called 'shrinks.' "

"Tina Sukhia is not the connection," I muttered.

"Still think there is one?"

"Yeah." But only Emily Woodrow knows it, I said to myself.

I left him, taking the files and an extra napkin-wrapped slice of Sara Lee with me. Now, I thought, would be a terrific time for a fat special-delivery envelope from Emily Woodrow to arrive at my front door.

Nothing came.

I studied the files, circling all references to Cephamycin. I hammered my fingers on my desk top and yanked at strands of wayward hair.

What did I know?

Five children had died at JHHI on the same day. *Five.*

Three, including Becca Woodrow, had been Tina Sukhia's patients.

Tina Sukhia administered chemotherapy drugs.

Cephamycin was a chemotherapy drug. All five patients had received Cephamycin the day they'd died.

Tina Sukhia was dead.

The CEO of Cephagen was dead.

My fingers moved to my temples and inscribed deep circles. Oh, for Chrisake, Emily, Emily, Emily.

I wished I'd made a copy of the anonymous note Mooney had shown me. *"She will live when you all die!"* Something like that.

Had Emily written the text? Who would die next?

I swallowed. Me. Mooney would kill me.

I took the photocopies of the file I'd lifted from Griffith Investigations out of my handbag. I'd been too tired to read it the night before. I couldn't take time to deal with it now. I stuffed it into a desk drawer. Locked it.

I changed from jeans to dark blue slacks. My white shirt would do, thank goodness. And I had a hat I'd once borrowed from a meter maid and forgotten to return.

I woke Roz. Placated by coffee cake, she agreed to take Paolina out to breakfast, then to the hospital to visit Marta. I admonished her to behave nicely and not frighten the nurses with obscene language or vulgar T-shirts.

"I'll be a good girl," she mumbled sleepily and sarcastically, her mouth full of crumbs.

"Then, if Marta's up to handling Paolina, I have a research job for you. Find out anything you can about a company called Cephagen. Not on any of the exchanges, so they're probably closely held. Offices in Orlando."

"Can I take a field trip?"

"No. And stay awake."

Downstairs, I hurriedly unlocked the desk drawer where I store dangerous or incriminating items, including my unloaded .38. I reached behind it to grab a set of slender picklocks—handcrafted by a former and future resident of the state prison at Walpole— thrust them into my handbag, and raced out to the car.

32

I had to crack my Arrow Street Guide to locate the Woodrow house, a huge mock-Georgian brick set on a couple of gently rolling acres bordering a golf course. Distant marker flags flapped in the breeze.

As a native Detroiter, I'm happiest surrounded by concrete, but I could see the charm of the area. Anyone who looked like Paolina's buddy, Paco, would be arrested on sight here. I, on the other hand, in my uniformlike dark slacks, with my meter maid's hat squashing my curls, would closely resemble the person who reads the gas meter, or delivers the mail.

B&Es, such as the one I now contemplated, are easier to pull off on busy city streets, where no one notices another car parked on a teeming block, a new face in the crowd. Your suburban crook banks on absence and indifference: closed curtains, housewives hypnotized by soap operas, dads and kids away.

I strolled up the walk and pressed the doorbell, feeling like a suspicious person.

Harold Woodrow yanked the door open and put an end to my criminal fantasies. He was dressed for the office, but his navy suit was wrinkled, his expensive tie askew, his thinning hair unkempt. The lines under his eyes had turned to gray pouches. *Pathetic* and *arrogant* don't generally go together, but he managed to look both down-in-the-mouth and insufferable at the same time.

I whipped off the hat and stuffed it under my arm. Maybe it was the shape of his nose that made him seem forever arrogant. I could sympathize with that: I've had my nose broken three times and it may say things about me that nature never intended.

I read recognition in Woodrow's eyes, anger.

"Savannah Cates," I shouted, leaning my weight against the rapidly closing door.

I almost fell into his arms when he suddenly reversed motion. A flicker of uncertainty crossed his face. He made a stab at denial. "Savannah who? What did you say?" He applied pressure to the door again.

I held my ground. "Don't try it," I advised. "Any jury would convict. Guilty as charged."

"What do you want? More money?"

"Let's discuss it inside," I said.

He released a pent-up breath and held the door ajar. "This way," he said tersely, leading me down a long hallway lined with framed hunting prints, into a room shelved with law books and furnished in deep red leather. I sat, without permission, on a buttoned-down loveseat.

"Have you heard from your wife?" I asked.

He remained standing. "No."

"Did you really have a burglary?"

"Someone broke in through the kitchen window."

"No burglar alarm?"

"Emily always sets it. I forgot."

"Let's look at this logically," I said. "If your wife had hired me to break in—to conduct a little asset search, let's say, just in case she were interested in divorcing you—would I need to crawl through the kitchen window? Don't you think she'd lend me a key?"

He contemplated the theory, his lips stretched into a tight line.

"Is anything missing?" I asked.

"I don't think so," he admitted.

"Where did this supposed burglar search?"

"There *was* a burglar, dammit. And he searched this office, for one."

"How do you know?"

"I keep my things extremely neat. Does this look neat?"

It looked average to me, papers strewn on the desk in multiple piles. Stacks of books on the floor.

"What was the burglar looking for?" I asked.

"I have no idea."

"Papers? An address book?"

"I have no idea," he repeated stubbornly.

"Do you keep files from your firm here? Legal documents?"

"My office has a safe."

"Savannah might be interested in your financial situation."

"She doesn't care about money," he said. I didn't see how his lips could draw themselves into a thinner line, but they succeeded.

"Yeah," I agreed. "Absolutely. She seemed like the spiritual type to me. But you probably don't entertain her here, what with a wife and curious neighbors and all. And she might just happen to have a friend in the burglar business."

"You're as bad as that oaf at the hospital," he said. "I consider that a racist remark."

"Which oaf is that?"

"Savannah's a beautiful woman, elegant, passionate—"

"And you'd be proud to introduce her as your bride at the next office Christmas party. I know. And the fact that she works for a temp agency and lives in a tenement, while your present bride has millions, that's never crossed your mind. So let's leave it be, and you answer my question, okay?"

He seemed to consider his options for a moment before angrily responding, "I resent your assumptions."

"Fine with me. Who was this oaf at JHHI?"

He sat on the companion loveseat, deftly yanking the knees of his trousers to preserve their careful crease. "A friend of Dr. Muir's saw us holding hands at a coffee shop near the hospital. An indiscreet bit of foolery. I'd met the man before. Socially and professionally. Renzel, Hank Renzel."

"Professionally?" I leapt on the word. "Does that mean you represent him? Do you legally represent anyone at JHHI? Jerome Muir, for instance?"

"I won't answer that. I won't answer a single one of those questions."

"Did Muir introduce you to Savannah?"

"No."

He'd answer questions, all right. As long as they didn't involve his legal practice.

I said, "Let's get back to Renzel. What oafish thing did he do?"

"Stared at me. Stared at Savannah. He knew us both. He—he shunned us. Like we carried the plague."

"Maybe he has a thing about infidelity."

"He has a thing about race," Woodrow blurted. "Before she started temping, Savannah had a steady job at the pharmacy. Until he forced her to resign."

"Really?" I made my tone skeptical.

My disbelief seemed to loosen his tongue. "He faked an incident, said she miscounted pills on purpose. It happens to every person of color who gets assigned to pharmacy," he finished awkwardly.

It never ceases to amaze me, this man-woman thing, this astonishing chemistry. "Person of color." Even Savannah's choice of words sounded wrong tripping off Harold Woodrow's staid establishment tongue. Oh, I could see what might be in it for him: a fling, a tonic for male menopause, escape from his wife's preoccupation with their daughter's illness and death, a way to forget his own pain at Becca's loss.

For Savannah, what?

"Let me ask you something," Woodrow said abruptly. "Do you think Emily will come back? What's happened to her?"

"I might be able to answer your questions after I go through her things."

"Impossible."

"Do you want a divorce?" I asked. "If she *is* alive, I'll find her. How do you think she'll react when I tell her you're having an affair with the receptionist at the hospital where your daughter died?"

"Get out of my house," he said, but there was no menace behind the words. He sounded exhausted, drained.

"As soon as you let me look through Emily's things."

"Let me understand this. If I allow you to invade Emily's privacy, you'll keep quiet about my, uh, personal business."

"Your wife never hired me to spy on you," I said.

"Why, then? Why did she hire you?"

"I won't answer that," I said, perversely echoing his earlier refusal.

"What could pawing through her belongings tell you? How would that help?"

I got to my feet.

He rose as well, took a deep breath, and stared around his study, seeming to view the disorder as a shambles, the rest of his life as the same. "The room at the top of the stairs to your left," he said.

"I won't be needing your company," I replied.

33

Top of the stairs to the left.

It was a large overdecorated room—finished, perfect, and yielding few signs of human habitation. The queen-size four-poster, shrouded in yellow-and-rust-flecked paisley, matched the chaise lounge and the curtains. The scallop-edged pillows contrasted. The framed watercolors looked as if they might have been selected for an upscale hotel room. Even the knickknacks seemed impersonal, like books chosen by the yard for their attractive spines.

I rested my meter maid's hat on the top of the bureau and started opening drawers.

Emily folded her sachet-scented bras and panties. Organized her closet rigorously by color. Harold maintained a separate closet and dressing room, also unimpeachably neat.

I wondered what Keith Donovan would make of the room. Compulsive personality disorder?

A full-time maid with too much time on her hands, I concluded.

The only papers in the tiny desk, which the decorator had doubtlessly called an "escritoire," were contained in a single drawer and amounted to one box of blameless blue stationery. Two gold pens huddled in a leather case.

Three skin magazines were crumpled at the back of a bedside drawer on what I assumed to be Harold's side of the bed. Very tame stuff.

I worked my way through Emily's scarves and stockings. Her jewelry box, a large leather case, gave me hope, but the only thing I discovered in a promising envelope was a handful of pearls awaiting restringing.

Nothing taped to the bottoms of the drawers. Nothing lurked under the mattress. I ran probing fingers over the back of each picture frame, hoping to find an attached manila envelope.

Where were these documents I was supposed to receive? Did Emily travel with them? I recalled her ultraslim handbag. Did she keep them in her car?

Mooney would be looking for her car.

The master bedroom's medicine chest was packed with over-the-counter cure-alls, vitamins, and bath oils. A muscle in my neck unknotted when I found the prescriptions Donovan had mentioned —Serax, Xanax, Dalmane—all intact, unsampled. I discovered a vial labeled Halcion.

Since the sleeping pill had received such unfavorable press, I counted the Halcion tablets carefully, slowly. None was missing.

I returned to the bedroom, sank into the desk's padded chair, and stared around me.

Was this where Emily had sat while slipping photos of her dead child into blue envelopes? Here, in front of a deep-red paperweight and a chunky crystal vase?

If Emily had wanted to keep secrets from Harold, she'd hardly have hidden them in a room he shared. I snatched my hat off the bureau, plunked it on my head so I wouldn't forget it. I listened for a moment at the head of the stairs, heard no footsteps, and hurried down the hall.

Of seven doors lining the second floor hallway, three were shut. I twisted the handles with care. They opened noiselessly, one to reveal a spacious linen closet, the next, a bathroom.

Rebecca's room had suffered under the same interior decorator as her mother's, resulting in an overblown "little-girl's" room, all pastels and florals. But the housekeeper had been kept away, and a bit of the child who'd lived there remained with the dust.

She'd collected stuffed animals. A large lion crouched in a cor-ner next to a propped-up giraffe and a kangaroo with a baby in its pouch. Smaller animals crowded the bed. Hippos had been a favorite.

A large wooden chair seemed out of place in a corner. I lifted it and found that the marks it left on the carpet were shallower, newer, than the marks left by a nearby rocker, the only other chair in the room. Had someone brought it in recently? Did Emily sit for hours in her late daughter's room?

Did she keep her secrets here?

I started with the bureau, opening each drawer, working methodically, bottom to top, left to right. My fingers sorted through piles of white undershirts, cotton panties, colored turtlenecks. Rebecca's socks were neatly rolled, some banded with lace.

I surveyed a shelf of dolls: worn Raggedy Anns and much-used baby dolls, stiff porcelain collectors' items, foreign figurines in exotic outfits, a row of Barbie dolls with wasp waists and clouds of hair.

Her closet was a miniature of her mother's, color coded, excessively neat. Her shoes were paired: patent leathers, sneakers, tiny pink-and-white saddle shoes.

I sat in the big chair, bit my tongue, and tugged at my hair. The chair was positioned oddly; it faced neither window nor bed. What had Emily looked at when she sat here? Why here?

Was the view unimportant, only the fact that she was in her daughter's bedroom, pretending Rebecca might rush upstairs, home from school, ready to change into play clothes? Did she keep her eyes closed to strengthen the fantasy? To better smell any lingering scent? At seven, Paolina had smelled of cherry Life Savers. Rebecca's room smelled of mint.

I stared at the ceiling and read nothing on its white surface. I glanced down.

Faint tracks led from the foot of the chair toward the closet, as if something had been dragged over the high-pile carpet. I traced the drag marks to a rectangular laundry hamper, hesitated. If the woman communed with her daughter's soiled clothes, I wasn't sure I wanted to know about it.

The hamper was heaped with photographs: scrapbooks, loose snapshots, paper envelopes from Fotomat and One Hour Photo. FREE DOUBLE PRINTS! screamed a coupon. JOIN OUR PHOTO CLUB! I hauled the hamper back to the chair, using the old track marks as a guide.

While Harold went to his office, Emily sat in a straight-backed chair and reviewed her daughter's life. I lifted five fat volumes from the left-hand side of the hamper. A pink and lacy baby book had a brass plate inscribed REBECCA, HER FIRST YEAR. Four subsequent albums in peacock-feather design—one per year—were as methodically organized as the color-coded clothing.

Most parents keep a baby book—even my erratic mother attempted one—but the majority decrease their obsessive photo taking after the second or third year. Emily had never tired of her subject matter. Was she validating her choice of motherhood over career by selecting her daughter as sole model over and over again? By choosing a cheap automatic camera, the kind so many mothers seem to use? By taking her too-well-composed photos to the one-hour developer?

A racehorse hauling hay? A promising poet penning limericks? A labor of love?

I'd leave stuff like that to Dr. Donovan.

I skimmed each book. Rebecca in a swimming pool, supported by a Mickey Mouse inner tube. Rebecca on her first sled, a red Flexible Flyer. Rebecca wearing a bright yellow dress, her white tights bagging at the knees and ankles, holding a toy camera made of bright red plastic, aiming it awkwardly, beaming.

All shots carefully preserved under plastic. I lifted each collection by the binding and shook it. No loose items fluttered to the floor. I stacked the books on the bed, started in on the packets and loose photos. More of the same.

She'd sent me photographs. She'd concealed photographs in a laundry hamper. Before her marriage, photographs had been her life.

I started to organize the envelopes by date, from Becca's final

birthday to her last days. I hefted each packet. None seemed notice-
ably lighter or heavier than the others.

She'd sent me photographs, dammit.

I started leafing through the most recent envelopes, dated just
before Becca's death, working my way backward through her life.

Nothing out of the ordinary. Nothing.

"What—what the hell are you—" I heard Harold Woodrow's
outraged splutter from the doorway. "Who said you could pry
through Becca's—through *her* things? How dare you?"

"Your wife must have had a darkroom," I observed calmly.

"No. Only a bathroom in the basement. And she hardly ever
used it. It smelled the place up. I didn't like it."

"After Becca died—"

"Don't use her nickname. You have no right."

"After your daughter died, did your wife use her darkroom?"

"She might have. Once, twice."

"Recently?"

"Get out of here. Get out. Put everything back exactly the way
it was, and get out!"

His mouth twitched with fury as he spoke. I stuffed photos into
envelopes, dumped them into the hamper, restored it to the closet.

"Before I leave," I said, facing off with Woodrow near the doorway, "I'm going to search the darkroom."

"There's nothing there."

"Not even a shot of Savannah Cates? Bet she's photogenic."

He pressed his lips together, parted them enough to say, "This
is nothing but blackmail. If I don't cooperate, you'll talk."

"At least you've got that straight," I said. "Could you show me
the basement stairs?"

34

If you want to know the age of a house, check the basement. Two hours ago, I'd thought the Woodrow place was practically brand-new. Now I recognized it as a modernization job, a good one. The basement, with its seamed cement floor and exposed beams, its old oil tank in one corner—just in case the modern gas furnace became obsolete—added fifty years.

Down a single step, in a corner that might once have housed a root cellar, a chemical smell oozed from under a partially open door.

If the door had been locked or closed, I might have hesitated, even with the picklocks screaming in my pocket. I don't know much about photography; my workaday needs in that area are met by Roz.

If I discovered undeveloped film inside, I'd need to call her, get her to come over.

Woodrow was sure to enjoy that. I shrugged. Who knew? Maybe a conservative lawyer type like Harold would get a charge out of Roz.

I eased down the step, shoved open the door, and ducked under the low transom.

E. J. Ruhly's career was represented by three newspaper clips, mounted in cheap black frames. As grainy news photos go, they were impressive, but the meager display was hardly in the same league as Dr. Muir's power wall.

I hoped the originals were superbly framed and proudly displayed on the Woodrows' living room walls. I doubted it.

Preconversion, the bathroom had been Spartan, with simple white fixtures, bare-bulb lighting. A sanded plywood workbench had been constructed to fit around the tiny sink, a larger metal sink installed nearby. A second bare bulb, this one red, stuck out of a wall-mounted socket.

Compared to Harold's leather-and-walnut office, Emily's dark-room looked like Cinderella's quarters. Inferior, indeed. Had it angered Emily, this dismissal of her work, this relegation to the cellar, this diminishment of her former career?

Maybe not, but it angered me. I studied the three grainy prints, the cheap frames. I always worry that if Vincent van Gogh had been Virginia van Gogh, she'd have been consigned to paint in the outhouse. Keep all the smelly things together, my dear.

I surveyed the room. It should have been easy going, such a small place. But the various pieces of machinery, of which I could only dubiously identify an enlarger, the shallow trays, the storage bins and files, were foreign to me, hardly everyday stuff like bureaus and desks.

I knew enough not to mess with lightproof envelopes.

There were three of them stacked on the toilet-seat cover. I examined them gingerly. Unsealed.

I flicked off the white bulb, located a second switch, and the room was bathed in a red glow. Now I couldn't inadvertently destroy what I was searching for.

The unsealed envelopes were empty.

Wooden shelves held large tinted-glass bottles. Fixative, developer, unlabeled liquids with sharp and pungent odors. Manila folders contained magazine clips of ancient, abandoned, stone dwellings.

Spider webs filled the corners.

I found the pictures strung like laundry on a line, over my head, across one end of the tiny room. Six shots, six photos that were definitely not of Rebecca.

Were these what Harold's break-in artist had sought?

My hands fumbled with the edges of the first photo. It was small, dark, grainy. The interior of a building. Metal pipes and buckets. Machinery.

I held up the next one. More pipes. Vats and coolers. Hoses. A cement floor with a drain. JHHI? Damn. Weren't there any identifying details in the dim shots? I studied each one. Drains and pipes and vats. No context. No meaning. No words.

I attacked the files. *Artists* consisted of a series of portraits, eight-by-ten blowups of unknown intriguing faces. *Bears* had been shot in zoos. Metal cages loomed and threatened, more terrifying than tooth or claw. No *Hospitals*. No helpful clues. No packets marked: Open in case of my disappearance or death. No explanation of the six photos. By the time I reached *Wampanoog* my fingers were stiff from opening and closing envelopes, my eyes tired of focusing, refocusing.

I flipped the light to full spectrum, blinking rapidly. I took one of the empty lightproof envelopes, tucked the six photos inside, and shoved the thin packet down the waistband of my slacks, snug against the small of my back.

Harold Woodrow saw me out. He didn't seem disposed to chat. As I got into my car, I knocked the long-forgotten meter maid's hat off my head and onto the grass. I retrieved it and stuffed it unceremoniously into the dash compartment.

Maybe Harold Woodrow thought I moonlighted as a meter maid. That could account for his hostility.

35

Before entering my house, I checked the side drive, the yard, even under the back porch where I usually store the garbage cans. No replacements. Was I going to have to send an illegally altered passport to the Feds, live through their intensive questioning, fill out forms for the rest of my life over eighty bucks' worth of trash containers?

I'd been so sure Paco Sanchez would jump at the deal.

One more bright idea gone awry. Now Roz and I would have to stuff the week's garbage into Hefty bags for the dogs to plunder. The neighbors would complain.

I dumped my purse on the hall table with a heavy thud. There were no messages on my answering machine. No packets from Emily Woodrow. Finding Emily was the key, dammit. Were there any bases Mooney wouldn't have covered? He'd check the local hospitals. Airports and bus stations. Credit card charges. The morgue.

If she'd killed Tina, and then killed herself . . . if she'd driven to one of the local beaches, disrobed, and kept on swimming out to sea—stroking, paddling, pushing her endurance until she was too exhausted to turn back, how long could her body stay submerged, undiscovered?

I'm a strong swimmer. When my mom died and I found myself wrenched away from everything I'd known, suddenly propelled from Detroit to Boston, the ocean had almost sucked me down. Dour November mornings, my seventeenth autumn, I'd ride the subway to East Boston, walk slowly to the sandy shore, all the time thinking that I could keep on walking, walking . . . walk till I had to swim, swim in cold, endless green till I'd never have to do anything again.

If Emily *had* killed herself after disposing of Tina Sukhia, then what about the death of the Cephagen CEO? Chalk it up to random urban crime?

Had Emily been murdered like the others?

In the kitchen, I popped the top on a Pepsi. Someone had killed the president of a pharmaceutical lab, a drug company that made a chemotherapy drug, this week of all weeks, in this town of all towns. Cephagen might not have employed Tina Sukhia, but there had to be a connection.

The *Globe* was hiding under the hall table this time; nothing is ever where it's supposed to be in this house. After the first bracing sip, the cola turned unappetizing, so I made myself a cup of instant soup from boiling water and a packet of powder and sat down to learn what I could about Cephagen's late David Menander.

Ringing tributes from colleagues, outraged cries for more police protection, those I could live without. Facts. Where were facts? The who, what, where, when, why journalists used to jam into the first paragraph, and now rarely bother to include at all if juicier details are available. I learned the per-night cost of his plush hotel room before I discovered that Menander had not come here as a tourist.

Body discovered after he'd failed to attend a scheduled meeting at the Jonas Hand/James Helping Institute. If that didn't raise a red flag for Mooney, I'd eat my picklocks.

Who would Menander have dealt with at JHHI? Not peons. CEOs were accustomed to dealing with CEOs. Muir, certainly. Renzel, as Chief of Pharmacy? A humble resident anesthesiologist like Peña?

The police were questioning several unnamed individuals. No one had heard the two shots, which indicated a silencer. A front-desk receptionist thought she remembered that flowers had been delivered to Mr. Menander's room.

As good a way as any to get his room number.

SNAPSHOT

Menander, thirty-nine, had been considered something of a whiz kid, although his company never seemed to take off after the early promise it had shown with the development and marketing of its premier drug, the costly but effective Cephamycin. Menander had been criticized for taking a soft approach to marketing, for keeping the company private, for not raising massive capital and diving headlong into the biotech future. His decision, some years ago, to repackage Cephamycin, using a fancy holographic logo, had been seen as sheer extravagance by several members of the board of directors who'd almost voted him out of office. Others had regarded it as a logical counterattack to the drug-tampering craze that had temporarily driven Tylenol off the shelves. This was from the business section, not the news update.

I finished the oversalted soup, rinsed the cup, shook it dry, and stuck it back in the cupboard. Then, returning to my desk, I spread out my borrowed treasures. Six dimly lit photographs. I rubbed my eyes, shook my head, went back to the kitchen, and burrowed in the fridge till I found the already-opened Pepsi. I ought to buy caffeine pills.

I went over the first photo with a magnifying lens, trying to identify the machinery. The lighting was so bad, the shadows so deep, I couldn't be sure what I was seeing.

Same with the second. Same with the third, although I could sense some order, some setup that made me think of an assembly line. A large metal vat had no visible markings in the fourth shot. The fifth and sixth were even darker and murkier.

Had Emily blundered in taking these shots, or deliberately misprinted them?

Disgusted, I turned them facedown on the blotter, and immediately noticed a legible symbol, a faintly penciled notation in the bottom left-hand corner of the fourth photo.

Tiny numerals: 6, 3, 2. A letter: L. A word: WOOD.

I stared at it until my head hurt, but no illumination came, so I unlocked the upper desk drawer and removed the file I'd forced Paolina's friend, Sanchez, to xerox. Working two or three cases at once isn't bad. When you hit a brick wall on one case, concentrating on the other can free enough brain cells to generate a breakthrough on the first.

Sometimes you just double your frustration level, shoot it straight into the danger zone.

The more I read about Mr. Thurman W. Vandenburg, the bastard who'd hired my garbage thief, the less I knew. An attorney, that most secretive of beasts, he was working for a client named Jaime Valdez Corroyo. Valdez Corroyo was interested in the whereabouts of one Marta Fuentes Giraldo, whom he believed to be his long-lost cousin. A question of inheritance was involved, but while he wished Mrs. Fuentes located, he did not wish to contact her directly. First, he needed assurance that she was not addicted to excessive gambling and drinking, as were so many other members of the Fuentes family. Codicils in the will could preclude her from inheriting if she were a gambler. Therefore it would be best not to raise her hopes until her character and her sources of income were evaluated by a reputable local firm.

Huh?

A list of Marta's "associates" was appended, with an asterisk preceding my name. The client was particularly interested in learning as much about me as possible, including my relationship with Marta's only daughter.

The phone rang. I let it go for three rings, trying to find the magic combination. Maybe the phantom caller would only hang up at the sound of my voice. I lifted the receiver, said nothing.

I heard faint muffled noises, grunts or groans.

"Hello?" I said softly. "Is that you, Emily?"

A slow, seemingly deliberate click.

Damn.

I closed the Vandenburg file, turned back to the photos.

Emily had developed them, therefore they were valuable. They meant something. They were part of the story she needed to tell. I would concentrate on the photos, the location shown in the photos.

632 L wood.

Six thirty-two Longwood Avenue?

Why not check it out? Paolina was safe, either with Roz or with Marta. If Sanchez chose to replace my trash cans, he wouldn't need me to greet him with a brass band.

I already had my picklocks in my pocket.

I sat back in my chair and closed my eyes. Less than a week ago, I'd met Emily Woodrow for the first and only time. . . . So many things remained unseen. Emily's daughter, Rebecca: I'd only viewed her snapshots. Tina: a single photograph. The CEO of Cephagen: a blurred likeness in a newspaper. For a moment the invisible dead seemed more real to me than Emily Woodrow. Through their photographs they had substance, a single frozen form. Emily had moved, walked, talked. Sobbed and whispered. If she entered my doorway, wearing other clothes, would I recognize her?

The intense blue eyes. The terse sudden speech.

"Do you own a gun?"

"Can you use it?"

"Have you used it?"

"Would you do it again?"

While I waited for darkness, I cleaned, oiled, and loaded my .38 police special.

36

Six thirty-two was the place I'd pegged as a former factory, an eye-sore lowering JHHI's property value. I drove around the block, circling it twice, checking the area.

You can learn a lot from looking. Cops who walk a regular beat know who keeps the lights on, who turns them out, who draws the curtains, the angle at which Mrs. Patterson sets her shutters before going to sleep every night at 9:37 P.M. sharp. Especially in small towns, or small neighborhood enclaves, such habits keep the police informed. If I'd known the cops working the medical area, I'd have bought them a few beers and steered the conversation around to 632.

If I'd known them. If I hadn't had the sense that time was running out for Emily.

If again. That ugly stammering word.

Since I saw no beat cop—nor was I likely to see one since most of Boston's patrolmen are locked into speeding vehicles—I decided to pretend that the cop on the beat was me.

I was still wearing my Winchester break-in outfit, so the imper-sonation was fairly convincing. The meter-maid hat had suffered slightly in the dash compartment, but a few pats straightened it enough for night wear. I added a black jacket, one of many articles of clothing I keep in my car, to blend in with the dark and hide my gun.

I strolled the perimeter of the block. Six thirty-two was larger than I'd expected, edging up against the narrow alleyway that ran behind JHHI. While it didn't share any walls with Helping Hand, one forty-foot section almost touched. I wondered if there was inside access from one to the other. An underground tunnel. If so, it might make the property a good acquisition for the hospital.

The front windows were plugged with plywood, crisscrossed with one-by-eight pine planks. Weathered boards. Rusty nails. Dust and cobwebs, dead leaves, and dirt. The front door didn't need plywood; a shuttered metal grille, padlocked and rusty, did the job.

Maybe the Boston Housing Authority had plans to destroy the structure, rebuild from scratch. I wondered when 632 had last been occupied. It was no architectural treasure, nothing worth renovating. Far as I knew, it wasn't an historic site. A few high windows had been smashed and left broken. A bird's nest bridged a gap in a gutter.

Did it already belong to JHHI? Was it awaiting a construction crew? Lying fallow till some golden goose passed on and bequeathed a substantial legacy?

Two winos gave me the eye as they passed. I nodded and one dropped his head in a tipsy greeting.

Instead of walking around the block this time, I found a way to squeeze between JHHI and 632, thinking I might gain access to an unobstructed interior view, a place from which Emily might have taken her snapshots. Why bother to nail plywood across a window that faced a brick wall? Most likely, I'd find no such opeining, but it couldn't be taken for granted. Builders erected their walls not knowing that five years later city planners would turn their picture windows into sunless, brick-view squares.

No window. I snagged my jacket on a nail and had to backtrack to keep the rip from becoming a triangular tear. A sharp smell permeated the narrow space.

I had to hold my breath to make it into the alleyway. The odor almost made me gag. In back, it was better. The windows were boarded and barred. The door mesh-grilled.

Somebody once warned me against learning to fire a gun. If

you know how, he said, you'll do it. Same thing with picking a lock. If you know how, if you take pride in it, you tend to do it. If your day's been frustrating and you don't know where your client is or who's going to sign your next paycheck—well, I admit my picklocks were weighing heavily in both my pocket and my mind.

I glanced right and left. A drizzle had thinned out the foot traffic, and while I could hear the occasional pedestrian, see car headlights shoot by the mouth of the alley, the temptation was high, and the risk seemed low.

The adjoining buildings were so close, so towering, it seemed almost as if I were in an air shaft, concealed by the sheer height of the surrounding walls. I reached in my shoulder bag and grabbed my flashlight, shining it on the back door lock.

It glistened. I knelt in front of the door, my tongue between my teeth, my pulse racing in my ears. The padlock reinforcing the Yale lock was almost new. Underneath it, a tiny plaque had been affixed to the doorjamb with two brass screws. Nothing fancy, the kind of item you could buy in any hardware store. Plastic-covered to keep out the rain, with a slot at the side big enough to insert a business card. DELIVERIES FOR CEE CO., it read in small precise letters.

I stood, ran the light over the edge of the door, felt the hinges. I rubbed my thumb and forefingers together, held them under my nose. Oil. The hinges had been recently oiled. I expanded the circle of light. Fresh tire tracks, deep wide tracks, scored the mud in the alleyway.

I'm not your meet-me-in-the-abandoned-warehouse-at-midnight kind of gal. I'm too tall to play a convincing damsel in distress. I've seen too many horror movies.

Still, I might have gone in. But the edge of the flashlight beam caught the crease of my pants as I got ready to kneel again.

Rust.

Spots of rust.

Like the ones on Tina Sukhia's dress.

Had it been Tina, not Emily, kneeling, camera at the ready?

Tina who'd taken the ill-defined shots? Given the precious film to Emily Woodrow?

I scurried out of the alley, listening for the faintest footfall. I checked the backseat before I got into my car.

No abandoned warehouses, thank you very much.

37

I drove straight home. I didn't even slip my jacket off before dialing Mooney. I tapped my fingers on my desk. Answer, dammit, answer.

Someone picked up.

Mooney was out. Could they reach him? Maybe. Yeah, if it was really urgent, they'd try.

"Have him call Carlotta."

"Yeah."

"Mister, this is not some boyfriend-girlfriend thing. This is business."

"Hey, I said I'd have him call."

"Fast," I said.

Draping my jacket over the back of my chair, I bent over and stared at the six grainy photographs. Rubbed dust off the magnifying glass. Turned on the desk light and edged the photos closer. My .38 dug into the base of my spine. I thought about returning it to the drawer, stuck it into my handbag instead.

I caught the phone before it completed one full ring.

"Mooney—"

"Hey? Hi? You there?"

The voice was slurred, familiar. I couldn't place it.

"Who is this?"

"This is Tony. 'Member? Tony Foley?"

Christ. I hoped he wasn't still at the Hyatt bar.

"Hi. How are you?"

"Rotten," he said with a quick, bitter laugh.

Struck by sudden suspicion, I said, "You haven't been pestering anybody with hang-up calls lately, have you, Tony?"

He stayed quiet so long, I thought I might have hit a nerve. "Tony? You there?"

"Look," he said, "I don't know what you're talking about hang-up calls. Maybe I got something for you. I dunno. Maybe I ought to throw it away, forget I saw it. I dunno what Tina would want me to do. I can't figure it."

"Are you okay?"

"You wanna have a drink with me?"

I glanced at my watch. Past midnight. "Now?"

"Hell, it's nothin'. I'll forget about it. Just make trouble is all—"

"Where are you?" I asked.

"My place. Tina's place."

"I can't leave here," I said.

"Oh, well . . . I'll just toss it—"

"Wait. Is it something you can carry?"

"Sure, but can't you come over here? I'm not feeling real good." Not sounding good, either. Sounding drunk.

"I need to stay by the phone," I said.

"Oh."

"Bring it to me."

"I dunno. I can't really—"

"You won't have to drive," I said quickly. "A cab will pick you up in fifteen minutes. A Green and White. He'll honk."

"A cab? I dunno."

"You won't have to pay," I promised. "Not even a tip. All taken care of."

"Hey, okay! Green and White?"

"Remember, bring it with you."

"I'm puttin' it in my pocket right now."

I dialed Gloria.

Maybe Mooney tried to reach me while the phone was busy.

38

The cabbie honked before discharging his cargo. The neighbors must have loved that, but when I saw Tony's condition I understood. The way he weaved across the sidewalk, Tony was as likely to wander into the bushes for a snooze as he was to ring my doorbell. The warning blast on the horn was pure courtesy.

"Hey," he said, trying not to stumble down the single step to the living room. "Nice."

"I'll make coffee," I said, backing off from a handshake that threatened to turn to a sodden embrace.

"Beer. Ya know, I could use a beer."

"Are you going to be sick?"

"I'm never sick."

"Yeah, well, don't sit on the couch, okay? I had it cleaned once."

Real coffee may taste better, but instant is a blessing. Tony Foley regarded it and me reproachfully. I centered the cracked blue mug carefully on an end table, where he'd be less likely to knock it to the floor.

I said, "Is this important or what?" Maybe the jerk was lonely.

"You're no cop, right?" He made no move toward the steaming coffee.

"I'm no cop."

"Maybe I don't want cops knowin' this, okay?"

"Tony, you phone me for advice at midnight, you gotta let me make the judgment calls."

He leaned back in my aunt's rocking chair and scowled. His eyes were half closed, puffy.

"It would help if I knew what you were talking about," I said.

"Once you're dead, it's over? Right?"

"I'm not in the mood for mind games, Tony."

He got a crafty look in his eye. "Gimme another beer. I'll trade for a beer."

Another beer, he'd probably pass out, I thought. One beer coming up.

He took a long swallow, tilting the Rolling Rock bottle toward the ceiling. A silly grin creased his face and he slumped in the chair.

"Tony, dammit—"

He didn't straighten up, but he opened his eyes. "I done nothin' but drink since I found it."

"Nothing but drink since you found *what*?"

"It doesn't make Tina look too good, you know what I mean? I don't want her mama hearin' this on the news."

"Hand it over, Tony."

The silly grin spread wider. "You wanna fight for it, lady?"

"Hell, no."

"C'mon, let's fight. Jus' wrestle a little, okay?"

"Jesus, Tony. You call me. I pay your cab fare. I bring you a cold beer. Don't you think you owe me?"

He considered it for a while, then stood on shaky legs, and dug his hand deep into the pocket of his stained khakis. "Sorry," he mumbled suddenly, slapping a hand over his mouth, dropping a crumpled envelope to the floor. "Which way's your—"

"Upstairs. First door on the right. Hurry."

I watched him lurch for the staircase. Either he'd make it or he wouldn't. I'd have to have the runner taken off the steps soon anyway. T.C.'s sprayed it once too often.

When I didn't hear any alarming noises, I strolled over and bent to pick up the envelope.

Addressed to the World Health Organization, Berne, Switzerland, it bore no street address, just two lines of block print. I examined the flap. It had never been sealed. Or stamped.

Handwritten in blue ball-point on onionskin sheets, the en-

closed letter could have been a first draft, or it might have been
written in a hurry. How else to account for the corrections and
alterations?

"Dear Mr. _____:" it began. That was crossed out and "To
whom it may concern:" had been substituted.

"Where'd you find this, Tony?" I yelled upstairs.

No answer.

I read:

Why haven't I heard from you? I don't know whether to call
the FDA or the police. Everyone who comes to my door, every
time the doorbell rings, I'm afraid they've come to arrest me.
Then I'm relieved, because if I'm arrested it will be over. And
even if I took the medicine from the wrong place, I know I'm not
really to blame. Dear God, if I could have one moment of my life
to live over again, that would be the one.

Maybe because I took the money, you think I was part of it
from the beginning. Maybe you don't trust me and that's why I
haven't heard anything. But I swear, I never would have taken a
penny if I'd known. To keep quiet about a mistake, that's one
thing. And I was scared for myself, too, scared he'd find a way to
make it seem all my fault.

One of the mothers I mentioned in my first letter is very
persistent, and I think I owe her an explanation.

That entire sentence had been crossed out with a single thin
blue line.

I haven't figured it all out yet, but I'm enclosing part of a
Cephamycin package, the kind that contains 25 mL (50) mg sin-
gle-dose vials. Can you check to see if the seal has been tampered
with in any way? You must have laboratories where you can do
that.

I saw another container that's ready to be shipped overseas,
to Karachi, like the rest. Before I send this, I'll get the exact

address so you can stop it and make sure it's what it's supposed to be.

My parents grew up in Karachi, and I'm glad that I can help people there. But in another way, it bothers me. I ask myself, if I weren't Pakistani, would I keep silent like the rest? There's so much money.

Please send someone quickly. I can't believe the people at JHHI know what's going on, but if they do, I need to find out. I need to know.

There was no signature.

I read it twice, then shifted my attention to Tony Foley, who was inching downstairs, clinging to the banister as if he were attempting a rope descent from a snow-capped peak. His head nodded to one side. His jaw was slack. I marched over, grabbed him by the arm, and deposited him in the nearest chair.

"Where's the package?" I demanded.

"Wha—"

"She enclosed part of a box. Where is it?"

"Huh?"

I waved the letter in his face. "Where'd you get this?"

"Wait. Wait. Slow down, okay? She forgot to return one of the library books. Books on Pakistan I told you about. I thought maybe I'd read it, see what was so excitin', why she had to spend so much time readin' and all. Damn book, I picked the thing up and threw it against the wall. And then I saw that letter on the floor."

"It just fell out?"

"Honest. Fell out."

"You haven't been holding back on me? Thinking you might keep Tina's money supply coming?"

"Hell, no."

"You still have the book?"

"At home."

"Did anything else fall out of it, Tony?"

He squirmed and swallowed, made a face as if he'd tasted

something sour and bitter. I hoped he hadn't left a mess in my bathroom. "Just a little slip of shiny paper."

Shiny paper. Shiny paper . . .

I dived across the living room, yanking open the top drawer of my desk so fast it nearly crashed to the floor. Where had I put it, the envelope with Rebecca's death certificate, the envelope Emily had handed me in secret?

I scrabbled through bills and letters. Shoved neat piles into disordered heaps.

There. I upended it and shook it onto the blotter. The shiny, Mylar-like stuff floated slowly to the floor.

"Tony? Wake up, dammit!"

"Hey, hey, there it is. There it is. What're you so upset for? I didn't lose it or nothin'. There's the stuff."

"This?"

"Yeah. Pretty, huh? You hold it right, you can see colors in it. Hologram. Neat, huh?"

I lifted it to the light. Blue, red, and green *C's*—a design I'd earlier misread as crescents—swam to the surface, wavered, and disappeared as I shifted the angle. Part of a Cephamycin package. Maybe the seal of a Cephamycin package.

The phone rang. Mooney, finally! I grabbed it.

"Hello?"

Nothing. Faint murmuring.

"Hello?" Was that a bell in the background?

I said, "Emily, please, where are you?"

Silence. I heard a distant beeping, a bell ringing again, but not like a telephone or a doorbell.

"Mrs. Hodges, dear, what do you think you're doing?" The voice was faint and far away, a voice I didn't know, a brisk voice, cheerful, but impersonal.

There was a clatter on the other end and a far away voice said, "Code Sixty, Code Sixty."

Then the phone clicked and went dead.

I held it to my ear for a long time.

3 9

I rang five times in quick succession, pressing my thumb against the bell until my knuckle hurt. I pounded the brass knocker, then hit the bell again. I was ready to kick in the door when I heard footsteps and the jangle of the chain lock.

The porch light snapped on.

"Goddamn," Keith Donovan said, hauling open the door. "This time I was *sure* you were Emily Woodrow."

He wore the same blue bathrobe. Blinking back sleep, his eyes looked unguarded and very young.

I stepped inside. "Code Sixty," I said. "I heard a Code Thirty called while I was at JHHI. Does Sixty mean it's some other hospital?"

"They call Sixty at JHHI," he said, looking bewildered. "Thirty's a child. Pediatric cardiac arrest."

"They double it," I guessed. "Sixty's an adult."

"Right. Can I—"

I said, "I need your help. Now."

He rubbed his hands over his eyes, then squinted at me as if he thought I might disappear. When I didn't, he followed me into the living room. I fumbled with the switch of a floor lamp, lifted the receiver on his desk phone.

"Call JHHI," I said. "Find out anything you can about a patient named Hodges. Mrs. Hodges."

"What the hell time is it?"

The floor lamp cast shadows against the deep green draperies, illuminated barely half the room. "Past two. It doesn't matter."

"Hodges?"

"That's all I know."

"You can't do this from your own house? In the morning?"

"I'm not a doctor," I said. "All I can do is call patient information and find out Mrs. Hodges's condition. Period. That's it."

"Have you tried that?"

I tugged at my hair. "Dammit, I should have." My fingers hit 411. I counted the rings. Five. Six. Pick up!

Donovan said, "JHHI's number is five five five seven three eight oh."

"Thanks."

I didn't know her first name, so I decided to let a quaver creep into my voice. I referred to the operator as "dear." I dithered and repeated myself. Yes, the operator said after a maddening pause, a Thelma Hodges was listed. Was that my friend? Yes? Well, she was in "guarded" condition.

"Over to you," I said to Donovan, reestablishing a dial tone, then brandishing the receiver.

"What? What's over to me?"

"Get me a room, a location. A diagnosis. A prognosis."

"If she's 'guarded,' they don't know the outcome."

"Get any information you can. Please," I said.

"Is this about your friend? The one who took the wrong pills?"

"This is about Emily Woodrow. Make the calls."

He stared at me as if I might want to make an immediate appointment for therapy, but then he leaned over the desk and started fanning through his Rolodex. I paced while he debated between two cards, dialed, and joked easily with someone on the other end of the line. Seemingly as an afterthought, he asked for Thelma Hodges's room number.

He did it well. The man was almost as good a liar as I am.

"Fifth floor west," he told me as he hung up. "It's a cancer ward. Adult patients. Why exactly am I doing this?"

"Do you know anybody who works on the fifth floor? Anybody who works nights?"

"I might know a couple of nurses."

"By name? By sight?"

"Both. Calm down, okay?"

I faced him. "Call a nurse. A specific nurse, by name. Ask her about Mrs. Hodges."

"What should I ask?"

I spied a notepad on his desk and started scribbling. "How long has she been there? Who admitted her? What's wrong with her?" I hesitated. "Is she confined to her room? Does she have access to a phone?"

"Anything else," he asked sarcastically.

"Lots. But let's start with these."

This time, with his permission, I listened in on the kitchen extension, holding my breath. Mrs. Hodges's care presented certain problems, he learned from a motherly sounding woman named Ava. Wasn't it a shame? So young and in such ill health. First the early onset of Alzheimer's Disease, so disorienting for the poor thing, and now the cancer as well. Hard to explain to her what they were doing, and that it was all for her own good. Like treating a child, really. But harder. Was Dr. Donovan doing some work on early-onset Alzheimer's?

Yes, well, Thelma Hodges wasn't confined, but they did their best to keep an eye on her. She tended to stumble around the hospital and disturb the other patients. And they were always finding phones off the hook. He probably should have placed her in a more secure facility, under greater restraint, but it must have been so hard for him, knowing that excellent care could be obtained for her right at JHHI.

He? Why, Dr. Muir, of course.

I wished I'd written more questions, different questions.

Donovan struck off on his own, started ad-libbing.

Dr. Muir? Oh, he never came to visit, but you really couldn't blame him. They'd been very close, Ava understood. Uncle and niece, yes, but really more like father and daughter. Poor Thelma's parents were separated, her mother dead. No one came to see the patient, no one at all. But then, Dr. Muir was such a busy man. And it would be so painful for him to see his niece the way she was now.

Yes, he'd engaged a private duty nurse. Would Dr. Donovan like to speak with her? Not now? Well, Mrs. Hodges was coping very nicely. Everything had been arranged with her comfort in mind.

And, might Ava ask, what exactly was Dr. Donovan's concern?

Enough, I urged Donovan silently. Don't push it. I tapped the phone stem up and down to make clicking noises, but he kept chatting away. I hung up and went after him, drawing a line across my throat with a finger to indicate that a quick farewell was in order.

"Hey, I thought you wanted to know all about her," he said defensively, rubbing sleep from his eyes. "Look, I suppose I owe you one. I barged in on you with a client, and now you get to barge in on me, but at least I phoned first—"

"She's Emily Woodrow," I said.

His finger stayed frozen at the corner of one eye. His lids blinked. He had dark lashes for a man with such pale hair. "What are you talking about?"

"Thelma Hodges is Emily Woodrow. Your Dr. Muir is holding her prisoner.

"Oh, come on," he said.

"She's probably drugged out of her mind."

His hair was cut so short it barely moved when he shook his head. "I can't believe that."

"Don't believe it," I said. "Come *see* it."

"Try me in the morning. After you get a good night's sleep."

I crossed the rug, so that only the width of the desk separated us. "This nurse you just talked to, Donovan—she doesn't exactly sound like the soul of discretion."

"Ava? She'll talk your ear off. You heard."

"Think she's gonna keep quiet about your call? Think she's not curious about why a psychiatrist's interested in Dr. Muir's sick niece? She's probably checking to see if Muir's on duty right now."

"It was Dr. Muir who recommended me, who brought me into this," Donovan protested. "To help Emily."

"And why didn't you tell me that before?"

Donovan lowered his eyes as if he were studying the grain of the desk. "He asked me to keep it confidential. He has other therapists he generally recommends. He didn't want them to feel that he was planning any major changes . . . didn't want them to feel threatened."

"So he doesn't normally refer patients your way?"

"She's actually the first. I'd hoped—"

"He chose you because you're inexperienced, Donovan. Or else to help him keep an eye on her. Was that part of the deal? Did you report to him?"

The therapist hesitated. "He asked about her occasionally."

"Did you tell him Emily had hired me?"

"No," he said. "You were essentially Emily's own idea. And I wasn't sure he'd approve."

"He's got her," I said. "He's holding her against her will."

"Why on earth would he? You wake me up in the middle of the night to tell me a—some kind of Gothic horror story! What? Do you think the man's suddenly gone mad? Do you imagine he keeps some kind of captive harem in the middle of a respectable hospital?"

I paced, pressing the heels of my hands against my temples. I could feel my pulse pounding. "Okay, try this," I said. "Come back to my house. There's a guy passed out in my living room."

"That's not my problem," he said angrily.

I softened my voice. "The man's name is Tony Foley. He lived with Tina Sukhia; they were engaged. He's drunk. Wake him and he'll tell you. And I can show you."

"Show me what?"

"Pictures of a bottling plant used to manufacture phony chemotherapy drugs."

He shook his head again, lifted a hand to the back of his neck. I wanted to grab his arm, force him to move. I made myself

LINDA BARNES

speak slowly, deliberately instead. "Someone's manufacturing phony Cephamycin right next door to JHHI. It killed Rebecca Woodrow and four other children. God knows how many other kids have been killed."

"Others?"

"Tina Sukhia used the wrong Cephamycin. She grabbed a package meant for faraway places, faraway deaths. Deaths where the mortality statistics are so grim that a few more deaths wouldn't be noticed."

Both of Donovan's hands were active now, kneading the muscles in his neck.

With effort, I kept my voice low. "Come with me. Talk to Tony. You're the one who told me you couldn't understand the relationship between Dr. Muir and Dr. Renzel. Well, here's a connection: they travel together, Chief of Staff and Chief of Pharmacy, to international conventions. They peddle phony drugs together, to backwater nations."

"You're absolutely wrong."

"Tina Sukhia didn't believe it. She's dead. Your hero's feet are not just made of clay, they're made of shit, and I can prove it."

He didn't bother with slippers or an overcoat. If any of the neighbors peered out from behind their closed blinds, they must have raised their eyebrows at the sight of us hustling across the damp grass.

In my living room, Tony Foley snored loudly. A red light flashed on my answering machine.

"Even if we could wake him—" Donovan began distastefully.

I waved the *Globe* in his direction. "Here. Four years ago, the Cephagen Company voluntarily repackaged Cephamycin, at great expense, to come up with a tamper-proof package, a package sealed with a trademark hologram. Why?"

"Why? Because of Chicago and the Tylenol scare."

"Cephamycin's not stocked on regular pharmacy shelves."

"So?"

"They must have *had* a counterfeiting problem. Or anticipated one. Do you know how much a dose of Cephamycin costs?"

"No."

"The *Globe* calls it extremely expensive."

"Research costs run high," he said.

"Hundreds of thousands?" I asked. "Millions?"

"Hundreds of millions," Donovan said, "to get a new drug on the market. Years of research."

"Could Cephamycin go for as much as a thousand dollars a dose?" I asked.

"I suppose it could. Maybe more."

Tina had mentioned fifty-dose cartons. Fifty thousand dollars a pop, I thought. Enough for expansion, a new wing, a whole new sterile floor. "Look at this," I said.

Donovan held the shiny paper gingerly between his index finger and thumb. I watched his expression shift while he read Tina Sukhia's appeal to the World Health Organization; he scanned it once, twice.

He lifted the silvery paper to the light, eyeing the three-dimensional *C*'s. "Was this enclosed with the letter?" he asked gravely. "Is this the genuine seal from a Cephamycin package?"

"I don't know for sure," I said. "Emily Woodrow gave it to me, the morning you brought her over. When she said she'd lost her glove."

"She didn't trust me."

"You had ties to JHHI," I said. "When I showed the hologram to Tony Foley, he swore it was the same as the one Tina'd enclosed in her letter."

"He's drunk. He might say anything."

"You want proof, help me load him into my car. The matching hologram should be at his place. You can see for yourself."

Donovan sank into the chair near my desk, fingered the sash of his robe. "Once we've got that kind of evidence," he said slowly, "we'd need to go to the authorities."

"Yes," I agreed. "Absolutely. The minute Emily Woodrow's out of that hospital."

The red light on my message machine flashed accusingly. I punched the button, listened long enough to hear Mooney's voice. Hit "reset."

I wouldn't call him back. I'd been a cop too long. I knew too much about bureaucratic delays and foul-ups. The police are a necessary force, not a perfect one. They're big and sloppy and secrets have a way of spreading like wildfire through the ranks.

You don't do brain surgery with a chain saw. It wasn't one of my grandmother's Yiddish maxims, but she would have agreed with the sentiment.

40

Cancers grow with no regard for the clock. Incisions heal and scar, babies wail indignant cries, and the elderly rattle their last breaths in their own due time. Hospitals know no night or day.

I fronted into a metered space scarcely a block from the hospital entrance. It was close to six A.M.

"I'm not sure we should do this," Keith Donovan said.

I ignored him. It wasn't the first time he'd voiced his doubts.

"Go home," I urged. "Walk. Take a cab."

"You won't know how to take care of her."

"I'm surrounded by hospitals. You did your part. I appreciate it. Now go home."

"I can't."

"Wait in the car, then. Can you drive?"

"Of course I can drive."

"Give me five minutes, then move to a loading zone or a fire hydrant, something right in front of the ER. Keep the engine running."

"I'm not afraid to go in."

"Then quit stalling."

Still harnessed by his safety belt, he stared at me searchingly.

Tina's white hospital smock was short and a trifle tight, but topping my own white pants, it looked okay. I hadn't bothered trying on any of her slacks when Donovan and I had deposited her drunken fiancé at the Buswell Street apartment. Donovan had helped me maneuver Foley's bulk into the tiny elevator, which had made lurching progess to the fourth floor. I doubted I could have handled Tony without him.

I'd certainly never have located the tiny but convincingly identical holographic seal without his help.

Donovan wore hospital greens, a relic of med school.

In addition to the smock, I'd taken a few props from Tina Sukhia's closet: a stethoscope, a clipboard, a flashlight more powerful than the one I normally keep in my handbag. A name tag hung from the pocket of the smock, but its photo ID was so small no one could distinguish Tina's dark smiling face from my own pale grim one. Not at a distance.

I'd yanked my hair back and up, wound it into a tight knot, and secured it with the dead woman's bobby pins, still scattered on a tray in the bathroom. I'd asked if I should bring the cap, but that was only for ceremony, Donovan said. For graduation photos.

A shaft of early sunlight pierced the windshield of my Toyota and scattered into dust motes.

"Please," Donovan said. "Leave the gun in the car."

"No," I replied firmly.

He released his seat belt, opened the door, and I breathed again.

We entered through the swinging doors of the ER, two doctors —or a doctor and a nurse, depending on the viewer's assumptions— in earnest conversation, heads bent over a clipboard, reviewing vital charts. Donovan had suggested the ER approach. The general lobby, he'd declared, was the stronghold of security guards.

We walked through the electric-eye doors of the first available elevator with a purposeful stride. No one stopped us; I didn't expect to be stopped. A tiny elderly Indian woman joined us, smiling and nodding as if she'd smiled and nodded to us a hundred times before. It was probably a nervous tic, but it gave me confidence, made me feel like we'd get away with the charade.

"Fifth floor," Donovan murmured, although my hand was already on the button.

"I know," I said. "If this is too interventionist for you, you can peel off on two."

"You'd get lost," he said.

We slipped past the second floor, the third. The Indian woman got off on four.

"I hope there's a wheelchair up there," I muttered.

"There's always a wheelchair. You bring one along, they'll wonder about you. Procedure."

"That's why you're here," I reminded him. "Just find the wheelchair, get the patient into it, and waltz," I continued.

"I still think we ought to wait. There's more confusion during visiting hours—"

"Look, we've been through this. I want it done now, before the shift changes. If news of your phone call gets to Muir, Emily might disappear along with the next wave of personnel. New name, new location, or worse. Tell you the truth, Donovan, the main thing I can't figure is why she's still alive."

"From the Alzheimer's and cancer diagnosis—the drugs indicated for that diagnosis—her memory may have been destroyed or altered in such a way that she could never be a credible witness," he said.

I said, "Maybe you should have stayed in the car."

The elevator slid to a stop. The doors opened.

"To the right," Donovan said crisply. "Past two corridors, hang left. We'll circle behind the nurses' station. If they see us coming out of the room with her, they might assume we went through proper channels. Out is easier than in."

We stopped at a utility closet, found and opened a lightweight chromium wheelchair.

"Good so far," I told Donovan.

Room 508 displayed the name HODGES to the left of the door. A private room. Nothing but the best for Dr. Muir's niece.

The quiet hum of the place jangled my nerves. I pushed down on the lever and noiselessly swung the door of 508 inward. Donovan scooted the wheelchair inside. I joined him and flipped the light switch.

On the narrow bed, a woman slept, her mouth open, a faint snore emerging. A sour smell issued from the twisted sheets.

Her resemblance to the photos of the little dead girl was all that connected the sleeper to my memory of Emily Woodrow. Her matted blond hair showed dark roots. Her hands were ringless, the nail polish stripped. The area around her eyes seemed swollen and dark, her cheeks rough and large-pored. All her surface elegance was gone.

I glanced at Donovan to make sure. He nodded.

I shook her, murmuring "Shhhh." She shifted, grunted in protest, but her eyes didn't open. Donovan lifted the chart at the end of the bed, studied it with pursed lips.

"What's she on?" I asked.

"I can hardly decipher a single word," he said.

The door opened. "Excuse me. Is there a problem?"

The private duty nurse hadn't wandered far. Maybe to the nurses' station to chat. Probably just to the bathroom; she had a nervous, rabbity look about her. She seemed to expect to be scolded for leaving her charge.

"Nothing you need concern yourself with, Nurse," Donovan snapped rudely. "Mrs. Hodges is taking a ride down to, uh, Radiology. Help me disconnect her from this monitor."

The nurse blinked pale lashes. "How long will she be gone?"

"Twenty minutes, half an hour. I'll have an orderly wheel her back up."

"Radiology?" She pressed her lips together firmly to keep them from shaking. "No one mentioned anything about Radiology."

Donovan said, "What's your name, Nurse?"

"Helen Robins. Sir."

"Helen. Make sure the IV line's secure."

She came, cowed by his arrogance. I briefly considered knocking her on the head, gagging her, dumping her in the bed. She seemed so harmless that I wavered, and then she was back near the door.

"May I go now?" she asked.

"Certainly," Donovan said.

The door hissed shut and we swung into action.

Moving an unconscious person is tricky. I'd hefted my share of drunks when I was a cop. Protesters who recommend passive resistance know what they're talking about.

"You should have ordered the nurse to jack her into the chair," I said. "They know how it's done."

"She made me nervous," Donovan responded. "I thought her nose was going to twitch."

"Forget the robe," I told him. "Let's just get her in the chair. She won't freeze to death."

"Protocol," he insisted. "We'll be stopped."

"Not if we don't get going," I snapped. "Take her legs, and for Chrisake, make sure the brakes are set on that thing."

"Make sure the IV unit's ready to roll," he said.

We were starting to shift her when the door opened. Our rabbity nurse had been joined by another, obviously her superior.

The more forbidding of the two said, "I've paged Dr. Muir. There is nothing in the written orders for this patient concerning Radiology."

I smiled at her winningly. "He must have hated getting such an early wake-up call."

"Hardly," she said. "He's right here at the hospital."

Great.

"When was the last time the patient was medicated?" Donovan asked.

"I gave her the regular meds when I came on at eleven," the little rabbit responded.

"What's your name?" The nursing supervisor stood toe to toe with Donovan.

"Woodrow," I said while he hesitated. "When Dr. Muir shows up, tell him Mrs. Woodrow's gone home."

"Home?"

"Home. And the name is Woodrow. Get it right."

"I thought you said Radiology." The older nurse turned on the younger accusingly.

"He did. He did," she said, wringing her hands, almost clasping them in prayer.

"Call security," the supervisor said.

"Um, can I see your badge?" our rabbity nurse asked Donovan, obviously more afraid of offending a doctor than a nurse. "Please?"

"I'll call them myself." The older nurse's footsteps thundered down the corridor. I quickly traded my clipboard for the chart Donovan had replaced at the foot of Emily's bed.

"Wake up," I said to her loudly, to no avail. We propped her with pillows, got a good hold and moved her to the wheelchair. She slumped forward and started to fall out. The young nurse gazed at us openmouthed.

I swore and jammed my body up against Emily's. They ought to make the things with shoulderbelts.

"Nurse!" Donovan ordered. "Give us a hand here."

She couldn't seem to help obeying. Must be the tone, I thought. The impersonalized "Nurse!"

Emily grunted and snored.

He entered the room quietly, a graying shadow of his portrait, his speckled bow tie askew, his mane of white hair tousled. Perhaps he had been sleeping. One corner of his mouth drooped.

He forced a ghastly smile and tried to seize control of the situation by sheer force of personality; he must have been able to do that easily in his prime.

"Oh, it's you, Keith," he said. "You've got the whole floor in a muddle. Ruth must have misunderstood. Radiology, my eye. Please explain yourself. What's this foolishness about taking a patient home?"

"Explain yourself," I returned sharply.

He eyed my mismatched uniform with distaste. "Who are you? Do you work here?"

"Does this patient suffer from Alzheimer's Disease?" I demanded. "Does she have cancer? Leukemia?"

He peered closely at the woman in the wheelchair. Raised a hand to his forehead, dropped it, and wiped it across his mouth.

"How dare you?" he said to Donovan, lowering his voice in fury. "This is outrageous. Where is her chart?"

"We know who she is," I said. "Dr. Donovan, can you identify this woman as your patient, Emily Woodrow?"

Donovan said, "I can and I do."

"You interfering bastard," Muir rumbled.

At the same time, Donovan said, "Dr. Muir, are you okay?"

"Mrs. Woodrow's leaving," I announced. "Now."

"Security," Muir said softly. He didn't call out to them; they were there. Two guards had silently materialized, one grizzled and stooped with age, one quite young.

"Take me as far as a phone," I told them. "You can even dial it for me: nine one one."

The guards seemed puzzled. I gave the wheelchair a push. It went nowhere. I released the brake. Donovan stood frozen.

Muir was blocking the way. His skin looked waxy in the overhead fluorescents. He said softly, "Give me her chart. You can't take a chart out of the hospital—"

I said, "Out of the way."

He rested a hand at his throat, breathed in and out audibly. "You may mean well," he said. "Please, just leave. I don't want trouble. Dr. Donovan, I'll speak with you later. I don't blame you for any of this."

"We're not going without Emily," I said.

Muir's face looked grayer by the minute.

"Out of the way," I repeated. "Or tell your guards to shoot. They're armed, aren't they?"

The younger one bobbed his head quickly, patted his holster as if he needed reassurance.

"Great," I said. "And then, after they shoot us, Doctor, you can try to save our lives. *Doctor*," I repeated scathingly. "Look what you've done to her."

If he'd brought the full authority of his presence to bear, the guards would have stopped us. Maybe not shot us, but stopped us. Muir stared at Emily, wiped his hand across his mouth again. He made his way to the edge of the rumpled hospital bed and sank onto it slowly, like an old man.

I wheeled Emily out the door.

The guards looked to Muir for instruction. The younger one said eagerly, "Should we stop them?"

"It doesn't matter," I heard Muir whisper.

I took off, walking with increasing speed. Down the corridor, past the nurses' station. I could feel eyes boring into my back. Donovan walked stony-faced at my side, a steadying hand on Emily's shoulder. The elevator took about two hours to make the ascent from the first floor.

No one stopped us as we pushed the wheelchair out of the ER. The automatic doors whooshed behind us and I took a deep breath.

"Where?" I said.

"The Brigham ER's closest," said Donovan. "I don't know how to get her down from these kinds of dosages without risking an MI and God knows what else."

"See," I said. "You know the lingo."

"You were good in there," he said.

"Thank you."

"You didn't shoot anybody," he said.

The Brigham's emergency room was jammed. While I was still reeling from the number of awkwardly bandaged arms and legs, the welter of wheelchairs and crutches, the incoherent cries of pain, Donovan collared a nurse, identified himself, and informed her that his patient had complained of chest pain just before collapsing.

In less than five minutes, Emily had moved to the head of the queue. In ten, she was in possession of a bed and full monitoring equipment.

41

I called Mooney from a pay phone. He answered immediately, and the more I talked, the angrier he sounded. He made the trip from Berkeley Street to Brigham and Women's in record time. He brought along two uniformed men.

"Look, I phoned," I said, as soon as I saw the tilt of his eyebrows. "We missed each other about a million times, but I did phone."

"I'm the only one in the department? Nobody else?"

"Mooney," I said, "this may surprise you, but I don't have great faith in the department. Especially when there might be political strings attached."

"Political?"

"There's money and power in hospitals. Politics can't be far behind."

Mooney's eyebrows lowered, and I took advantage of the lull to introduce him to Keith Donovan.

"She really sick?" Mooney said skeptically, as soon as I mentioned the word *psychiatrist*.

"Not only is Emily Woodrow really sick, Mooney," I said, "she didn't kill anybody, so we wouldn't have to pretend she was sick if she wasn't. I *want* you to talk to her."

"You couldn't have waited until I was available before you went stealing her out of Helping Hand?"

"Stay in your office."

"Soon as people quit knifing each other, I'll be delighted." Back from a ruckus in the South End, he was less than cheerful. "I'm not the only cop in town."

"The only one I trust, Mooney. You want to put me in jail for that?"

"Has her husband been notified?"

I said, "I didn't call him."

"Nice," Mooney said. "I guess you leave us a few scraps."

"C'mon, Moon."

He made a face. "The way I understand it," he said, "you've got some pictures, you've got two bits of shiny stuff, and you've got an unmailed letter."

"Right. And we've got Emily Woodrow."

"Who might not remember anything," Donovan added.

"That's it?" Mooney asked.

"Yeah," I said defensively. "That ought to be enough."

Mooney said, "Give me details. The pictures are of some kind of machinery—"

"It's a bottling plant," I said, "an assembly-line kind of thing."

"Wait—and you think it's at six thirty-two Longwood Avenue?"

"Soon as you get a warrant, we'll know," I said.

"I need probable cause for a warrant."

"Find out who owns the place. I'll give you ten to one it's JHHI. Check the ground near the rear door. It's covered with rust —again ten to one it matches the stains on Tina Sukhia's dress. There's some kind of chemical smell. Brand-new locks on the back door. A tiny sign that says 'Deliveries for Cee Co.' Cee Co.'s got to be a knock-off of Cephagen Company—the cut-rate division."

I remembered what Tony Foley had told me. That Tina Sukhia had laughed when she'd told him her money came from Cee Co. Muir must have had fun selecting the name.

"Jerome Muir is a respected and powerful man," Mooney said. "Even with all that—"

"Jesus, Mooney," I exploded, "don't you know a judge who owes you a favor?"

"I know a lot of people who owe me a favor," he said pointedly.

"Donovan," I said. "Tell him."

"Tell him what?" Donovan and Mooney had disliked each other

on sight. Mooney hates psychiatrists. As for Donovan, I guess he was only fascinated with women who felt comfortable with violence, not men.

"What you told me," I urged. "About how much it costs to manufacture and market a drug like Cephamycin."

"It costs plenty," Donovan said shortly.

It seemed like I was in this on my own.

"I'm worried about Dr. Muir," Donovan continued. "He must be ill. You can see that, just looking at him. Did you notice the left side of his mouth?"

I kept a close watch on the door to Emily's room. It stayed ominously shut.

Donovan said, "We have to be missing something. It doesn't make psychological sense."

"Psychological sense," Mooney echoed. "What's that called? An oxy-something? Oxymoron? Psychology doesn't make sense most of the time, Doctor."

"Donovan," I said. "You *saw* Muir. You saw his face when he realized we recognized Emily."

"I saw him," Donovan agreed, "but I can't comprehend it. It's like—like learning my father was a thief, or a casual adulterer— someone who betrayed my trust over and over again, in terrible ways. I know it can happen. I've heard it from patients. But I know the man."

"Yeah," Mooney said, "but what do you know about his lousy childhood?"

"*I know the man*," Donovan repeated.

"You called him a genius," I said quietly. "He could have fooled you."

"But this sort of thing, this basic lack of caring . . ."

"Mooney," I demanded as Donovan's voice trailed off into anxious silence. "Did you find out why the president of the Cephagen Company was up here? Who he was meeting with?"

"You could have paid back a lot of favors by making that connection for me, Carlotta."

"We can argue that later, Moon. Did you find out?"

"The meeting was supposed to be with Muir, but Muir says he had no idea of the agenda. Never spoke to Menander directly. Hang on, okay?"

He spent two minutes conferring with his uniforms, gesturing and talking full speed. In another two minutes, he'd have a team scouring city records, searching for paper concerning JHHI, 632 Longwood Avenue, Cephagen, and Cee Company.

Maybe they'd run into Roz.

"You need to get in touch with somebody at the World Health Organization," I reminded him when he turned his attention back to me. "About Tina's letter."

"Oh, yeah," Mooney said, raising an eyebrow. "Switzerland."

"Berne."

"Narrows it down."

A doctor hurried out of Emily's room. Mooney clapped a hand on his shoulder, blocked his way.

"How is she?"

"Hard to say at this point. She's unconscious."

"When can I see her?" Mooney demanded.

"She's not going anywhere," the doctor said. "What's so urgent?"

"Tell me when I can speak to her."

"You can see her when she wakes up. Now, ask me when she'll wake up, and I'll say I don't know, okay? It could be five minutes; it could be five hours. She's not a hunk of machinery, officer."

I got between them. "Is she going to wake up?" I asked quietly.

His voice softened. "Are you family, miss?"

"No," I said.

He stiffened up again. "If's she's not responding in twelve hours, we'll try a stimulant. She's not in a coma. That's our major concern, making sure she doesn't slip into one. It would be better if she woke up on her own." With that, the doctor broke away and strode down the hall.

"Shit. I'll have to assign somebody. I can't wait around," Mooney said.

"I'll stay," Donovan said.

"Me, too," I volunteered.

Mooney reconsidered. "I can give it a little while," he said grudgingly. "Until the warrant comes through, anyway."

Half an hour later, with Emily still asleep, a uniformed officer bustled in, a young guy I'd never seen before. He stopped at the nurses' station and held a whispered confab. A white-haired woman pointed him in our direction.

"Lieutenant Mooney?"

"Yeah."

"We got a stiff. Nearby. Called it in, and Officer Triola said to get you on it right away."

"Where?"

"Helping Hand. My partner and I caught the squeal. Doctor name of Muir. Important guy, I guess."

Suicide, I thought, slamming my hand down angrily on a nearby seat back. Dammit to hell.

42

Donovan stayed at the Brigham. I trailed Mooney out to the cruiser and either he didn't notice or else he'd forgotten that I no longer worked for him.

The young cop sped the two hundred yards, siren blaring, lights flashing, and dropped us in front of the ER doors. Two nurses greeted us with a stretcher, but Mooney waved them off. Guided by the cop's directions, we boarded an elevator.

Someone had posted a hospital security guard on the fifth floor. He opened his mouth to question us. Mooney flashed his badge in response.

"Room five forty-six," the security guard said excitedly. "Head of the whole damn hospital croaks. And not a thing they can do about it." He sounded perversely satisfied, as if death's triumph over a doctor was something to cheer about.

Two uniformed cops controlled the scene.

"Randall," one announced with a military snap, apparently recognizing Mooney.

"Talk."

The man consulted a spiral-bound notebook gripped tightly in his left hand, began haltingly, then spoke with increasing confidence. "According to the nurse who found him, Doreen Gleeson— that's two E's in Gleeson—this Dr. Muir was found in a supply room. Got a man there, but a whole medical team's already tramped through it. She, uh, Gleeson, yelled for help and another nurse sounded the alarm. Carried him in here and tried to resuscitate. Thought he'd had a heart attack or something. Used those paddle things, a defibrillator, right? A bust. Couldn't get his heart started.

Gleeson, the nurse, goes back into the supply room and spots a syringe lying on the floor. I've got it safe in an evidence bag, but I had to practically threaten three doctors to make her give it to me. They wanted to send it to the hospital lab, have it analyzed here, can you believe it?"

"I'm surprised they bothered to call us," Mooney said.

"Doreen Gleeson did that. After she saw the syringe."

"Observant."

"And she knew that other nurse who died here."

Mooney said, "A syringe on the floor doesn't make it homicide. What's against the doc using the needle on himself and then dropping it? Or it could have fallen out of his arm or wherever when the medical team grabbed him."

"Yeah, I suppose," the cop said, his nonchalance not quite hiding an underlying excitement, "but I've got a witness—not to the moment of death or anything—but a witness who says he saw somebody leaving the supply room, kind of sneaking out, and he says he can describe her."

"Her?"

"Yeah. A woman."

"Crime-scene unit ought to be here by now," Mooney said, checking his wristwatch.

"Yeah, well, they're on the way."

"Witness?"

"Guy named Renzel. A doctor. But I don't know what kind."

"He's involved, Moon." That's all I had time to murmur before the man himself was in earshot. His tan had yellowed and paled, and behind his glasses he looked older, sunken, almost as old as Muir had looked the last time I saw him.

"God, I don't know if I can talk about this," Hank Renzel said. "He was my best friend."

Mooney gave me a long look. "Let's find a place to sit down," he said.

He didn't tell me to stay away, so I followed. I figured he

wanted me as a witness, in case Renzel decided to do any confessing about the phony drug setup. Juries prefer nonpolice witnesses.

We found an empty lounge across from the double steel doors of an operating theater, the kind of place where anxious relatives await word.

Renzel looked like he'd already heard the worst. He sank into a blue couch and Mooney sat next to him. I took a chair facing them both. Renzel gave me a single glance, didn't recognize me without my blond wig.

"I can't believe it," he mumbled. "Muir. Like that. It was bad enough with the nurse . . ."

"Tina Sukhia."

Renzel nodded at Mooney. He seemed surprised that he'd spoken loud enough for anyone else to hear. "Yes. Her. And now him. Who else, I wonder? Who else?"

He was silent so long I wondered if he'd fallen asleep behind his heavy frames and staring eyes. I took Interrogation 101 from Mooney. I know how reluctant he is to prompt a witness, but even he was finally forced to talk.

"Can you tell me what you saw, Dr. Renzel?" Mooney asked.

"I told the other officer."

"Tell me. Sometimes, when you go over it, you remember something."

"I'd never have seen anything out of the ordinary if I hadn't felt like taking a stroll. I pass that supply room on the way to the cafeteria. I wanted a brownie. They make good brownies. Sometimes the pharmacy workers bring them in for me. They know I like them . . ."

This time Mooney and I outwaited him.

"I saw a woman come out of the room."

"How sure are you that she came out of the supply room and not out of one of the adjoining rooms?"

"Well, I'm absolutely sure of it because I thought to myself, why is she coming out of the supply room, what was she doing in there? You know, you read things where doctors have all these, well, sordid meetings, trysts? In magazines. Made-up things. I've never seen behavior like that at an actual hospital. Not here, anyway, and so I just took notice."

Renzel paused. "Do you want me to describe her?" he asked.

"Yes."

"She seemed to be a patient."

"A patient," Mooney repeated.

"Or else she was wearing a patient's johnny and robe," Renzel said, sounding as if he'd just that minute considered the possibility of such a deception.

Had Muir and Renzel decided to keep Emily alive in case they needed a patsy for Tina's killing? Someone to blame for the death of the Cephagen Company's president?

Had Renzel alone decided to make use of her again? Why kill Muir? Why now?

I bit my lip. Why didn't the Chief of Pharmacy know that Emily was no longer trapped in her JHHI cell? Why hadn't Muir confided in his partner?

"I'd say she was forty," Renzel continued, giving each word due weight and consideration. "Maybe older than that. Very fair skin. Blond hair, medium length. Not anyone you'd consider the criminal type."

"What do you mean?" Mooney asked gently. "By 'the criminal type'?"

"Well," Renzel said in a low confiding tone. "Around here, in this neighborhood, it's the minorities who generally cause trouble."

"Ah," Mooney said. "Do you remember when I spoke to you before, right after Tina Sukhia died? You thought she might have been stealing drugs from the pharmacy. Was that, in part, because she was dark-skinned?"

"The woman I saw today was definitely Caucasian," Renzel said quickly, defensively.

Was he going to try to sell Mooney some tale about Emily Woodrow admitting herself to the hospital under a false name? Feigning cancer, so she could get a good shot at Muir? How was he planning to explain "Thelma Hodges's" medical chart, with Muir's handwriting all over it?

My throat felt dry. I wished I'd paid closer attention to that chart. Undecipherable, that's what Donovan had said. Undecipherable.

Mooney glanced at me and I gazed steadily back at him. He didn't nod or smile. Maybe he moved a fraction of a second slower. Maybe his jaw worked.

Renzel slapped both hands to his head, then leaned abruptly forward. His hand smacked against Mooney's thigh.

"Oh, my God," he said. "If I'd checked right then, gone to see what was going on, I might have saved him. I'll never forgive myself. Never. Muir was a fine man. A decent man. He treated me like a son."

He was good, this Renzel guy, very good.

"What time was it?" I asked quietly, speaking to him for the first time, "when you saw this woman?"

"Not even fifteen minutes before Jerome—before his body was found in the supply room. She could still be posing as a patient. She could be anywhere by now. I know your man posted guards, but there would be no reason for her to stay once she'd done what she did—"

Hadn't he had time to check "Mrs. Hodges's" whereabouts? Doreen Gleeson, the observant nurse, must have discovered the body too soon.

"You know that a syringe was found in the supply room?" Mooney asked.

"I didn't. You mean . . ." He paused and licked his lips. "It's almost like the other one. I know this: Jerome got a threatening letter, an anonymous letter. I told Jerome he ought to take the letter to the police, but ignoring it would be more like him. He wouldn't want to make trouble for the poor woman."

"The poor woman," I repeated. "Then Dr. Muir knew who'd sent the letter?"

"He suspected the mother of a former patient," Renzel said.

"Did he tell you her name?" Mooney asked.

How far would Renzel go? I wondered.

"I might recognize it," he said, waiting for Mooney to name Emily Woodrow.

Instead Mooney said, "Dr. Renzel, I think we should continue this conversation downtown."

Mooney didn't say a word about calling an attorney. He didn't do anything stupid like trying to cuff Renzel or read him his rights. It must have been in Mooney's eyes, the knowledge that he'd caught a killer.

"Don't move, don't speak, don't do anything," Renzel commanded. He was staring at me as if Mooney's compliance was a foregone conclusion.

It was. Mooney sagged on the couch, his eyes unfocused, his mouth open. He was trying to speak, but he couldn't.

"What—"

"Shut up." Renzel's hand came out of his pocket and I got a glimpse of the tiny syringe tight between his index and middle fingers. Mooney hadn't seen it at all. Had he felt the jab?

"Stand up."

I did.

"Stand next to me."

My feet moved.

"Walk to the elevator." He grabbed my right arm above the elbow in a firm left-handed grip. The syringe, in his right hand, shrouded by the folds of his lab coat, was close to my side.

If it were a gun, I'd know. Know whether it was cocked, whether the safety was off, know what my chances were, what organs the bullet would pierce. I'd know whether it was a .22, which would give me a faint chance, or a .9mm cannon, which wouldn't.

But a syringe . . . what had its poison done to Mooney? Was it the same stuff that had killed Tina Sukhia? Jerome Muir?

"That cop *knew*. You knew," Renzel said, his hand biting into my arm. "What did I do wrong?"

"Emily Woodrow's not a prisoner anymore. Didn't Muir get a chance to mention that before you killed him?"

"Where is she?" was all he said.

"Police custody."

"Push the button," he said. "Down."

Most drugs, you have to hit the vein. Intramuscular's not as good. I learned that from junkies. Had he hit a vein with Mooney? How much time did Mooney have?

I stared at a silent loudspeaker, willing it to life. Code Something. Call the code for reviving a police lieutenant pumped full of a substance that might or might not prove lethal.

I didn't intend to get into any elevator with a maniac holding a loaded needle. Once inside, it would be too easy. A quick slap on the butt, a shot in the vein if he got fancy. Carlyle on the floor, and him out the door, and on the way to the airport.

My handbag hung over my left shoulder, occasionally bumping my hip. My handbag with my gun inside, the gun I'd taken because of Emily's insistent questions.

"Can you use it?"

"Would you do it again?"

Not when I can't reach it, dammit. Could I manage to swing the handbag, knock the syringe away?

I had a quick vision of Mooney, head lolling against the arm of the couch. How long before anyone strolled over to the lounge by the operating theater? How long before someone went looking for the officer in charge?

How long before they searched the elevators?

"Dammit. Why doesn't this thing come?" Sweat was beading on Renzel's forehead. Obviously, this wasn't his style, this immediate, physical crime. He preferred long-distance hits, where you never got to see your victim.

"I thought Muir was the boss," I said. "But I guess it was your show all the way."

"Shut up. We're going to try a staircase."

That was fine with me.

Maybe security had turned off the juice to the elevators. That would mean someone had found Mooney, someone knew what was going on. They'd be looking for us.

The silent speaker suddenly boomed. Code Red.

Dammit, I thought they used numbers here.

"What's that?" I asked.

"They probably found your cop friend."

"Did you kill him?"

"I'm not a killer," he said.

"What do *you* call it?"

"Profit and loss. Business, that's what I call it."

How much could the man see without those heavy glasses? How could I knock them off?

"It's hard to believe Muir never knew what was going on," I said.

Renzel flushed, and I realized it was with pleasure. Pleasure at having duped Muir, the man who'd "treated him like a son."

"Muir's a fool." The Chief of Pharmacy's voice seemed harsh, grating. How could I have ever thought it appealing? "He's been losing it for years, but they all cover up for him. They know what his name's worth."

Dr. Jerome Muir. An M.D. doctor, a medical doctor, like Renzel's father, the well-known surgeon. Was that the root of Renzel's delight? That he'd put one over on the substitute old man?

If I survived, I'd ask Donovan.

"Dr. Muir never knew you were holding Emily Woodrow prisoner? Even though you used his name," I said, my voice full of pretended admiration.

"I sign his name better than he does," Renzel said.

"But how did you manage the drugs, the medical chart? You're not an M.D."

"I'm as good a doctor as anyone here," he said. "Better than most."

Renzel's glasses had sidepieces that curved firmly around his ears. It would take more than a quick sideswipe to dislodge them.

"Now stop jabbering and walk faster," he ordered.

"Where's the staircase?"

"Keep going. There's one around the next corner. Not many people use it."

We were walking down a broad, empty corridor. If someone had found Mooney, the place ought to be a hive of police activity. I imagined Renzel's profile in cross hairs, a target for unseen sharpshooters. Suddenly I envisioned them everywhere, siting just a little off, high and to the right, at my head.

"Backward," I muttered, my mouth dry as dust, speaking to keep my mind off the shooters.

"What?"

"I got it backward," I said. "Once I started to believe Emily's statement, to accept what she'd seen—a man shoving a mask over her daughter's face—I called it all wrong. I assumed the man—I assumed you were trying to kill Rebecca, not save her."

Renzel said nothing, kept walking.

"Why did you bother?"

"I don't expect you to understand."

"I'd like to understand."

He swallowed. "It . . . the children here . . . Rebecca's death was different."

"You ran into the chemotherapy room. You pushed Emily Woodrow out the door. You risked your entire operation."

"Look, the other stuff I do . . . No one cares. Everyone does it. I ship bogus high-tech drugs to sink-hole countries with no sewage treatment. Sick people—people who'd have died anyway, from bad water or third-rate physicians—die a little sooner. Keep it off the U.S. market and nobody cares. The profits are unimaginable. Millions. I would have gotten everything I wanted."

"What?"

He stared at me blankly.

"What?" I repeated. "What was it you wanted?"

"Everything." His eyes blinked rapidly behind his thick glasses. "Money," he said carefully, as if he were explaining a difficult concept to a child. "Here we are. Now shut up and open the door."

The stairwell was cool. Silent. Gray walls. Gray steps.

"You're nuts," I said.

He held more tightly to my arm. I didn't think he'd do anything while we were actually on the stairs. The landings, where he'd have better footing—I'd have to watch for the landings.

"I would hate to have to kill you," he said softly, his face so close I could feel his breath on my neck.

"Like you killed Tina," I said.

"If she hadn't taken the carton off my desk—if she'd followed standard procedure, none of this would have happened. But she was in a hurry and she grabbed the first carton she saw."

"Why was it on your desk? Why not keep the mess over at six thirty-two? Why risk contaminating your own hospital?"

"I needed to check the bar codes, make sure the packaging was current. It was her error. Not mine."

"Why didn't you kill Emily Woodrow?"

"I could have. I found them prowling the hospital together: proof that Tina'd never keep quiet no matter how much I paid her. But it would have been too many deaths too fast. Even old Muir might have woken up and asked questions. And I had plans for Emily. You might call her a little pharmaceutical research project of mine. The police will probably find her quite willing to confess to Tina's death. Any death. Even her daughter's."

I studied the concrete-block walls, listened for approaching sirens, ascending or descending footfalls. Nothing.

"The black nurse," Renzel said confidingly, "Tina. Killing her . . . I have no regrets about it. No feelings. Except possibly . . ."

"Yes?"

"That I'd have preferred to kill a black doctor. Yes. A minority M.D. Someone my own age."

"Someone whose acceptance to medical school meant you didn't get in?"

"Exactly," he said coolly. "Perceptive of you. But I do regret the children *here*. I regret Emily Woodrow's child."

I stared down at Renzel's feet, left, right, left, right. He wore brown loafers, well polished, expensive. Leather soles, I thought. No traction. I watched my own feet in conjunction with his. I couldn't do anything obvious, but I tried to match my stride to his, to measure the distance my foot would have to kick in order to trip him up.

"The doors are probably guarded," I warned, just before we reached the landing. "You'll need me. You'll need me, as your ticket out."

I could feel his hesitation.

"You might not be so lucky with your next hostage," I said hastily. "Cops are very careful when a woman's taken hostage."

"We'll go out the ER," he said.

How many steps could I fall and still get up? How quickly would he have to stab with the syringe? Could I count on his impulse to throw out his arms and save himself? Would his damn glasses fall off?

I watched and counted, felt his rhythm. When he was between steps with his right foot I lurched as far away from him as I could, hurled myself down the stairs.

He shouted, toppled as well.

Seven steps was all I wanted to fall. And I was ready for it. And it hurt like hell.

When I dive on the volleyball court, my knees and elbows are padded, and the floor is level, forgiving wood. Dammit, dammit, dammit. The staircase was cold concrete and hard right angles. It's the knees and elbows that get it every time. Knees and elbows because I was rolled in a ball to protect my head.

He wasn't holding on to me. Even as I was falling, I knew that. And somebody was yelling. Me.

I grasped my handbag to my chest and hugged it. I could feel the outline of the gun.

Would the tiny syringe break? Would he squeeze it inadvertently? Disarm it? Would he break his goddamn hand?

We landed in a tangle of limbs and I found I could move. I threw myself on top of him and I kept yelling and thrusting my hand in my handbag until I could bring out my weapon and hold it at the base of his skull.

I couldn't see the syringe.

"Just lie there," I told him.

He squirmed and I dug the barrel into his neck. "Don't move!" I yelled, my mouth an inch from his ear.

He lay still.

"I can pay you," he said.

"Like you paid Tina Sukhia?"

"Listen," he said softly, like he was imparting a great secret. "There's nothing you can't fix with money."

"Yeah," I said. My knees ached. I could feel wetness under one of them and hoped the cut wasn't deep. I felt bruised and shaken. Time for some cop to open the door.

"Nothing money can't fix," I said. "Be sure and tell that to Emily Woodrow."

43

It took two days for the fallout to hit. I don't mean the newspaper headlines; those were fast and immediate, and mostly inaccurate as hospital PR kicked into overdrive, handing out misleading press releases by the bushel. But the reaction to my role in Renzel's arrest came more slowly.

Part of the delay was due to Mooney's hospitalization. Some of it was weekend inertia. Another element was jet lag, but I didn't know anything about that until after my Monday morning summons to Mooney's office.

Mooney had taken a 1-cc intramuscular jolt of a drug called Ketamine. Hospitals don't keep Ketamine under lock and key; you can find it on any anesthesia cart. It's what they call a dissociative anesthetic. Keith Donovan told me about it.

He stayed at the Brigham, camping outside Emily Woodrow's door, leaving only to see his regular patients. I don't know if he acted out of guilt; I don't much care. I just liked the way he remained after others went home, noting the changing shifts of nurses and police guards, reading psychiatric journals, chatting.

We talked about anesthesia, third-world medicine, general topics, skating-on-the-surface stuff. He brushed my hair back from my face once, when the arguing got a bit heated.

He offered to see me to my Toyota when I left. In the descending elevator he asked if I wanted to talk about it.

"What?" I said.

"Did you feel tempted to use the gun? When you had him down on the floor, when you had him cornered?"

I considered possible replies. I thought about dating, even sleeping with a very attractive guy who'd analyze my every move.

I got in the car and drove away, watching Donovan grow small in my rearview mirror.

The next day, while I was at JHHI waiting to visit Mooney, a bouquet of wilting jonquils in my hand, Pablo Peña, the sleepy anesthesiologist, told me more about Ketamine. They use it on kids. Horses, too, he believed. Unless given supplemental drugs to offset its effect, patients wake from Ketamine-induced sleep soaked in sweat, screaming of gruesome nightmares. A biker he'd once sedated had specifically requested Ketamine, asking for that "angel dust stuff." He'd come down shrieking, "They're ripping my flesh off! Man, I'm charred by fireballs!"

Over the weekend I wondered about Mooney's dreams.

Monday morning, at headquarters, I thought I might actually be offered a congratulatory handshake, a collegial pat on the back. Mooney hadn't died. Emily Woodrow hadn't died. The poison plant at 632 Longwood had been shut down. A receptionist at David Menander's hotel had picked Renzel out of a lineup as the "flower delivery man."

"Mooney? In a meeting," I was told when I arrived. I waited long enough to drink one cup of coffee. Long enough to hunt for doughnuts, tracking their cinnamon smell to an empty box in the trash.

Through a slit in the shade on Mooney's door, I could see that he was entertaining two suits. They didn't look like plainclothes cops. They looked like politicians or businessmen. Possibly lawyers. Maybe I ought to take a hike, call, and reschedule.

"Hey, thank goodness," JoAnn Triola said when she caught sight of me.

I glanced behind me. We went to the police academy together and we get along okay, but Jo doesn't usually offer up prayers of thanksgiving on making visual contact.

"What?" I said cautiously.

"You'd better go right in."

"Why?"

"Mooney's been asking for you every five minutes," she said.

"Maybe I'll leave," I said.

She took two long strides across the floor and rapped on his glass before I could stop her. He glanced up, startled, saw me and pushed back his chair.

The door opened.

"Carlotta, get in here."

"I hope you're feeling better," I said sweetly.

One of the men in the office popped out of his chair like a jack-in-the-box. He was wearing a pin-striped navy suit. A crisp white handkerchief peeped from his breast pocket. On his lap, he cradled a small round hat with a flipped-up brim. The other man rose more slowly. He wore wire-rimmed glasses, a brown suit.

If I'd known it was going to be formal, I'd have worn a suit, too.

"Sit down," Mooney ordered firmly, nodding me into a chair. "This is Mr. Kuh—"

"Kurundi, madame." The man who'd popped had a clipped, almost British accent, dark skin.

Mooney said, "Mr. Kurundi is a representative of the World Health Organization, and this is Mr. Wiley from the FDA."

"Food and Drug Administration," I said warily. "Hi. Carlotta Carlyle. Let me guess. You got a letter from a woman named Tina Sukhia."

Wiley said, "We should have been contacted immediately."

I shrugged, gestured at Mooney, said, "He was in the hospital. I was busy sitting on a killer."

Mr. Kurundi spoke in a high voice with a melodic lilt. "You read a letter which was intended for the World Health Organization."

"It hadn't been sent," I said. "I didn't exactly tamper with the mail."

His tone became more severe. "Nevertheless, once you read such a letter, we should have been informed with utmost speed."

"In Switzerland? What's going on here?" I asked.

"Exactly this," Wiley, the Food and Drug man said. "If the proper authorities had been activated at the proper time, we would now know the names of Renzel's suppliers, wholesalers, middle men, exporters. The whole bag."

"And Emily Woodrow would be dead," I pointed out. "Unless she was getting ready to stand trial for multiple murder. Sounds to me like your beef's with this Kurundi guy. Ask him what the hell he's been doing with the letter Tina Sukhia sent him months ago."

"Excuse me, madame," Kurundi said, fiddling with his hat, "but you did not read that letter. It was, shall I say, both a vague and confusing communication. Also, the World Health Organization is a large tree with many branches. Prompt action was indeed taken once Miss Sukhia's letter reached its correct destination. However, we began our investigation from the other end, you might say. We were grateful to Miss Sukhia for pointing us toward Cephamycin. We discovered it was, as she implied, arriving into several third-world countries in a contaminated form—"

"I'm sure she appreciates your gratitude," I said. Mooney fired me a warning glance.

"In conjunction with the Food and Drug Administration of your country, we were working with the Cephagen Company's president—"

"Menander? The guy who got shot?"

"Yes," Wiley admitted.

"I'm sure he appreciates your work as well," I said.

Mooney said, "Menander had noticed that his orders from JHHI had picked up considerably."

"So Renzel would have access to more packaging materials," I said. "While Muir and JHHI paid the bill."

"Renzel could counterfeit the drug at minimal cost," Mooney added, "but he couldn't counterfeit the holograms. When the World Health Organization started questioning Menander about unusual ordering practices—"

Kurundi interrupted. "Which we did because the packaging was so perfect, everything absolutely correct. We assumed the counterfeit drug must have been coming directly from the Orlando manufacturing plant."

"Menander must have realized that JHHI's orders had more than doubled," Mooney continued. "But he couldn't believe Helping Hand would have any truck with counterfeiters. He came up here, figuring Muir must have a good explanation."

"And Renzel got to him first," I said. "Renzel had a hell of a nerve. And Muir—I can't believe he didn't figure it out. Five deaths in one day."

Mooney said, "He didn't want to figure it out, Carlotta. He knew he had a problem; we've got that in his own writing, notes and letters left in his desk. He was trying to hold off a scandal until a bequest came through. He was expecting a twenty-million-dollar legacy—"

"Why didn't he hide the medical records?" I asked Mooney.

"He did."

"No," I said. "Donovan got them."

"He hid them in plain sight," Mooney said. "Shunted them into general records instead of bringing them up for review. He planned to recall them, after the bequest—"

Mr. Kurundi interrupted again. "Madame, you perhaps do not take this seriously enough. Counterfeiting of drugs is a major problem worldwide. In Africa, in Nigeria, more than a quarter of the medicines on the market are not what they seem to be. Millions and billions of dollars are involved. In Burma, men, women, and children believe they are taking good medicine to counter the effects of malaria, and they die from it. Hundreds of them die."

Wiley broke in. "And now, what do we have? A minor operation closed, a tiny dent in an enormous machine. We could have placed operatives inside this plant. We could have traced shipments and made arrests up and down the chain of command."

"You've got Renzel," I said.

"He's not talking."

"Make a deal with him. Isn't that what you guys do? Offer him a cushy cell in a country club jail."

"Maybe I should have said that he's talking," Wiley admitted slowly, "but he doesn't make a lot of sense."

"A team of psychiatrists could have a field day on that guy," Mooney offered.

"He tried to save the kids," I said, "the children at JHHI. He seemed genuinely grieved by their deaths."

Wiley said, "Self-interest. You don't shit in your own backyard."

Kurundi looked so shocked at the FDA man's language that Wiley colored and apologized. To me.

"Renzel's reaction seemed like more than self-interest to me," I said. "He had some kind of moral code. Them and us. Black and white. The code got so twisted, it probably snapped."

"Him along with it," Mooney muttered.

Kurundi ran his fingers around his hat brim. "It seems," he said bitterly, "that the Sukhia woman was correct. I read your newspapers: An airplane crashes; no Americans are aboard, so all is well. You dump cigarettes on foreign markets. You dump waste products, some of them toxic, on any country so poor and debt-ridden they cannot refuse. You move slowly, cautiously, in this case, even though the suspect lab itself is located here—"

"Now wait a darn minute," the Food and Drug man said. "Most of the labs aren't here. This stuff mainly goes on in Turkey and Greece—"

Maybe I could get the two of them going and slink out the door. I stood, and they immediately ceased arguing.

"Mooney," I said, "why am I here?"

"These gentlemen are gonna try to suspend your PI license, Carlotta. Yank your ticket. They're gonna do their best."

"I don't believe this."

"Believe it."

"I had to move in a hurry, Mooney. You know that. Emily Woodrow would be dead if I hadn't—"

"Madame, you say it yourself," Kurundi observed. "You saved one life. We could have saved thousands of lives."

I counted to ten, counted to ten again. "Excuse me," I said. "What exactly would you have found out, in this perfect situation, if I hadn't acted so hastily?"

"We've told you."

"Repeat it, please."

"Renzel's suppliers."

"He used water. Arrest the water company. He probably used red food dye. Arrest whoever the hell makes food coloring for birthday cake frosting."

"Suppliers of machinery," Kurundi went on, "pharmaceutical bottling machinery. And especially, we would like to net the wholesaler, probably someone this man Renzel met at one of his international conferences. The wholesaler would then sell to a brokerage house. It's a vast network, a chain. You break it at one place, it starts up again. It's a huge industry, this counterfeiting, as bad, even more dangerous, than illegal drugs."

Illegal drugs. I could almost hear the puzzle pieces click in my mind. *Illegal drugs.*

"Carlotta?" Mooney said. "You okay?"

"I'm not the one got shot full of dope, Mooney."

"You looked funny for a minute."

"Mr. Kurundi," I said. "Mr. Wiley. If you were to get a lead to the next link in this chain, the wholesaler, would you consider ignoring the matter of my license? You probably have more important things to do than pick on me."

"What do you know, Carlotta?" Mooney said too quietly.

"Absolutely nothing, Mooney. Pleased to make your acquaintances, gentlemen."

"Carlotta—" Mooney said.

"Arrest me, or I'm gone," I said on my way out the door. Under my breath, I added, "I hope you have technicolor nightmares, Moon." He didn't hear me, or if he did, he ignored it.

44

"Professional pride, Patsy," I said insistently, "don't you have any?"

"Carlotta, look, I'm sorry I didn't get back to you with the woman's job history—"

"It's water under the bridge. But I want a little satisfaction here."

"Sounds like you want a freebie."

"This is right up your alley and I'm gonna sit on your phone till I get it, Patsy. Miami lawyer named Vandenburg. Thurman W. Vandenburg. I want to know if he's a defense attorney, and I want to know if he defends drug runners—"

"He's earning a living in Miami? Of course he does."

"In particular, a guy named Jaime Valdez Corroyo. I want to know if Valdez Corroyo's ever been arrested, if Vandenburg ever got him off. I want to know if Valdez Corroyo was tried alone or with anybody else."

"When can I—"

"Start punching names right now, Patsy. Time-and-a-half rates."

"Double?"

"No way."

I could hear her fingernails tapping the keys. I spelled Vandenburg and Valdez Corroyo, and within eight minutes she hit gold.

"Bingo," I said. "Send me the bill."

"Will do."

"While it's on your screen, read me Vandenburg's phone number, okay?"

The lawyer's secretary took my "absolutely urgent" at face

value. Thurman W. Vandenburg returned my call within six minutes.

"Get in touch with C.R.G.," I said, after giving my name and phone number. "Or I could call him Carlos. Have him call me. I'll be sitting by this phone for the next four hours—and if I don't hear from him, tell him I doubt he'll ever see his daughter."

That was bullshit, but I wanted a call fast.

"I don't understand you, miss."

"You don't have to understand. What you *do* have is a number to call on the 'Jaime Valdez Corroyo' business. Not Valdez Corroyo's real number. No point in phoning the state pen, huh? Do yourself a favor and call Carlos."

Vandenburg said nothing.

"Time is passing," I warned.

"I may have, uh, some little difficulty reaching this man you speak of," the lawyer said.

"That's life," I said.

I fidgeted around for a while, trying to organize my files. Gave that up, brought my National steel guitar downstairs, and started picking out old fiddle tunes, playing faster and faster until the fingerwork required total concentration. Usually music can fill my mind, empty it of everything but melody and harmony, bass line and chords.

I jumped when the phone rang half an hour later. Vandenburg again.

"The man we spoke of earlier cannot call you on your own line."

"Can he call me on somebody else's line?"

"I am not trying to amuse you. Is there a pay phone near your house?"

"Yes."

"Somewhere quiet?"

That would rule out any phone in Harvard Square. There was a booth in the back of a drugstore on Huron Avenue. "Yes."

"Go there now, call collect, and give me the number."

"Okay."

"I warn you. I'll check to see that it really is a pay phone."

"Hey, I'm not trying to set the guy up."

"Our friend is a cautious man."

"No kidding."

"He has business enemies."

"I'm not surprised."

We did the whole song and dance. I was relieved he didn't make me change pay phones until he found one he liked. At the drugstore, I bought a copy of the *Globe*, read a lengthy article about restructuring at the top at JHHI, and waited. Twenty, thirty, forty-five minutes went by. I studied the Op/Ed page, the funnies, Ann Landers, "Ask Beth." She advised a self-described "mature" ten-year-old to avoid attending sex parties with her best friend's father.

The phone rang. I grabbed the receiver, heard a hollow sound, a faint hum, a click.

"Señora?"

"Señorita, and I'd rather speak English."

"I can do that."

"Who am I speaking to?"

"The man you wish to speak to. We will avoid names, I think."

"Are you her father? Paol—my sister's father?"

"Let us say this: A woman you know well made a trip to my country last year, to beg an old man for money. She was accompanied by her daughter. Soon afterward the old man, my father, died. My father and I, we were not reconciled at the time of his death, you understand, but the housekeeper, an old and faithful friend, spoke to me of this visit."

"And you hired somebody to kidnap her, just in case she turned out to be your daughter? To check her out?"

"What is this?"

"What do you call it?"

"We speak at odds, señorita. I no longer understand you." There was an echo after every phrase. Pauses made the conversation

313

awkward. The man's voice was deep and smooth, heavily accented. It had both warmth and power. A caressing voice.

"The girl was encouraged to take a plane ride," I said.

He sounded puzzled. "Not on my orders," he said.

The trip could have been Paolina's idea. But Paco Sanchez had loaned her money, encouraged her, obtained a false passport for her, planned to accompany her.

"If you're telling the truth, you may have a problem, señor," I said. "In the future."

"I may have many problems in the future," he said evenly.

"In all innocence, your—my sister may have confided a secret to a man who would take advantage of it," I said slowly. Paco Sanchez had asked Paolina leading questions about herself. Most likely he'd learned of the connection to Roldan Gonzales. Figured a rich father would be willing to pay for his daughter's safety. Figured the chance to get in good with a big-time drug dealer would be worth the price of plane fare.

I went on. "If you should come in contact with a man named Paco Sanchez, a man who says he knows your daughter, and could arrange to bring your daughter to you—"

"It would not be advisable for her to visit," Roldan said. "I will speak to my attorney about this matter."

"Will you deal with Sanchez?"

"As it is necessary," he said in a tone that almost made me shiver. "Is that all?"

"No," I said quickly. "May I ask, why the need to find out about her? After all these years?"

There was a long pause and I wondered if the connection had been broken. The deep voice, when it spoke again, seemed uncertain. "I don't know. How do you say it? A whim of mine, perhaps. Maybe old age approaches. A child—she is part of me. My friend, the old housekeeper, said she looks very much like me."

"Then you must be a handsome man," I said. "Your daughter— my sister—this girl—is lovely."

He chuckled. It amazed me, this monster I'd read about, this killer. He chuckled.

"I know about you, señorita," he said.

"Yeah? What?"

"Many things I like. Some I dislike."

"Such as?"

"You are a divorced woman, and you sleep with a man whose father is not in a good line of work."

"Yeah. That's good, coming from you!"

"You don't know me," he said somberly.

"Oh, yeah, but you know me, right? You think you found out anything about me by hiring a thug too dumb to steal my trash without getting caught? Mister, if it's true that you know somebody by the caliber of people they hire, I'm wasting my time here, you're too dumb to help me."

I heard a sharp intake of breath, a long hollow pause, and then the chuckle again. This time it grew into a laugh.

"What is it you want, señorita?" he said. "Much as I might enjoy trading these insults, I cannot stay on the line."

"The connection isn't very good."

"I can hear you."

"Do you want her? With you?"

"No. She would be no good to me here. She would be someone my enemies could use against me. It would be dangerous for her. All I want is to know about her. To help her, if I can. I have money to send, for her education. Enough for anything she wants."

"You should talk to her mother."

"If I send money, it will be for the child alone."

"You could send it to me," I said into a long echoing pause.

"I hear the beginning of a bargain."

"You're a businessman."

"I can smell a deal," he said.

"Listen. I need to know something about your business. Or rather, a related business, and I can't find it out any other way. A small counterfeit drug company called Cee Co."

"Counterfeiters of regular medicines? That's a nasty business."

Nasty. Coming from someone like Carlos Roldan Gonzales. Nasty.

"Our two worlds don't often intersect," he said.

"My world doesn't intersect at all."

"Understand this, señorita. What I sell, people want to buy. I make no pretense about what I sell. I am not a thief or a murderer."

"I make no accusations," I said flatly. "I made a request. I asked a favor."

The silence stretched. I swallowed, remembered to breathe.

"I might be able to find out something," he said reluctantly. "But these are dirty people."

"I need a wholesaler of a fake chemotherapy drug called Cephamycin—a name, a place to start."

"Do you know in what country this person operates?"

"The drug enters Karachi. In Pakistan. That's all I know."

"Is this important to the girl, to Paolina?" It was the first time I'd heard him speak her name. He hesitated before he said it.

"If I get an answer I'll stay employed, so I'll be able to look after her a little."

He said, "I must go now."

"How will you—"

"The man from Miami will contact you."

"If I get no information, there'll be no money conduit to Paolina. Not through me."

"Will it trouble you? The origins of this money?"

"I'll have to think about it," I said. "It would bother me to tell Paolina she can't go to college."

"You have been saving money for her. This I know about you."

"Yes."

"But not enough."

"I'm working on it. She might not need your money."

"I would like to give it to her. It surprises me that I would."

"Why?"

"I'm a man of causes. I thought I would always only give my money to causes."

"Maybe you should keep on doing that."

"Why?"

"I like Paolina the way she is. I don't know how you bring up an heiress."

"Not as I was brought up, señorita." Across thousands of miles I heard a deep sigh. "That is all I can tell you."

The line went dead.

Señor Carlos Roldan Gonzales had hung up first.

45

"Ma nish-ta-nah ha-lai-lah ha-zeh mi-kol ha-lay-los?"

"Why is this night different from all other nights?"

At their best, my seders bear little resemblance even to my mother's radical gatherings, little resemblance to most seders at all. Haphazard is the word I'd use to describe them, and true to form, this year I was celebrating belatedly, having missed the traditional first-night and second-night observances. A small group assembled at my house on the eighth and final night, to eat, sing, and drink. I rarely miss the holiday altogether.

We each have our appointed tasks. Gloria makes potato kugel, a kind of enormous rectangular pancake, because she has a knack for greasy and fattening dishes. When she brings along one or more of her huge brothers, she makes multiple kugels. Roz buys enormous jars of gefilte fish at the supermarket, and white horseradish sharp enough to make your eyes water. She also brings men. Lemon's a regular.

This year, to my surprise and chagrin, Roz had invited the therapist-almost-next-door, Keith Donovan, evidently her latest conquest. Donovan's eyes met mine more than once during the evening, and I'm pleased to report that, on each occasion, he was the one who glanced away.

Ah, well, I thought philosophically, she's more his age. And he could continue his study of women comfortable with violence, even branch off into the behavior of women who wear strange T-shirts and shave their heads. Roz's shirt of the evening was hot pink and read: WILL WORK FOR SEX.

I make the chicken soup. From scratch. Its slow simmering

constitutes my major religious observance of the year. I have no recipe. No matter what quantity I make, there always seems to be enough. No matzoh balls ever remain in the pot. Sometimes I can almost feel my grandmother's hand guiding me as I add water, salt, and dill, debate the merit of a parsnip over a sweet potato.

I never met my grandmother, my mother's mother, the dispenser of Yiddish sayings.

Fish, kugel, soup, that's it. The entire menu. Chopped liver is traditional, but no one at my seders has a taste for liver except the cat, and T.C. shares his liver 'n' onions with no one.

At my mother's seders, fish, soup, matzoh balls, and kugel were all appetizers. The entrées—dried-out soup chicken, overcooked beef—were so anticlimactic no one ever ate them. So I forget about them. If anybody complains of hunger, we go to Herrell's for ice cream.

I skipped seders for years after my aunt Bea died, started them up hesitantly, almost secretively. I'm often the only Jew present.

Sam Gianelli brings good Italian wine. Mooney came once. His mother, who hates me, told him attending a seder was an occasion of sin.

Paolina attends. So do Marta and the boys. It's a time for families to be together.

I hadn't told Paolina anything about the phone call. I hadn't mentioned it to Marta either. Carlos Roldan Gonzales had come through with a single name and an address. I was off the hook with the WHO and the FDA, and Mooney now regarded me as a probable member of the underworld.

I'd have to deal with Roldan Gonzales's largesse, his guilt money, in some way. Some way that would satisfy the tax man. That would satisfy me.

Charities, maybe—with Paolina the major beneficiary.

Marta's smallest boy squirmed and wiggled when it came time for the youngest participant to ask the four questions, the set piece around which the Passover ritual revolves. Eventually Paolina read them, speaking hesitantly in her clear sweet voice.

" 'Why is this night different from all other nights?' " she began.

My *Haggadah*, the official rendition of the Passover story, gets pared down every year until it's more a distillation than a discussion. "Because on this night we celebrate the going forth of the Hebrew people. Because we were slaves and now we are free."

We take turns reading, in English, not Hebrew. Marta refuses to take part, embarrassed by her illiteracy. Sam reads in a rich deep baritone that reminds me oddly of Roldan Gonzales's voice.

Two days earlier, I'd gone to visit Emily Woodrow. In the waiting room, I'd met up with her husband, who'd beckoned me closer with a stiff and imperious gesture.

"I'm just leaving. Back to the office. I've been here for hours," he said. "She hardly talks."

I said nothing. I didn't know what he wanted to hear.

"I'm grateful to you," he muttered. "The police have mentioned your role."

Kind of them, I thought.

He went on. "What I'd—excuse me. My wife, have you told her about me?"

"I don't think she needs any additional burdens right now, Mr. Woodrow."

"I intend to stick by her through this, you know," he said.

How does he see himself? I wondered. What does he glimpse when he looks in the shaving mirror each morning? A hero forswearing his true love for an invalid spouse? A martyr?

"Well," he said lamely, glancing at his gold Rolex, "I have to go now."

"Are you planning legal action?" The words came out of my mouth. I hadn't planned to ask.

"Yes," he said. "I am. You may be called to testify."

"If your *wife* asks me to, I will."

I watched him as he waited impatiently for the elevator, wondering uncharitably if he'd come back to Emily for the imagined profits of the lawsuit.

I knocked on her door. No one answered. I entered slowly, in case she was asleep. The television in her private room was on, but she stared out the window at the parking lot below. Her hair was neatly parted and combed. The dark roots showed.

It seemed impossible that we'd met once, just once while she was conscious. I'd seen her through her husband's eyes, her therapist's eyes. I'd seen her through her photographs.

Her face looked puffy and swollen, her eyes bewildered. On the television screen Fred Astaire danced with Ginger Rogers, spinning her in widening circles.

She was fine, Emily murmured. Just fine. Was there ice water? Oh, yes, there was. How nice. Ice water.

A nurse described her as disoriented. The doctors weren't sure what she remembered, what she would remember.

She remembered that her daughter was dead.

At the seder table, I thumbed through my *Haggadah*. It's more than a story of slavery and freedom. It's a tale of God's wrath. There are dreadful events. Plagues.

I remember the plagues from my childhood seders as nothing more than a game. Stick your finger into your wine cup and splash a drop of sticky redness on the edge of your plate, one drop for each plague. Chant the unfamiliar, meaningless words:

Daam. Tz'far-day-a. Keeneem. O-rov. Dever. Sh'cheen. Ba-rad. Ar-beh. Cho-shech. Ma-kat B'cho-rot.

Don't suck the wine off your fingertip, Carlotta, my mother would say.

Why, Mama?

It's bad luck to taste a plague.

Ma-kat B'cho-rot. I know what it means now. The killing of the firstborn.

I know that killing is not the Passover message. I know we spill the wine to show that we cannot rejoice in full measure when our enemies have been so harshly treated.

But a single drop of wine for the killing of the firstborn? I turn the page quickly. My mouth will not shape the words: *Ma-kat B'cho-rot.*

I remember Emily, what she said to me, glancing up suddenly. I'm not sure she recognized me or knew who I was.

"It's just—I don't know. I think I'm dying." Her voice was still rough, her tone flat, unexpressive.

"That's not what I heard. The doctors say you're going home soon," I said.

She murmured on. I had to bend low to hear her words. "No. It's not—it's that I don't know how to keep going. I kept on all this time, because I thought I'd find out what happened and then I'd—I don't know—that it would change things. That if I found out how she died, I'd see things differently. That if someone had to pay for her death, if someone else had to die even, it would make it easier."

"But it isn't?"

"It doesn't make anything different. It doesn't make anything easier. They gave me drugs—Renzel, I think I remember, he gave them to me—and there are things I forget. He made me forget. I'd hallucinate. I thought she was alive. He should have wiped my memory clean. I remember the wrong things. I forget the wrong things. He should have killed me and let that other woman live. She was young, you know. Tina. A beautiful woman. Young. She could have had children."

"You can still have a life, Mrs. Woodrow."

"It's like you read about people who've lost limbs, an arm or a leg, and they still feel pain in them."

"Phantom pain," I said.

Fred Astaire and Ginger Rogers pirouetted and bowed.

"Yes," she said. "I have a phantom daughter."

On this night that is different from all other nights, I wish I could tell the story of the coming out from Egypt to Emily Woodrow, tell it the only way I can understand it.

"It's April, Mrs. Woodrow . . . Emily," I would say. "I don't know if you're a religious woman. I'm not. But I was raised a Jew, and April is when Jews celebrate the Passover. It was always a hard holiday for me as a kid, and it hasn't gotten easier. Do you know the story?

"I'm going to explain this badly," I'd say. "I'm no rabbi. But this is the part that always gets to me. God punishes the Egyptians for enslaving the Israelites, and not obeying the word of God. There are ten punishments, ten plagues: blood, frogs, gnats, flies, cattle disease, boils, hail, locusts, darkness—and the last plague is the slaying of the firstborn."

"God does that?" she might ask.

"The God of my fathers," I'd admit. "But first this God tells all the Hebrews to put a mark on their front doors—lamb's blood—so the Angel of Death will pass over their houses. Passover."

I see her in my mind's eye, turning her face to the wall.

"I think about it," I would say, "especially in April. And I think sometimes that if God had told the mothers, it might have turned out differently. They might have acted the way you did. Because you did it, Emily. You defeated the Angel of Death. You marked the doors with the blood of the lamb. Strangers' doors, the doors of Egyptians and Nigerians and Pakistanis. You made the Angel of Death pass over their houses. You saved their children, the children of strangers."

"It doesn't help," she would say faintly.

"Maybe someday it will."

"Carlotta," Paolina said. "You're not listening."

"Sorry."

"Can I have wine? Please? A little?"

"If your mother says okay, you can taste the wine. Taste."

Marta, her arthritis under temporary medical control, smiled broadly and poured a thimbleful of Barolo into a stemmed glass. I stared at my little sister, a girl in search of a father, and saw Emily Woodrow, a mother in search of a daughter.

"Carlotta?" Sam said. "More wine?"

"Yeah," I answered, my voice sounding too loud in my ears. "Is it the fourth cup yet?"

"Way past the fourth."

"Good."

When I heard the rumbling outside, I thought it was distant thunder. It grew louder, gave a curious squeak. At the first crash, I was on my feet.

What with all the shouts and questions, the delay while I found my keys, I got outside just in time to see a car's taillights disappear around the corner.

I'd run straight down to the sidewalk, over the grass. I almost tripped over them heading up the walk.

"What?" Sam called to me from the stoop.

It took me a while to answer. I was laughing.

"What is it?"

"The trash cans, Sam," I said. "They came home."